The Lakestown Rebellion

KRISTIN LATTANY

FOREWORD BY SANDRA ADELL

COFFEE HOUSE PRESS is an independent nonprofit literary publisher. Major support was received for this project through a grant from The Medtronic Foundation, the Star Tribune Foundation, the Jay and Rose Phillips Family Foundation, and the Laura Jane Musser Fund. Additional oranizational support has been provided by the Minnesota State Arts Board, through an appropriation by the Minnesota State Legislature, and in part by a grant from the National Endowment for the Arts, and from the McKnight Foundation; Marshall Field's Project Imagine with support from the Target Foundation; the Elmer L. & Eleanor J. Andersen Foundation; the Athwin Foundation; the Bush Foundation; the Patrick and Aimee Butler Family Foundation; the Buuck Family Foundation; the Lerner Foundation; The St. Paul Companies, Inc. Foundation; Star Tribune Foundation; James R. Thorpe Foundation; the law firm of Schwegman, Lundberg, Woessner & Kluth, P.A.; Archie D. and Bertha H. Walker Foundation; the Wells Fargo Foundation Minnesota; West Group; and many individual donors. To you and our many readers across the country, we send our thanks for your continuing support.

LIBRARY OF CONGRESS CIP INFORMATION

Hunter (Lattany), Kristin
  The Lakestown rebellion
  1. Title.
PZ4.H9457LAK {PS3558.U483}   813'.5'4   78-1085
ISBN 1-56689-125-6

COFFEE HOUSE PRESS books are available to the trade through our primary distributor, Consortium Book Sales & Distribution, 1045 Westgate Drive, Saint Paul, MN 55114. For personal orders, catalogs, or other information, write to: Coffee House Press, 27 North Fourth Street, Suite 400, Minneapolis, MN 55401.

Originally published by Scribners in 1978.

10 9 8 7 6 5 4 3 2 1
PRINTED IN CANADA

To the conservative who raised me to excel:
GEORGE LORENZO EGGLESTON (1902–1976);
And the radical who raised me to raise hell:
MABEL L. MANIGAULT EGGLESTON (1904–1953);
this book is gratefully dedicated

THE COFFEE HOUSE PRESS
BLACK ARTS MOVEMENT SERIES

The postwar 1920s was the decade of the "New Negro" and the Jazz Age "Harlem Renaissance," or first Black Renaissance of literary, visual, and performing arts. In the 1960s and 70s Vietnam War era, counterpointing the white backlash against the civil rights movement and rising Black Power insurgencies of SNCC, CORE, and the Black Panthers, a self-proclaimed "New Breed" generation of black artists and intellectuals orchestrated what they called the Black Arts Movement.

This energetic and highly self-conscious Black Arts Movement accompanied and helped foster an explosion of urban black popular culture analogous in many ways to the cultural renaissance of the earlier era: Broadway shows and off-Broadway independent black theater; African inspired painting and sculpture and postmodern graphics; music-minded performance poetry and streetcorner "rapping"; avant-garde "free jazz" with consciously cultivated Afro-Asian references and mystical spirituality; independent and Hollywood-based black cinema riveted on street life and the politics of the urban ghettos; politico-religious sects and charismatic orators like Malcolm X and Stokely Carmichael; "soul music" performers such as Ray Charles, James Brown, Aretha Franklin—and a host of writers—who celebrated and critiqued it all from the vantage point of a newly articulated Third World conscious "Black Aesthetic."

Although most of the literary commentary on the movement emphasizes Black Arts poetry and drama, African American novelists too walked the walk. The transformations of black consciousness produced corollary changes in the forms, styles, techniques, and ethos of all the African American literary modes. The Coffee House Press Black Arts Movement Series is devoted to reprinting unavailable works of the period. In selecting the titles, the editorial panel of African American authors and scholars has employed no fixed guidelines. We have looked for works with distinctive voices, with historical value as windows on the literary and social world of the time, and with that subjective and impressionistic quality of "aliveness" that crosses boundaries of audience, era, and topicality. We have tried to choose work that is masterful, that deserves another chance and other audiences, and that will help us keep the windows to the future open.

The year 1963 heralded several major events that radically transformed the structure of American society. Through the efforts of civil rights activists, especially in Birmingham, Alabama, where dogs and fire hoses were regularly unleashed on nonviolent protestors, the evils of racial segregation were exposed to the world as the country inched painfully toward a more integrated society. The assassinations in Mississippi of the NAACP's secretary Medgar Evers and of President John F. Kennedy in Dallas, Texas, put the country on alert that nonviolence was more rhetoric than reality, despite the optimism of Martin Luther King's "I Have a Dream" speech, which he presented that year before more than 250,000 people who had gathered at the Lincoln Memorial in support of the struggle for civil rights. After the president of Vietnam, Ngo Dinh Diem, was ousted by a military coup, the United States intensified its involvement in a very unpopular war. As a result of these and other social and political events that were forcing the country to change its ways, for many people 1963 was not a happy time. But for Kristin Hunter Lattany, this tumultuous year proved to be a good one. With the pressures of a disintegrating marriage out of the way—she and her first husband, Joseph Hunter, whom she married in 1952 at age twenty, were divorced in 1962—Lattany quit her job as a copywriter for a Philadelphia advertising agency and took off for Atlantic City where she spent the summer completing her first novel, *God Bless the Child.* It was published in 1964.

In retrospect, Lattany's accomplishment was a milestone for black women writers. According to Gloria Wade-Gayles's study of black women writers in *No Crystal Stair: Visions of Race and Gender in Black Women's Fiction*, between 1946 and 1976, black women published only "twenty-six major novels," of which "twelve cut most brilliantly 'through layers of institutionalized racism and sexism' and take us to the core of black women's humanity."[1] Wade-Gayle attributes the dearth of fiction by black women to "double jeopardy": the "unnatural thwarting" of black women's creativity by racism and sexism (Wade-Gayle 11). But the fact that Lattany does not make her list of twelve—only one of which, Sarah Wright's *This Child's Gonna Live*, was published in the

1960s—suggests that the literary establishment did not quite know what to do with a novel by a black woman that, as Henrietta Buckmaster described it in her review for *The Christian Science Monitor*,

> is a lively sharp swarming story of people. But they are people who have had the doors slammed on them once too often, who have been hobbled by the moral deformities of a fabricated society. The life they lead is like an immense, macabre charade which acts out conditions of privilege and security. When the unreality becomes too great then the police arrive, the bottles fly, the nightsticks crack, and the rest of the world watches from the safe side of the invisible boundary.[2]

At the center of all these people is a young girl, Rosalie Fleming. Rosie is so obsessed with achieving her version of the American Dream that she becomes hopelessly entrapped by the very thing she tries to escape: an environment infested with destructive insects and with people who mercilessly prey on each other. Encouraged by her grandmother's descriptions of the house of the white family where she works as a live-in maid, Rosie quits high school in her senior year and literally works herself to death as a clerk in a dress shop, a nightclub waitress, and a numbers banker in an effort to acquire the material things she thinks define success.

God Bless the Child is a bleak novel. Like most novels that can be described as naturalistic, it does not offer a happy ending. One gets the sense at the end of the novel that the cycles of petty crime and greed that helped to precipitate Rosie's demise will continue unabated. Yet, as Henrietta Buckmaster pointed out, by focusing on "a ferociously alive little Negro girl," Lattany had "added a little more depth to the picture, a few more fresh details" to a world that had been written about by "Negro writers" such as "Richard Wright, Ann Petry, James Baldwin, Willard Motley, Ralph Ellison, John Killens, Paule Marshall."[3] That Lattany received little media attention in the 1960s had as much to do with the literary mainstream's benign neglect of black writers, and particularly black women novelists, as it did with her need to stay put and write rather than going out and promoting her work. Lattany explained in a 1983 interview with Claudia Tate for *Black Women Writers at Work*, that she does not find it easy to fit writing novels into her busy life:

> To do a novel one needs a lot of time. I integrate living as a wife and woman, as a person and a teacher, with writing. I'm not complaining about this; I want a full life. But I do pay a price . . . Writing is harder than anything else; at least *starting* to write is. It's much easier to wash dishes. When I'm writing I set myself a daily quota of pages, but nine times out of ten I'm doing those pages at four o'clock in the afternoon because I've done everything else first. This I don't blame on anyone but my reluctance to face the writing. But once I get flowing with it, I wonder what took me so long. That's why I say I don't have my own priorities straight all the time.[4]

Writing also requires that one has lived a while and profited, for better or worse, from one's lived experiences. By the time she had reached her thirties, Lattany felt that she had lived long enough and experienced life fully enough to have something to say about being black and female in the world. She told Claudia Tate that her inspiration for Rosie in *God Bless the Child* came from a girl she met only once: "I knew she was working two jobs in order to buy a house. I went home and said I was going to write a book about her. Of course, nobody believed me."[5] That nobody believed Lattany would write a book comes somewhat as a surprise, considering the household in which she was raised and her deep commitment to literature and to writing.

Kristin Hunter Lattany was born on September 12, 1931, in Philadelphia. Both her parents were educators. Her father, George Lorenzo Eggleston, was an elementary school principal. Her mother, Mable Lucretia Manigault Eggleston, taught school until she was forced to retire under a New Jersey state law that "forbade teachers to be mothers."[6] Growing up as the only child of two teachers, Lattany undoubtedly spent a great deal of time reading. By age fourteen she had become accomplished enough as a writer to start a social column for teenagers in the *Pittsburgh Courier*. She continued writing for the paper while attending the University of Pennsylvania, where she graduated in 1951 with a degree in education. In 1952 Lattany was assigned to cover the civil rights provisions of New Jersey's new constitution. Lattany also worked briefly as a third grade teacher in Camden, New Jersey, before accepting a job with the Lavenson Bureau of Advertising in Philadelphia, where she remained until 1959. In 1961 she returned to her alma mater, the University of Pennsylvania, as a research assistant in the School of Social Work. Her second book, *The Landlord*, was published in 1966. She married John Lattany in 1968, but continued to publish under the name Kristin Hunter. She joined the faculty in the English Department at the University of Pennsylvania in 1972. Lattany retired from teaching in 1995.

The Landlord is unique in two ways: its protagonist, Elgar Enders, is a wealthy white man with psychological problems stemming from his relationship with his millionaire father and doting mother; it is a fine example of a black woman writer's command of wit, humor, and satire.[7] Enders, in his effort to liberate himself from his parents, his psychologist, and his stock broker, buys an apartment building in an inner-city neighborhood. However, his efforts to prove to his parents and his managers that he can handle his own affairs are foiled by his tenants, an eccentric group of black people whose idea of revolution is putting one over on their white landlord. In one hilarious episode after another, they contrive against him until he all but gives up trying to collect his rent. In the end, he wins the confidence of his tenants, and some of the rent money they owe him, after he defeats a city proposal to demolish the building for an urban renewal project that would have left them homeless. Lattany explained to Claudia Tate that the idea for *The Landlord* presented itself to her "one day on a street corner":

> A rich, white person I knew fairly well bought an apartment house and showed me these rent receipt books. He said, "I've got my apartment house. I'll collect my rents. Doc's going to see me next Thursday; he's a truck driver, and he'll be back next Thursday. Minnie's not going to pay me until two weeks from Thursday; that's

when she gets paid." I listened to him with a straight face, but inside I was cracking up. I said to myself, "Boy, are you in trouble." I had my story. . . . I could tell from what he was saying and from the names that they were inner-city blacks and everybody was running a game on him. I just knew this rich, white boy was about to be taken. (Tate 82)

Apparently, Lattany's readers did not find this "rich, white boy" and his black tenants as amusing as she did. The African American poet, Gwendolyn Brooks, for one, was not pleased. In a review for *Book Week* magazine, Brooks wrote,

> Certain items of this narrative may occasion some tightening of Negro lips, or, perhaps, some hot reproofs. There is calm extension of that old stereotype, the invariably loose and oh-so-sexually-able Negro woman ("attractive and uninhibited," praises the jacket). There is a static gift of that newer stereotype, the noisy Black Nationalist puppet, flat-charactered (and there are not and could not be any flat-charactered Black Nationalists) and steadily recommending the ejection of the Enemy.
>
> These reproductions may not seem especially entertaining to Negroes who are working hard to confront themselves as well as others, with estimable images. Miss Hunter might exclaim "But these are *persons!* There *are* such persons, whether Negroes want to admit it or not! And it is my permitted privilege to present them!" The author would be argued back to the responsibilities of the I-am-here premise (which *seems* to be hers).
>
> It is entirely true that *persons* have a right in fiction, whatever may be their tone or temper. When, however, this is the fundamental, bare, and pleasant premise, the author's manipulation should be magnificent enough, or surprising enough, or warmly poignant enough to cajole us into the hearty acceptance—once again—of that I-am-here which is recurrent in contemporary story telling.[8]

For Brooks, Lattany had violated some of the basic principles of the black aesthetic. Not only had she made a white man the central character, or protagonist of her novel; she failed to render her black characters "lovable or loathable."[9] Instead, she mirrored the very stereotypes that the Black Arts Movement was trying to eradicate in order to raise the self-esteem of black people and make them proud of their blackness.

Abraham Chapman's review of *The Landlord* for *The Saturday Review* was the exact opposite of that by Brooks. Hailing the novel for its theme of "the American quest for identity, meaning, and purpose in the age of alienation," Chapman wrote,

> Kristin Hunter's second novel is a fresh and refreshing expression of the diversity of American Negro writing, an elaborate spoof that somehow manages to combine touches of the absurd and intimations of the surreal, strokes of caricature, slapstick, and the grotesque, with an inherent, down-to-earth sanity and realism."

Chapman also praised Lattany for writing a book that "negates the idea that all American Negro writing is didactic and dead earnest and bitter and full of the mystique of race; she explodes the stereotype of the so-called 'Negro novel.'"[10] With the exception of these two reviews, critics were silent about *The Landlord.* The explosion either was not very loud, or it was muted by the more strident voices of writers more closely aligned with the Black Arts Movement than was Kristin Lattany.

In 1970 *The Landlord* was made into a feature-length movie with Beau Bridges in the lead role and Pearl Bailey, Diana Sands, and Louis Gossett, Jr., as his rowdy tenants. Another Philadelphia native, the African American director Bill Gunn, wrote the screenplay. The movie was distributed by United Artists. Although *The Landlord* was far from a box office success, it was, as Gerald Early points out in his essay on *God Bless the Child*, a milestone that most critics have overlooked.[11] Lattany was the first black woman to have her novel adapted into a feature-length movie. That historical fact was overshadowed in 1985 by the phenomenal success of the movie version of Alice Walker's *The Color Purple.*[12]

Likewise, Lattany's foray into literature for adolescents has gone unnoticed by most critics of African American literature despite the popularity of her novel, *The Soul Brothers and Sister Lou* (1968), its sequel, *Lou in the Limelight* (1981), and an award-winning collection of stories titled *Guests in the Promised Land* (1973). She also published a delightful story for younger readers about a little black kitten and its new family titled *Boss Cat* (1971).

Lattany began writing for young readers because her publisher asked her to. Her plan was to "alternate between writing an adult book and a young adult book." Things didn't quite work out that way, in part because of the "huge and unmanageable project" that the adult book she was working on at the time, *The Lakestown Rebellion*, had become as a result of her extensive research about the building of Highway 295 in the small black town of Lawnside, New Jersey, in the 1950s.[13] She worked on it on and off for years and finally finished the manuscript between 1973 and 1975. In the meanwhile, as she told Claudia Tate, kids kept writing her about *The Soul Brothers and Sister Lou* and "asking what happened to those characters as if they were real people," but she didn't complete the sequel until 1979 (Tate 82-83).

Like most of her early fiction, *The Soul Brothers and Sister Lou* is set in the 1960s. It deals with a group of kids who manage to resist the temptation to get involved with gangs by focusing on their natural talent to make music. With the help of Lou's brother William, an elderly blues man named Blind Eddie, and two of their favorite teachers, Lou and her friends form a singing group that attracts the attention of the vice president of a recording company. The kids are signed on and their first recording, "Lament for Jethro," which they wrote in honor of a friend who was killed by a racist white cop, becomes an instant hit. The novel ends with Lou questioning her new found celebrity and the way it has changed her life and those of the boys in her group.

The Lou that emerges in *Lou in the Limelight* resembles Rosie Fleming in *God Bless the Child*. Like Rosie, this Lou is worldly beyond her years. At age sixteen she is able to hold her own against the men who try to exploit her until the Soul Brothers begin experimenting with cocaine that is supplied to them by the manager of the Las Vegas hotel where they are performing. Taking the advice of a friendly prostitute named Tina who urges her either to leave Las Vegas or write her mother and ask her to come and look after her, Lou does the latter. Instead of her mother, who disapproves of her daughter being involved with the "devil's music," Lou and the Soul Brothers get their murdered friend's mother, the lively Mrs. Jerutha Jackson. With the help of an African American attorney, Mrs. Jackson gets the teens out of their contract and eventually they return home, but not before Lou's health fails and she nearly dies during an extended tour of the South. Although it is more naturalistic than *The Soul Brothers and Sister Lou*, *Lou in the Limelight* ends on a hopeful note. After traveling "thousands of miles, from East to West, from North to South," Lou finds her spiritual and psychological home in a small town in Georgia among some cousins she never knew she had.

Lattany's response to Claudia Tate regarding a writer's responsibility is in relation to her young adult novels and their muted optimism:

> I have been optimistic in most of my books, almost compulsively so at the endings, with the exception of the first book [*God Bless the Child*] and [*The Soul Brothers*] sequel, *Lou in the Limelight*. I'm not sorry that's been the case. I feel I'm at a transition though I don't know what direction I'm going in. As I said, as a group blacks must give up their illusions . . . . I can't have kids living in a dream world. The boys think they can all be athletes, and the girls think they can all be singers. That's the way to fame and success. That's a delusion. I was compelled to do this book, and yet I wonder what kind of teenage book it is going to be because every chapter I've written has a real shocking event. The ending isn't jubilant optimism, but it isn't absolute horror either. (Tate 83-84)

Lattany's third novel for adults, *The Survivors* (1975) also has its share of "shocking" events and another child, B.J., who is worldly beyond his years. B.J. finds his way into the basement of Miss Lena Ricks's dressmaking shop and from there begins to change her life, first by helping her with her errands and chores and finally, after she suffers a stroke, by practically running her business for her. Their relationship is not without its problems, though. B.J. is a little crook. He is also the son, by another marriage, of the husband Miss Lena Ricks had convinced herself was dead. Although some of the interactions between the characters in this novel seem implausible, the relationship between B.J. and Miss Lena and her transformation from a lonely woman in her mid-fifties who is totally estranged from other blacks, to the boy's surrogate mother recall the manner in which Elgar Enders in *The Landlord* takes charge of his black mistress's children after her black revolutionary husband goes insane. While not exactly "jubilant optimism," both novels end on a positive note. It is with her next adult novel, *The Lakestown Rebellion* that Lattany achieves "jubilant optimism" and a spirit of rebelliousness that has as much to do with her "own feelings of rebellion" (Tate 81) as it does the people in her novel who band together in order to keep their land.

Set in the fictional all-black town of Lakestown, New Jersey, *The Lakestown Rebellion* presents an array of eccentric characters who share one thing in common: they have mastered the African American art of masking. Their form of masking—hiding their true selves behind a mask of ignorance, simple-mindedness, and buffoonish behavior—once served their enslaved ancestors as an effective strategy for survival. It is now 1965 and that same survival strategy becomes the primary weapon used by the citizens of Lakestown to save their town from destruction. The towns-people also engage in masking for their own amusement and, like modern-day "Brer Rabbits," to put one over on their white boss men whenever they can. For the town's intellectual, Ronald P. Roaney, or "Fess," as he is called, the ease with which his neighbors don their masks of servility is one of the "many contradictions in his immediate environment" that made research for his Ph.D. dissertation in social psychology, which he abandoned twenty years ago, seem "empty and irrelevant." Fess realized that social psychology, with its "single-premise" hypotheses, would be of little value when it came to analyzing and interpreting the social conditions that helped to shape people like Lonnie Jenkins, Josh Hawkins and his son Lukey, each of whom is an expert at masking, and Essie Mae Merchant and the Grimes sisters, to name but a few of Lakestown's more colorful citizens.

The topology of Lakestown and the inhabitants of this insular black New Jersey community, "the largest all-black community in the United States and the only one in the North," are introduced from the perspective of Fess Roaney. As he makes his way through the streets of Lakestown to the office of his physician and friend, Walter "Doc" Thompson, Fess is aware of what lies behind him—"the hideous reality created by men's machines and their greed," a "bleak, inhuman scar" left in the earth by the construction company that is destroying entire neighborhoods to make way for a superhighway. But he prefers to look ahead at the "pastoral lushness and peace" which he knows is "the dream" rather than the reality of Lakestown.

Lakestown is anything but pastoral. It is a town of hardworking women and men who do their best to make ends meet. It is a town of "laborers and construction workers and stevedores"—heroes in Fess's mind: "a breed of supermen who stood up not only to grueling jobs but to the unpredictable cruelties of white boss men."

An event that stands out in Fess's mind, during which "the roles had been miraculously reversed and one white boss man had spent the whole summer working for blacks in Lakestown," occurred in 1961 or '62—Fess isn't sure about the year. Through the wily antics and masking of Lonnie Jenkins, who made his boss believe that he and his neighbors were too ignorant to repair their houses, the whole community enjoyed the spectacle of seeing a white man working hard to complete their home improvement projects. The man never caught on that Lonnie and his neighbors were manipulating his sense of pride and superiority to their advantage. After having completed the projects that Jenkins, Nunc Farmer, and some of the other men swore they didn't know how to do, the boss man left with "his heart cheered, his soul elevated, and his ignorance and ego still secure," while the townsfolk enjoyed a good joke and the "concrete basketball court" they talked him into building.

Recalling that event, Fess marvels at the ease with which his people play their historically stereotypical roles but wonders why they have become so complacent that they would allow that same boss man, McCoy, and his construction crew to literally displace them. After leaving Josh Hawkins's country store where he witnessed yet another instance of masking raised to the level of art, Fess can hardly believe his eyes as Dunce Cap Carter's house comes "trundling along at about five miles per hour on a wooden platform." Carter's is the first house to be physically moved to make way for the highway. Watching the house trundle along, Fess wonders what happened to the "fierce pride" that motivated the town's founding families, "those first Lakeses and Merchants and Carters and Farmers, to flee slavery in South Carolina" and to endure tremendous hardships and deprivation in order to secure for themselves a "free, black, and independent" township. It troubles Fess that the "fires of revolution" that, by 1965, "were raging everywhere else" had barely begun to flicker in Lakestown and that "there was no one in Lakestown who gave a damn what the white man did, even if he picked up their houses and moved them away."

Unbeknownst to him at that moment, there are several people who not only "gave a damn," but who are trying to do something about it. One of them, Lukey Hawkins, had just described to Fess how he had inadvertently been recruited into the "freedom cause," which he claims he doesn't understand, and spent six weeks in New York City at the invitation of one of "them [white] N double-A lawyers." Both Lukey and his father Josh play their roles of simple-minded country folk so well during Lukey's recounting of his experience that Fess leaves Hawkins's country store convinced that the boy's limited "political consciousness" is "shared by everyone in this isolated, insulated little town." His play acting was so real that Fess was unable to see beneath the mask Lukey decided to wear for his and his father's amusement, even after Lukey dropped his southern drawl and spoke to Fess about college in an accent that was "suddenly crisp and northern." A first-year student at Duke University in North Carolina, where he undoubtedly had more exposure to the freedom movement than he is willing to admit to Fess, Lukey is also the president or "chief" of the Young Warriors.

The young men who call themselves the Young Warriors meet every Saturday at Mount Moriah A.M.E. Church in a room reserved for them by the church's radical but ineffective minister, Reverend Bream. It is there, in the room they call their clubhouse, that Lukey Hawkins is igniting the "fires of revolution" that Fess believes have bypassed Lakestown. The Young Warriors have given themselves African and Arab names such as "Daoud," "Hakim," "Rashid," "Nazzam," and "Sulik," and have adopted "Umoja," the Swahili word for unity, as their guiding principle. That unity nearly falls apart after one of them drowns in the local "whites only" swimming pool and the boy who tried to save him is shot by the police. Lukey Hawkins, who just the day before had fooled

Fess into believing that he had no interest in the social and political changes occurring around him, reveals a very different persona to his fellow Warriors in the privacy of their clubhouse.

Lukey Hawkins is a strategist. He knows that the Warriors must control their anger if they expect to be a part of the "main action" and work with their elders to keep other houses from being demolished or moved. His manner is far from that of the simple country boy he pretended to be when Fess was in his father's store. Lukey is thoughtful, firm, and probing as he tries to get to the bottom of what happened at the swimming pool. Likewise, his remarks during the Lakestown Borough Council meeting are those of a young man who has learned how to challenge the authority of his elders without alienating them. Responding to Mayor Abe Lakes's arguments about eminent domain and the importance of saving the "certified historical sites" of the adjacent all-white town of Edgehill, Lukey reminds the mayor that Lakestown's history as the "first northeastern stop on the Underground Railroad" is also worth saving.

> . . . the Underground Railroad dates back to before the American Revolution. Way back to the seventeenth century, not just the eighteenth. Seems to me like the white folks' revolution didn't amount to that much, anyway, if they still admire that king enough to preserve his houses and enforce his laws. But *our* revolution is still going on!

Voices young and old respond enthusiastically to Lukey's pronouncements about the historical significance of Lakestown and its monuments. The Reverends Bream and Bird, building on the momentum of Lukey's speech, each take a turn at addressing the Council, with the latter proclaiming, "If my understanding is correct, their revolution was a mockery. Their history is a fraud. They are still kneeling before royalty over there in Edgehill. The people in this town bend their knees only to *Gawd!*" With that, the flamboyant Reverend Bird succeeds in turning the already disorderly crowd at the Council meeting "into a congregation. There were a half dozen amens, three cries of 'Yes, Jesus!,' and one fainting in the congested center of the crowd."

The fainting person is Vinnie Coddums, one of Reverend Bird's most faithful parishioners. She is quickly revived by Doc Thompson and before Abe Lakes can move to have the now unruly meeting adjourned, she demands to have her say: "Abe Lakes, when I get finished tellin' these people what a hypocrite you are, you'll wish you'd never laid eyes on this town *or* on me." Not only does Mayor Lakes already wish he'd never laid eyes on her; after she threatens to expose his complicity with the people who want to destroy their town, he wishes that she was dead. Riled by the prospect of losing her home and her house of worship, Coddums is transformed overnight from a placid and overworked domestic to a shotgun-wielding firebrand.

Until she arrived the previous evening at Doc Thompson's office with the three sets of plans she stole from the office of her employer, Senator Grafton, Fess had always thought of Vinnie Coddums as a woman who "seemed to care only about her white folks, her Jesus, and her child, in that order." But he also knows his people well enough to know that "When Sapphire gets mad at Whitey . . . that's when he's through. For years he's been able to count on her loyalty, but he should never take it for granted, because when that goes, he goes." That is precisely what Grafton did while entertaining his business partner, a "greasy little Eyetalian contractor" named Dominick Luciano. He was so sure of Vinnie's loyalty to him and his family that it never occurred to him that she might be greatly disturbed to hear them discuss disposing of Merchant Avenue, including her house and her beloved church, "as if it were soiled toilet paper." Vinnie had worn her mask of servility so well over the past twenty-five years that Grafton assured Dom that they could discuss their plans in front of her. "Oh, you don't have to worry about Vinnie. She looks like a witch, and sometimes I think she is one, but she is absolutely loyal. She's been with us twenty-five years, you know. She's just like one of the family. She loves us." He was wrong. After Grafton passed out from the strong drinks she had been serving him and his guests, Vinnie went into his office and stole the blueprints he and his partners had been studying. Unable to read them herself, Vinnie had taken the plans to Reverend Bird, hoping he would read them to her. Finding the Reverend in one of his hashish-induced trances, she turned next to Mayor Abe Lakes, her arch-enemy and the father of her fifteen-year-old child, Cindy.

Abe Lakes is an opportunist. His greatest ambition is to be what he looks like—a white man. He identifies so strongly with Senator Grafton and his men that he quickly suppresses his anger at being tricked into endorsing plans they had not shown him and tries to persuade Vinnie to leave the papers with him so he can have a "chance to study them." Vinnie refuses to fall for his ploy. She accuses him of being a sellout and takes her papers to the only other person she feels she can trust to tell her what they contain—Doc Thompson.

Vinnie arrives at Doc's office shortly after Fess, who had been following her. She hands the papers over to Doc, who confirms that, according to the most recent set of blueprints, "the line of destruction" will take "half the town." Doc makes a copy of the blueprints and returns the originals to Vinnie. After she leaves, he and Fess begin planning their next move—to recruit as many people as possible to attend the Borough meeting and demand that Mayor Lakes explain, based on the most recent set of plans, what is really going to happen to their town. In the meanwhile, Abe Lakes is at home trying to figure out a way—short of murder—to rid himself of Vinnie Coddums. He calls on his right-hand man, the Chief of Police, Benson Maimonides Boyd, to serve a notice that her house is condemned property and must be vacated immediately.

Tall, imposing, and fearless in the dispatch of his duties, the Chief heads to Vinnie's house with no inkling that "he was about to come up against the only object his irresistible force could not move: an angry and obdurate black woman." Not even the brush fire raging near her back door can move Vinnie, who greets the chief with her loaded double-barreled shotgun aimed at his belly. In one of the novel's many comical scenes, Vinnie and Cindy put on the "'crazy' act" Vinnie often used to get rid of pesky bill collectors. "And it always worked; it was a dramatic masterpiece with only one flaw—Cindy's tendency to giggle." The act usually includes Vinnie throwing things at her uninvited guests. This time the act almost ends in tragedy when the shotgun accidentally discharges while Vinnie flings a heavy vase in the Chief's direction: ". . . the flinging of breakables were all part of Vinnie's performance but, just as in the real theatre, nobody was ever supposed to actually get hurt. She almost stepped out of her role to see about his injury, but her daughter saved her from spoiling the show." A master at playacting herself, Cindy has spent her life as a mute. Now, after having found her voice and revealed it to Abe Lakes's wife, Bella, and to her mother, she picks up where her mother momentarily leaves off to see about the chief, giggling all the while: "'I crazy too. Hallelujah!' cried Cindy, who was now thoroughly enjoying herself. She had always wanted to take part in her mother's mad scenes, but this was the first time she dared. Imitating the 'happy' dance Vinnie often performed in church, she trucked over to the far wall, took down a picture of Martin Luther King, and sent it spinning in the chief's direction." Vinnie and Cindy end their performance with a hearty rendition of the spiritual, "We Shall Not Be Moved," as the unharmed Chief Boyd quietly slips away.

Abe Lakes later visits Vinnie himself to offer her five thousand dollars for the house and walks right into a shotgun wedding. Vinnie holds her loaded shotgun on one of the Young Warriors, Tommy Adams. Reverend Bird officiates. Lakes's wife Bella, Tommy's father Carl, and the construction site's foreman, Dom Luciano, who insists that Vinnie kidnapped him at gunpoint, make up the wedding party. Abe interrupts the ceremony long enough to protest that *his daughter,* the child he had not publicly acknowledged until this moment, isn't old enough to be married. Vinnie's shotgun convinces him otherwise, and after Bella orders Vinnie to put the gun down and to change into something more appropriate than the "pink chenille bathrobe" she's wearing, Abe Lakes tearfully gives his daughter away.

Abe Lakes is one of the novel's more complex characters. Light complexioned and determined to maintain a distance from other, darker complexioned people whom he despises, Abe Lakes strives to be accepted by the white men who maintain political power over the town and its people. He measures his success by the degree to which he is accepted into their social circles. For him, Lakestown is but "his bridge to higher ground." His ambition is to be named the state's highway commissioner. An obstacle to that ambition, at least in Abe's mind, is his wife Bella. Through their relationship, Lattany tackles the sensitive topics of intraracial racism and incestuous relationships within black communities. Like her husband, Bella Lakes's physical features are more caucasian than African American. Yet, to Abe's disappointment, she shares none of her husband's ambitions or his need to distance himself from other black people. Bella's identity as a black woman is grounded in the experiences she shares with women like the proprietor of the Blue Moon Hotel and Restaurant, Mame Porritt and her working girls, Lily and Booty. Her affair with her brother-in-law, Ikie, and her tendency to adopt a southern drawl during her infrequent conversations with her husband are her ways of getting back at Abe for constantly criticizing her for not being what he thought he had married: his version of an idealized white woman.

Orphaned as a child after the rest of her family lost their lives in a car accident, Bella married Abe when she was only sixteen. The Claypool community where she grew up "was an ingrown, incestuous little community where marriages between cousins and resultant birth defects were common." That is why Abe offered to marry her "on the condition that there be no children." Bella, however, was not his first choice. He wanted to marry an even lighter complexioned, blond woman, but she married someone else, "a Claypool boy as blond as herself." After twenty-five years of marriage, Bella remains troubled by her husband's obsession with the world of white people. Her concern, as she tells Ikie, is that Abe as a child never experienced the trauma of finding out "what it meant to be a nigger." They both agree that the psychological impact of learning that, in the eyes of white folks, one is black and therefore inferior is "worse the older you get." Bella mentions a friend who was forty when she arrived on a job for which she had been hired over the phone and "got told the usual jive story about how the position was already filled. It hit her all at once. Like getting smacked in the face with a wet dishrag." The blow apparently was too great for the woman. Bella tells Ikie, "I go to see her at the hospital, . . . when she's allowed to have visitors . . . That's what happened to somebody who found out at forty. Ikie, Abe is *fifty*, and he hasn't found out yet! It scares me." Abe finally finds out during his final telephone conversation with Senator Grafton. The Senator calls him a "nigger" and he feels the hurt. "'He called me a nigger, Bella,' he said in a voice as shocked and small as a five-year-old's."

This was not the first time Grafton called Abe a "nigger." He did so during a dinner party Abe insisted that Bella prepare for Grafton and his gang of "tightly suited white men." But Abe, believing he had a good chance of being appointed the state's highway commissioner, ignored the insult. Now that the townspeople succeeded, with the help of a sudden three-day thunderstorm, to turn the construction site into a large lake, thereby permanently ending the highway project and Abe's chances of becoming highway commissioner, he reacts with pain and disbelief:

> "*Me,* Bella," Abe said, and began reciting his credentials. "Me, Abraham Lincoln Lakes, B.A. Howard, 1937; M.A. Rutgers, 1939; Ll.B. Yale, 1941; Major, u.s. Army; Phi Beta Kappa; Alpha Phi Alpha; thirty-third degree Mason *and* Boulé. *Me!*"

With Bella by his side, Abe recovers quickly and, at a stand-off with Grafton and his men on the edge of the new lake during which Grafton shouts the racial epithet at him, "Abe remained silent, giving Grafton plenty of rope—no, wire, amplified wire—with which to hang himself." Bella was holding a microphone through which Grafton's remarks were broadcast to the "enormous crowd of people" which had gathered to marvel at the miracle they had helped to create. When Abe finally speaks, it is to shout his own insults at Grafton: "*Ethnic!* . . . This isn't your country, so you don't care what happens to it. You'll destroy every inch of it if we don't stop you." Grafton leaves defeated, not by Abe Lakes, but by the people of Lakestown. Grafton admits, "I don't know how this latest sabotage was accomplished. Redfern's men can't get anything out of your people, they all seem to be hopelessly retarded, but this section of the highway is definitely abandoned, finished."

These seemingly "hopelessly retarded" people accomplished all of their acts of sabotage by outsmarting their adversaries. They found the construction workers' vulnerability—their pride—and exploited it. Pretending to be "hopelessly retarded," some of the men who just the night before had expertly handled the construction equipment to refill an enormous crater the crew had dug, returned to the site the next day and tricked one of Redfern's men into explaining and demonstrating over and over again how to work the equipment.

> Pride made him an easy victim—he was proud of his skill at operating the marigold yellow dynamo, proud of the pay it earned him (which was, he said, triple the wages of unskilled laborers), and as proud of the machine itself as if he owned it.

Other carefully coordinated work stoppages occurred when workers fell prey to the charms of Mame Porritt's girls, Lily and Booty, and followed them to the Blue Moon Hotel, and when a group of toddlers wandered onto the work site to make mud pies and some of the older children decided to hold their "marbles tournament" on the site right in front of a piece of equipment. Lattany is at her comic best in describing the chaos created by the townspeople and the efforts of Maxwell Berger, the "state engineer in charge of the project," to find out if anyone lives close enough to the site to have heard or seen something that might explain how tons of dirt got moved back into the big hole "in two days."

> Raising his voice, gesturing with his arms, and speaking very slowly, as if addressing the natives of a newly discovered isle, the engineer asked, "Does anybody live close to where we're working here? *Real* close? Close *by?*" He brought his hands together in a kind of sign language, in case these natives didn't understand any English at all.

Berger throws his hands up in despair after listening to Baretta Farmer go on and on about how she heard nothing but the "crickets crickin' in the weeds out back" of her house and Vinnie explains, with great authority, that the refilled hole is the work of "sperits."

> "Sperits is what done it. Sperits picked up that dirt and moved it back where it was before."
> "Why would they do that?" Josh Hawkins asked in pop-eyed innocence.
> "'Cause, long 'bout the end of last week, them shovels started diggin' up old graves in the corner of Mount Moriah churchyard. It wasn't people done it, mister. People ain't been out after dark all weekend, 'cause they knew the graves was disturbed and the sperits was restless."

Lattany, in addition to her ease with writing comedy, masterfully manipulates the black vernacular. Characters like Vinnie Coddums and Baretta

Farmer speak the language of transplanted southern black women; whereas, Mame Porritt, Lily, and Booty are more urban in their speech. Lattany also introduces the supernatural as part of the black vernacular tradition.

For all of her urbanity, Mame Porritt believes as strongly as Vinnie in the spirit world. Suspecting that the creepy embalmer, Baron Sam Potter, has been sent by Death to the Blue Moon Hotel where a distraught Bella Lakes sought solace from her husband, Abe, Mame sets about doing "a lot of spirit work" with the goods she purchased from Josh Hawkins's store.

> Mame bustled back and forth between the dining room and the kitchen, lighting sulfur candles, sprinkling sulfur powder at all the doors, placing cut onions and garlic cloves in odd corners. Then she came over to their table and set a cup of tea in front of Bella. "Drink this. It's not as good as what I sent for, but it'll help."

Under Mame's ministrations, Bella soon recovers from her depression; the undertaker Greta Grimes ends up with the seven-day itch for sending Death, in the form of the Baron, to "fetch" Bella Lakes; and Bella's lover Ikie Lakes refocuses his attention on the big hole that for Fess, ". . . seemed to happen all by itself, like a miracle." Ikie attributes the mess they have created to something else—a natural impulse on the part of black people to rebel.

> "No miracle," Ikie said. "Just a couple of basic sociological facts you of all people should understand. One, every black person in this country is by nature an outlaw. Most of us don't dare risk overt action, because we are outnumbered, but the more we have to conform outwardly, the more we want to rebel. So, dig it: there's nothing we love better than finding sly ways of getting over on the Man. And nothing we're better at doing."

Ikie's "basic sociological facts" convey some of what Lattany feels about violent confrontation. Since black people are outnumbered, there cannot be open confrontation without them being annihilated. If her novel has a message, it is that black people must unite and defeat their enemies through subversive acts rather than through the kind of armed confrontation that was proposed by the militants of the Black Power Movement. The people of Lakestown get over, but not without their share of tragedy. The tragic in *The Lakestown Rebellion*, however, only occasionally shows its mask. This is one of those rare novels that treats the serious subject of the effects of racism on the lives of black people in such a way that one cannot help but laugh. Gregory B. Witcher, writing for *The Washington Post* described *The Lakestown Rebellion* as "a timely, insightful and very readable novel whose call to unity deserves attention. Hunter's novel of the recent past is a refreshing word of encouragement and instruction for the future. Today, when Americans seem overly concerned with individual gratification, 'The Lakestown Rebellion' reminds us of the greater rewards that can be had when we work together."[14]

Two of Kristin Lattany's more recent books, *Kinfolks* (1996) and *Do Unto Others* (2000), mark a transformation in her adult fiction insofar as they both use first person narrators and they both deal with black women who have enjoyed a degree of success in their personal and professional lives. (Lattany also uses first person narrators in some of the stories in *Guests in the Promised Land*.) The central characters of *Kinfolks* are Patrice Barber and Cherry Hopkins. The women are best friends. In the opening chapters their children, Toussaint and Aisha, are engaged, although neither of them is particularly enthusiastic about getting married. The wedding is called off after Toussaint's mother, Patrice, notices that Aisha's birthmark is exactly like her son's. Curiously, considering the closeness of the two women's friendship, Cherry has never revealed to Patrice the name of her child's father. He turns out to be Eugene Dessalines Green, the same man who sired Toussaint. A poet and self-styled revolutionary who, during the Black Power Movement, obliged Patrice and several other liberated women who wanted to have children and raise them on their own, Green has long disappeared from their lives. Patrice and Cherry use the organizational skills they learned during their years of Black Power activism to locate the other women and children and Green—who by now is blind, homeless, and suffering from alcoholism. This odd extended family is finally united, and although some of the women resent the way their children dote on their newly discovered "dad," they realize with pride that their children are all independent and gifted young people who don't need them anymore.

Motherhood is the theme of *Do Unto Others*. The novel's central character, Zena, believes that she can instantly assume the role of mother to a beautiful young African woman she has just met. Ignoring warnings from her young friend and employee, Vyester, that Ifa, as the girl is called, is anything but a child in need of a mother, Zena takes her into her home and soon finds out that Ifa is using her and her husband, Lucius, to acquire visas for her and her very large extended African family. Just as Vyester predicted, Ifa seduces Lucius, but the couple manages to repair the harm that had been done and Zena, finally cured of her desire to be someone's surrogate mother, settles for the role of godmother to Vyester's new baby, A'Zena. She soon realizes that her little godchild requires a lot of attention and that "Motherhood was probably something I was not cut out for, for all my talk about wanting a child."[15] She settles instead for the two her husband already has and for little A'Zena, whom she quickly hands over to Vyester whenever the novelty of God-motherhood wears off as it often does for this woman who, when all is said and done, knows that she is blessed.

Breaking Away (2003), Lattany's third novel in six years, begins with an African American woman, Dr. Bethesda Barnes, counting her blessings. Everything is going well for the English professor. But the peace and "sense of security" she experiences as she finishes her routine swim in the campus swimming pool is later disrupted when four black women undergraduates describe how a group of white male students insulted them by calling them "Water Buffalos." They ask her to support their efforts to force their university to take actions against the men. Beth is reluctant to do so at first, but soon becomes deeply involved in their case to the detriment of her career. Based loosely on an incident that occurred at the University of Pennsylvania in 1994, *Breaking Away* is a more serious look at racism than her previous fiction. It also lacks the humor of her other novels, mainly because Lattany feels that she has become more "angry" over the years. During the 1960s when she wrote some of her best satire, Lattany claims not to have felt the anger that motivated the artists and writers who were more involved than she with the Black Power and Civil Rights Movements.[16] Part of that anger might have to do with what Lattany sees as a dilution of gains made by blacks during the 1960s. She told Claudia Tate,

> I do think the black movement has waned in America. Certainly I can see a bunch of followers just walking around in circles looking for a leader. From what I hear, the sisters had a lot to do with the disintegration, namely their concern about their men talking black and sleeping white.
>
> I'm not a part of the women's movement, nor do I know anyone who is. It's still growing. I think it has climbed on the back of the black movement along with a great many other social movements: the Gray Panthers, gay lib, handicap lib . . . and almost crushed it. The women's movement has eclipsed many black concerns and diluted black gains. I think we are back where we were before. (Tate 80)

Not only was Lattany not involved with the Women's Movement, she was not directly involved in the Black Power or Civil Rights Movements, although she was a keen observer of the way they were transforming the American cultural landscape. A fiercely independent writer and thinker, Lattany has always marched to the beat of her own drum, cultivating her writing skills by simply writing and rewriting and living her life to the fullest. But the 1960s has greatly influenced her writing and the way she views the world today. Much of the humor in her fiction comes as a result of what she calls "Off-Timing." In a 1993 essay titled "Off-Timing: Stepping to the Different Drummer," she describes "Off-Timing" as "the subversive attitude we had to maintain if we were to survive in the man's society."[17] She describes her generation as "the Off-Timers" and asserts that they may "have been the first to develop a unified black consciousness, with the help of the fiery younger ones born in the 1940s who for a time became our teachers. Led by them, we moved from off-timing to rocking steady on straight doses of rhythm, blues, and Motown soul. I call the sixties radicals, with a nod to Amiri Baraka, the Soul People."[18]

The Soul People were superceded in the 1970s and 1980s by a generation who benefited from the "civil rights and integrationist struggles" but for whom those struggles "have been efficiently erased from their memories" by a "white consciousness,"[19] the result of growing up in "predominantly white suburbs" and attending "predominantly white schools." For Lattany, the hope for a new black consciousness resides in the present generation of young blacks. She advises us to "take hope, and, maybe, take cover," because this generation is unlike any that came before:

> This newest group, the Rap Generation, now under twenty-five, has come striding angrily on the scene in fade haircuts, kente, and beads. These youngsters are the first group of African Americans to have a purely black consciousness. They either do not know or do not care that if they are honest with the man he is likely to kill them, as is his historic habit. They do not believe, as I did in my youth, that subversion is necessary for survival, or perhaps they sense that their survival is at best tenuous, under the current conditions of race hatred, a failing economy, and the sick planet. Whatever the reasons, they are very open, and foolish, and vulnerable, and brave. Perhaps they sense that the millennium is at hand, and with it, the end of white power. But because I know that the powerful do not give up control easily, and because I love these young people, and want them to survive, I am afraid for them, even as I admire them.[20]

The lesson Lattany tries to convey in *The Lakestown Rebellion*, and in her fiction for young readers and adults alike, is precisely that subversion *and* unity are necessary for survival. The people of Lakestown survive. But that town is a fiction. In reality, the people of Lawnside, New Jersey, were not able to stop the building of Highway 295. Like her other fiction, *The Lakestown Rebellion* is based on reality, but the outcome is not what actually happened. Through the power of her imagination, Kristin Lattany created a community of "lovable" people, to quote Gwendolyn Brooks, working together against enormous odds to make their world what they wanted it to be.

Endnotes

[1] Gloria Wade-Gayles, *No Crystal Stair: Visions of Race and Gender in Black Women's Fiction*, 2nd. edition (Cleveland, Ohio: Pilgrim Press, 1997), 13. The works included in Wade-Gayle's list of twelve are:

> 1946: Ann Petry, *The Street*
> 1948: Dorothy West, *The Living is Easy*
> 1953: Gwendolyn Brooks, *Maud Martha*
> 1959: Paule Marshall, *Brown Girl, Brownstones*
> 1969: Sarah Wright, *This Child's Gonna Live*
> 1970: Louise Meriwether, *Daddy Was a Numbers Runner*
> 1970: Toni Morrison, *The Bluest Eye*
> 1970: Alice Walker, *The Third Life of Grange Copeland*
> 1973: Toni Morrison, *Sula*
> 1975: Gayl Jones, *Corregidora*
> 1976: Gayl Jones, *Eva's Man*
> 1976: Alice Walker, *Meridian*

[2] Henrietta Buckmaster, "The Girl Who Wanted Out," *The Christian Science Monitor* (10 September, 1964), C 7.

[3] Buckmaster, C7.

[4] *Black Women Writers at Work*, ed. Claudia Tate (New York: Continuum, 1983), 82-83.

[5] Tate, 82.

[6] Sondra O'Neale, "Kristin Hunter," *Dictionary of Literary Biography: African American Fiction Writers After 1955*, Vol. 33, 119-124.

[7] For an excellent discussion of humor and satire in African American literature, see John S. Wright's introduction to the 2000 Coffee House edition of William Melvin Kelley's novel, *dem*.

[8] Gwendolyn Brooks, "Tenant Problems," *New York Herald Tribune Book Week Magazine*, Vol. 4 (8 May, 1966).

[9] Ibid.

[10] Abraham Chapman, "White Invisible Man," *The Saturday Review* (14 May, 1966), 45.

[11] Gerald Early, "Working Girl Blues: Mothers, Daughters, and the Image of Billie Holiday in Kristin Hunter's *God Bless the Child*, in *Black American Literature Forum*, Vol. 20, No. 4 (Winter 1986), 423-442.

[12] Early, 423.

[13] From a November 17, 2002 telephone interview with Kristin Lattany.

[14] Gregory B. Witcher, "Timely, Readable Tale of Civics and Courage," *The Washington Post* (29 June, 1978), B9. Interestingly, Witcher's review appeared in an issue of *The Washington Post* that was dominated by news of what many black people felt would greatly undermine the gains that had been made during the Civil Rights Movement and create yet more divisiveness—the Supreme Court's landmark ruling in favor of Allan P. Bakke in his case against race-based admissions policies at the University of California-Davis Medical School.

[15] Kristin Lattany, *Do Unto Others* (New York: Ballantine Books, 2000), 262.

[16] From a November 17, 2002 telephone interview with Kristin Lattany.

[17] Kristin Lattany, "Off-Timing: Stepping to the Different Drummer," *Lure and Loathing: Essays on Race, Identity and the Ambivalence of Assimilation*, ed. Gerald Early (New York: Penguin Press, 1993), 166.

[18] Ibid.

[19] Ibid.

[20] Ibid., 167.

The Lakestown Rebellion

It was a drowsy, buzzing day in July, the sort of day when you could believe that summer was perpetual and everything in it perfect and immutable, fixed in time under glass like the vivid butterfly collection that adorned Doc Thompson's otherwise dingy waiting room. That was, of course, Fess Roaney thought, if you kept your eyes fixed resolutely in only one direction, the west end of Lakestown, toward Stony Mill. If you turned around and looked the other way, toward Edgehill—but Fess did not need to look over his shoulder at the nightmare, no, the hideous reality created by men's machines and their greed. That bleak, inhuman scar behind him was the reality; this in front of him, this pastoral lushness and peace, was the dream. He knew it and yet went on drinking it in, drowning in it, a willing fool.

For the day to be at the height of perfection (and this one was) it had to be not only midsummer but Friday, a late Friday afternoon at that. The sun had slid down from its point of highest intensity and no longer fried the landscape. Lakestown merely simmered gently, like a fine sauce on the back of the stove. Cool blue shadows were already forming under the oaks in the Mount Moriah churchyard. The excitement of a baseball game occupied the adjoining vacant lot as usual and, as usual, frequent high flies had to be retrieved from among the tombstones. Reverend Bream and his parishioners chased the young outfielders whenever they caught them, but in Fess's view the boys did no harm. The tenants of the churchyard could hardly be disturbed, and there was little enough else for the kids to do all summer. Beyond the house of God's worship the sun worshipers, a crowd the color of boiled shrimp, gathered around a glare of light on blue water that both hurt and affronted Fess's eyes. The Dorsettown Swim Club, built on a spit of Dorsettown land but plainly visible to all of black Lakestown through an eight-foot chain-link fence, was for members—whites—only. It was time to turn his eyes and his steps in another direction, south toward Low Point and Josh Hawkins's country store.

The first thing that met his eyes was Bella Lakes, plump and golden as her giant marigolds, weeding her flower border, a mighty rich and pleasing, if disturbing, sight—but in shorts her upended rear and lush thighs were a good disturbance. Fess sighed and felt better. This, the best Friday evening of summer, was no time to become possessed by bitterness. The hard-working men of the town, the laborers and construction workers and stevedores, were already home with their paychecks and out of their work clothes into something softer and more comfortable. If a Lakestown workingman didn't change out of his work clothes on Friday night, it was because he had grown so used to them over the years that nothing else seemed as comfortable. And also because, wherever in Lakestown the workingman planned to spend part of his pay, his work clothes were socially acceptable; in fact, they were a badge of hard-earned manhood and therefore as much a mark of distinction as white tie and tails in other towns.

Fess was not one of the workingmen, but the town did not penalize him for it. Lakestowners had enough space in their living arrangements and enough room in their large minds to allow a wide margin of tolerance for all of God's deviations. They accepted Cindy, Vinnie Coddums's perpetual three-year-old—now there, by God, was someone who had managed to arrest time—just as they accepted Ronald P. "Fess" Roaney, a pensioned-off navy veteran with a small, frail body and a bulbous, overactive head that sometimes went haywire, and honored the claim that he was still working on the Ph.D. dissertation that had been abandoned twenty years ago.

He had abandoned it with good reason, Fess believed; his dissertation had seemed empty and irrelevant after a year back home in Lakestown. There were just too many contradictions in his immediate environment to allow him to endorse a single-premise hypothesis in social psychology. So, perhaps searching for a new thesis, perhaps not, he wandered about, listened, observed, and marveled. Sometimes so many excited observations and ideas were circulating in his head at once that it felt like a spinning top. When that happened, he called Doc Thompson in case he went into a coma, then anesthetized himself with some of Mame Porritt's moonshine and went to sleep until things made sense again. There was so much material here—too much for someone with time to think. Right now Fess was thinking about Lakestown's laborers and why they wore their drab work clothes like the uniforms of heroes. He decided that they were heroes, a breed of supermen who stood up not only to grueling jobs but to the unpredictable cruelties of white boss men.

Fess smiled suddenly, remembering the year—had it been '61 or '62?—when the roles had been miraculously reversed and one white boss man had spent the whole summer working for blacks in Lakestown.

Lonnie Jenkins, a road laborer, had lured his boss to Lakestown by a show of that simple-minded ignorance that white folks found irresistible. It had been just that, a show, when Lonnie went whining to him about his sudden problem with water in his cellar. "I just don't know where it come from, Boss," he had said. "I just don't know what to do." Or something like that; something compellingly hopeless and pitiful.

First thing Saturday morning, the boss man was seen arriving at Lonnie's place in his golf clothes and his sleek silver Mercedes-Benz. An hour later, after being softened up by Jerutha's ham and hot biscuits, the children's charm, and some more of Lonnie's whining, he departed and returned in his work truck and coveralls. And from then on, and for three weekends thereafter, Bossman was to be seen digging around the soggy foundation walls of Lonnie's house.

A crowd gathered to watch, to cheer him on, and to marvel at his competence, and long before Lonnie's problem had been solved, Bossman was listening to other pitiful complaints. Someone's chimney was bulging more dangerously every year, and though their prayers were holding it up so far, they didn't know how much longer the Lord would let it defy gravity and keep from tumbling in a heap on the ground. Someone else had front steps that were flaking away into a heap of powder while the owners watched and wrung their hands helplessly. A third party had a kitchen at the back of his house that sagged at a forty-five-degree angle, making the cook dizzy and the cakes lopsided. Why, the whole goddamned town was falling apart, and only Bossman could save it!

Bossman responded heroically. Every weekend he was in Lakestown shortly after daybreak both Saturday and Sunday, and every weekend the crowd gathered to watch him work; and their praise warmed him, and their complaints multiplied.

Bossman's wife threatened to divorce him when she learned they were giving up the traditional two-week family vacation so he could go on working out his guilt or whatever he was doing over there in that nigger town. But by then he was a man in the grip of an obsession and, recklessly, he almost threw it all away—his beautiful blonde expensive wife, his three adorable children, his two cars, his five-bedroom house, his swimming pool—rather than give up the first work he had ever really enjoyed. "They need me," he had snarled at her in self-justification, "a helluva lot more than you do." But if the truth were known, the most satisfying fruit of his labor was the feeling of superiority it gave him.

Nunc Farmer had expressed a desire for a concrete basketball court "to keep these chirren out of mischief," but, like his fellow citizens, he hadn't the slightest idea of how to make his project a reality. Nor, apparently—like the rest of them—had he the slightest acquaintance with money.

Bossman, smoothing away with his trowel, did not feel the heat of the day as it grew torrid enough to melt a glacier. He felt only the milder warmth generated by the praise of his cheering section. Fortunately, he never heard the comments from the fringes of the crowd, the ones not meant for his ears.

"Look at that, will you? Just look at that white man work. Ain't it wonderful?"

"Praise the Lord. I never thought it would happen, but at last they're sending *us* slaves."

"That's Lonnie Jenkins' boss man," another neighbor said.

"I know," a giggling woman responded. "You can tell he's the boss man 'cause he's down on his knees."

The summer had ended with all of Bossman's projects completed, his heart cheered, his soul elevated, and his ignorance and ego still secure.

Fess grinned at the memory. It had been wonderful while it lasted. It would never happen again; too many torches had been applied since to too many structures, including the white man's fortfications of illusion. Now, in 1965, America's boss men were angry and wary and no longer ashamed of their cruelty, feeling it justified. But at least the week that belonged to them was over and Lakestown was free to contemplate its blessings.

Those blessings were not much, maybe, to those who were at ease with money and power and could casually order desecrations like the one at his back without a second thought—but to the people of Lakestown, who had made them, they were miracles. The most splendid structures in town were, in order, the school, which had cost everyone a 20 percent tax increase; the fire hall, maintained by teen-age pay dances and adult socials; the Grimes place, a rambling ruin that still had grandeur when viewed from a distance; the Loveland and Satin Club bars down on Rowdy Row, and the half dozen new houses that were situated on a little triangle of land that jutted into Edgehill and tried to pretend they were not in Lakestown at all.

Many other less pretentious houses, like Abe and Bella Lakes's snug stucco rancher, were in a finished and stable condition, but just as many others seemed to be perpetually undergoing some process of completion or renewal. Fess had heard them called shacks and shanties, but to him, as to their owners, they were both original and beautiful. He admired Nunc Farmer's place, with pink shingles on the first story and bare lath beyond; Doc Thompson's carport, held up crookedly by one column of cement, one of cinder block, and two of wood, as if waiting for the leisurely old doctor to make up his mind, and the Adamses' grandiose design for a rancher, as yet only a blueprint of a house. Still underground like their dreams, it consisted of a tarpaper roof covering a rambling basement partitioned into seven spacious chambers in which nine people lived like happy moles. Fess liked the houses in progress better than the completed ones. To him they represented creativity, one of the town's strongest assets and something that white folks lacked. Maybe that was why they were so damned destructive, he thought. And he liked, too, the fact that Lakestown people took their time about their creations. One or two more good business weeks and maybe Josh Hawkins would finish covering his tall, skinny frame house and store with imitation stone siding, unless he decided to paint it yellow again or to build a chicken house first.

For Lakestown people raised food as well as children, knowing, among other ancient truths, that children must be fed and food does not originate in supermarkets. In the matter of gardens, as in everything else, the town was as individualistic as hell. Fess felt a thrust of his old, youthful anger rise up and take charge of him—a contradiction in his own psyche, since he both admired and deplored this individualism. If only these people were less original they could be organized, they could be led, they could be made to fight! His fit of militancy ebbed as quickly as it had risen, his mental fist unclenched as he remembered that he was, after all, in his forties now and lucky to have reached them. Anger was both futile and bad for a walking compendium of all the major human ailments; a philosophic attitude was healthier. And in a more conformist sort of place, an oddity like Fess—unsightly, unhealthy, unmarried, unoccupied because he would rather learn than teach, and contumacious—would have been run out of town long ago. He decided to appreciate both his blessings and the gardens.

The Carter family went in for patriotically painted cans, shells, and rocks arranged in intricate designs, all red, white, and blue. Next door, the Jenkins yard had a jungle of flowers, dozens of varieties, running wild inside and outside the fence, hospitably inviting passersby to stop and pick. The Adamses' corner lot was sensibly landscaped with neatly staked tomato plants, flourishing pole beans, collards and cabbages in front of their sunken house, and old-fashioned flowers—cleomes and daisies and snapdragons—behind it. This, Fess felt, was the proper order of things for a man with seven children; Bunky Adams was putting first things first. The Grimes Funeral Home went in for topiary designs—hedges that were baskets, hedges that were urns, were columns, were birds—everything but hedges. He rather preferred the ragged, untrimmed growth around the Grimes residence, but the topiary work went well with its next-door neighbors, Doc Thompson's fantastic cement sculptures, obelisks, pyramids, towers, wishing wells, goldfish ponds, and waterfalls, all encrusted like crown jewels with sparkling bits of china and glass. Then, refreshingly plain after so much ornament, came Josh Hawkins's country style yard, a bare, dusty patch of earth raked in circular patterns each morning, its only occupant a single frizzly rooster said to keep evil spirits away.

The children, beneficiaries of so much of this cultivation, were just as colorful: tan kids, chocolate kids, copper skinned, golden, near white, and purple black—screaming, fighting, laughing, playing, but mostly dancing, the affluent ones to transistor radios, the rest to the authoritative rhythms of their own pulsebeats. Tuesday's children, every one of them, full of grace: from the time they could walk they were doing the latest steps—the slop, the shuffle, the bump, the hustle—and so moved about town, bopping, slopping, and bumping instead of walking, digging on the music and their own limber, tireless bodies and on each other, knowing all the lyrics of all the latest songs even though they could not tell you the name of a single capital of a single state. And also knowing no fury or fears, or they would be marching on Trenton, the capital of this one, at this very moment.

The only marcher in sight at the moment was Lakestown's august mayor, Abe Lakes, who crossed Edgehill Road to avoid a cluster of the kids and continued at his usual brisk pace: head up, chest out, shoulders back, back straight, as if reviewing invisible troops. Fess saluted, but the mayor passed him by without noticing, his nostrils flared as if assailed by a bad smell. Fess wondered whether he had caught a whiff of live pigs from the Wright place down in Froggy Bottom, or was it the aroma of butchered and barbecuing pig coming from the opposite direction? Fess sniffed, recognized the smoky tang of Jerutha Jenkins's sauce, considered doubling back in that direction, then decided against it. Today he would keep his pride.

Cooked or alive, pork in any form would offend the mayor, Fess was sure. Anything visually or culturally black offended him, which must make it difficult to be the mayor of the largest all-black community in the United States and the only one in the North. Bella had told Fess once that, after eating a fruit cup containing watermelon and being informed of the fact, her husband had instantly broken out into hives. And she, no doubt, had made it worse by breaking into hearty laughter. Bella loved watermelon and barbecue too, and people— especially kids, and music, especially raunchy music—and humor, especially the earthy variety: in fact, she loved life with an intensity that must make her a bitter disappointment to Abe. He had married her for her white appearance, Fess was sure, but anyone who loved life as much as Bella had to be blacker than her ivory skin and horse-tail hair would lead a man like Abe to believe.

Bella seemed not to know what was wrong, why Abe disapproved of her. For years she had tried with pathetic eagerness to meet the exacting standards of the strange, rigid man she had married, but no matter how painstakingly she dressed, in half an hour she looked flushed and rumpled, like a whore after a busy, exhilarating night; and no matter how carefully she did up her hair, it slipped out of place, just as no matter how hard she tried to restrain her mouth, blunt truths kept slipping out of it. Lately, Fess had observed, she had stopped trying so hard. Abe did not seem to notice; it was his way never to seem to notice anything that was beneath his dignity. Thus he avoided being associated with anyone who did not meet with his approval, which, his standards being so inscrutably high, must make him a very lonely man.

I wonder what he thinks? Fess asked himself. Does he think he's white, and therefore better than the rest of us? No, he answered himself, for he had heard the mayor curse white folks with the sincere bitterness of a frustrated man. Why frustrated? Because he's so near to white and yet so far; because he refuses to be a nigger, but they won't let him share their powers and privileges.

2

What Abe Lakes was thinking, at this or any other moment, was nobody's business. His motives were seldom understood; he knew this, and strove to keep it that way. He had left the sidewalk to avoid not children but his brother Isaac's disreputable establishment and the crew of loafers who always lounged in its precincts. A sign advertised it as Ikie's Pool Room, but Abe, who was fond of long-winded euphemisms, particularly when he wished to disparage something, thought of it with distaste as a billiard parlor. One or the other of its habitués would have been sure to speak to him, and it was to discourage the familiarity of a "hello, brother" from anyone, including the only person who had the right to so address him, that he had crossed the street. Familiarity was distasteful to him, and intimacy, especially these days, was downright dangerous. Abe guarded the information in his head the way a crab guards its vital organs, with a hard shell of indifference. Not that anyone would dare approach him with prying questions, but caution was his long-standing habit, and in his present position he could afford no confidants.

He was thinking, with a rich pleasure not visible on his stern, hawklike face, of a certain meeting in a certain private dining room in Edgehill, a gathering that was to be convened again next week. The walls had been paneled with real wood of a venerable patina, the carpets had been thick as moss, the air conditioning had been silent and efficient, the service bone china and fragile crystal. He had taken one Gibson from a properly deferential black woman in a black uniform and then, uncharacteristically, reached for a second brimming bubble, with a reckless jubilation because he was *there*. Where, exactly, was *there*? Why, the place where he had always known he belonged but had almost despaired of reaching. Now it had happened; he had, in the most satisfying sense, arrived. And it was all, ironically, due to his father, whom he had often cursed with saddling him with the responsibility of this wretched, backward black town. Well, things had a way of working out. Lakestown would be his bridge to higher ground, and then he would be able to forget it existed.

The men in the room had all been white except Abe, and they had all been on cordial terms. Here was the respect, the equality, he had for so long been denied. With the second round of drinks had come amiability; Mr. Grafton had become Harry; Mr. Luciano, Dom; Mr. Lakes, Abe. First-name usage was an American custom, fine if—but only if—it were mutual. This time it was. Over lunch (chicken breasts with white cheese, rice, string beans with almonds, a pale lettuce salad) details had been discussed and no problems foreseen.

His problem—no, his role—would be to sell the advantages of the project to Lakestown and keep the dissident elements, the ones who would complain if the Lord sent them chocolate-flavored manna instead of vanilla, from causing trouble. With the help of the man he came closest to calling a friend, his police chief, Benson Boyd, it would not be difficult. Together he and Boyd would send the malcontents back to church, there to wail until their Jesus turned stone-deaf. Perhaps, he thought, it would not hurt to have a little private talk with the ministers. Bird could be reached with an appeal to his self-interest; Bream, a half-baked idealist, with the very real advantages of the plan. There would be new ratables, a balanced budget, even local jobs. He was satisfied; he was not selling the townspeople out, and he expected no real trouble from them. Not that his future lay here. No, he had been promised something in the capital: something impressive and wonderful, a deputy commissionership, at the very least. Abe was the sort of man who habitually looked gift horses in the mouth and, seeing no reason why he should have been promised anything, sensed that this one might have a few rotten back teeth, but he did not wish to inspect it more closely. He honestly saw nothing wrong with the highway plans, and he had waited so long for this, so long.

Only one problem really troubled him. A man who held high office must have a suitable wife, and already, on the first rung of his climb to the top, Bella was a potential source of embarrassment. The masculine get-togethers had not included her, of course, but there had been one mixed gathering, at the Grafton mansion in Edgehill, where her absence had caused comment. Asked "where's your wife?" he had mumbled something about a visit to her relatives, ashamed to admit that he did not know. And that tarry witch, Vinnie Coddums, who *would* be their maid, had eyeballed him mockingly, knowing Bella had no living relatives.

He would not go out to meet trouble; he would let Bella slide for the present, but when his appointment came through, she would have to change or be left behind. Abe was not a sentimental man; the substance had long gone out of his marriage, but he could live without that and was, in fact, relieved at no longer having to grapple with it. But in the world into which he was destined to rise, appearances counted a great deal. Bella could make a splendid appearance, if only she would cooperate, if only he could make her understand the importance of good taste, manners, and discretion. He did not care even if she had affairs, as long as she had them discreetly. After all, a few wisely granted favors could help his career. Why, in the right clothes, with the right behavior, she could be as good as any high-class white woman! But she seemed stubbornly determined to remain low-class. Her lack of discrimination; her democratic attitudes; her motley friends; her earthy tastes; her blunt, frank speech; her bouncing, uncorseted figure—all were acceptable in a country town like this, but not on the Hill, let alone in the Capitol. Let her slide, let her slide. The time was not yet here.

So, his fierce eyes turned inward, Abe Lakes walked through crowds of attractive children and pungent waves of barbecue, past jungles of vivid flowers and knots of laughing adults, dreaming of silently air-conditioned rooms with no odors, in which pale people ate paler chicken breasts and lettuce.

3

Keeping his back turned on that barbecue and walking firmly into Josh Hawkins's store required a mighty moral effort, but Fess managed to do it and felt proud of himself. This town was so relaxed and relaxing that he was like a British colonial overseer in the days of the Empire: he felt the need to impose little disciplines on himself to keep jungle rot from setting in.

Josh's store seemed to have been picked up and moved intact from a rural county in Georgia. The floor was bare wood worn smooth by many footprints; the walls were rough, unpainted pine boards. The place smelled of a wonderfully narcotic mixture of spices, hickory smoke, chicken blood, and sawdust. The stock consisted of things most northerners had never heard of, let alone seen or tasted. There were cracklin's, fried pork rinds in a big tin can, and every other product of the pig, from black, smoked hams to white globs of lard. There were huge croker sacks of field peas, black-eyed peas, pinto beans, hominy, cornmeal, pecans, and peanuts, both roasted and raw. There was homemade sausage in oddly shaped lumps, heavily flecked with sage, that could never have come from a factory. There was cold sarsaparilla to drink and birch beer, and stronger things too, if you had a real thirst and Josh knew you well. And there was a delicacy Fess loved, souse, which consisted of many mysterious little snips and bits of the pig floating in their own gel like tropical fish in a pink lagoon.

"A souse sandwich," he requested of the proprietor, a very tall, very black man with the build and grace of a sprinter and the deceptively slow, soft, stupid-seeming speech of a deep southerner. The accent was deceptive because Josh Hawkins was gentle only with gentle people; and he was never stupid, though he had the southern black man's knack of playing dumb when it served his ends. Fess sometimes suspected that the southern drawl itself was an art form invented by the earliest American blacks to give them time to think up ways of outwitting the white man.

"Got fish today," Hawkins said, without moving toward his counter. "Nunc Farmer brought by some porgies he caught this morning. Mae's fryin' 'em now."

The smell of frying fish, overpowering all the other odors, was irresistible. "I'll have a souse sandwich and a fish sandwich," Fess said.

"Got some ribs left over from lunchtime, too," Josh said, still without moving. "Barbecued 'em myself this morning."

"I'll have a souse sandwich, a fish sandwich, and some barbecue."

"Heeee," went Josh's high-pitched, artificial-sounding giggle, like a siren about to go off full blast. "Heeee. You gonna eat all that at once? Where you gonna put it?" He pretended astonishment, letting his eyeballs enlarge, but Fess knew Josh had seen him eat that much and more at one sitting—or rather standing, since there was no place to sit in his store.

"I am," said Fess, "but not all at once. Only one bite at a time." He knew he was supposed to keep his weight down, but goddamn it, it *was* down, and he had already walked away from one temptation today.

"Heeee. I better get you a beer," said Josh, who was not licensed to dispense alcoholic beverages. "What you want first?"

"The fish, then the beer."

Josh went into the back room and came out with two cans of beer in one of his giant hands and in the other two slices of white bread from which several fins peeped coyly. Fess took the sandwich gratefully and devoured it the proper way, enjoying the texture added by the bones, spitting out the big ones but crunching the small ones thoroughly, along with the flesh and the crisp cornmeal-batter crust.

Josh waited considerately until Fess had taken the edge off his hunger before he spoke. And that was true politeness, for, as slowly and casually as he talked, he was bursting with news.

"My boy just got back from New York City," he announced. "He had a big time up there. Heard about it?"

"No," Fess said, genuinely surprised, for news traveled through Lakestown faster than one cat chasing another. "I thought he went to Georgia."

"He did," Josh said. "But something happened down there and he ended up in New York. I don't rightly understand it myself. I'll let him tell you about it. Hey, Lukey! Lukey!"

"I'm right here, Pa," said the soft-spoken boy, who was as tall and slender as his father, with the same big-footed grace, which had allowed him to come in soundlessly in his size-thirteen sneakers. "But I don't understand what happened either. One minute I was on a bus coming back from Grandma's house in Valdosta and the next thing I know I'm in New York and people are buying me dinners at them big hotels and asking me to make speeches and all."

"What'd you say in them speeches, boy?" his father asked.

"I didn't say nothing, Pa. I told them I didn't know how to make a speech, then I just said thank you and sat down. They liked that a lot, though. I think they liked it better than if I'd really made a speech, 'cause they applauded so long I had to keep getting up and taking bows."

"Ain't you forgetting something?"

"What, Pa?" the young man asked, with what Fess felt sure was feigned innocence.

"What happened between the bus out of Valdosta and the other bus, the one to New York?" his father prodded.

The youth dropped his eyes and shifted from foot to foot, an exact imitation of his father's parody of embarrassment. "I thought you wouldn't want me to tell people I was in jail, Pa."

"Heck, boy, why not? Didn't them white folks in New York think it was the greatest thing ever happened?"

"Yeah, Pa, but that was them, and they was kind of weird and crazy anyhow, and, well, folks around here might think I done something wrong."

"Well, son, maybe you're right, maybe you shouldn't tell everybody in town. But Professor Roaney here, he's an educated man, he'll understand."

"I hope so, Pa, 'cause I don't understand it myself."

"Why were you in jail, Luke?" Fess asked, sucking on barbecued ribs.

"I don't know, Mr. Roaney, and that's a fact. See, the bus going down was half empty, but coming back it got plenty crowded. A funny thing, too; most everybody on it was my age. They were all students at them Negro colleges down there. We all got seats, but we had to squeeze in any way we could. Squeezed up like that, we got pretty friendly. They was a nice bunch of kids, even though I didn't understand half of what they were talking about, shouting "freedom now" and "move on over or we'll move on you," stuff like that. And they was singing on the bus; I didn't think that was polite. But maybe I would have understood them better if we'd talked more. We didn't have half a chance to get acquainted, 'cause the bus hadn't gone five miles out of town before the police stopped us. And they put us all in vans and hauled us off to the county jail.

"After that, I only got to know my cell mate. His name was Raymond Williams, from Albany. Albany, New York, I mean. He had come all the way down there just to go to jail, can you beat that? I mean he seemed *happy* to be in jail, like that was his whole reason for making the trip. I could hardly believe it, but I don't think he would lie.

"Jail wasn't all that bad, except I couldn't talk to anybody but Raymond, and I guess the others were lonely too, 'cause they kept singing songs. They usually sang all night, so I didn't get much rest. And I got hungry, too, 'cause the other kids had decided to go without eating, and that meant I didn't get no meals either."

Luke's mother, Mae, a woman so tiny it was hard to believe she had given birth to this giant and two others, brought him a fish sandwich, as if to make up for his recent deprivation.

"Thanks, Ma. But I ain't hungry no more, not after all them fund-raising banquets and parties in New York. It wasn't as good as the food you fix, though."

"Of course it wasn't. White folks don't season their food," she said calmly.

"But really, it wasn't so bad, what happened to me. I was only in jail four days; less than that, really. Three days, twelve hours, and twenty-five minutes. Them N double-A lawyers came right down from New York and fixed up our bail and got us out. And one of them was white. I never knew the N double-A had white lawyers, did you, Pa? Anyway, he was the one asked me would I be his guest in New York. Said it would help the cause."

"What cause?" Fess wanted to know, though he was beginning to suspect the answer.

"That's what I asked him. The freedom cause, he said. Well, of course I'm for freedom, got to be for freedom, 'cause I'm an American and this is the land of the free, so I said yes and I went. I sure didn't know I'd have to show up at all them fancy places, though, and be introduced and asked to make speeches."

His mother sighed. "I just wish you'd had some of your good clothes. Why didn't you call us? We would've sent them to you."

"Oh, I didn't need them, Ma. They wanted people to see me like this, in my overalls. They said overalls made me look like one of the people. Personally, I couldn't see why I couldn't be people in a nice suit, but I went along with it. But I wouldn't go out looking beat up and dirty like they wanted me to. I washed my clothes every night and pressed them every morning."

"Well, I should hope so," his mother said. "I raised you."

So, Fess realized, work clothes had become heroic uniforms outside of Lakestown. Every time black folks adopted a costume it became the fashion, and most blacks had to find something new. But the men here would go on wearing their overalls and dark twill work pants, because Lakestown was outside fashion, or so far behind it that it stayed ahead. Quite rightly, too; people here knew what became them. This tall, limber father and son, who would look stiff in sharp-edged new suits, were at ease and elegant in their neat, dark denims. "How long did you stay in New York?" he asked the boy.

"Six weeks," Luke replied, reaching for a rib. "It was all right, but I was getting tired of going to all them banquets and parties to raise money for the cause, and the air conditioning didn't agree with me, and neither did the champagne.

"They didn't want me to leave. They said I could do lots more for the cause, but I found a way to fix it so they sent me back here right away."

Josh chuckled and urged his son to tell just how he had fixed it.

"Well, I finally made a speech. Not a long one. I just said I thanked them all very much, but I didn't want to take up any more of their time, 'cause I never meant to be a freedom rider, I just wanted to go see my grandma, and I didn't know why they was making such a fuss over me anyhow."

"I don't know why, neither," his father said. "But I'm just an old country boy. Maybe the professor can explain it."

"I sure hope so, Pa, 'cause I don't know why they did it either."

Then father and son both laughed, mutually slapping knees, sly, high-pitched laughter that made it clear they both understood every bit of it and were not about to drop the masks of ignorance that let them make the most of every situation.

KRISTIN LATTANY

"Aren't you in college down south too, Luke?" Fess inquired.

Now that he had finished his story, Luke's accent was suddenly crisp and northern. "Yes, I go to Duke. That was another reason I had to get back here. Basketball practice starts early."

Josh, too, had clipped his drawl. "He's majoring in finance and economics. Too many colored get money and don't know what to do with it. We want him to be different."

"But I don't know what it's all about yet, Pa," the boy said. "I only had one year."

"Hell no, he don't understand what he's studyin'. But he's tryin', and he's started him a pretty little collection of stocks, Texaco and IBM and Hilton Hotels and ITT. His ma and me, we bought some of them too, just to encourage the boy. But I guess they ain't worth nothing."

"I suppose not," Fess said, poker-faced. "But you never know."

"You still want that souse sandwich?" Josh asked, seemingly suppressing another fit of laughter.

"Yes, I'll take it with me. And I'll have another beer," he added recklessly, even though he was due at Doc Thompson's next for his compulsory six-month checkup and the beer would surely raise his blood-sugar level. On the other hand, it might relax him enough to lower his blood pressure. When a man had almost every serious ailment in the book, he had to kind of balance things out.

He shook the boy's eleven-inch hand and added by way of parting, "Glad you're home, Luke."

"Me too. I didn't like staying cooped up twenty stories high in those little air-conditioned boxes they call houses, but I didn't like coming down to the street, neither, on account of the noise and the crowds. I been home two weeks, and I just got back to sleeping my normal ten hours a night. But say, Professor?"

"Yes?"

"Don't tell anybody about what I got into up there. It got to be an awful strain, being a hero."

4

Munching his sandwich on the steps of Josh's emporium, Fess heard high squeals from somewhere behind him. Were they laughing at him, or was Josh merely slaughtering a pig?

Moving on, he wondered how much of the scene he had just witnessed had been a performance for his benefit. Just when he thought he understood people like the Hawkinses, they confused him.

"I'm for freedom 'cause I'm an American," young Lukey had said, "and this is the land of the free." Was that some more of the family irony, or was it really the extent of the boy's political consciousness? He had shown that he was not really that simple, and yet Fess thought that that statement at least was sincere. What was worse, he suspected that Luke's attitude was shared by everyone in this isolated, insulated little town. The fires of revolution were raging everywhere else, but Lakestown would be the last place in America to ignite.

The lowest species of animal would fight over its territory, but Lakestown people saw their land threatened by a superhighway and did nothing. The town tolerated aggression just as good-naturedly as it tolerated characters like Essie Mae Merchant, who dressed up daily in elaborate finery to go about on her imaginary errands. Whenever she got tired she stopped, and wherever she stopped she was fed. Informal but efficient; that was Lakestown's system of public welfare. Tipping along Edgehill Road in high-heeled silver sandals, Essie Mae wore a ratty fur cape secured with a big safety pin, a flowing red satin gown, a black straw coolie hat bobbing with cherries, and her usual vacant grin. Biker Boyd, the police chief's harmless, moronic brother (all the town's officials had embarrassing brothers, it seemed) glided up beside her on his brilliantly decorated bike, braked, and tipped his hat. There was a moment's hesitation, then the grin on Essie's face spread wider. She hoisted her long skirt and climbed aboard the back of Boyd's vehicle, which was redecorated every month to reflect the seasons and their holidays. This being July, the bike was resplendent with red, white, and blue streamers woven into spokes, American flags fluttering from handlebars, and glued-on stars.

Essie made herself comfortable, Biker reseated himself, and they took off together down the road, a gaudy, improbable, and splendid spectacle.

Fess found himself smiling because they were so splendid and because this was a splendid town to let such people roam free instead of locking them up in institutions, until he saw an even more improbable sight that spoiled his pleasure. He rubbed his eyes, but he had not been mistaken. It was a house on wheels trundling along at about five miles per hour on a wooden platform, a recognizable house, Dunce Cap Carter's home. Square, gray, and Victorian, it moved along with serene dignity as if unconscious of its humiliation. Nothing about it seemed disturbed, not the curtains at the windows, not the flowerpots on the sills, certainly not the owners.

"Damn!" Fess cried aloud in pain. The original Lakestown settlers had not been so complacent. They had risked cruel punishment or death, those first Lakeses and Merchants and Carters and Farmers, to flee slavery in South Carolina for a precarious hope of freedom in the north. They had lived with danger, fighting off bounty hunters with shotguns until Emancipation, and after that with hardship and deprivation. The last fierce Lakes, Abe's father, old "Freedom George," had piled on more hardship when he fought to secede from Dorset Township—and won. After that, Lakestown was on its own, free, black, and independent and, like most independent black ventures at the start, broke.

Where had all that fierce pride gone? Into the history books, probably, Fess sighed. There was money in the borough treasury now, there were fat chickens in the backyards, and there was no one in Lakestown who gave a damn what the white man did, even if he picked up their houses and moved them away. Creatures who would not fight for their own preservation were doomed; any high-school biology student could tell you that. Perhaps he had miscalculated; perhaps there was hope somewhere. . . .

The small Edgehill-Lakestown bus, a jitney in all but name, rumbled past him, whined to a stop, and spewed out Vinnie Coddums and a half dozen other maids home from another day of serving white folks. People called the bus line the Cook's Tour; almost no one rode it but domestics. In the old days, before Freedom George achieved secession, the bus had been larger and packed with standees. Domestics, salaried slaves, had been the main support of the settlement that existed, like so many small black hamlets near prosperous white towns, on the edge of the Hill, its economy truly marginal, its only function to serve white families. The town had no other source of income then and no identity except a nickname, The Edge, a sad comedown from its proud original designation, New Freedom. But old George Lakes had changed all that back in '29. He could hardly have picked a worse year for Lakestown's declaration of independence. Times were suddenly hard, even for the rich, and service jobs had grown scarce, not that the Edgehill whites hadn't been mad enough to fire their newly uppity help anyway. Lakestown was incorporated with a fine new name, the name of its largest founding family, and little else. Somehow it had survived. But at what price—the loss of memory, the loss of pride?

The small bus seemed to ride several inches higher after relieving itself of Vinnie's weight. She looked tired, hot, evil, and sweaty, as she well might, being both overweight and overworked, but she also looked like a person determined to go somewhere and do something.

Fess felt a sudden, unreasonable excitement. This seemingly ignorant woman might possess the key to saving Lakestown. Her boss, Senator Grafton, a fearsome power in state politics was said to be the author of the project that was cutting the guts out of the town. Vinnie seemed to care only about her white folks, her Jesus, and her child, in that order, but he had just been reminded that people in Lakestown were seldom as simple as they seemed. She might know a great deal; might have seen and heard things that were helpful, might even be angry about something besides the party she'd had to serve this evening after scrubbing and waxing nine floors. The set of her jaw as she trudged straight up Merchant Avenue instead of turning toward her house certainly gave that impression.

When Sapphire gets mad at Whitey, Fess thought, that's when he's through. For years he's been able to count on her loyalty, but he should never take it for granted, because when that goes, he goes.

He was probably wrong about Vinnie, but he decided to follow her.

5

Vinnie Coddums's mind resembled a darkroom, a small black closet in which a single red bulb cast an angry glow. Twenty—no, closer to thirty years—scrubbing their toilets, their floors, and their babies' behinds; bringing up the babies, too, and this was her thanks. They spat in her face. She was mad at her white folks, but madder at herself for being so slow to catch on to them.

Not that they had ever fooled her completely. She knew they lied when they gushed how they loved her, how she was just like one of the family. When they got off by themselves and their liquor got into them, the truth came out. She had simply not known the whole of that truth, never peered into the slimy depths of their souls, until this evening.

She had mixed the cocktails herself as usual and served them to them and their business guests—she wouldn't dream of tasting the nasty things, but she had learned to make them perfectly—and they had all had more than one too many.

Mrs. Grafton had already gone upstairs and passed out on her bed when that greasy little Eyetalian contractor had said, "Merchant Avenue will have to go too."

"All right, Dom," her employer had responded easily, disposing of Merchant Avenue as if it were soiled toilet paper. "If you say it goes, it goes. What's on it?"

"Nothing but a few nigger shacks and a church."

"So? They can always build more shacks." The senator's voice was mellow, rich as a radio announcer's, as always after three of Vinnie's Gibsons. "And you know they'll build another church right away, even if they have to—what's that line?—sleep in hollow logs." He chuckled. "This is a lethal potion you make, Vinnie, a regular witches' brew. Pour me another one. Give my friend one too." Like she was a machine.

"Yessir, Mr. Grafton," she mumbled. Merchant Avenue was *her* street. One of those shacks was hers and Cindy's, the house Vinnie had lived in all her life. Shack or no, it had sheltered her comfortably for forty-seven years. And the church, Peace Baptist, was hers too, her sanctuary, the closest place she knew to Heaven. Reverend Bird was so beautiful in the pulpit on Sunday morning, his hair pomaded and shining in the rainbow light coming through the stained-glass windows, one of them paid for by Vinnie herself out of five years' hoarded savings. Seeing him up there, his large, liquid eyes rolling as he preached that beautiful gospel, was the closest she might ever get to seeing Glory. In her mind the church and Heaven, her minister and the Lord, were one and the same, and when she muttered, "He will punish them," she was not clear as to the subject of her sentence but had no doubt of His powers.

She was panting as she struggled up the hill, past the church to the parsonage, but she wasn't thinking of her fatigue; she was thinking only of her need to get to her minister and unburden herself to the Lord.

That little wop had noticed her too late. He whispered to his host, "She's one of those Lakestown niggers, isn't she? You think we can talk in front of her?"

Her boss laughed complacently. "Oh, you don't have to worry about Vinnie. She looks like a witch, and sometimes I think she is one, but she's absolutely loyal. She's been with us twenty-five years, you know. She's just like one of the family. She loves us. Pour us another, Vinnie."

And she had poured the drinks silently, not bothering to say "Yessir" this time, wishing she had put poison in them, thinking of stealing some from the garden shed for the next batch. Or better yet, of gathering some wild herbs and berries she knew where to find over the weekend. She could brew them and put the concoction in their food or their drinks, it wouldn't matter; they would die and no one, not even a doctor, would be able to detect why. Nor would she be blamed; after all, they believed she loved them. White folks were fools; they were so careless, and so easy to kill.

She urgently needed to confess these thoughts to Reverend Bird. Her soul was in danger; she had been deliberately planning murder. A contemplated sin was as bad as a committed one, she knew, so she badly needed forgiveness. If one were as bad as the other, though, why not do the deed? She had been severely provoked, and the Lord's mercy was infinite, the Reverend had said.

Still, she had not put anything in their drinks this evening except the usual six parts of gin to one of vermouth. Instead, after her employer had seen his last guest to the door, then staggered to the living room sofa and passed out, she had gone into his office, opened the filing cabinet, and extracted the folder they had been studying. It contained three sets of plans. She could not read maps or anything else, but Reverend Bird could read them to her, just as he read her the Bible, the heavenly words that saved her soul. Once before she had contemplated murder, of the child then in her womb, and he had talked her out of it, soothed her, saved both her and Cindy. But after Cindy turned two, only her body continued to grow. Her daughter had never learned to talk, only to sing, in a mysteriously beautiful and moving voice, the sacred songs she had learned from constantly hearing them. Vinnie saw this as her own punishment, the cross she must bear to her grave for having wanted to kill her child. But perhaps, as Reverend Bird had suggested, Cindy was blessed in a way beyond their earthly understanding; perhaps, in her own way, she knew better than anyone else the meaning of the holy songs and was already in the kingdom.

The door to the parsonage was open. Vinnie walked in, passing with her heavy-footed tread through the front parlor, glowing dimly with stained-glass lamps and unlit crystal chandeliers, into the den that the Reverend LeRoy Bird had furnished with a large antique desk, leather chairs and ottomans, Oriental rugs, and burnished-brass Persian tables. Lounging in one of the leather chairs in a paisley robe, smiling like a beautiful brown Buddha, he seemed to be staring straight at her.

But when he spoke it was to the wall behind her. He said, or rather chanted, "And the angel came down in a shower of gold, and said, 'Behold, I will bring to some destruction and torment, but to others, I will bring great glory.'"

Vinnie saw the amber glass bubble pipe, with its snakelike cord and ivory mouthpiece, on the table beside him and realized that her visit was useless. The pipe helped Reverend Bird see holy visions, he said. Many prophets and saints had used it too, but she was not to tell anyone about it; some of his parishioners might not understand. Thrilled at sharing one of her pastor's secrets, she had kept strict silence. But why, why did he have to be in a holy trance tonight?

"And there were three wise men and three and thirty fools, and they went together in company to Gethsemane. And there they drank the juice of the poisoned fruit, and the wise men died, but the fools rose up unharmed. Therefore I say unto you, be as little children and fools, and ye shall be saved."

Vinnie pondered his words, trying to draw some direction or inspiration from them. She was afraid to assume they were instructions to poison her boss and his gang. They might refer to Cindy, that she was saved because she would always be a child and a fool, but they shed no light on her immediate problem, which had her too upset to wait till morning. Casting about for what to do next, she reluctantly reached a decision. He was worse than a white man, he was one of her own who treated her like dirt, but he would know what to do and could do it. He was, in fact, the man she should have gone to in the first place. This matter was too important to let personal feelings or pride interfere.

The squat impassive face across from him often haunted Abe Lakes's nightmares, but he had avoided encountering it during his waking hours for so long that he had forgotten its details: A squaw's obstinate features stamped on southern riverbank clay: a broad, high brow, muddy red skin, big nose, big protruding teeth, long silky braids now half gray. And unblinking, hypnotic, amber-colored eyes. How had he ever seen anything attractive in that doglike face? It must have been her hair, he thought; he had always been drawn to long, straight, shining hair. But, God, she was ugly now. And mean—not just nigger-mean, but squaw-mean. With all their other handicaps, why did half the niggers in the country have to be cursed with crazy Indian blood? he wondered, so miserably conscious of the kinky growth on his head that he was completely unaware of his own high cheekbones, hawk nose, and squinty eyes.

Since she was too stubborn to speak first, he cleared his throat. "Well, good evening, Lavinia. How are you?"

"No use complaining."

"Lucinda is all right, I hope?"

"As all right as she'll ever be. I'm gonna have to take her out of school this year. The teachers say she can't keep up."

"Tsk. A pity. Is that what you wanted to see me about?"

"No." There was a brusque movement below his line of vision across the desk, probably a dipping into one of the swollen shopping bags women like Vinnie always carried. Then a folder of papers stamped with the state seal was thrust in front of his eyes. "I thought you ought to have a look at these, Mayor."

He was grateful for her use of the title; it put things on an impersonal basis and created a distance between them. "What are they?"

"The plans for the highway. I heard my boss and his friends talking tonight. They said Merchant Avenue would have to go, and since that's the first I ever heard of it, I wanted you to look and see if it's true."

It was the first he had heard of it too, but no one would have guessed. Abe's keen-featured face was as impassive and Indian as her broad, blunt one. They would have made excellent opponents in a poker game.

"Won't you be in trouble if these are missed, Vinnie?" he asked, stalling.

"I'm already in worse trouble if they meant what they said."

"Hmmmm. I see," he murmured, and opened the folder with deliberate casualness. He almost dismissed the top set, dated October of the previous year, then decided to give them a quick look. This, apparently the original plan for Interstate 27, did not touch Lakestown at all. It went straight through the heart of Edgehill instead. On the reduced state map it was clear that this plan made more sense. Edgehill stood directly in the highway's north-south path, but the road would have to curve far out of its way to go through Lakestown.

Abe was mildly surprised but not shocked. Half the politicians who controlled the state lived in Edgehill. They would hardly agree to have their valuable, historic, A-I real estate destroyed.

The second set of plans, dated June of this year, was the one he had already seen: a grade-level, six-lane highway running through Lakestown, its width covering everything from Nestor Avenue to Piney Road, requiring the condemnation or relocation of forty-two properties in all, most of very low valuation.

But the folder also contained a third set of plans dated this month, July, which he had not been shown. In them the highway was widened from six lanes to eight and was divided by a twenty-foot medial strip. This expansion would take all of Merchant Avenue, just as Vinnie had said, and part of Grimes Road, too. He would have to look at the borough tax maps to be certain, but Abe guessed that would double the number of condemned properties and quadruple their value. Worst of all, in these plans the highway was not at grade level but depressed, a gorge containing a rapid river of traffic. So much for the possibilities of ribbon development along its borders, the likely jobs and ratables he had been promised. If travelers on Interstate Route 27 wanted to stop for a night's lodging or for Yum-Burgers, Sweety-Freez, or Licken Chicken, it would not be in Lakestown.

Abe was angry. Clearly, he had been tricked. Drumming his long beige fingers on his desk, he considered calling Grafton to demand an explanation, considered calling the newspapers to make a statement, considered calling a borough council meeting to draft a resolution of protest. Slowly his fingers went limp and he relaxed, realizing that it made no difference to him in the long run. If he kept quiet, his future was assured in a place far away from Lakestown.

It was one of those critical moments when a man learns once and for all where his commitment lies. Abe's, he discovered, was to himself alone.

Vinnie, he knew, could not read; she had only heard a chance remark, and she might be persuaded she had heard wrong.

"Uh, Lavinia," he said in his most genial voice, "I've been thinking about Lucinda's school problem. The Board of Education's funds are limited here, of course, but I know of places that are staffed and equipped to take care of special children like Lucinda. They can teach her to be independent, teach her a useful trade. I know of an excellent training facility in Branch Creek . . ."

The amber eyes glowed balefully like yellow warning lights. "I don't live in Branch Creek."

"I was about to say that it might be possible to send you there. Or to send Lucinda there, board her there during the week, and bring her home on weekends. If it's only a question of money . . ."

"My girl's better off here, where people understand her. Why should I send her off someplace strange where they might mock her and make her feel bad? And why . . ." her gaze narrowed suspiciously, "should you pay for it?"

"Well, I, er, I feel a certain responsibility."

"You ain't felt none all these years. How come you feeling it all of a sudden?"

"Be reasonable, Lavinia. I didn't want to harm the child, so I never breathed a word, and I never interfered as long as she didn't seem to need my assistance. But now that she does, I'm glad to do whatever I can."

"Hah!" she barked. "I came to see you about them plans, not about Cindy. What's in them, Mayor? Is the highway going to take my house and my church or isn't it?"

"I haven't really had a chance to study them, Lavinia," he lied. "But I'll keep them and go over them carefully when I have the time. Then I'll be able to let you know."

"Oh no you ain't," she said, her voice a low growl, her face more than ever like a bulldog's. "What's happened to you is a sorry thing to see, Abe Lakes. I'm only glad for one thing: your father ain't alive to see it. Them white folks have bought you somehow, and you just finished trying to buy me. But I ain't for sale, and neither is Cindy. So I'll just take what I came with and leave."

"Vinnie, wait. You're jumping to conclusions. We can still talk— work things out—have a sensible discussion. After all, we're old friends ..."

His front door slammed behind the determined tread of her swollen, clumsy feet and heavy legs.

6

Fess followed Vinnie to the Peace Baptist parsonage, saw her come out soon after she entered, and surmised that Crow, his nickname for the suave Baptist minister, was lost in another of his hash-pipe dreams. Like almost everything else in Lakestown, the Reverend Bird's vice was no secret to Fess. Nor was Bird's preference for his own sex, though to give the Reverend credit, he channeled it discreetly. His female parishioners either ignored or were ignorant of Reverend Bird's predilection. They were unanimously, adoringly in love with their silky-haired, smooth-skinned, velvet-voiced minister and contributed enough to the church collections to provide him with all the antiques and hashish he required for his happiness. And since *their* happiness required that their pastor be transported in a large, elegant car and the Reverend Bird did not drive, they could hardly object to his series of chauffeurs.

At least Bird had used some of their contributions to build his congregation a fine church constructed of wood along sparse classic lines, with a slim, dainty spire, all of it annually repainted a sparkling white. A Christopher Wren church, in fact; Bird's built us a Wren! Fess thought, and smothered a laugh. Well, give the man some more grudging credit; he knew his architecture as well as his art and music, and both his church and his choir, trained to produce precise cascades of Handel and Bach as well as mellow spirituals, brought high culture to the community. There was something to be said for choosing intelligent rogues as leaders over zealous fools; Bird was a positive force in the town, and his congregation included some of its most stable citizens. Whereas Reverend Bream, the Methodist minister, whom Fess privately called Fish, had a ragged, rundown church and a confused congregation blown this way and that by his intense, shifting enthusiasms for secular causes, usually lost ones.

Fess hid behind one of the parsonage's giant sycamore trees until Vinnie passed him, then doubled back to follow her until he realized that she was approaching the mayor's house. He was surprised and puzzled. Those two had not spoken, as far as he knew, for twelve years. Something was definitely up. He began to be excited. But he did not want to get caught skulking around the mayor's property, which was guarded by two vicious Dobermans and an electrified chain-link fence. From the side garden, now dark, he heard an unearthly voice singing—what else—"In the Garden." He paused, listening to the liquid, effortless notes, sounds rarer than a nightingale's, that were the chief ornament of Bird's choir.

The mayor evidently disliked children, since he had none, at least none that bore his name. Recently Bella Lakes, denied motherhood until it was too late, had taken up a substitute mothering of Cindy Coddums that must be a particularly painful thorn in Abe's side. The child was with Bella all the time Vinnie worked, which often went on into the night, helping in the Lakes kitchen and in the garden, never talking, of course, but constantly listening unless she was singing. And of course no one dared talk to Bella about Cindy, Abe least of all. Fess was sure she did not know who Cindy's father was, but Fess knew and, more devastatingly, Abe knew.

A light went out behind him, across Edgehill Road. Fess turned and saw that it was Doc Thompson's illuminated office sign, their signal. Doc liked to arrange for Fess to be his last patient so they could enjoy their long, leisurely conversations on everything from politics to philosophy, and he always extinguished the light to let Fess know when the waiting room had been emptied.

The waiting-room door was still unlocked, though, an absent-minded mistake of Doc's, since more patients could always straggle in. Fess took the precaution of locking it behind him. The room was darkened, probably to discourage unwelcome entry. Fess announced himself with a soft "Roaney" and the old metal desk lamp went on. The butterflies glowed like jewels from the dirty brown walls, and the fat, heavy-jowled old doctor appeared in chiaroscuro behind his desk, his magnifying glass poised above a specimen. Not blood or sputum or urine, all three of which Fess had come to deposit, but *Lepidoptera*. "Is that a rare one?" he asked.

"Not rare, but pretty. A Red Admiral. The top markings are not that unusual, but the underwings are really special. Come have a look."

Fess moved the glass until the upside-down specimen came into sharp focus. "Gorgeous," he said. "It reminds me of a pheasant's tail feathers."

"It's exactly like a pheasant's tail feathers," the doctor corrected him. "Another of nature's mysteries. The pheasant is reproduced in the butterfly, which emerges from a worm. Did I ever show you my Peacock?"

He took one of the framed specimens from the wall, a pair, one mounted right side up, the other upside down. "This one has the bird markings on top of his wings; his underwings are as drab as mud. But mud can be interesting, too."

"I know," said Fess, who was aware of the doctor's strange, sensuous pleasure in handling mud and clay and cement. Especially cement.

"Nothing is lost in nature, Roaney, nothing! Oh, the dross is lost, the mistakes are sloughed away, but nothing valuable ever dies. Everything that is really fine, really worth preserving, reappears somewhere else. It's the only rational basis I know for a belief in immortality, the only faith I have. When I look at *Vanessa atalanta* here and see how it reincarnates the pheasant, or vice versa, I know I am looking at something holy."

"Is he local?"

"Yes. I don't know about the 'he.' What gender do you assign to an Admiral named *Vanessa?* Something else very interesting, Roaney. Sex is often rather indistinct in nature. It's the last thing to develop in the human embryo, did you know that? The other night I delivered an infant with both sets of reproductive organs."

"Good God. What did you tell the parents?"

The doctor chuckled. "I just told them to wait a while before naming the baby. It'll take a little time, a few tests, till we know which sex is dominant. Then I'll order a minor operation, and they can start buying pink or blue booties. Hermaphroditism is fairly common, you know. And it's not really a serious problem, not anymore, as long as the infant is normal and healthy in all other respects, and this one was."

While talking, the doctor had listened to Fess's chest, thumped his back, and tightened a sphygmomanometer cuff around his arm. "Good," he grunted as he got the second reading.

"I'll live?" Fess inquired.

"Technically, Roaney, as I've told you before, you've been dead for fifteen years. You're a moving miracle, like these butterflies. But I believe in miracles, I see them every day, and at least your pressure's under control." He pointed to the little bathroom door at one side of the cluttered room. "You know the rest of the routine. Might as well get it over with."

Fess, who was feeling pressure in his bladder from the beers, went gladly into the little cubicle and produced a urine sample. Next he coughed up sputum into the waiting cup and last, since he was thoroughly accustomed to using a hypodermic to inject himself with insulin, he drew his own blood sample with the needle Doc had provided. He brought all three containers back to the doctor, who was breaking the seal on a more attractive bottle.

"I've just discovered this. A domestic cream sherry as good as anything they make in England." Doc half filled two huge snifters and handed one to Fess. "To California and its vines."

"What about my blood sugar?"

"You've already given me your sample, haven't you?"

Fess nodded and joined him in laughing.

"So it won't be affected. And if you go into coma, I'm here to bring you out of it. Drink up, friend. Life is too short to restrict it so severely you stop really living."

"No lectures?" Fess asked mockingly. "No prescriptions? No doctor's orders?"

"This," Doc Thompson said, raising his glass appreciatively, "is your prescription. Tastes good, feels good going down, relaxes you so we can have a decent conversation. I'm selfish, you see. If I were an altruist I'd order you to Arizona for the air. But if I did that, who would I have to talk to? So I'm only going to order you over to Edgehill Hospital next week for your regular chest X-ray. Don't let those ghouls over there do anything else to you, though. Just have them send the report to me, and let nature go on working her miracles. You're one of them, you know. But don't get conceited, Roaney. You're only one of many. I see a half dozen others every day." He gestured with the hand that held a stinking Turkish cigarette. "These butterflies. And a turtle down at Crump's Creek. I turned it over and its underbelly had the exact markings of the lily pads that grow in the dammed-up pond there. A leaf I found with a perfect tracing of the human venous system. And a fifty-year-old woman delivering a viable infant that, if I weren't planning to remove a few excess endowments, might well grow up to be both mother and father to its own children. And I'd bet the children would be normal. But not interesting. Nature needs variety to make things interesting.

"I really don't think Arizona could do you any more good than this place, Roaney. Sometimes I think there's something curative about

Lakestown air, that maybe even those vile fogs down in Froggy Bottom are salubrious. People over eighty are so common here nobody even notices them. If the Census Bureau ever catches on and puts the scientists on to us, we've had it. Ready for a refill?"

"Why not?"

The doctor paused professionally before tilting the bottle. "You *have* eaten, I hope."

"Amply," Fess sighed, remembering his meal at Josh Hawkins's. "Bread, fish, and pig. Mostly pig."

"Was it greasy?" the doctor asked, still withholding the bottle.

"Extremely," Fess replied, and smacked his lips at the memory. "Deliciously."

At last the doctor refilled his glass. "Then this won't hurt what's left of your ulcer. I know what they say about cholesterol, but I have my own theory that grease is what keeps our race going. Grease in our skillets, in our greens, in our hair, on our skin—all of it lubricating our engines. I would never be cruel enough to put anyone on a low-fat diet. Unless they were white." He raised his own glass. "To the glory that is grease."

"*Salud,*" Fess said. He understood the source of Doc's grease theory. Cars, after all, required lubrication, and the doctor now owned six, managing to keep at least one running with parts borrowed from the other five. But Fess had faith in Dr. Thompson. Though he would rather tinker with concrete structures and engines than with the human body, he had better success with his patients than with his automobiles, approximately in an inverse ratio: he kept at least five out of every six of them in good running condition.

"I added some antique running lights to the Ford, real beauties," Doc said. "Want to see them?"

"Not really," Fess admitted, staring morosely into his glass. "I'm just moody, I guess. I was thinking about what you said before, about this healthy Lakestown air. It has a new ingredient I don't think is so healthy."

"What's that?" asked the doctor, replenishing his own glass but offering no more to Fess.

"Dust. From digging."

The doctor's pouchy face took on a lugubrious expression. "I know. I've seen it. Can't stop looking at it, as a matter of fact. Like any other fascinating horror. It's monstrous. Evil. No resemblance to the earth. More like a crater on the moon."

"And after the dust, there'll be worse pollution. Car fumes."

"Yes, it's dreadful. It's depressing." Doc picked up the bottle and set it down again. "I really should put this away. You shouldn't have any more, and I shouldn't be a pig in front of you."

"Go ahead, if it'll help you think of a way to stop the highway."

"You might as well ask me to stop evil, Roaney. Evil is inevitable. And so is that thing."

"Why?"

"Money, for one thing. Greed. The Federal Highway Trust Fund has been compounding interest for decades. By now it's a monstrous fortune. The biggest pork barrel in the country, maybe in the world. Every politician and every contractor who's a politician's third cousin wants to get his hands in it. The government practically begs them to take that money. The highway fund's grown so big they have problems administering it."

Fess considered another idea. "A little while ago you said nothing valuable ever dies. Then what happened to the spirit that started Lakestown? I mean those first runaway slaves, the fight that was in them, the determination? Did it die?"

"I don't think so, no," Doc said. "I think it's just been put to sleep by comfort and prosperity. Like the whites in America; they revolted once too, remember? I think all it needs is something to shock it awake."

"If cutting the guts out of this town doesn't shock people, what can?" Fess shook his head slowly, despairingly. "For a while tonight I thought there just might be some hope. I saw Vinnie Coddums in a strange mood, and I started wondering . . ."

"Forget it," the doctor said shortly. "She's hopeless. The last of the good old house niggers."

"But think of the house she's the nigger in."

"Don't you think I haven't thought of it?" the shrewd old doctor replied.

They were interrupted by a loud rapping at the door, so heavy it sounded like a club instead of a hand. "Don't they know my office hours are over? Don't I deserve any time to myself?" Doc grumbled. "Stop that damn banging, and come the hell in!" he called.

"I locked it," Fess said.

"Who's there?" Doc called, rising and waddling, on large feet and thick legs that resembled two of his concrete columns, to the door.

"Miss Lavinia Coddums," was the formal answer.

"Speak of the devil," the doctor said softly, and opened the door, revealing Vinnie still carrying her shopping bags. "Are you ill, Lavinia?"

"No more than usual, just my legs and my back paining me like they always do. But you can't do nothing about that."

"Quite right," he said. "You know my limitations, and so do I. So why this visit?"

He had not invited her in, but she did not wait for an invitation. She plodded forward and stood, rooted stubbornly as an old tree, in the middle of the room.

Doc Thompson, just as stubborn, stood glaring at her in his old house slippers and dirty coveralls.

Abruptly, with no warning, she produced some papers from her shopping bag and announced, "These are the plans for that devilish highway. I stole them from my boss's office tonight, after I heard them white folks talking. I heard them say they were going to take all of Merchant Avenue. That means my house and my church, too. I figured I better find out was it true. I already took these to the mayor, and he tried to get slick on me, so I had to find another colleged person to read them for me. The only one I know . . ."; for the first time she noticed Fess, and ducked her head in his direction; ". . .the only two others I know are here."

"Miracles," Fess said.

"What was that, Roaney?" asked the old doctor, who had already spread the papers under his desk lamp and was peering at them through his magnifying lens.

"I said, 'miracles.' An awful lot of them seem to happen in this room."

"Is it true what they said?" Vinnie asked.

"Yes. Oh God, yes. This is a disgrace. A disaster." Fess looked over his shoulder but, having no experience with maps or blueprints, did not know what he was looking at until the doctor pointed it out to him.

"This line here. That's the line of destruction, what they would call construction, progress. All the way to the north end of Grimes Road.

Half the town, Roaney. Half the town. And they lied to us." He opened the other plans. "Here, see. It was only supposed to go this far."

"What are you going to do? Bring it before the council?" Fess asked the doctor, the only council member he trusted.

"Probably. There's a meeting tomorrow night. But I can tell you now it won't do any good. The state has the right of eminent domain; it can chew up anything it wants. Politics, legal methods, lawsuits—they can stall things for a while, but they won't get us anywhere in the long run."

"What we need," Fess said sadly, "is another miracle."

"Good thinking, Roaney," said the doctor. "I think we'd better call in one of the ministers."

"Fish or Crow?" Fess asked, forgetting who else was in the room.

"I don't appreciate you calling my pastor out of his name," said Vinnie, with a quickness that surprised them both. "Suppose I called you Frog, Mr. Roaney, how would you like that?"

Fess made a little bow of apology. He knew what he looked like: bowed legs, oversized head, and pop eyes. Her name for him was cruelly accurate.

"Anyway," she said, "I can tell you it's no use calling my pastor tonight. I was just by there, and he was sleeping."

"I was thinking of Fish—er, the Reverend Bream," the doctor replied. "He has zeal, he has energy, he has imagination, and he has a following that will do anything he says, however crazy it seems."

Fess groaned, remembering the latest Fish crusade, a chain-store boycott that had lasted six months and resulted in the hiring of a single black employee. "Don't you have any better ideas?" he asked.

"Not at the moment," the doctor admitted.

"I was thinking of poison, myself," Vinnie said calmly.

"What?" the doctor roared.

"I'm the cook. I could poison all of them, my boss and his friends, everyone who's in this devilish thing. I bet you got something in there, in them bottles, that I could use."

"Yes, I do. And I won't let you have it. But, God, how I love your spirit! Forgive me, Lavinia, I have misjudged you." And to Vinnie's astonishment the doctor embraced her—bent her stiff body backward and planted a long, firm kiss on her stunned lips.

"Well, I never," she said when it was over, her clay-colored complexion turning redder.

"I think I love you," the doctor said. "Lavinia, did I ever tell you you're beautiful?"

"Go on with you," she said, smiling in spite of herself, looking somewhat like an alligator after a large meal.

"Thank you for your suggestion," the doctor teased. "I don't think we want anyone killed just yet. But we'll think of something for you to do, Vinnie. We can't let all that magnificent spirit go to waste."

"I'll do anything," she said.

"I know. That's why I love you." The doctor advanced toward her again, but Vinnie was ready for him this time. She brought her large, heavy pocketbook down on top of his head.

"Ow! Is that any way to treat a man who has just declared his love for you?"

"You're full of you know what."

"Yes, I know what I am full of. Hope. And joy. And a considerable amount of sherry, and tons of gratitude. From the bottom of my heart, I thank you, Lavinia."

"You're welcome," she said humorlessly.

"I'll copy these plans on my machine and give you back the originals, so you can put them back where you got them, hopefully before they're missed. You can be very valuable, Vinnie. You can be a heroine. Keep your eyes and ears open, and see what else you can find out. But no poison, not yet. Dead men can't talk."

"They can't dig holes, either."

"No," he said thoughtfully, "they can only lie in them. Give this town your prayers, Vinnie; it can use them. And a little voodoo wouldn't hurt, either, if you happen to know any."

"I know plenty," she said. "But it's against my religion."

And murder isn't? the doctor wondered, and continued to wonder, staring at the ceiling for a long time after she was gone.

7

Abe charged through the house like a robot with circuits gone haywire, stiff legs pumping, wheels and gears clicking, transistors melting and giving off angry sparks. A dry, scorched odor like an electrical fire clung to him.

His first thought had been of murder. Women as evil and ignorant as Vinnie Coddums should not be allowed to live. Now, as when Vinnie had told him she was pregnant, his conscience had not stopped him, but thoughts of his position had. He was ambitious, therefore vulnerable; he could not risk killing someone and getting caught. Vinnie would have to be run out of town.

Abe had called Borough Hall, only to be told by the dispatcher that Chief Boyd was out either dispersing a traffic accident or quelling a disturbance on Rowdy Row. He had not reported back, so there was no telling where he was now or when he could be reached. Abe felt he was running against the weight of deep water, with time ticking away at triple speed. He needed Boyd now, this instant, before that old witch talked and turned the whole town against him. Together he and his police chief could work out something; declare the house unfit for habitation and Vinnie mentally incompetent and in need of custodial care. There was, of course, no question about the child's mental incompetence and, in Abe's mind, no question about its source. The mother, of course. He scarcely ever admitted, even to himself, that she had a father.

After a brief stop in the bathroom, Abe headed for the kitchen, hardly knowing where he was going or why. The brandy in the cupboard, that was it.

In his present mood, the familiar females he found there were as startling as two creatures from an alien planet. Two dark, sleek heads bent over a bowl, snapping string beans from the garden. His wife and— he almost choked—his daughter.

Bella and Cindy looked up at him with equal shock, as if he were an intruder, probably armed and dangerous.

"What are you looking at?" he snapped.

"Nothin', dear," Bella murmured.

"Doesn't a man have a right to walk around his own house?"

"Sholy," she said, in tones meant to be soothing but that only exacerbated his nerves, "sholy he does."

"Why do you talk like that?" he raged, going to the cupboard for the brandy and a glass, pouring himself a stiff one. "You've never set foot in the South. Why do you have a southern accent?"

"Cayunt rahtly say," she drawled maddeningly. "Hayunt no accountin' foah it."

"And why," he continued peevishly, "do you insist on us having a vegetable garden like poor farm niggers? We can afford to buy at the best stores in Edgehill and have things delivered. We can afford damn near anything you want, including a maid. So why do you have to be kneeling down digging in the dirt all day, like some sharecropping slavey?"

"Oh," Bella said, pushing back a damp lock of hair with a shockingly grubby hand, "hit just give me somethin' to do."

"Well, I wish you'd find something else to do. For instance, I wish you'd scrub those hands before you cook my dinner. Especially under the nails."

Bella looked down at the blackened tips of her long, elegant fingers in surprise.

"Sholy, dear," she said again, and leaned back in the kitchen chair, propping her feet on the rungs of the one opposite, which held Cindy, sitting up prim and straight as a reed. Bella's sprawled legs, in contrast to Cindy's bird-thin ones, were the big legs so admired by black men, plump and round and, considering her age, amazingly smooth, with no creases or visible veins. They were a gorgeous pair, his full-blown rose of a wife and his slim, tan, fragile-faced daughter, both with luxuriant heads of black hair.

"Must you sit like that?" he roared at Bella.

"Liyuk what, dear?" she asked innocently.

"Like *that,* with your legs open! There's a rip in the crotch of your shorts. Why do you wear shorts, anyhow? For God's sake, Bella, you're an adult woman."

"I know how old I am," she said, in clear, crisp tones that made her previous drawl seem a mockery. "I also know there's nobody here to look up my snatch but you and Cindy, and neither one of you is interested."

The same reason, he thought angrily, that she never bothered to shut the bathroom door, no matter what disgusting animal functions she was performing in there. "Must you use words like that?" he shouted.

"What words, dear?"

He gave up. "It's time you sent that child home. Her mother's waiting for her."

Bella lowered her tilted chair and her legs languidly. Lately, all her movements had become unaccountably provocative. "Wait till I wash up and change, Cindy honey," she said. "I'll drive you home."

"You're going to *drive* her?" asked Abe, who regarded Cindy as a combination pet and unpaid maid.

"It's after dark. She's got no business walking home alone, with all the big, horny boys running loose in this town. Cindy's getting to be a big girl now. Or hadn't you noticed?"

He had, fearfully and guiltily, noticed the almost imperceptible signs of early womanhood, the lengthening torso, the beginning of a waistline, the gently swelling breasts. And he had noticed too, with trepidation, the attentions of a boy called Lou. But Abe was one of those people who feared that speaking about unpleasant things would make them more real. His acknowledgment of them now was a brusque nod.

"Don't worry," Bella reassured him. "Any boy messes with this baby, he got to deal with Vinnie *and* me." Cindy followed her progress toward the kitchen door with a sly, sidewise glance that already seemed to contain centuries of experience.

"You might be too late," he warned.

"I doubt it," she replied, and waited for him to step aside.

He was blocking the door. "Why are you changing?"

"You don't like my shorts," she replied unanswerably.

He had to let her go, but not yet. In some obscure way he did not understand she had challenged him, and he felt he had to force her to submit to his authority. He touched her shoulder and felt her flinch. There was a strong repulsion between them, as if they were magnets advancing to meet at the same pole. He cleared his throat.

"Er, Bella, I feel I have to answer that remark about my lack of interest in your—er—pudenda. At your age, the chances of having a Mongoloid child are five in a hundred. And since you refuse to use any prophylactic measures—well, what can I do?" He shrugged. "There are enough congenital idiots running around this town without our contributing more."

Bella gave him a piercing, black look. "You can use that for an excuse if you want, Lakes. Course I could turn that around and say my chances of having a normal baby are ninety-five in a hundred, and that sounds pretty good to me. But don't worry. I won't surprise you with a baby." She laughed in his face, a flash of strong, predatory teeth. "Only thing is, you ought to be careful what you say around Cindy. She understands more than you know. Just because she can't speak doesn't mean she can't hear."

He had lost, and his stinging pride flooded him with reckless anger. "Then let her hear this. As you said, she's getting grown now, and she's a menace to herself. There's no way you can make her understand the dangers, and no matter what you and Vinnie do, you can't watch over her every minute. That's why I intend to have her sent away somewhere where she'll be protected."

"An institution, you mean? A home?"

The small, exquisite face at the kitchen table became distorted with anguish. Soundless tears began running down the buff cheeks.

"I *told* you she understands more than you know. Don't worry, Cindy, I won't let him do it."

The silent crying bothered him more than noisy tears would have, but he had to hurt Bella and frighten her. "It won't be me doing it. There are higher authorities who would take an interest, and once the machinery was set in motion, you wouldn't be able to stop it. What I suggest, Bella, is that you break off your attachment to this unfortunate child. Stop spending so much time with her. Busy yourself with something else."

"Like what?" Her tone was not saucy, merely puzzled.

"Well, you might try helping me with my career," he said ironically. "I'm going places in politics, Bella. I need the right sort of partner."

"Sholy," she said meekly, in that infuriating sham drawl. "Anything you say, Lakes."

He had won, seemingly, but he was not satisfied. He had no idea what, if anything, his wife was thinking, but he was sure her meek compliance was as much a pretense as was her southern drawl.

Bella went to the bathroom, where Abe, in his rage or whatever it was, had relieved himself without flushing the toilet. For once she shut the door, and even locked it. Then she scrubbed her hands and her vulva, squatted and inserted the diaphragm Abe did not know she possessed, scrubbed her hands again, removed the offending shorts, and tied on a long skirt that matched the blue and green blouse she was still wearing. All this took her less than two minutes. It would look as though she had simply tied the skirt on over the shorts, but actually she was naked under the skirt, producing an awareness of her own body which, she knew from experience, always aroused her.

She hesitated at the door. In her haste, she had used one of Abe's five washcloths instead of her own. But which one—the one for his face, the one for his feet, the one for his armpits, the one for his privates, or the one for the rest of him? With sudden, reckless glee, she wiped herself with each cloth in turn, impregnating them with her female odor, then deliberately, maliciously, mixed them all up.

It was the first time she had allowed herself to make even a secret gesture of hostility toward her husband, and it filled her with exultation. She'd always been too grateful to Abe to admit anger against him, even to herself.

An orphan at sixteen, the frightened remnant of an auto crash that had killed both her parents and her brothers, she'd accepted Abe's proposal of marriage as if he were the doorman of heaven. Coming back from a football game in which her older brother had run up record points, her family had slammed into the side of a new abutment that carried an overpass over a congested curve. Ever since, Bella had hated highways and driven only on back roads. There had been the security of her surrounding family, the cheering excitement of the game, the snug warmth of the car, an icy patch on the highway, and then—nothing. Bella found herself with no money, no people, no home she could afford to keep, and no negotiable assets but her exceptional beauty.

She was all the more isolated because she and her parents were products of Claypool, a little ghetto pocket of Low Point where everyone was almost white but not quite, and people of either distinct racial heritage were unwelcome. It was an ingrown, incestuous little community where marriages between cousins and resultant birth defects were common. Abe, fearing the Claypool taint in her blood, had offered marriage on the condition that there be no children. She'd agreed readily; it was him or nothing. Nine years older than Bella, already out of college and law school, he was a tall, morose spectator on the fringes of Claypool parties, rarely speaking but seemingly preferring blondes, especially her best friend, Ellie Polite, until Ellie married Beau Parker, a Claypool boy as blond as herself. Almost immediately afterward, Abe proposed to Bella, who scarcely knew him. After twenty-five years, she could still say that.

Having no basis for comparison, she thought for a long time that all husbands were like Abe, distant and moody and disapproving, and that she had no cause for complaint. But lately, something in Bella was bursting free after all those years of restraint.

She had hesitated to perfume herself, because it might arouse Abe's suspicion. But she had too much catch-up living to do to waste time worrying about him. Waiting out there were a child who made her feel like a mother and a man who made her feel like a woman, both for the first time. She recklessly sprayed herself with a shower of Chanel and sailed out of the house on a wave of fragrance.

Deciding that Abe's Lincoln would be too conspicuous, Bella slid behind the wheel of her lithe little Volvo and opened the passenger door for Cindy. She got some finger-popping sounds on the radio, rolled the window down, and took off, alternately humming and talking.

"You all right, Cindy? He didn't scare you, did he?"

The delicate profile beside her bobbed up and down vigorously, then moved from side to side, more slowly and less convincingly.

This car steered easily with one hand. Bella put her right arm around the girl's bony shoulders and drew her protectively close. "I won't let him do it, Cindy. Nobody's going to take you away from me."

The heart against her side was beating ninety to the minute. "How you gone stop him?"

Bella's own heart flopped in her chest on hearing that almost perfect sentence. The last time, last Monday when the bulldozers first appeared, Cindy had only uttered three words, and there had been a desert of silence since.

"I'll find a way. Just trust me. You trust me, don't you?"

"Sure, Miss Bella."

Bella released her after a hard squeeze. "That's a good girl. You *are* a good girl, aren't you, Cindy?"

She was staring at the dark contours of Merchant Avenue now, but the corner of her eye caught the startled jerk of the child's head. "Ma'am?"

"I mean, you don't let boys touch you, do you?" She pointed to her own excitable crotch. "That Lou Adams—has he ever tried to touch you down here?"

Cindy was clearly shocked. Her answer was a decisive, "No, *ma'am.*"

"Good. But he *will* try. Never mind how I know; he will. When he does, what will you do?"

Bella slowed the car to look at Cindy. Her forehead was knotted in puzzlement. Bella wondered fleetingly if she were pushing too far too fast, bringing up matters that were too disturbing for the child's seeming innocence. But she was going on fifteen: time she learned.

Apparently, Cindy was not struggling with the problem, though; only with the words. Finally they came: "Kick him ass."

Bella roared approvingly. She was feeling good now—loose, mellow, relaxed, *good.* "That's my girl. Stop him any way you have to. If you don't, you might like it. And then you'd be sorry."

"Because it's bad."

"No." Bella thumped the steering wheel angrily. "Hell no. It's good, but only for big people."

"I big now."

"Not big enough."

"When I be big enough?"

Bella sighed, swore, and swerved to avoid a jackrabbit and one of Lakestown's many potholes. Parents had more problems than she had ever imagined. But no one had ever told her anything about life, and she had sworn, if a child ever came her way, to do better. "When I tell you," she said shortly. "Not one minute before. And then I'll tell you all the things big girls need to know.

And that had better be soon, Bella decided. Her mellow feeling had vanished. She was annoyed with her own tension and with the awkward situation she had created. One hurdle had been cleared, but ten new ones had sprouted ahead. She tossed her cigarette out the window, lit another, tossed the match after the butt, and stomped angrily on the gas pedal. If Vinnie Coddums knew, she would call her a meddling bitch, Bella thought. And she would be right. Cindy, as if exhausted by her unaccustomed effort at speech, had lapsed into her usual silent passivity. Bella could only hope she had done more good than harm.

"I'll take you for a little ride before we go home. You'd like that, wouldn't you?"

There was no answer. Cindy's hands were over her ears, as if to prevent hearing anything more.

Bella went on chattering nervously. "Lou Adams has the same name as you, did you know that? Lucinda. Sounds strange for a boy, I know, but half the mothers in this town named their babies after old Miss Lucinda Lakes a few years back, hoping she'd leave them something. But every penny she had went right back to the white folks she got it from, the people in her religious thing. I forget what it was, not Christian Science, but something like it. And those hymn-singin' white folks got all her property, too, even the waterfront land she had down by Crump's Creek, back when it was a lake."

Bella began to remember her own childhood. "And oh, it was a lovely lake, Cindy. You could swim in it and fish in it, you could row a boat on it, and you could ice skate on it in the winter. There was a sandy beach, and dunes to run through, and a pier we used to dive from.

"You aren't listening, are you?"

Cindy was slumped down low in her seat, her hands tightly pressed over her hair.

"What is it—your hair?"

The girl nodded.

"I thought so. We've got blow hair, it's the only thing Abe likes about us, so why not let it blow? Let it blow, let it blow, let it blow, let it blow . . ."

"Let It Be" by 'Retha was on the radio, and Bella was singing along. But Cindy did not join in. Her lips remained closed, her hands tightly pressed to her head. Bella gave up.

"I can tell you're not enjoying this ride," she said. "Neither am I. I think I'll take you straight home; your mother's probably waiting. I know what she thinks; she thinks the night air will make your hair nappy. But she's wrong, she's dead wrong; the most it can do is curl it. And who cares, anyhow; curls or naps, what's the difference? We're all niggers anyway. But I shouldn't say that. I shouldn't say anything. *She's* your mother, not me."

Bella executed a quick, vicious U turn, enjoying, in spite of her anger, the way the car swiveled on a dime. In less than a minute she stopped at the door of Vinnie's small frame house. A light on the porch indicated that Vinnie was indeed home and that her daughter was expected.

Bella reached across for Cindy's hand. "Nobody knows you can talk but you and me. Let's keep it our secret for a while."

The child nodded, but the hand Bella held was cold and lifeless.

"Let's save it up for a surprise. It might help me keep you here in Lakestown. Okay?"

With another nod, the child was out of the car and skipping up the sagging steps. For once Bella was glad to get rid of her. The easy companionship they had enjoyed during Cindy's childhood, baking cakes together, gardening, going fishing, picking wild blackberries, had abruptly ended. It was thrilling that Cindy was talking at last, that all Bella's patient efforts to teach her were finally paying off, but the thorny, difficult adolescent years had begun, and speech was not going to make them any easier. In fact, Bella suspected it was going to make them harder.

She nosed her car back in the direction she had come, then executed another swift pivot, this one planned. In the thicket where she had tossed a lighted cigarette, a hundred yards from Vinnie's house, the fire was still hidden, too small to catch her eye as she passed, bound for the back way to Rowdy Row. She turned up the radio and lit another, hoping she would soon feel sensual and mellow again. The music, a righteous sermon by Lou Rawls, was helping. Soon she would have a drink, and that would help more. And then soon she would be with someone who made her feel good, and that would help most of all. Bella had a lot of living to pack into the short time left before the years of merely maintaining life began.

8

Although Chief Benson Maimonides Boyd was considered black, he looked like the furthest thing imaginable from a soul brother, in his high, glossy boots and crisp blue uniform decorated with rows of bullets instead of medals. He looked more like an S.S. captain, complete with steel gray eyes. Only his crinkly dark hair and mustache saved him from being a pure example of the mythical Aryan breed. He had a military bearing, the lordly height of seventy-six inches, and the habit of command. People usually followed his orders. Thirty minutes ago he had walked calmly into a melee of flailing fists and knives at the Satin Club, discharged two soft-nosed .38-magnum bullets into the ceiling, and produced instant order and decorum. Now he stood fearlessly in the middle of Route 80, the Dorset Turnpike, and traffic obediently parted itself like the Red Sea to flow around him and the debris of a multiple-vehicle accident. Chief Boyd did not know he was about to come up against the only object his irresistible force could not move: an angry and obdurate black woman.

Vinnie Coddums inspected her child anxiously the moment she walked into the smoky little kitchen, touching and sniffing and poking at Cindy like a she-bear examining a strayed cub. She was looking for signs of what she called worldliness: a trace of forbidden lipstick, a hint of cologne or something worse out of a bottle, a cheeky attitude or any other change in the girl's manner that might betray lost innocence. The inspection was accompanied by little grunts and growls that sounded threatening but were more akin to a cat's deep purr of affection. To Cindy, who did not know how much her mother loved her, the sounds were frightening and the inspection an insult. Worst of all, in the last year her mother had added a new, humiliating item, which she never omitted, to the nightly ritual. Resignedly Cindy stepped out of her panties, handed them over, and waited until she was permitted to put them back on.

From now until Monday morning Vinnie's daughter would not be out of her sight, but that did not ease her worries, any more than did the satisfactory outcome of her inspection. The long hours during the week when she had to be away from Cindy working were a sheer torment. She knew Cindy was with Bella Lakes most of the time, but Bella had other things to do besides watch Cindy, and it took only fifteen minutes to ruin a girl. The Reverend Bird counseled faith, but faith was one thing and human nature another. Vinnie was too experienced to mix up the two.

The child's affliction, and Vinnie's conviction that it was a punishment for her own sins, made her anguish all the worse. If only she could question her daughter and get some answers, she might feel better. She knew this was impossible, but just as she did every other night, she questioned Cindy anyway, between mouthfuls of the succulent neck bones and pinto beans she had cooked before dawn that morning. She wanted to tell Cindy how ashamed she was that her anxiety compelled her to show distrust; how the depths of her fears only matched the heights of her love; how grateful she was to the Lord for bringing her such a precious burden, and how unworthy and incapable she felt, in her ignorance and gracelessness, of discharging the responsibility. But Vinnie could not have said these things even if she thought Cindy could have understood them and responded. Instead, she just grumbled, "What did you do today? Huh? Were you at the mayor's?"

Cindy nodded.

"Humph. I wonder why Bella Lakes wants you around all the time. Do you mind her and do what she says?"

Cindy nodded again.

"You better," her mother said gruffly. "And she better not tell me no different when I see her. She's been good to you, buying you that dress for church and them shoes. And she's got enough to put up with, being married to *him,* without having any trouble out of you. Do you help her around the house, like I taught you?"

Another nod responded affirmatively.

"Well, doing what, for instance? What did you do today? Dusting and sweeping? Washing dishes?"

Cindy's head ducked twice, meaning two yeses.

"Working in the yard? Getting supper?"

Cindy responded with two more affirmative nods.

"Humph. If you doing all that, maybe it's time she paid you a little salary."

Cindy smiled radiantly. From inside the almost-flat bosom of her dress she pulled a little wad and passed it across to her mother. It consisted of four one-dollar bills.

"Well, the Lord knows we can sure use that. It'll buy us a little chicken for Sunday. The electric bill was so bad, we was gonna have to eat beans all weekend. And the taxes on this house are due, too. Still, I don't know if I ought to take it. She's been looking after you for me. Maybe you ought to give it back."

Cindy shook her head and opened her lips. A sibilant hiss came from between them. "Sh . . . sh . . ."

Noting her daughter's attempt at speech, Vinnie leaned forward eagerly. "What is it, honey? What you trying to say?"

Cindy picked up the money from the table, folded it again, and folded her mother's stiff, callused fingers around it.

"She wanted you to have it, and you want *me* to have it? Is that what you mean?"

Cindy nodded, and lit up the room with another of her incandescent smiles.

Vinnie, blinded by so much beauty and by something else, an emotion she could not name, rubbed her sleeve across her eyes. "Lord, girl, the Reverend Bird said you would be a blessing and a comfort to me, and I didn't believe him at the time, but he was right. I never told you before, but the mayor wants me to send you away to one of those schools where you can learn the sign language, and I been thinking about it, especially since you *got* a woman, but now I know I was right to tell him no. We understand each other all right, baby. We can manage. You're stayin' right here with me."

Cindy jumped up and flung grateful arms around her mother's neck, but Vinnie, fearing another show of tears, pushed her away and said gruffly, "That's enough now. Sit down and finish your supper. Were you at Miss Bella's all day?"

The child was truthful as well as good. She could have easily lied, but she shook her head, no.

Instant alarm seized Vinnie. "Well, where were you, then?"

Cindy pointed at the window. Out there were Vinnie's small vegetable garden and packed-clay yard, with next to them a field where a house had once stood, now vacant and golden with wild daisies, and beyond that a large thicket of scrub pines and weeds. Between the daisy field and the woods was a barren ditch, a new tentacle of the highway construction, that greedy octopus whose head was a vast crater four blocks away.

"I saw monsters!"

It was the same sentence Cindy had startled Bella with on Monday. Vinnie's arms fell stunned to her sides. "Oh, Jesus, it's a miracle!"

Cindy ran to the window and pointed. "Out there. Monsters that eat dirt. See?"

Normally, it would have been too dark for the highway construction crew's equipment to be visible. But tonight there was a greedy red glow in the woods beyond the field, and in front of it the silhouetted shapes of the power shovel and the crane were indeed like dinosaurs, looming black and evil against their lurid background.

The Devil was out there, but in this little house God ruled. "Praise the Lord," Vinnie exulted, heedless of the fire and the prehistoric dragons. "He has cast out the devils and made you whole! He has loosed your tongue! Use it to praise Him." When the religious fervor was on her, Vinnie frequently spoke in Biblical apostrophes. "Down on your knees, girl, and thank Jesus."

"First stop fire," Cindy urged practically.

"I do believe that fire can't touch us, baby. Nothing can hurt us now. We are under the protection of His almighty arm."

But when Cindy flung open the window and pushed her mother toward it, the scorched smell of the air shocked Vinnie out of her holy happiness and out of the house as well. Dragging Cindy with her, she ran across the road to Reverend Bird's, where there was a telephone.

Again she found the parsonage door open and the parson still smiling beatifically at his drug-induced vision.

"Reverend, wake up! We came to praise Jesus!"

This was accompanied by vigorous shakings of the Reverend's shoulders until his eyes focused on her angrily. She released him and stepped back in horror at what she had just done. It was the first time she had dared lay hands on his sacred person.

"Woman, are you out of your mind?" Reverend Bird demanded, rearranging his robe with an irritated series of little pats and shrugs. "What do you mean, coming in this hour of the night and attacking me?"

"Reverend, I'm sorry. It's just that the Lord has worked a miracle. Cindy can talk!"

The Reverend subdued her with an angry stare while he smoothed his hair and continued to groom his robe until its neatness satisfied him. He was fully awake now, and this activity gave his quick mind time to work. If what Vinnie said was true, here was an opportunity for him to gain a nationwide reputation as a healer.

"You were saying, Sister Coddums . . . ?" he inquired blandly.

"Show him, Cindy. Say something."

The child was, as usual, mute. He looked at her mother with raised eyebrows. Perhaps this old fool woman was getting senile, hearing voices. He shrugged. At least it was worth a try. Laying a hand on the child's head, he closed his eyes piously and said in his most sonorous voice, "Speak, child. Through the power of the Lord Jesus Christ invested in me, I command you to speak if you can."

"Fire," Cindy said.

The Reverend's eyes widened in surprise, but he kept his serene demeanor. "Through the power of the Lord God Almighty which is channeled through me, you have been healed. All praise to Him. Let us pray. . . . Perhaps she has seen a holy vision, a burning bush," he said aside, to Vinnie.

"Fire!" Cindy screamed this time, and ran to the window of the Reverend's study. She pulled frantically at the cords that opened his velvet drapes to reveal the fiery glow of not one but many burning bushes. The flames were higher and appeared to be getting closer to her mother's house. The Reverend Bird could feel their heat. Thanking God Vinnie had awakened him, he pointed to the French phone on the library table. "Call Borough Hall. Get the firemen out here."

Vinnie was disappointed. "Ain't we gonna pray first?" she complained. "If the Lord healed Cindy, he can surely stop that fire."

"The Lord helps those who help themselves," the Reverend reminded her. "Dial 6060, that's the emergency dispatch number."

The white and gold French contraption looked like a toy, but

Vinnie was familiar with it because Mrs. Grafton had one in her bedroom. Like her mistress's, this one worked. She dialed and got a busy signal.

"It's busy," she said, and hung up.

"Jane Grimes is the auxiliary dispatcher. I think her number is 6341. No, wait." He smacked his recently dream-sodden forehead to make it remember. "Yes, that's right, 6341. Dial it!" Lakestown had only one exchange, so four numbers were all one needed to remember to call anyone within its borders. It was one of the many simplifications that made life pleasant here.

But that line was busy too, Vinnie informed him.

"Then," the Reverend intoned, "let us pray."

The main emergency dispatch line at Borough Hall was being used for a long conversation between the mayor and the chief of police. It was dangerous to tie up the line so long, especially on a Friday night, but there was nothing the dispatcher, who could see his worried face reflected in the gleaming tops of Chief Boyd's boots, could do. The mayor had top priority when it came to the use of the line, and he was talking to his highest ranking official, who had second priority. Yet this was a peak crisis hour. He considered pulling the tail of the chief's jacket to remind him of the risk but looked up, saw the .38 in its holster, and reconsidered. His name was Morris Merchant, he was frail and nearing eighty, and when he stood up his eyes were on a level with the chief's shining belt buckle. The dispatcher sat down and reconsidered some more.

The conversation was taking so long because the mayor was being even more mysterious than usual. He always had a tendency to beat around the bush, especially on the telephone, but tonight he was being positively cryptic about the reason why the chief's presence at his house was required immediately. Just as Boyd was deciding that it would take less time to run over to the mayor's and get the straight of it than try to decipher his problem on the phone, the mayor said tersely, "Goddamn it, Boyd, if you aren't over here in two minutes, you're fired."

"I'll be there," the chief said, and hung up two seconds after Vinnie did the same thing, a busy signal having responded to her fifth call to Borough Hall.

Miss Jane Grimes, stretched out luxuriously on the ivory satin cover of the king-sized bed she shared with her sister Greta, was talking long distance to Atlanta when the emergency operator broke in. She was annoyed. No, furious.

"Sorry to interrupt, but I have an emergency call for Miss Jane Grimes from the Reverend LeRoy Bird," the operator said.

"I didn't know they could do that. Did you?" Jane asked her sister, who was studying the effect of a new wig in the mirror of their double vanity.

"Do what?" asked Greta. As usual, she was sitting on Jane's side of the vanity, which increased her sister's annoyance.

"Oh, put him through, operator. What is it?"

Reverend Bird explained that there was a fire in the woods on Merchant Avenue next to Vinnie Coddums's house, across the street from his.

"Well, what am *I* supposed to do about it?" Jane asked peevishly.

"Get the firemen over here. You're still the volunteer dispatcher, aren't you?"

"I don't know. I guess so," Jane said doubtfully. "Greta, are we still supposed to be the dispatchers for the fires?"

Greta shrugged to indicate that she did not know either. The Grimes girls had inherited this civic duty along with their profitable funeral business from their father, Jolly Grimes, but since the dispatcher's desk had been installed in Borough Hall, no fire calls had come through in so long that they had forgotten all about the responsibility.

"I think you're supposed to call Borough Hall," Jane told the Reverend.

"That line is busy. I'll keep trying, but in the meantime, please get the firemen over here. It's spreading fast."

"All right," Jane said, and hung up. "That was an emergency call from Reverend Bird. I thought it was a body, but it's only a fire."

"Where?"

"Vinnie Coddums's place on Merchant Avenue. I do wish you wouldn't use my brush, Greta. Do I have to make all those tiresome calls, or shall we let it burn?"

It was a game they had often played in the big, warm bed, years ago, when neither of them felt like getting up in the cold night and making calls. If the burning property were an eyesore they both felt the town would be better off without, they had often gone back to sleep with a virtuous feeling of having discharged their civic responsibility, since their omission amounted to a program of selective urban renewal.

"That raggedy shack? Let it burn, of course," Greta said languidly. "Besides, I don't even know where the list of the firemen is."

"Well, what do I *do?*" Jane wailed, betraying her petulance and nervousness. Greta was, after all, the elder and the family decision maker.

"Call Borough Hall, of course. 6060."

"And if I can't get through?"

"I told you. Let it burn." Greta calmly continued to arrange the curls on her wig with Jane's brush. Underneath it she was almost completely bald, just as underneath her auburn dye job Jane was almost completely gray, but both sisters literally intended to fight to the death for their right to go on being called the Grimes girls.

9

"We rockin' . . . we rollin' . . . even when we jes' be's strollin' . . ."

The wooden frame structure that was Lakestown's fire hall shook
to the stompings of a hundred feet and the pounding of music amplified
to a punishing decibel level. The noise was deafening, the inside temper-
ature a steamy 110 degrees, the funk of sweaty adolescent bodies so thick
it could have been packaged and sold like margarine, and the lighting
was dim. It was, in short, teen-age heaven. The price of admission to
heaven was one dollar every Friday night, and the place was packed with
half the teen-agers in Lakestown. Outside were most of the other half,
lounging and smoking and cooling off in the relatively temperate July
night before plunging once more into the social steambath.

The group outdoors was the first to hear the rude blast of the
siren that meant the building was about to be used for its fundamental
purpose. So deafening was the noise inside that the others went on
dancing, couples and solos alike posturing and profiling in the new nar-
cissistic way, for another minute. Then Fire Chief Freeman "Nunc"
Farmer, the first to arrive on the scene, threw a switch that simultaneously cut off the music and cut in a microphone. Not that he needed
amplification: Lakestown's fire chief, a big, barrel-chested man, was a
Juilliard-trained basso profundo and his deep voice had boomed out
over far larger halls than this one. "Clear the hall," he sang out in
ominous Wagnerian tones. "Clear the hall!"

And then, since his command had not cleared the building as
rapidly as he wished, Nunc reverted to basic black English.

"HAUL ASS!"

"Where's the fire?" an irreverent youngster asked.

"Up your rear end, if you don't move," came the sincere response.
At the same time Nunc turned on the hall's brightest lights, illuminating
a scene of boisterous confusion: firemen, half in and half out of their
slickers, struggling to get to their equipment through the packed bodies
of boys and girls in the two extremes of high fashion: brilliant plumage
and dingy jeans. The sudden glare did the trick. Nunc knew that

teen-agers disliked bright lights and tended to prefer congregating in darkness. The youngsters groaned their unanimous disgust at this interruption in their fun, but they scrambled out of the way.

And not a moment too soon. Engine Number One, an antique kept running by prayer, mojo, and Dunce Cap Carter's loving ministrations, was already moving out of its berth in the station, and Number Two, the gleaming new pride of the borough, was revving up its engines to follow it.

"Any auxiliaries out there, get aboard!" the fire chief thundered at the few remaining teen-agers. "We need you. But we don't need spectators. All the rest go home. You know the rules. You get a rebate tomorrow. Number Two, MOVE OUT!"

A half dozen young men trained as auxiliary firefighters, Lukey Hawkins among them, found handholds and swung athletically aboard Number Two as it moved out of the fire hall, gathered speed, and careened around the corner. The rest of the under-twenty crowd did not linger. The floodlights outside the fire hall were even brighter than the lights inside. They scuttled like sand crabs for the cover of darkness, complaining loudly about their disappointment, except for a few who were strangely silent. This group, who had not possessed the dollar price of admission, cherished a secret happiness. Tomorrow night they, along with all who had paid, would get in free.

A strange, fatalistic calm came over Vinnie after she had tried for the fifth time to report the fire and failed. The Reverend Bird tried to persuade her and Cindy to stay, pointing out that at his house there was at least a road to make a barrier of safety between them and the fire, but she refused.

"We'll be all right, Reverend," she assured him. "This evening I made a decision. I prayed to the Lord to let me know was I right or wrong. And He answered me! Them was His words coming out of my little girl's mouth. Nothing can shake my faith now." And, like a squat Joan of Arc, she took her daughter by the hand and went joyously toward her immolation.

"We'll be all right," she repeated to Cindy as they sat together in the little kitchen, which was now illuminated brightly by the fire outside.

She patted the child's cold, trembling hand. "You hear me? We'll be just fine. The Lord gave me a sign. This here is my time of trial, and I ain't going to fail. Your hands are cold. You want some hot cocoa?"

Cindy shook her head.

"You can do better than that, child. You got a tongue now. Use it!"

"No," Cindy said, and broke immediately into a spasm of coughing. They had closed the doors and windows, but smoke was coming into the house through every unsealed crack.

"Thank you, Jesus!" her mother cried, with a clap of her hands and a happy little jerk of her body. "Amen. He done worked a miracle, honey, healing you. Now we gotta thank Him by standing fast in our faith."

Cindy was used to her mother's religious apostrophes and normally accepted remarks like "eat your grits" and "hallelujah!" with equal composure, since they came from Vinnie with equal frequency, often in the same sentence. But now all her senses were tremblingly alert to danger. The smoke in the little house was burning her eyes and throat, causing her to cry and choke and cough, and still her crazy old mother sat immobile, talking in identically enraptured tones about hot cocoa and thanking Jesus. Her instincts urged her to flee.

Before she could reach the door, though, strong, callused fingers seized her arm and dragged her back. "Aw, no, Cindy. Come back here. We got to stand fast against the infidels."

"And burn?" Cindy cried. Wide-eyed, with ears and nostrils twitching, she resembled an immature doe poised for flight.

But her mother paid no attention, though she tightened her grip on Cindy's arm. "Here they come!" she cried triumphantly. "Look, child. Screaming red-eyed demons, straight out of hell! But they can't hurt us."

The parade of vehicles that came rushing down Merchant Avenue with spinning red lights and screaming sirens did resemble a procession of demons. But only one, a Lakestown police car, continued all the way to Vinnie's door. The others stopped at the woods a hundred yards away and quickly deployed their equipment.

There was a series of hard knocks. "Police! Open this door!"

Vinnie did as she was commanded but, blocking the doorway with her wide hips, did nothing more. There was no way Chief Boyd could maneuver past her into the house, and no way he could budge her short of using dynamite. There was a surprised expression on his usually impassive face. The knocking had been a pure formality. With the fire so near, he had not expected to find anyone at home. He had considered the fire a lucky accident that would make his uncomfortable task of sealing the house and posting Board of Health warnings easier. Now, confronted with its implacable owner, he was confused. "I have orders from the Board of Health . . ." he began.

"I don't take orders from nobody but God," Vinnie informed him. "And tonight He told me to stay right where I am. They gonna have to run that devilish highway right over my dead body, and Cindy's too, if they want to build it here!"

Chief Boyd pulled an official-looking document out of his pocket. "I am authorized to make an inspection of your premises," he said.

Vinnie stepped back a pace, twisted, and bent to reach behind the door. Chief Boyd used the interval to get one of his large, polished boots inside the house. But before he could take a second step, he felt cold steel prodding the tender area above his belt. It was the loaded, double-barreled shotgun Vinnie kept behind the door.

"I keep this thing loaded," she told him, "and I know how to use it. Now you go on and obey your orders, and I'll obey mine." She braced herself, wide legged, and pushed the shotgun against him.

The chief's pale eyes narrowed. "The mayor's right. You *are* crazy."

"I knew that rotten old Abe Lakes sent you here. But I'm ready for him, too. There's two barrels in this shotgun. Tell him that, Law. And tell him, if he says I'm crazy, that's fine with me. Crazy people don't go to jail for what they do."

Vinnie backed off a few paces, still holding the shotgun level with Chief Boyd's belly. "Why don't you come on in and inspect, Law? You ain't scared of an old woman, is you? Course a crazy old woman might do anything, and I'm not right in the head. You said it yourself. I'm not responsible. Hallelujah!"

"Hallelujah!" Cindy echoed, forgetting in her excitement to be frightened. This "crazy" act of her mother's was nothing new to her; Vinnie had used it often to fend off bill collectors. And it always worked; it was a dramatic masterpiece with only one flaw—Cindy's tendency to giggle.

Vinnie was going into her familiar warm-up now. "You better watch out, Law. My head was buzzin' when I got up this morning, and I knew an attack was coming on. But this is the worst one I ever had. This time I'm hearing voices. I even thought I heard my daughter talking just now. Everybody knows she can't talk, so that proves I'm crazy. I might do anything! Praise Jesus!" Momentarily lowering the shotgun, she picked up a heavy vase and flung it in the chief's direction, carefully aiming wide of her mark. Unfortunately, the chief, having quick reflexes, swerved to avoid the jug and caught it on his right hip. This was a mistake; the shotgun, the reported head noises, and the flinging of breakables were all part of Vinnie's performance but, just as in the real theatre, nobody was ever supposed to actually get hurt. She almost stepped out of her role to see about his injury, but her daughter saved her from spoiling the show.

"I crazy too. Hallelujah!" cried Cindy, who was now thoroughly enjoying herself. She had always wanted to take part in her mother's mad scenes, but this was the first time she dared. Imitating the "happy" dance Vinnie often performed in church, she trucked over to the far wall, took down a picture of Martin Luther King, and sent it spinning in the chief's direction. Now there were two white rectangles on the yellowed wall above the sofa. The other picture, a framed photograph of Marcus Garvey, had been sacrificed to hasten the departure of a finance company's bill collector.

"Ugh," the chief grunted as the picture crashed against his skull. He was not hurt, but it took him two minutes to find that out, minutes in which he was kept busy picking fragments of glass from his immaculate person. "I bet you never had blood on that pretty uniform before," Vinnie taunted. "You better run on home and tell your wife to soak it in cold water."

"Mrs. Coddums," he said, "defying me is one thing. I'm sure you have your reasons. But it's foolish to stay in here and defy that fire."

"What fire?" Vinnie responded instantly. "Cindy, look around. Do you see any fire?"

Cindy, still play acting, was making an elaborate game of looking for the fire in corners and under furniture.

"Surely you know that field out there is burning," the chief said impatiently.

Cindy ran with feigned surprise to a window, yanked down the shade to its full length, and released it. It rolled up to the top of the casing with a sharp report. The chief instantly drew his gun and fired back. Then, sheepishly, he replaced the gun in its holster. He had been more nervous than he thought.

"Sorry about that window, ma'am."

"Sorry don't fix nothin'," Vinnie grumbled.

"I'll take care of it tomorrow."

"Better do it tonight, 'less you want to be in trouble. I got a witness. You see any fire out there, Cindy?"

Cindy shook her head vigorously, then remembered she could now speak. "No."

The only redness visible through the shattered window came from the many engines, including one Dorset and two Edgehill companies, which had responded to the alarm phoned in by Jane Grimes. One by one, they were already making their departure. Inside, the color of their lights was matched by the shade of Chief Boyd's usually creamy cheeks.

"*Now* who's crazy?" Vinnie demanded of an imaginary audience. "I don't know what to say about people who come in here talkin' about fires that ain't real and shootin' out my windows. Maybe they should be reported. Maybe they shouldn't be wearin' police uniforms."

"Ma'am," the chief said with a tremor in his voice, "m-maybe you're not crazy." He advanced half a step in her direction.

"Hold it!" Vinnie commanded, swinging the gun barrel upward. "Maybe you ain't one of the infidels, either. But I can't trust you till I'm sure."

"Infidels?" he echoed in puzzlement.

"I mean the devils who is building that highway. They've already torn up half the town, and they want my house. My house, and my pastor's house, and the church too. Didn't you know that?"

The chief did not; he was as ignorant of the latest revision in the highway plans as the mayor had been a few hours ago.

His expression must have shown it, because Vinnie's tone of voice softened, though she kept the gun high. "Maybe you ain't one of them, but you work for them, and that's the same thing." She began to preach, excoriating the sinners like an experienced Bible thumper. "They tried to plan me out, and that didn't work. Praise Jesus! They tried to burn me out, and *that* didn't work. Have mercy! Then they tried to throw me out, and they sent you here to do it. Now didn't they? Answer me! *Testify!*"

The chief was familiar with the last word, but only in its legal sense. "My orders say . . ." he began.

Vinnie interrupted with scorn, "Is that all you can do, obey orders? Ain't there no brains in that big good-lookin' head of yours? Listen to me, Benson Boyd. Unless you as white as you look—and you ain't, 'cause I knew your mama and your daddy, and I used to hold you on my knee—you better start to *think.*"

Thinking was hard work for Chief Boyd. Stiff from years of following the rule book, his mind suffered from exercise like the muscles of an untrained athlete. It was stirred, though, by the memory of a young woman who had held him and soothed him with sweetly sung hymns before he reached school age.

It was her voice, a gentle voice, that spoke now. "Listen, Benson Boyd, I been a fool longer than you. Forty-seven years I been obeyin' folks' orders. But them days is over now. From now on, I don't obey nobody but my Lord. I got to thinkin', and I decided maybe the white folks don't want us to have a town of our own. And my Lord worked a miracle to tell me I was right. He told me, no matter what happens, to stand fast. Me and my girl, we gonna do just that. You go back to the people who give you your orders and tell them we ain't goin' nowhere."

Chief Boyd's head hurt from unaccustomed effort. Nevertheless, he persevered. There might be truth in what Vinnie was saying. He had thought there was something funny about this business all along, because the mayor had not been straight with him. Two things were certain: Cindy Coddums was not as afflicted as the mayor made her out to be, and her mother was not crazy. She had made more sense in the last five minutes than the Honorable Abe Lakes had in the past two years.

"Tell them," Vinnie continued, "to take their highway someplace else, 'cause we shall not be moved! Come on, Cindy. Sing it for me!" She sat down at the old upright in her parlor and struck a thunderous chord, a righteous, rippling introduction, and some more stately chords to accompany her daughter:

KRISTIN LATTANY

Weeeeeeeeee
Shall not,
We shall not be moved.
We
Shall not,
We shall not be moved.
Jus' like a tree
Standin' by the water,
We shall not be moved.

"Oh, yes! Tell 'em. We ain't movin' nowhere but on to Glory!" Vinnie shouted, pounding out a bridge to the second stanza. It was the perfect opportunity for Chief Boyd to make his move and carry out the purpose of his visit. But, for the first time in many years, a crowd of thoughts and emotions were knocking down barriers in his disciplined, military mind. Painful recollections of the mayor's peremptory orders: like anyone else, this seemingly impassive giant was discovering that he had feelings that could be hurt. Doubts, for the first time in his career, about the correctness of his mission. Respect for the stubborn old woman who had blocked it. Awe for the richness and depth of her daughter's voice, singing their defiant message. The mighty sound issuing from that slender throat was unbelievable, almost frightening. It had to come from God.

Moved in a different sense, Chief Boyd took off his hat and left, gently closing the door behind him.

10

The Blue Moon Tavern and Rest was a large, ramshackle building with a row of six scabby tourist cabins out back. Mame Porritt, its feisty owner, served meals when she could get the help, but she had been forced to fire so many chefs for temperament and intemperance that the availability of food at the Blue Moon was a sometime thing. Rest at the Blue Moon was also an uncertain thing, since there was likely to be a noisy party going on all night in at least one of the cabins.

Fess Roaney, approaching the good old B.M. with the limp that gave his walk a jaunty bounce, admired the blue neon sign. To him it was a triumph of ambiguity. He recalled that it had finished shrinking on the day about two years ago when Mame fired her last full-time chef, bibulous Benny Mingle. On the same day the last of Mame's six tourist cabins was completed.

Mame had only planned to build one cabin, a shrine to her hope of keeping at least one full-time man on the premises, but the carpenter's work was not true, and a second cabin had to be erected to keep the first from falling in the direction in which it so alarmingly leaned. The final *t* in *Restaurant* went out for good the day the last shingle was nailed on the roof of the first, crooked cabin. If she had been alert, Mame said, she would have known then and there that her chef Benny would not stay on. But she ordered the work to proceed, and the *n* went out as soon as the leaning cabin was propped up by its new neighbor.

Soon the second cabin was leaning too, the fault, the carpenter said, of the shifting of Mame's land caused by the underground springs that fed Crump's Creek, which bordered her property. But as the first two cabins were already profitably rented, Mame told him to build another. As soon as the third cabin was finished, it too was occupied, by the first of her "girls," Lily, and three letters were blank at the end of the sign. Transient couples were already requesting the use of the cabins, incommoding the permanent tenants. Mame told the carpenter to build three more cabins.

On the day all six cabins were completed, the row stood straight and true as an arrow. But Benny could not stand at all, and Mame was forced to fire him. That evening, the sign finished amputating itself for good. Wisely, Mame had never had it fixed. The Blue Moon Tavern and Rest the place remained, and it was, Fess thought, the best possible name for it: promising everything and guaranteeing nothing. No advertising genius could have done better.

Many people had described the Blue Moon in other terms, but few had been accurate. To the respectable citizens of Lakestown it was lumped in with all the other establishments of Rowdy Row as a disreputable, even dangerous, place. To Chief Boyd and the other Lakestown law enforcement officers who knew better than the respectable citizens, the Blue Moon was strictly off-limits except for off-duty relaxation, since the locals who frequented the Blue Moon policed themselves, loving debate and discussion but never permitting a friendly argument to turn unfriendly. Violence was reserved to the big-city tourists who frequented Lakestown's other cabarets and considered the Blue Moon tacky and countrified.

Fess did not care what the city people called the Blue Moon; as the longest-standing resident of the tourist cabins, he called it home, and recognized it for what it was: a comfortable country inn in the earliest American tradition, enriched by the quality of intimacy known as soul. That sign, an accidental poem topped by a winking blue crescent, was a beacon guiding him to a night of rest after his lengthy excursions and explorations or, if he was not too tired, to an hour or two of sociability before bed. Actually, he was always too tired and never too tired. Each night he promised himself he would go straight to his cabin and sleep, but he could never resist the lights of the main building and stopping in for a quick nightcap and a look around to see who was there.

Tonight enough people were in the common room, as Fess called it, to make it clear that his nightcap would be a slow one. Across the way at Loveland, Big Bertha Barnes was belting out a welcome blues, but in here Big Bill Pritchett's intermittent cry from behind the bar, "SpeNNNDDD MONEY!," was music enough.

Besides, an impromptu songfest was erupting at the piano, a group consisting of Mame's girls Lily and Booty, with, of all people, Bella Lakes leading the chorus. She was in good voice tonight, and as she put her whole self into her singing of "Put the Blame on Mame," her long, wraparound skirt unwrapped itself most becomingly.

"They ought to call her Bella *Legs,*" Fess commented appreciatively as he took a chair at one of the old wooden tables opposite Doc Thompson.

"Sotto voce, sotto voce, friend," warned the doctor, who enjoyed a good pun but also understood the importance of discretion. "Remember she's a lady, the first lady of our community. A true queen, one who does not hesitate to mingle with whores." The doctor attempted a pun of his own. "Mame ought to call this *Barbe-Chili,*" he said, dipping a spoon into the steaming bowl in front of him.

"What does she call it?" Fess wondered, looking with some alarm at the indecipherable contents of the bowl.

"A Bowl of Heaven. Mere mortals are not supposed to question its ingredients," the doctor said, and smacked his lips. "Well named. Mame's gone in for astrology lately. Last night we had Tauruscue—beef barbecue, of course, to initiates. This must be Gemini; it has a double personality." Doc sniffed and tasted again. "Yep. Yesterday's beef and today's beans." He inclined his ponderous head toward the door. "Better feast your eyes while you can. She won't be onstage long."

Fess followed Doc's meaningful gaze and saw his next-door neighbor, the long-term occupant of Cabin Two, stroll into the room and take up a negligent pose against the far wall. He did not seem to be looking for anyone in particular, but a moment later the song broke off in mid-phrase. The fabulous legs twinkled across the room toward Fess's neighbor and the two disappeared into a booth.

Fess sighed. "Oh, well. I'll just feast my belly instead."

"That's the idea," Doc approved. "Better hurry, though. I wouldn't want you to get the next item on the zodiac."

"What's that?" Fess asked.

"Cancer," Doc said, with a gleeful grin. He clapped his hands and yelled, "Innkeeper!"

"What you want, you old elephant-leg devil?" demanded the proprietor, a wisp of a woman with a voice like a buzz saw. "Why can't you call me by my right name?"

Doc ogled the proprietor's trim figure. "I didn't think you wanted me calling you 'darling' in front of all these strangers."

"You damn right," Mame said, thin arms folded across her pleasantly rounded bosom. "I want you to call me Mrs. Porritt, and say it with some respect. And if you want service around here, I want you to call the waitress."

She pointed to a long, gawky girl leaning listlessly against the bar, order pad in one hand, cigarette in the other.

"Is *that* what she is?" Doc asked in amazement. "I thought she was part of the decorations, like that cardboard Santa Claus that's been standing in the corner since Christmas. She hasn't moved in an hour."

Mame grunted. "And won't move, neither, till I make her. Tried to pull a slick one on me tonight. Called in sick and sent her boyfriend for her paycheck. I told him she had to come pick it up in person. Sure is funny how quick she got well."

"I don't want a waitress, sweetheart. I want *you*," Doc said, grabbing her waist and pulling her onto his lap.

Mame, who was wiry and strong, struggled gamely until she was free, knocking her wig askew in the process. Cocked over one eye, it was like a rakish beret. "What's wrong with you, you old fool? You been takin' some of your own drugs, or what?"

"Shhh, Mame," the doctor said, with a finger to his lips. "You're making a public spectacle out of something very private and precious. Let our romance remain our little secret."

"Look at him," Mame said disgustedly to Fess, in a way that let him know she was not really angry. "Ain't had but one drink, and already he's cuttin' the fool."

"I am intoxicated by your powerful allure, my love."

"Well, get intoxicated on some of that other stuff I sell," Mame ordered. "I ain't got time to be standin' here talkin' trash with you. It takes eight pairs of hands to run this place, and I only got two. My cook quit on me tonight and that lazy gal over there is tryin' to make me fire *her*.

"And you," she accused, turning suddenly and glaring at Fess, "you don't lift a finger to help out around here. The least you could do is pick up some of that trash out back."

Fess ducked his head guiltily. This was the only drawback to living at the Blue Moon. No matter how firmly he insisted on being a mere tenant, he could never rid Mame of the fixed idea that he was the full-time, live-in male help she had been counting on for so long.

"This is the perfect spot for a retired man like you. No heavy work or nothing. All you'd have to do is relieve Bill at the bar, keep an eye on the cash register for me, stuff like that, and you could live rent free."

This was the same appeal Fess heard around the first of every month when, scrupulously, he paid his rent and, grudgingly, Mame accepted it.

"Well, there's work to do, and as usual I got to do it myself. No time to stand here funnin' with you, you old walrus. Thank God I'm retired from *that* part of the business. I'll send Lily or Booty over to keep you company. That's *their* job."

"I don't want them, my sweet," Doc objected. "I want you."

"Lily! Booty!" she called, ignoring him. "Where are those triflin' girls? Five minutes ago they were here, mocking me with that low-down song, and now they've gone and disappeared. Do I have to fire them, too? Lily! Booty!

"I should have known," she said a moment later, as a high-pitched chorus of giggles emerged from the booth into which Bella and her friend had disappeared. "Every time that Ikie Lakes shows up, you'd think Congress had declared a damn national Hookers' Holiday. You two want anything before I go over there and light up their behinds?"

"A Bowl of Heaven for Mr. Roaney here."

Mame acknowledged the order with a little nod, then lingered a moment longer. "Ted Crump brought by a new movie with some Mexican girls. It's running in Cabin Six, if you're interested."

"Only if you'll watch it with me," the incorrigible doctor said.

Mame snorted indignantly. "Not me! Ain't nothin' them movies can show me I ain't already seen. Half the stuff in them I invented."

Her tight rump moved briskly out of Doc's swatting range. She hurried to the kitchen, pausing only to order her hustlers out of Ikie's booth. "Lily! Booty! Can't you see the gentleman's already got company?"

Tall Lily and compact Booty stood up, respectively resplendent in long white and black gowns, only to sit down in the booth again the moment Mame was safely back in the kitchen.

"One man with three women," Fess observed resentfully, "and here we sit, alone. It doesn't seem fair. What's his secret, anyway?"

"Isaac likes women," Doc said. "That's the only secret, really, if you want to make a hit with them."

"Well, the women may like Ikie, but not everybody else does."

"Who, for instance? Are you suggesting that no man likes a ladies' man?"

"No-ooo," Fess admitted reluctantly. "The guy's all right with me. I mean, he's never done anything to make me dislike him. I can't figure him out, that's all."

"What is it," Doc asked, "that you have trouble figuring out?"

"Hell," Fess exploded in righteous indignation, "he has a college education and he lives like a bum. Sleeps in one of Mame's tourist cabins, and if he owns more than one jacket and one pair of jeans I've never seen them on him. And besides running that poolroom, which practically runs itself, what does he do with his time?"

The doctor burst into such an explosion of laughter he scattered beans over Mame's tabletop.

"What's so funny?" Fess wanted to know, glaring at him.

"Just that every one of your objections to Ikie's life-style could also be raised about yours."

Fess stared at him in anger for a moment, then burst into laughter of his own. "Got me that time. You're right. But—hell, you know what a mess I am. Messed up in the body and mixed up in the head. Maybe I've soaked up so much knowledge I'm like a sick computer. Going 'beep, beep, beep' in my beer. But Ikie's healthy, isn't he?"

"Extremely," Doc Thompson said.

"Then what's his excuse?"

"For not being a model citizen like his brother?"

"Ooh," Fess squealed in masochistic pleasure, "you're sharp tonight. That was right on target. You knew all the time, didn't you, that I meant the mayor when I said everyone doesn't like Ikie."

"Of course." The doctor took out his pipe and lit it, signaling the start of one of his longer narratives. "I knew their father, you know," he said when he had it going. "Splendid man. But somewhat hard to live with, I imagine, especially for a spirited young boy. Heroes usually are."

"And their mother?"

"A fine woman, too, in her own way. Had to be, to cope with George. One of those strong, stoic types, blank-faced like an Indian. Matter of fact, I think she was half Cuffee and half Cherokee. A mighty heritage. But George's zeal finally wore her out. She died when Isaac was only two years old. Abraham was . . . let's see, twelve. No, thirteen. And George never bothered to marry again. No time for courting, he said. Too busy saving this town and its sinners."

"He was a preacher, then?"

"And how. Hell-fire-and-brimstone Methodist. For the Lord thy God is a jealous God, a wrathful God, and all that. Consigning sinners to hell left and right, seven days a week, not just on Sundays."

"We could use him now," Fess said wistfully.

"Yes. I had a conversation with Reverend Bream this evening and, frankly, I was disappointed. But that's another story. The one I'm telling you now . . ."

"Explains a lot about our mayor," Fess interrupted.

"Yes. I think he accepted his father's precepts. The older son usually does, you know. But Isaac took the opposite route. Decided he might as well enjoy original sin, since he was born with it, just as he was born with straight hair."

"I wonder which his brother hates most about him?"

"Pardon?"

"His enjoyment of sin, or his hair?"

"That," the doctor said, "is the most profound piece of insight to emerge from this entire discussion. It's unanswerable, and it's worth every bottle on Mame's shelf. I shall now order and pay for one, if it's possible to call that waitress."

Fess bowed modestly, acknowledging this praise, while Doc made a dramatic bid for the waitress's attention.

"O chaste Diana! O haughty Artemis! Unattainable goddess, wouldst deign to bring a libation to thirsty mortals?"

This loud declamation having failed to produce any results, the doctor said in his normal voice, "Nothing can bring that girl to life. I'm convinced she's a statue. Speaking of statues, you should know that Isaac does have an occupation. He's a sculptor. Not a potterer like me, a true artist. He moved into the cabins because the apartment over the poolroom is crammed with his work. I've been up there, and some of it is breathtaking."

"I should have known," Fess grumbled, still unwilling to grant legitimacy to the subject of their discussion. "He has one of those hippie vans."

"Yes. Not, as you and the other arch-conservatives imagine, for drug and sex orgies, but for transporting his work to New York. Where, I understand, he recently had a very successful show. This is top secret, you understand. He uses a pseudonym in the art world. News travels fast, and Lakestown isn't ready to accept a serious artist."

"Oh, come on," Fess said impatiently. "This town accepts everybody."

"*Almost* everybody," the doctor corrected him. "Fools and failures of all kinds, yes. Also people who are successful in occupations they understand, like undertaking and dentistry. But if it became known that Ikie was a successful sculptor—of nudes, mind you, *female* nudes—he'd be run out of town. The way it is, he's free to go his way in peace, tolerated and even loved, like the town idiots and the town drunks."

"Humph," was Fess's skeptical reply.

"All I ask is that you keep an open mind, my friend. If you can win Isaac's trust, he might let you see some of his work. That should convince you. Though I doubt he'll show you his latest piece." The doctor clapped a hand to his mouth. "God, but that was an unfortunate choice of words."

"He's done a nude of Bella," Fess said instantly.

"I never said that. Don't you dare repeat it."

But Fess knew he was right. As for repeating anything Doc said—"I thought I had *your* trust," he said.

"You do. But your suspicion of Isaac might be an overriding factor. It's too bad. We need allies, and I think he might be a formidable one."

"Oh, nonsense," Fess said irritably. "I'm just not going to feel sorry for Boy Beautiful over there, that's all. But if he can help us fight that road, I'll forgive him his talent and maybe even his glamor."

"I hope so," his friend said gravely.

The female chattering in the booth had become too loud to ignore.

"I swear, Ikie," Lily crooned, "you got the prettiest hair I ever seen, 'cept in a wig. How come I wasn't born with hair like that?"

"'Cause you wasn't born, bitch, your mother plucked you out of a pigpen. She doesn't bathe, Ikie. Me, I take three baths a day."

"He ain't interested in you, bitch. You so old your pussy's bald, just like your head. She ain't got no hair under that dress, Ikie, or under that wig, neither."

"I'll bald *you*, you lying bitch!" Booty screamed.

From the scuffling and screeching noises that ensued, Booty was trying to carry out her threat.

"I think our friend could use a little help right now," Doc said, and stood up. "Let's join the party."

Fess, who had just decided he did not crave the company of women after all, followed several reluctant paces behind his wide friend.

11

His straining arm muscles showing the effort it took to keep two angry whores apart, Ikie Lakes grinned a welcome. "Evenin', Doc. My man. Evenin', Professor. Sorry I can't shake hands. But you see how I'm occupied."

"Carry on," Doc said with a cheerful little semisalute, maneuvering his bulk into the space beside Bella.

"Evening, ladies. Evening, Lakes," Fess said gruffly, and regarded the object of his hostility.

By general standards Ikie Lakes was not handsome. On the contrary, he looked as if God had dipped into His grab bag of races and put him together in a hurry, producing one of the oddest-looking individuals on earth. He had the flat nose and full lips of an African; the Oriental skin fold at the inner corners of his eyes, slanting and diminishing them, especially when he was angry; and a complexion like varnished maple that could have come from anywhere—Colorado, Calabria, or the Congo. Capping this hodgepodge of features was a crest of wavy black hair badly in need of barbering.

Yet women found him extremely attractive, often, as now, to his peril.

Doc addressed one of his admirers. "You're looking ravishing tonight, Madame. I hope that means you're enjoying the evening."

Bella's lovely brow became furrowed. "I came to see Ikie," she said defensively, "on some family business."

"Never explain, my dear," Doc boomed paternally, patting her nervous hand. "Be like the daughter of Juno you are. Be Olympian. Never explain. No one here is curious. We only hope you're having a good time."

"I am," she said emphatically. "Hell, yes. For the first time in my life, I am."

"Will somebody," Ikie asked petulantly, "please help me get these women off my back? Ow! You girls stop that, now. I don't want to have to hurt anybody."

Fess thought he detected a clue to Ikie's mysterious sex appeal in that speech. It had an endearing country quality, a soft-spoken gentleness that reminded him of Josh Hawkins. Bigfooted, broad-shouldered, at least seventy-five inches tall, Ikie looked and talked more like a country bumpkin than like a sophisticate who, if Doc were to be believed, was at home in the New York art world. You felt he sincerely did not want to hurt anybody and that it was with the greatest regret that he had dislodged the front teeth of certain local wiseacres who had once called him L'il Abner. Now, for all his pleasantness, no one called him that anymore.

Lily and Booty continued to arch and hiss at each other like a pair of cobras.

"How about a little game of cards?" Doc suggested.

"Beautiful idea, Doc," Ikie said, "Reach in my left-hand pocket, Booty, that's a good girl. There's a deck in there. We'll play poker."

"And where," Fess inquired, "do you carry the dice? In your shoes? Your feet must hurt all the time."

"I'll ignore that for now, Roaney," Ikie said, his eyes dangerously small. "But I won't forget it."

"Five-card draw," Lily said, shuffling and cutting.

"Fine," Ikie said. "Everybody ante up a dime. I'll deal."

They were suddenly so quiet, studying their hands, that Fess ventured to draw up a chair. He refused to be dealt in, preferring to study the others. Bella had no consistent style of playing. She would throw in with a good hand, then hold out with a bad one. Clearly, she was just marking time. Ikie seldom bluffed. A true gambler, he risked his coins only when he could back them up with two pairs or better. Doc tended to bluff to the limit, but he was no match for Booty. A chubby, compact nut of a girl, she won the pot with a crazy-quilt hand consisting of a jack and the queen of spades and the seven, eight, and ten of clubs.

"Shee-it," Lily said. "Look at them cards. She didn't have nothin'."

"I did too," Booty argued. "That there's a straight."

"Where's the nine?" Lily wondered.

"What's it matter?" Booty retorted. "I got everybody's money, ain't I?" And she went on serenely raking the coins into a large beaded bag she carried.

Lily seemed determined to rekindle their argument. "Ikie, you never did answer me. Where'd you get your pretty hair?"

The doctor, hoping perhaps to stave off renewed hostilities, cleared his throat. "Uh . . . this may not be the right time, Isaac. I don't want to interrupt your fun, but we came over to enlist your help in a subversive enterprise."

Delight at the last two words brightened and enlarged Ikie's eyes. "I am a direct descendant," he answered them both, "of Curly, the famous black Indian. Whom General Custer employed as his trusted and loyal scout. Heh heh. A black Indian. That should've told Massa Custer something, but it didn't. My ancestor, Curly, was the sole survivor of Custer's forces at Little Big Horn. Naturally, there were rumors and suspicions. But no one could prove he had joined forces with his relatives who were, heh heh, the enemy."

"You say all that to say what?" Lily asked impatiently.

"That I come by my hair—and my subversive tendencies—naturally."

"Is you really a descendant of a curly-headed Indian?" Booty asked, wide-eyed and serious.

"Better than that. I am his reincarnated spirit."

"In this action," Doc Thompson warned, "your relatives might again be the enemy."

Ikie poured himself a double shot of Old Overcoat and tossed it down. "I had to get ready for that. Now I am. Lay it on me."

At that moment Mame showed up and announced that she was tired of doing everything herself, that she needed some help around the place, and if the girls didn't hustle and hoo-rah this minute, they could go back to standing on street corners. In her hands she carried a chef's cap and two aprons.

Thus the Blue Moon's dining service acquired the most elegant help in its history—a formally gowned waitress gliding among the tables, and a cook who screeched each time she burned herself trying to retrieve a rhinestone earring that had fallen into the chili. They were not very efficient, but they were decorative, and at least Ikie could breathe.

"Told you before, I'm ready," he said to Doc. "What you got in mind?"

"The evening's young," the doctor said, "and there's still a lady present."

"The lady's with me," Ikie said defiantly.

"You may remember I mentioned," Doc said, "that you might have to oppose your relatives."

Ikie understood instantly. He patted Bella's hand. "Listen, baby," he said, "there's a pint in the cabin, and that good FM station on the stereo. Why don't you go make yourself comfortable and wait for me?"

Bella bridled. "I've been waiting for you all week."

"Yeah, baby, I know, it was hard on me, too. But these fellas came to see me on some special business."

"Well, go ahead and get your business over with, and then we'll leave together."

"Didn't you hear the doc say I might have to go against my relatives?"

"So?"

"How many relatives have I got in this town?"

"Hundreds," Bella said truthfully.

"He didn't mean them," Ikie said. "Look. I don't want to put you in a worse position than you're in already, baby."

Bella understood. A flush of mauve rose into her cheeks. But she did not move.

The doctor cleared his throat. "Perhaps another time. . . ."

Fess was a little drunk. "Time," he said loudly, "is just what we don't have. They've already started digging on Merchant Avenue."

Doc shrugged, as if abandoning his hope of secrecy. "All right. I talked to Reverend Bream tonight. He is enthusiastic. But he has no new tactics in mind. He still prefers what I call the way of the Book. He is all for marching, singing, and praying, with a legal permit for every demonstration. All in the hope of appealing to the white man's conscience."

"He hasn't got one," Bella said.

"I know that," Doc agreed, "and I think Reverend Bream knows it too, deep down, but he refuses to admit it. He's built his whole life around the quaint belief that all people have souls."

"Applying for a permit to demonstrate! Shee-it." Ikie spat into an ashtray. "Boyd and the state troopers would have 'em all locked up before the demonstration even got started."

"It's happened before," Fess said gloomily, remembering the Reverend's ragtag march on the capitol to secure income supplements for senior citizens. It had produced no results except thirty-nine arrests, for which the senior citizens who had stayed home had to provide bail money.

"The Reverend Bream is concerned, though," Doc went on, "about a younger faction in his congregation, the ones who call themselves the Young Warriors. They prefer, er—" he searched for a phrase— "what I might call the way of the sword."

"Now you're talking," Fess said eagerly.

"He's talking *crap*," Ikie said in disgust. He got up and began to pace, colliding with Booty, aproned and demure and tottering on high heels, causing her to spill the bowl of chili Fess no longer wanted. Kneeling to help her clean it up, he continued, "There's ten of them for every one of us. That's nationwide, you understand. Locally it's more. And besides, this is a *federal* project. That means troops, machine guns, tanks. That takes care of your Young Warriors and their swords. Ever see a sword go up against a tank? Nothing takes a tank but another tank."

Fess, brimming with anger and liquid courage, then made a remark he was to regret for a long, long time. Turning to Bella, he said, "What's wrong with you? With all you have to offer, can't you find yourself a real man?"

Instantly a pair of fierce little black eyes were boring into his. "Take that back, nigger." The hands around his throat were surprisingly hard and callused to be those of a man who did no work.

"You two stop it," Bella said. "You're just proving their point."

"What point?" Ikie asked, startled enough to release some of the pressure on Fess's windpipe.

"White folks say blacks can't work together because they always start fighting among themselves."

"I'll stop if he'll take it back," Ikie said, and removed his hands.

"I . . . take . . . it . . . back," Fess croaked, rubbing his sore neck.

"You never said it." Ikie sat down again, this time very close to Fess. As if to emphasize the menace of his presence, he took out a wicked-looking knife and began cleaning his nails. "Just how young are these Young Warriors?" he asked Doc Thompson.

"Middle teens, mostly. Average sixteen. Couple of old heads nineteen, twenty."

"My point was," Ikie said, keeping a watchful eye on Fess, who did not intend to say another word to arouse this easily angered man, "that I don't believe in dying early. If they kill off all our young men, how much future will this town have?"

"If they dig up all our land and pave it over with cement, how much *town* will we have?" Fess rejoined, then began to shake at his own daring. Doc gave him a massive kick under the table to remind him that they were not supposed to get this specific around Bella or whoever else might be listening. But Fess was past caring about secrecy.

"Do we have a town now? Or is this just another reservation?" Ikie's eyes were large again, his face impassive. "Abe doesn't understand reality because our parents raised him. But my Indian grandmother raised me, and I learned history from both sides of my family. The white man never lets Indians or niggers own anything. They took the land from my grandmother's people and herded them onto a concentration camp called a reservation. She escaped by marrying Afro. Thought she was one of the lucky ones; thought she was gaining her freedom. Hah! What is this but a northern slave pen? A fancy labor camp to supply their kitchens and their factories? We don't own it; they only loaned it to us. I never paid any attention to what my father said. I knew he was crazy, that the white man would take this town back any time he got ready. Well, now he's ready. And there's not a damn thing we can do about it."

Fess was awed by this speech and momentarily ashamed of his taunting remark. Ikie's heritage, not any cowardice, explained his passivity and resignation. He bore a double burden of bitterness.

"You're wrong, my friend," Doc said gravely. "Brave men founded this town. They risked death to get here via the Underground Railroad. And when they got here, they didn't give up just because the risks were almost as bad. They stayed on, knowing they were in constant danger of being captured. And they paid for this land in money and in blood. They bought every inch of this town, and they fought to keep it. That was a long time before Emancipation, remember. Right here where we're sitting, white bodies are buried—the bodies of slave owners who came to hunt down and recapture your ancestors. None of them completed their missions. Oh no, my friend. This town is *owned* by us, not loaned to us.

At the mention of white bodies, Ikie flashed a wide smile. "That's a pretty story. Tell it to me again sometime."

"It's not just a pretty story. It's true," said Fess, who had done most of the research. "Dig deep enough in almost any backyard around here and you'll find human bones; *white* human bones."

"I like that," Ikie said, flashing another of his rare smiles. His teeth were huge, like beavers' teeth; they looked big enough to cut down trees. "I can even believe it. But even if it's true, how can it help us? They didn't have tanks in those days, or machine guns. I believe right *does* make might if you keep technology out of it. But now—" he shrugged and slumped in his chair. "We might as well just get drunk. You, boy, get us another bottle."

Fess reacted with a more honest and direct rage, now that he was understanding and liking Ikie more. "Don't call me 'boy.' I'm older than you. I know more history than you, too. And I can tell you, it does help. It can give people determination and courage. A Lakes fought in every one of those battles. Doesn't that do anything for you, man?"

"Yes," Ikie said. "It tells me how far we've degenerated." He pounded his fist on the table and shouted, "Get me a bottle!"

"Please don't," Bella said. "You know drinking's no good for you when you're like this."

He cut his eyes at her. "I'm not going to smash up my statues again, if that's what you're afraid of."

"I'm not afraid of anything," Bella said in an exciting, husky voice. She hesitated, then began to speak very carefully, as if all their fates depended on her choosing the precisely appropriate words. "I don't know what you all were talking about, you understand. I didn't understand any of it. I have no idea what you were planning. I wasn't even here tonight, for that matter. I was at a meeting of the scholarship committee. But I was thinking . . . there might be another way."

"We hear you." Doc nodded. "Go on."

"The way of the Book is no good. Preaching, marching, praying. All that depresses me, somehow. But the way of the sword won't work either. Ikie's right—they'd simply kill us all. But there's another way black people have always used in tight situations."

"And that is?"

Instead of answering immediately, she picked up the cards, toyed with them, shuffled them so rapidly they blurred like the blades of an electric fan, made them dance up and down her arm, let them cascade from hand to hand, then set down the deck and turned over the top card. It was an ace of spades. She cut and picked up the top card again. It was the same ace. "You might call it," she said, "the way of the game."

"Beautiful card trick, baby," Ikie complimented her. "I wish I'd let you deal. But you should've gone to the cabin when I asked you. This is a men's discussion, and we're not playing games."

"Neither am I," she said, and flashed him a hard, brilliant look. "And I'm not your squaw, either, so stop ordering me into the tepee. Maybe your mother was a squaw, but I'm an *Afro* woman." The way she said it seemed to darken her ivory skin. The tilt of her head and the tone of her voice were pure Dahomey.

"Black people," she said softly, "have to work together as a tribe. We're surrounded and outnumbered. We can't afford to let the men take all the risks alone. And this is something that could involve every man, woman, and child in town."

"The way of the game," Ikie repeated scornfully.

"Yes."

Fess's imagination quickened. He thought of Lukey Hawkins's mistaken-identity spree in New York and of Lonnie Jenkins's boss man metamorphosing into a slave. "Gaming," he said, unconsciously adopting the pedantic lecturing tone he had used at the university, "is the black man's traditional method of getting over, as reflected in the folklore. Brer Rabbit; the signifying monkey; Anansi, the African spider; all clever creatures, but weak and small, underdogs like us. Like us, using their wits to beat a larger, stronger enemy."

"You said women and children could take part in this plan of yours?" Doc asked.

"Women have weapons men don't possess," Bella said meaningfully.

All of them felt the power of her gaze. "That's true," Doc said.

"As I said," she went on in her careful, hesitant way, "I don't know what you're planning. But I assume there are men who oppose you, white men. Let's say they have a job to do. Think how a woman, or women, might distract them from that job."

Ikie laughed. But Doc did not; he nodded gravely.

Bella continued in low tones, "I'm just talking hypothetically, you understand. But suppose it were—a construction site you were talking about. And suppose Booty were to wander across that construction site. Wearing, say, shorts and a halter. How much work do you think would get done that day?"

Doc eyed Booty as she moved sinuously among the tables. "The lady makes sense," he said excitedly. "She's on to something. That project has deadlines, federal deadlines. Anything that slows it up, causes enough delays, could block it. Conceivably, Washington would cut off the money if we managed to hold it up long enough."

"I like it," Fess said.

"It stinks," Ikie said disgustedly.

"No one is suspicious of children," Bella went on. "That's *their* big advantage. I don't know what this project is, you understand. But let's say it involves hard work. This is summertime. Men get thirsty doing hard work outdoors in the summertime. Suppose a few small children show up with pitchers of lemonade?"

"Awwww," Ikie vented his disgust. "This is getting worse and worse. Children with lemonade. Get me something stronger before I puke."

"Suppose," Bella continued sweetly, "that it is not really lemonade. Suppose something stronger has been added to it, something that makes the men tired and sleepy. Perhaps even ill."

"Some of Mame's private-label stock?" Doc asked, referring to the home-brewed corn liquor that he called Universal Solvent.

Bella shrugged. "I wouldn't know. Whatever. These are the only ideas I have right now. I'm sure you men can think up much better ones and work out the details."

"The lady's a marvel," Doc said. "Only my respect for you keeps me from kissing her, Isaac."

"The lady's nuts," Ikie said sourly. "Beautiful, yes, but crazy. I want to save the young men, so instead she wants to sacrifice the children."

"Nothing will happen to the children," Fess said authoritatively. "They will escape because they appear to be so harmless. And because they are small, nimble, and quick, just like the monkey." And he quoted:

The lion stepped back and squared off for a fight
And that slick little monkey jumped clean out of sight.

Ikie tossed back his leonine mane and said, "You ain't got that right, Professor. You been signifyin' about me all night, so it's up to me to straighten you out. This is how it ends":

Now the monkey is in his grave.
No more signifying will he crave.
And on his tombstone these words are writ:
He died as he lived.
By his
Signifying
Shit.

Keeping a murderous stare trained on Fess, he caught Bella's hand and pulled her to her feet. "Come on, baby. I've already wasted too much of my life sitting around bullshitting with niggers. I've lived long enough to know they ain't never gonna do nothing but talk, and I've got better things in mind."

"I still think she had some pretty good ideas," Fess said after the couple had gone.

"So did I," said Doc Thompson.

"And so did he," echoed Mame, startling them both by suddenly materializing over the back of the booth. "That's why he was mad. You got to understand about Ikie. He's an Aries, he's got to think up all the ideas himself. You wait and see. By tomorrow night, everything she said will be *his* idea."

"Did you hear everything she said?" Fess asked, wondering how long Mame had been sitting in the next booth.

"No, of course not," Mame said indignantly. "I don't eavesdrop on my customers. Bad for business. But here. See can you taste what I put in this lemonade."

And, putting two glasses of innocent-looking liquid on the table, she left. Fess and Doc sat there eyeing the drinks suspiciously. Neither of them was willing to take the first sip.

Doc finally solved the problem. "I think I'll send these to my lab for analysis. We don't want to *kill* the poor bastards."

"Why not?"

Doc could think of no good answer to that. "Well," he amended, "at least we don't want to kill ourselves."

12

Turned out of the fire hall, the dispossessed young of Lakestown split into two groups. Those with money jingling in their pockets headed for the Jump Shop next to the school, where canned music and sodas were dispensed in return for the jingle; those without, for the vacant lot, the daytime baseball field, next to Mount Moriah A.M.E. Most of the young men who gathered on the lot were members of the Young Warriors, a club that met every Saturday at the church.

But among them was one who did not belong, Theodore Crump by name. He was built like a long stick, and on his scarecrow frame hung clothes more ragged than the ones worn by cornfield effigies. As usual, his pockets had been too empty to purchase a soda, let alone admission to the dance. Another outsider had tagged along—sneaky little Rudy Merchant, called Runt for his size—but he was too young and insignificant to be worthy of a nineteen-year-old man's attention. So, waiting with an angry alertness for an opportunity to join in, Crump lurked on the edge of the Warriors as he had on the fringe of the dancers, listening to the members discuss club business.

Tommy Adams, at seventeen the oldest of Bunky Adams's basement dwellers, was speaking excitedly. "The Rev won't let us take action, man. We got to do this thing ourselves."

"I say, let's tear up the man's machines," said Forrest "Foxy" Carter, Dunce Cap's tall son, whose head, like his father's, culminated in a steeple but, again like his father's, contained a generous supply of brains. Foxy, who had just turned seventeen, said excitedly, "You just let me at one of those bulldozers. I can strip fourteen gears in two minutes. Or let me go to work on one of them tractors. I'll have it throwing rods faster than a machine gun spits bullets."

"Let's wait and decide at the meeting tomorrow," counseled Tonio Farmer, the oldest and coolest head of the group.

"Hell, man," Foxy replied angrily, "you know the Rev ain't gonna let us go for no action like that. I mean, you know, the Rev's all right with me—that room he gave us is cool, with the masks and the spears and the posters and all—but he still got that old-timey Christian attitude. Love thy enemies. Bless them that curse you. Shee-it."

The chorus of disgust that responded to this argument signaled agreement.

"I mean," Foxy continued, "are we Warriors, or are we punk choirboys, like the Rev wants?"

"I wasn't thinking about the Rev," Tonio said. "I was thinking about the chief. We shouldn't decide on strategy when he's not here."

"He's right," chimed in Lou Adams, Tommy's younger brother. "Lukey Hawkins is the president. He ought to be in on all our strategy meetings."

"The chief," Tonio gently corrected him. "'President' is a white Western term."

"The chief, then," Lou said. "I don't think we ought to decide on any action without him."

"Shut up, Lou," Foxy ordered. "What you know about it? You too young to be out this late, anyway. Whatsa matter, your little tongue-tied sweetheart stand you up again?"

"Lay offa her, man," said Lou, his small fists raised.

"And you lay offa my brother, man," said Tommy, striking an identical pose.

"Peace, brothers," said Tonio. "We can't afford to be fighting among ourselves. That's our first rule, remember? Umoja."

"Umoja," echoed the others, repeating the word for unity.

"All I want to say is," Foxy continued, "we got to stop talkin' and start doin'. While we're standin' around talkin' strategy, the white man is diggin' the ground right from under us. Pretty soon this town will be one big hole, and we'll all fall in it. Then all he'll have to do is cover up our dumb black asses."

"Hawk's got heart," said Tommy, who had seemingly been converted like his little brother by Tonio's reasoning. "I think he'll go along with your program. I just think he ought to be here when we decide on it."

"I ain't so sure," Foxy said. "Seems to me he's been stallin' us along."

"He wants to see what the older men decide to do," Tonio explained, "so we can coordinate with their efforts."

"Let me tell you fools somethin'," Foxy declared. "Them old farts ain't gonna do nothin'. They moved our house today. Just picked it up and put it on some logs and rolled it away. And my old man stood there and watched and *didn't say a word.*"

"Maybe they paid him, Foxy," Lou offered.

"Sure they paid him," Foxy agreed. "That's what's wrong with the old heads. They can all be bought. Cheap, too. Can't see their own black faces for lookin' at the white one on a dollar bill."

"I'm not so sure," Tonio said. "I hear some of the older people are gettin' mad. I hear council meeting tomorrow night is gonna be bust wide open. I think we should wait for that."

"Where you get your information, Tonio?" Foxy wanted to know.

"I can't say. I promised not to. And stop callin' me by my Christian name. Never know who might be listenin'." He glanced meaningfully over his shoulder toward the shadows, where Ted Crump stood.

"Sorry, Daoud."

"It's okay, Hakim. Are you willing to wait for the chief before we act?"

"Just tell Lukey—"

"Rashid," Tonio-Daoud corrected gently.

"Just tell the chief, if he don't let me work on them machines, I'm gonna work on some whiteys' heads."

A rousing "Yeah!" came from several throats.

"And I can tell," Foxy continued, "that *some* brothers are with me. I don't know who you with, the CIA or what, but let me tell you something, Daoud. When I saw my father stand there and watch while they took our house away, and I saw he wasn't gonna do nothin' about it, I wanted to kill him, or cry. I got to do somethin' tonight, *right now,* or bust."

Ted Crump edged forward. The pain of exclusion was so familiar he had almost grown used to it, like any other chronic condition, but that did not prevent him from seeking relief. He lived in a shack near the creek that bore his name with his father, Ted Senior, ex-prizefighter, ex-truck farmer, and ex-convict, the latter the result of his having shot and killed a six-year-old girl caught stealing peaches from his orchard. The following year the peach tree died, as did Mrs. Crump. The year after that, Crump was paroled to the frustration of working barren orchards and acres that no longer yielded crops; land that was, in fact, as bare as a baboon's behind. The rumor spread that "grass won't grow where them Crump niggers go," and the superstition that became attached to them, that their very presence was lethal to living things, left them in isolation as well as poverty. Ted Senior was now a peddler of filmed, recorded, and printed pornography, a lucrative enough business for most men but a poor one for him, because the smut seemed somehow dirtier to people after it had passed through his hands. As for Ted Junior, isolation had fueled enough hatred in his skinny frame to scorch the whole earth.

He stepped forward and said lightly, "Why don't we go swimming?"

"Who's that?" Foxy Carter asked. "Oh, Crump. Why don't you go someplace and scare somebody?"

"Yeah," Tommy Adams chimed in. "I heard Doc Thompson has a job for you, Crump. Standin' out in front of his office, makin' people sick."

Ted refused to react to their taunts. "It's a hot night," he observed. "Anybody hot besides me?"

"Yeah," Foxy cracked, "but all the girls went home."

"He don't mean that kind of hot, Carter," Runt Merchant said.

"Well, what else could the fool mean? Ain't no place to swim around here."

"Yes there is," Ted said. "Right over there. Right in front of your eyes."

As if mesmerized by his voice, they turned in unison and stared at the eight-foot chain-link fence surrounding the private Dorsettown Swim Club, darkened since its closing two hours ago.

Now it was Ted's turn to jeer. "Call yourselves proud black warriors, and yet you walk past that place every day and pretend it isn't there. Hot as a motherfucker out, and you pretend you don't even know there's an Olympic-sized pool two feet from your noses. That's cause Whitey's got control of your minds."

"It's guarded," someone objected.

Ted laughed derisively "You mean those jive Hartz Protective Agency signs? They don't mean nothin'. That's just somethin' Whitey stuck up there to scare dumb niggers off his property. But he doesn't give a damn about our property, does he?"

"Right on," Foxy approved.

"Well, then, why don't we cool off?"

"Crump," said Foxy, "I like your ideas. Why don't you come to our meetings sometime?"

The truth was, nothing could induce Ted Crump to enter a church except his own funeral, but all he said was, "I wasn't invited."

"I'm inviting you now," Foxy said. "And . . ."

"Wait—" Tonio counseled, but he was overridden by the younger fellow's enthusiasm.

"And I'll give you a name," Foxy said, and thought for a moment. "Karim. Course it don't really count till you mix your blood with one of ours."

"Solid," Ted said. "Now I guess I can go get baptized."

The newly named Karim stripped rapidly, then hooked his claws and toes into the interstices of the fence. Soon he was straddling it, looking down at the inside. "It's lookin' good down there," he reported. Then he stood up, a gaunt, eerie silhouette, flapping his arms like a buzzard's wings for balance.

Tonio, the twenty-year-old voice of reason, tried desperately to dissuade them. "Brothers," he said, "the chief isn't here, but if he were, I know he'd ask one question: is this action constructive? What is its purpose?"

"To cool us off, of course!" answered young Lou Adams with a laugh.

"And another thing," Tonio reminded them, "why are you following an outsider instead of your elected leaders?"

"'Cause he had an idea, fool," answered Foxy, who had already stripped to his shorts and was heading for the fence. "Last one in is a boy soprano!"

Only Tommy Adams lingered a moment, then shrugged and began to pull his shirt over his head. "If you don't want to get wet, will you stand watch, Daoud? We need somebody to watch out for the Man."

Tall, grave Tonio nodded, relinquishing the command he had already lost. Already a half-dozen piles of clothing had appeared around him on the ground; a moment later, a half-dozen bodies scrambled to the top of the fence and briefly appeared silhouetted there, until one by one they disappeared with loud splashes.

KRISTIN LATTANY

"Hold your pee!" Foxy shouted over the splashing. "After we're done swimming, we're gonna pollute Whitey's pool for him."

"I'm saving something better than that," Ted Crump announced.

"Nasty old Crump," Foxy observed, and tried to duck him.

But in the water, the skinny young Crump, who had practically grown up in the creek near his shack, was as slippery as an eel, and just as much at home. He swam underwater and surfaced at the opposite end of the pool, where Tommy Adams lay floating on his back and jetting water like a whale. A few feet away, his younger brother Lou was treading water. Crump had not known until he saw the boy that he had been searching for a victim.

Filling his lungs, he submerged again, caught Lou's feet, and dragged him underwater. Having no conscious intention beyond torture, Ted calculated how long the struggling boy could hold his breath by the tension in his own lungs. When they were about to burst, he let go of the feet that had already stopped kicking a few moments ago without his noticing. They rose to the surface sluggishly, without a struggle. Crump had expected at least a kick in the jaw. Puzzled, he surfaced again and looked around.

It was too dark for anyone to notice what had happened. The pool's floodlights had been turned off hours ago, of course. There were no stars, and even the moon had gone behind a cloud. They seemed to be swimming in an inkwell.

A sudden uneasiness seemed to strike all the boys at the same time. Quite near him, Crump heard Runt cry out, "Yo, Carter! Let's go!" Then from a great distance came Foxy's voice calling "Tommy! Where are you? Let's split, man!"

In response, Tommy turned over, looked around, and missed his younger brother for the first time. "Lou? Where are you? Hey, you guys, help me find my brother!" Silently, Crump submerged again and glided to the far end of the pool like a water moccasin.

That end of the pool was empty. Foxy Carter had left it to join Tommy Adams with a half-dozen powerful strokes. "What's happenin', ace?" he asked.

Tommy's voice was troubled. "I found Lou. But something's the matter with him."

"Shit," Foxy cursed as he supported the boy's head, holding it out of the water while Tommy pounded his back. "What a fucked-up situation. What do we do now?"

"What's happenin', brothers?" a strong voice called down from the top of the fence.

"It's Louie, Tonio!" Tommy yelled. "I think he stayed under too long."

Their guard did not hesitate. He kicked off his shoes and executed a straight dive from the top of the fence, surfacing directly at the spot where Foxy and Tommy were supporting the younger boy and trying to revive him. With a muttered curse of his own at their stupidity, Tonio hooked his elbow under Lou's chin, backstroked him swiftly to the edge, hauled him half over it, and started working on him while his legs were still in the pool. Quantities of water gushed out of the boy's mouth as soon as Tonio applied pressure.

The other boys gathered around anxiously.

"Is he breathing?" Tommy asked.

"Not yet," said Tonio, who was still working on Lou's shoulders.

"Try mouth-to-mouth," Tommy urged desperately.

"I am," said Tonio, flipping the boy over. "But somebody's got to go for an ambulance."

Ted Crump had slithered out of the pool last, unnoticed. "I'll go," he volunteered.

Tonio raised his lips from the other's long enough to say, "Not you."

"Let me," Tommy urged. There was another long kiss of life, then Tonio turned to say, "No, Nazzam. Stay with your brother. You go, Hakim."

"Right," said Foxy, and began to scale the fence.

"Let's all get out of here," wailed Runt Merchant, who was suddenly sounding very young indeed and was climbing right behind him.

"Come back here!" cried Tommy. "We're all in this together."

"Let him go," Tonio panted. "He's useless."

"Breathe," Tommy commanded, as Tonio continued to work on his brother. "Damn you, breathe!" Forgetting the others' part in the diversion, he thought, "It's all my fault." Tears started down his cheeks. But he was wet anyway, and in the dark, who would notice?

All that changed in a flash, as the floodlights came on and the pool was lit up like noon. For the second time that night they were blinded by glare and their ears were assaulted by sirens.

"That damn Rudy," Tommy muttered. "He must've tripped the alarm. Or else Crump did. Where's Crump, anyway?"

"Right here," came a spooky voice with no visible source. Ted Crump was back in the pool, clinging to the edge, out of sight.

Another invisible person called with authority from the glare of the floodlights, "Come out of there, or we'll shoot!"

"We can't. My brother's hurt!" Tommy shouted back.

But his voice was lost in the screeching of the burglar alarm and the sirens of the arriving Dorsettown police.

The warning was repeated. Again Tommy tried to answer, but again his voice was lost in the bedlam. The next sound he heard was the *ping* of a bullet as it whizzed past his ear. He touched his head; he was not hurt. But when he looked down, Tonio had collapsed atop the boy he was trying to save.

"Later, brothers," Ted whispered, after reaching a snakelike arm out of the pool and touching Tonio. "There's nothing I can do now."

He swam underwater to the opposite side of the pool and vanished in a way that to Tommy was spectral. The club, knowing their pool was offensive to Lakestown, had planted Lombardy poplars outside the fence in an attempt at concealment. Their thin shadows would have offered no protection from the floodlights to anyone except the gaunt Crump, who seemed to merge with one shadow, flow from that one to the next, and finally to disappear.

Later, by the candlelight in his cabin, Ted Crump, Jr., studied the bloodstain on his right palm and the stigma on his left where it had caught on a barb of the fence. Assiduously he rubbed the two palms together, performing his own rite of initiation.

"Now," he exulted aloud, "I'm *really* Karim!"

13

The stereo was playing softly, those lonely, despairing moans called progressive jazz. Bella, restless, smoking, switched stations several times until she found some music that wanted her response; warm, soulful sounds instead of cool ones. There was no room for pacing or dancing, so she sat on the edge of Ikie's narrow bed, her skirt wrapped tightly around her legs, feet tapping in time to the primitive beat.

Ikie sat on his only chair, a straight one borrowed from the Blue Moon's dining room. "Gonna jack off all by yourself?" he inquired coarsely.

"God, but you're gross tonight. I just might. Will you give me a drink?"

"Why?"

"'Cause I want one, fool!"

"Oh, the drink. Sure," he said in his mild, courteous voice, and poured some warm rye into his two enameled cups. "I meant, why do you want to fly solo when I'm right here with you?"

She tossed the liquor down, suppressing her nausea by sheer willpower. It tasted terrible, even worse than the bottom-shelf bourbon Doc had bought. "Because," she said when she felt no more risk of retching or coughing, "you don't respect me."

Ikie's brow resembled a newly plowed field. "Baby," he said, "I can't deal with that. It's too heavy. I figured it would come up sometime. After all, you're my brother's wife. But we've been lovers for so long now—five months, six—I thought I could relax and forget about it. Why'd you pick this time to throw your shit on me?"

"God, men are dumb," Bella said, banging her knees with her fist as if to lock them together permanently. "I wasn't talking about whose wife I am. That's my problem, not yours. What I meant was, you don't respect my *mind*."

Ikie began to laugh. "Is that all's bothering you?"

"I may not be a genius," she went on, smoking furiously, "but I do not like the way you laughed at my ideas out there."

KRISTIN LATTANY

Ikie shrugged. This, she knew, was the most she would ever get from him by way of apology. "What can I say? Sometimes I laugh to keep from crying, you know? Like all us happy darkies."

Her voice softened. "You have no hope, you mean."

"How can I? It's a hopeless situation."

"Which one?"

"You name it. This town and that road. You and me. Both."

"You might be wrong about one of them."

"Which one?"

"Oh, I don't know, I don't know," she said, her head tossing in the beginning of passion, for she had stopped resisting; at least part of her had stopped, the part below her waist that had a life of its own, a life she had tried to cage forcibly between locked knees and failed. One touch from him and they had sprung open. But her head was full of conflicts that did not leave enough room for her to concentrate on passion, only enough to notice little things—a rancid odor from his hair, a lack of freshness about his general person—that were distasteful. He was spent all too soon and she was still unsatisfied.

"No good, huh, baby?" he gasped. "You didn't moan or cry out or nothin'."

"You're more than a cock to me," she said, fondling it absently, as if she were stroking a soft pet. "How come I can't be more than a cunt to you?"

"Because the rest of you belongs to someone else. And that someone happens to be my brother." He groaned. "That makes it worse. Almost incest."

"That should make it more interesting," she said with a bawdy laugh, becoming the rough, reckless Bella he had known at first but had never really believed in. He did not believe her now.

"You're crazy. No, you're acting crazy, like you always do when somethin' really bothers you. You know bein' my brother's wife only makes things more worrisome. I don't need hassles."

"Does anybody?" she asked, stroking the hair that had repelled her a moment ago. "But sometimes they just come up and stare you in the face, and you have to deal with them."

"I can deal," he said pridefully, "with anything." Looking at his broad shoulders, thick arms, and wide, hairless chest, she could believe it.

"Anything but you. With you I'm nothing but a big, helpless hunk of butter. I'm a fool to admit this; any man would be. But all you have to do is walk in a room, shaking all that beautiful stuff you got, and I just melt. Do it now," he pleaded. "I'm not ordering you, I'm begging you. Please, do it now."

"Do what?" she asked in puzzlement.

"Get up and walk around the room."

Ikie's cabin room, an eight-by-ten cell, contained, in addition to its furniture (a single bunk, dresser, and chair) numerous heaps of clothing, books, wood, and carving implements, as well as crocks of clay and plaster. She had been unable to push the door open because of all the junk piled behind it, and it had taken all his strength to open it for her. She looked at his earnest, pleading eyes and began to laugh.

"That's right. Laugh at me. I deserve it for being fool enough to get in your power."

"I wasn't laughing at you. Only at your idea."

It was his turn to be baffled. "Huh? What idea?"

"That there could possibly be enough space in here for me to walk around. There's no room for a *cockroach* to turn around in here."

Ikie looked ruefully around at his heaped-up possessions and began to laugh too, his usual stoic countenance taking on a rare, appealing, boyish look.

"Clean it out and put it in your van," she said, "and I promise you my most spectacular walk ever."

"The van's full too." Ikie raked despairing fingers through his long hair, disarranging it even more. "God, how I hate possessions. I try not to have any, but they keep accumulating anyhow. Sometimes I think they get together late at night and make little possessions. They must. They multiply like rabbits."

Bella's laugh went all the way up and down three octaves that time.

"You don't have to walk," he said, frowning, but still looking youthful. "You can sit there all night like Miss Prim if you want, with your knees stuck together. I still won't be able to keep my hands offa you."

"Your hands were too busy to touch me out there in the dining room, I suppose," she said archly.

"You're faking again. I know you aren't jealous of those pitiful bitches."

She nodded. "You're right. I was faking just then. For fun. I don't mind Lily and Booty. It sounds strange, I know, but I think they're good girls."

"Sure they are. The only trouble with them is, they have to *act* sexy. It's their trade. Sex is just a job to them, so they're bored with it, and they have to pretend. That turns me off. Now, you—you don't have to act sexy; you just *are*. You can't help being sexy any more than you can help breathing. All you have to do is be yourself. Promise me you won't ever try to be anybody else."

"I promise. What is it you like best about me? My legs, or what?"

"All of it. It's *you* I like. That womanly nature deep down inside you. Course the outside is plenty fine too, and that's cool, but it ain't the main thing. You say men are dumb. Well, maybe so, but most women are dumb, too. They think men are just interested in their outsides—in their shapes, or their legs, or in some makeup they bought in the dime store. Women like that are nothing but empty dolls. What makes a woman is what's inside. And all the paint in the world won't turn a doll into a woman."

He had said the right things, the things she wanted to hear, but she had to test him a little more. "You say you like everything about me. Does that include my mind?"

"Even that. Sure. It's all you. Except sometimes your mind gets in the way of more important things."

"Damn you," she said, but he was not listening. He was seeing a picture from the past.

"The sexiest I ever saw you look," he said dreamily, "was before we got together. You was wearing an old raggedy sweatshirt and some sneakers, walking in the woods around here. You had scratches on your legs, and you had a bucket in one hand for picking berries. . . ."

His mouth had curved into the tender smile she saw so seldom and loved for its gentleness. "What *I* like most about *you*," she said, and bent to kiss him, "is your mouth. Sometimes. When it isn't talking."

"Mmmm," he said, his eyes still seeing a mental picture from the past even while his hands were walking up her legs. "And with your other hand you were leading that little girl—what's her name?—my niece . . ."

"Your *what?*" Bella cried, pulling away, breaking the mellow spell.

"Oh, God. I thought you knew."

She shook her head.

"You must be the only person in Lakestown who doesn't."

"You mean Cindy—"

"Is Abe's daughter. By Vinnie Coddums." He knelt on the floor, removed her sandals, and began to kiss her toes. "Oh, Lord, why did I have to say that? I'm sorry, sweetheart. Please don't start thinking about it. Not now. Please don't think now."

With his irresistible mouth working its way up her ankles and her legs to the inside of her thighs, Bella managed not to think for a while. But later, after her release and his, as they lay cramped together in the bunk, her mind became active again.

"I can't believe it," she said, aware that she had always known it at some deep, unconscious level. "But it must be true."

"Maybe it's good I told you," he said sleepily. "Make you less guilty."

"For once and for all, I am not guilty about us. I don't need cheap excuses for what I do. I belong to *myself*, not to him or to you either, mister. If he wanted me in bed, I might feel differently; but as it is, I don't think I have a thing to be guilty about."

"What I can't understand," he said, "is how he can keep his hands off you."

"What I can't understand," she said, slapping the one of his that was busy under her skirt again, "is how he can deny that lovely little girl. Oh, I know she's supposed to be retarded, but she's not, Ikie. She's quick, quick as lightning. She learns faster than I can teach her. She—well, it's supposed to be a secret, nobody knows it yet, but I can tell *you*—she's even learning to talk."

"He's guilty, that's why," her lover said.

"About me?" Bella threw back her head and roared. "That's really funny. When all these years I've been hoping he had someone else to keep him from exploding."

"Boy," Ikie said, "you two sure do need to talk to each other. But that wasn't all I meant. See, you didn't know our father. The first word we learned to say was 'da-da.' The second was 'sin,' and the third was 'repent.' Plus, Abe has a white man's mind—"

"I know that much," she interjected.

"Well, then, you ought to know that a white-minded nigger Christian is ten times guiltier than a white one. Abe soaked up all that stuff about sin instead of choking on it and vomiting it up like I did."

"So?" she asked flippantly.

"So somebody like Vinnie, an ignorant stump who does day's work, is okay to screw, because she's lower than he is. In fact, he can only screw somebody he thinks is beneath him. But he's ashamed of it, too, because he thinks she's so low, and because he thinks all screwing's sinful. And he's even more ashamed of Cindy, because she's the living proof he did it."

"Whew," Bella half said, half whistled at this glimpse of the torture chamber that was her husband's mind. "Where do I fit into all this?"

"You're supposed to be a high-class white lady. Pure. On a pedestal. Above sex, and all those other dirty things."

"Maybe," she said with a dim glint of understanding, "that's why he gets mad when I don't shut the bathroom door."

"You leave it open?" he asked with astonishment.

"Sure. Why not? I'm his wife, aren't I? What do I have to hide?"

Ikie began to laugh. "Baby, how long you been married to my brother? You sure don't understand him. You may be his wife, but you're not his woman. As his wife, you're supposed to be like a high-class white lady. You ain't even supposed to have to go to the bathroom. Hell, you ain't even supposed to *perspire.*"

"Well, I do. I sweat a lot. Especially in this little hot box of yours."

"Well, you ain't supposed to. Remember, you're supposed to be an imitation white lady. Real white ladies perspire sometimes, but imitation ones never do. And they don't even *say* 'sweat,' let alone do it."

Bella sighed. "I suppose they don't come, either."

"Horrors!" Ikie mocked. "Of course not. They don't have anything down there but silk drawers. You ain't even supposed to know what the word means, except when you see it on an invitation that says 'Come to cocktails.'"

Bella rolled over on her face so that her laugh was muffled in his pillow.

"Are you laughing or crying, baby?" he asked, touching her shoulders with concern.

She looked up. "I don't know. I guess I'm doing like you were.

Laughing to keep from crying. What an impossible way to want somebody to be. It's unreal. Nobody can be like that. Shit." She pounded the pillow with her fists. "Ikie," she asked, "what the hell am I going to do? All these years, I never knew what he wanted. Now I know, and I know I can never be it. But I can't leave him, either."

"Why not?" He waved at his cubicle. "Look around you. All this could be yours."

"Ikie, please be serious. Of course I'd love to live with you. I'd live with you in a chicken coop. But I'm too worried about him." She propped herself up and stared at him gravely. "How can I make you understand? Listen. Can you remember how old you were when you first found out what it meant to be a nigger?"

Ikie didn't need to give the question much thought. "Sure. About five, when I first went to nursery school, and got beat up by the little white kids. Then came home and got a worse beating, 'cause they were white, so they *had* to be right, even if they were wrong."

"It took me a little longer," Bella said. "I was thirteen. Just starting high school, integrated high school, and dating—the whole boy-girl scene. All of a sudden the same white kids I'd played with all my life started acting like I didn't exist. And the teachers kept mixing me up with the other black ones till I realized we really did all look alike to them."

"Thirteen," he said. "Yep, I guess that's about the normal age. Painful, wasn't it?"

"Sure. But I'm glad it happened when it did. I think it's worse the older you get."

"How much older *can* you get in this country without realizing you're a nigger?"

"You'd be surprised," she said. "I had a friend who didn't find out till she was forty. She was single, lived alone; stayed by herself too much, I guess. Then one day she got hired for a job over the phone, walked in and let them see her black face, and got told the usual jive story about how the position was already filled. It hit her all at once. Like getting smacked in the face with a wet dishrag."

"What happened to her?"

"I go to see her at the hospital," Bella said, "when she's allowed to have visitors." She gripped Ikie's hand, digging into it with her nails as if to make the words penetrate. "That's what happened to somebody who found out at forty. Ikie, Abe is *fifty,* and he hasn't found out yet! It scares me."

"It should. It scares *me,*" he said.

"And that's why I can't leave him. He's heading for a big crash, Ikie. Just like my mother and father. Only they were lucky; they had a real crash and died still thinking they were practically white. But Abe's heading for a crack-up that won't kill him, only break him into a thousand little pieces. Who's going to be there to pick them up, if I don't?"

"I don't know," he said. "I just don't see why you have to take on the job."

"Because he doesn't have anybody else," she explained. "And because I made some kind of a promise in church, in front of a minister, about sticking by him in sickness and in health. That's what I think a marriage vow means: not keeping my pussy in cold storage for life, just in case he gets around to wanting it; just being there to look after him when he needs it. And I think he's going to need it bad."

"Have you tried to let him know he's heading for a fall?"

"Sure I try. I do everything I can to remind him we're niggers. I cuss, I scratch, I talk like a Geechee, I eat chitlins and greens and water-melon. Hell, I even *grow* watermelon in the backyard. And all it does is make him mad."

"Of course," Ikie said. "You're just waving red flags in front of him."

"You drive a truck. When you see red flags on the highway, what do they mean?"

"Slow down. Danger ahead," Ikie said.

"Well, all right," Bella said. "That's what I'm trying to do. Warn him. Slow him down. But all he sees in my—uh, niggerisms—are obstacles to his progress. I offend him, so he avoids me."

"He avoids me, too. It must be my body odor."

"Your sweat, love. And your dirty old funky poolroom."

"Please. My perspiration. And my *billiard parlor.*"

"And your sexy statues. Pornography, he calls them."

"Yes. My pornographic statues. And my prison record."

"You were in jail?" she asked, awed as a teen-ager.

"Like a Legion of Honor citation these days, ain't it?" he said sourly. "Only I don't deserve any medals. I was just transporting some dudes to Martin's March on Washington in my van, and they didn't bother to tell me they were carrying sidearms and ammunition. But somebody told the FBI."

"Poor Ikie," she said, stroking his chest. "Didn't you get the message? You were supposed to be a teacher or a preacher. Or an undertaker, at least."

"Mortician," he corrected her. "Specialist in death. Pays good, I hear. Better than trucking," said Ikie, who drove a tractor-trailer six months of the year to help him afford six months of sculpting.

"Hands that touch dead bodies," she said with a shudder, "will never touch this live one."

"I don't blame you," he said. "I'll give up that particular ambition for your sake. I only ask one thing in return. I don't have the right to make any claims on you, Bella . . . but please, go on being yourself. Don't distort your personality for anybody. Don't act white for him—and don't act blacker than you are for his sake, either. Because all I want is for you to be you. If he had any sense it would be all he wanted, too."

"I guess I can promise that. I'm no good at tea sipping, and my minstrel-show act doesn't seem to be discouraging him."

"Of course not. You have to let him go on the way he's going."

"Until he crashes and breaks up into little pieces?"

"Yes. You have to let him crack up and break, and feel the pain. Otherwise he'll never learn."

"I know," she said with a sigh. "It's just that . . . it's so hard to learn anything new at his age."

"Christ, I feel like a fuckin' marriage counselor," Ikie growled, rumpling his spiky hair. "And I don't even want to save this particular marriage. Let's not talk about Abe anymore."

"I'm sorry," she said. "Of all the people to pick to dump these problems on . . ."

"Your problems I don't mind, baby. I'd just rather not deal with his."

"But don't you see," she asked softly, "that they can't be separated?"

"Of course, I see it. I never stopped seeing it. That's why I don't want to see you mixed up in anything we do to stop that highway. I think he has a whole lot riding on it. I think, if we stop it, he stands to lose everything."

KRISTIN LATTANY

"I know," she said. "That's why I have to stick by him. But it doesn't keep me from wanting to help you. You don't know how much I hate highways. A highway killed my whole family. And I love this town. The people here are the only family I have now. Sure, I feel a duty toward Abe, but I'm not about to sacrifice Lakestown to save him."

"I think," he said, "you've got your loyalties separated very nicely."

Bella did not like that acute remark. She countered with, "So do you, don't you? I thought truckers were supposed to be in favor of highways."

"You know I only drive a truck so I can afford to be a sculptor. I've got about as much interest in trucking as your husband has in fucking."

"Copulating," she corrected. "Fornicating."

"That may be what white people do," he said, "but it ain't what we do. Is it? Is it?"

"No," she said, barely able to speak under the crushing weight of him.

"Say it. What are we doing? Say it."

She did and he did and they did, frantically purging themselves of the evening's sadness.

As she stirred and began dressing to leave, he murmured sleepily, "Stay with me, baby."

"I can't," she said, tying her skirt securely, poking around for a misplaced shoe.

"Why not? He don't need you."

"Maybe not now. But he will."

He opened sleep-thickened eyes and said, "Aaah, forget what I said, will you? I must've been drunk. Go home."

She found the shoe and threw it at him, hard.

14

Bella was surprised to see the lights on all over the house when she got home. Abe never stayed up this late. Ever since his three happiest years, the ones he had spent in the army, he was a stern believer in the well-regimented life, including early to bed and early to rise. But when she let herself in the kitchen door, he confronted her with reddened, angry eyes. Bella was so startled she lost her balance and almost fell.

"Drunk, huh?" he sneered. Her usually fastidious husband was haggard, rumpled, and stained. And the brandy bottle, which had been nearly full when she left the house, lay on its side, empty, on the kitchen table.

"Where've you been? Oh, never mind, never mind," he said, and flopped crookedly into a chair, nearly missing it. "'s too late anyway. When a man doesn't want to be bothered with people, they're all stuck up in his face." He waggled angry illustrative fingers in front of his nose. "But when he really needs people, he can't find them. You're no use anyway. You can't help. I need Boyd." He banged the table angrily. "Where's Boyd? I've been calling Dispatch all night. They can't find him." He pointed to the phone. "You call, will you?"

Bella glided over to the wall phone, dialed 6060, and was told that Chief Boyd had not called in since his last assignment, on Merchant Avenue.

"They said there was a fire at Vinnie's," she said, replacing the receiver. "Is everything all right?"

"Everything's all *wrong,*" he said, his head bowed over the table, his shoulders shaking in some dreadful agitation. Bella thought he might even be crying until he looked up, dry-eyed. "Oh, they got the fire out, if that's what you're worrying about. Your precious child is safe."

"*My* precious child?" she echoed in wonderment. Abe's remarks tonight seemed loaded with ironies.

"Yes. And I wish to God they'd been burned to ashes, both of them. But they weren't, and at least one of them can talk. So I'm ruined. I don't suppose you care, but I'm ruined. Ruined, d'ya hear?" he yelled, and recommenced banging on the table.

"Naow, Lakes, don't go gettin' youahself all wukked up," Bella said in her drawl. "That won't hep nothin'."

"Only thing that would help me is another drink. Why isn't there ever anything to drink in this house?"

Bella glanced eloquently at the empty brandy bottle but said nothing.

Her husband tried shakily to get to his feet, succeeded by holding onto the table, stood there, wavering for a few moments, then crashed down into the chair again. "If I could walk," he said, "I'd go down there and take care of it myself. Two bullets would do it. No, one. The brat can't talk. But it ought to be a silver bullet, the way that witch haunts me." His back straightened as he arrived at a decision. "Maybe I can't walk, but I can drive. Get my gun, Bella. It's in the left-hand drawer of my desk. The ammunition is in the middle drawer. Go get it. Load it for me."

Bella had not known he owned a gun, but she was not surprised; there were so many things she did not know about her husband. Thinking quickly, she offered the lesser of two evils. "First you need a drink to pull yourself together, Lakes. I just remembered where there might be some."

She went to his bedroom closet, dragged out the leather portable bar she had given him for Christmas many years ago, and opened it. Like the rest of her Christmas gifts to him, it had never been used. Among its elegant fittings were three flasks with silver caps and labels, each filled with top-shelf booze. She snatched up one and brought it out to him.

"Aaah," he said, after draining a quarter of the flask in one gulp. "That's what I needed, all right. Now, where's my gun?"

Instead of answering, Bella got out a juice glass for herself, sat down at the table opposite him, poured herself a shot, and sipped it slowly. "Now tell me, Lakes. What's the trouble?"

"Miyash well," he said. "By tomorrow the whole town'll know anyway. If they don't know already. Shows you how a man's luck can turn. He can work for years and years, come *this close* to his goal"—he pressed his thumbnail against the end of his forefinger—"and one ignorant darky who thinks she knows something can stop him. One ignorant darky with a grudge 'gainst him, maybe 'gainst the whole world. But I'll fix her. Boyd was supposed to fix her, but I haven't heard from him. Can't wait for Boyd anymore. Got to do it myself."

"Better have another drink first," Bella suggested, proffering the flask.

He tipped it up and sucked on it like an infant nursing a bottle. "'s all gone," he said, looking at the empty flask as ruefully as a child.

"There's more," she said quickly. "I'll get it."

"Wait," he said, catching her wrist in one of his beige claws, using the other to wipe his wet mouth. "Don't leave me again tonight, Bella."

"I won't," she promised.

"I wish I could believe you. Why are you always running to niggers, Bella? You don't belong down there with those Neanderthals. Where you belong is—on a throne! At my right hand, on a *throne!*"

"I ain't goin' nowhere, Lakes," she said.

"Aaagh," he said, with disgust at her put-on poor grammar, but he released her.

When she returned with the second flask, he was already well launched into a rant that had evidently begun while she was out of the room. ". . . always take your whip, I say. If you don't, they'll turn on you like a bunch of wild animals."

"Who?" she asked, getting a glass for him, because she had decided to measure his drinks.

"Told you who," he said with a red, angry stare. "Niggers! It doesn't pay to treat them like human beings. They like to be knocked around. Abused. Exploited. Only way to make them respect you."

"What are we, then?" Bella asked softly, knowing he was at least temporarily mad, knowing that she, too, must be a little crazy or she would not be trying to make sense out of his madness.

"You mean you don't know?" he asked incredulously.

"Tell me."

"We're peolas, of course."

"Oh."

"Do you know why God created peolas, Bella?"

"No. Why?" she asked, withholding the liquor from him.

"To rule over niggers," he answered triumphantly. "To rule over them, and keep them in line! *Some*body has to do it. They can't be trusted to think for themselves. They're like children, only more dangerous, because they're much stronger. Your average nigger is ten times stronger than a gorilla. All brawn and no brains. But he has a temper, just like that gorilla you see in his cage. One minute he's laughing and playing, the next he's angry, for no special reason. And a whole mob of niggers is more dangerous than a hurricane. It'll sweep right over you and stomp you to death and pass on without even remembering why. Shhh," he said suddenly, finger to his lips. "Did you hear something?"

"No."

"Shhh. Keep your voice down. They might be out there, listening."

"Who, Lakes?"

"Told you who. Look out there and see if you see them sneaking around."

"Lakes, *please*—"she objected.

"Look outside," he whispered compellingly, "and see if you see anyone out there. Be careful, now. Don't let them see you looking. Sneak up to all the windows sideways, and look out. Then pull the shades."

She followed his instructions, tiptoeing to the side of each window, peering outside, then pulling each shade to the sill. An unreasonable fear grew in her as she did this. She realized for the first time that insanity was contagious.

"There's no one out there, Lakes." She managed to say it calmly, though her heart was skipping beats as she returned to the table. "Who'd you think was there?"

"The mob," he muttered. "Coming to get me. Oh, they're out there, all right. They're hiding, that's all. They can be cunning when they have to."

She saw now there was no curbing his paranoia. It had the power and the rapid mobility of water; if she dammed up one channel with logic, it would immediately flow into another. She saw also that she should have recognized this tendency in him six months ago, when he first put up that high fence, then wired the fence, then bought the Dobermans for added protection. Protection against what? she had wondered then, but only passively, in the bovine state of contentment a new lover had brought her.

"Who, Lakes?" she asked.

"Niggers, of course!" he screamed. "Why are you so stupid? They don't want us to get away from them, Bella. I'd almost gotten away, and they know it. That's why they hate me. Might still get away, too, if I play my cards right. If I shut her fat mouth before she tells them, if she hasn't *already* told them . . ."

"Maybe you'd better tell me."

"No. You're on their side," he said with an accuracy that made her shiver. His eyes were angry slits, almost disappearing into his cheekbones, just like Ikie's. It was the first time she had seen a resemblance between them. "Why are you always trying to be one of them, Bella? Why do you want to be a nigger?"

"Well, I'm not white," she said reasonably.

To her surprise he roared back, "Of course you're not white! You're better than white! Better than black, too. A mixture of both is always better than either one. We're the best people on God's earth, Bella. We're the chosen ones the Bible talks about. That's why we're going to win!"

His perverse grounds for arrogance were not unfamiliar. After all, her parents had felt that way too—superior to white *and* black—only they hadn't been crazy enough to mix God and the Bible up in it.

"Listen. There's a high-level job waiting for me in Trenton. And after that, Washington. Probably a cabinet post. My reward for half a lifetime spent overseeing these backward niggers. We've got six months to wait, a year at the most. Then we can kiss Lakestown good-bye. No, tell them to kiss *us* good-bye. Leave them behind, and tell them to kiss *our* behinds." He giggled childishly at his joke. "But right now, we've got to be careful, Bella. All these years, they've been docile. They *would* pick this time to get unruly. We're treading on thin ice. Very thin ice indeed. I want some."

"What?"

"Ice, of course. And some more of that bourbon. I've decided to tell you what we're up against. But we've got to be careful. They're out there listening. Come closer so I can whisper."

She obeyed.

"No, don't sit down yet. Take the phone off the hook first. That's how they bug a house when they want to listen in on your conversations. Through the phone."

She did as he asked, marveling at the contradictions of a mind that saw blacks as savage children, yet credited them with enough electronic sophistication to bug his entire house.

"That's better. Now come over here and sit beside me. I can't risk speaking above a whisper. No, better not talk at all. Ears are everywhere. Give me pencil and paper."

Wordlessly she handed him the pad and pencil she used for writing shopping lists.

While he wrote furiously there was no sound inside or outside the house until the phone began its nasty little snarls. He tore off a piece of paper and handed it to her. In large, sprawling print it said:

> The Road
> (1- 27)
> Is Not
> What
> They Think

She studied it and nodded seriously, as if it made sense.
He wrote swiftly on another page, then handed it to her.

> It
> (1-27)
> Is
> Much Bigger

"Ohh," she said, expelling a lot of air. "How much bigger?"
"Shh. Don't talk!" He began to write rapidly.

He shoved a third piece of paper at her. On it he had drawn a crude map and written:

> Not from
> Here (Nestor Avenue)
> to
> Here (Piney Road)
> MUCH BIGGER

She read it, wisely keeping silent this time.

He was scribbling furiously, pausing at intervals to clutch his forehead as if it hurt him. Finally he handed her another piece of paper:

8 Lanes not 6
Everything on Merchant Ave.
       "   Windsor Ave.
       "   Thomas Ave.
       "   Grimes Ave.
to Crump's Crk.

He snatched it back and added, in oversized letters:

VINNIE KNOWS.

"Now," he shouted almost triumphantly, "do you see?"

She made a deliberate effort to be as calm as he was excited, as casual as he was tense. "I think so, Lakes. Let me look at this a minute." In her mind she was picturing the beloved places that would be chewed up by the bulldozers: Lonnie and Jerutha Jenkins's house, where she had spent many happy mornings and evenings; Vinnie's cottage; the Baptist church where she had often sneaked off to services that lifted her spirits more than the Anglican ones Abe considered more suitable to their status; and the Blue Moon; and the fields where she and Cindy had gone berrying; and the woods behind her own house; and . . .

She was so startled she spoke aloud. "Why, it'll even take *our* house!" she cried.

"Won't need it," he said with a malicious cackle. "We'll be far, far away."

"My cabinets," was all she could say. She stood up and ran her fingers over the satiny edges of the birch kitchen cabinets she had sanded and finished herself. "I don't want to lose my cabinets," she said, knowing that at that moment she was as mad as he.

There was a series of firm knocks on the front door.

"Destroy those papers," her husband ordered, and went, on legs grown miraculously firm, to answer it.

Bella took out the flask, set it on the kitchen table, and cached the

                      KRISTIN LATTANY

papers in her skirt pocket instead. She moved fast, and it was fortunate that she did. In a moment her husband returned with Police Chief Benson Boyd looming behind him.

Chief Boyd had always seemed unreal to Bella, like a windup toy soldier: so perfect he must have been manufactured and painted by someone. But tonight he was as shockingly changed as her husband had been when she came home. She saw dirt on his hands, spots on his trousers, and what looked like bloodstains on his shirt.

Her husband clapped him on the back. "Well, at last you're here, Boyd. What kept you so long?"

"Rough night," the chief said.

"Sit down. Have a drink. Relax, man. You're not on duty now."

"Bad business tonight," Chief Boyd said. "Bunch of kids trespassing on the swim club property. Jumped into the pool after closing hours. Two of them in serious condition over in Edgehill Hospital."

"Oh, well," Abe said airily, "just a little prank. Boys will be boys, won't they?"

That remark was just enough off-key to make the chief look edgy for a moment, but he apparently decided to ignore it. "That's the way *I* would look at it. Unfortunately, I wasn't first on the scene. The Dorsettown police were, and they got nervous. Shot the Farmer boy while he was trying to revive the young Adams boy."

"Which one? Lou?" Bella asked, breaking her resolve to keep quiet, for she was sympathetic to Cindy's puppy love, in spite of her admonitions.

"Yes, ma'am," the chief responded. "It doesn't look too good for him. He's still unconscious. The Farmer boy will probably make it. Bullet in the left shoulder, just touched his lung."

"Serves 'em right, I say."

"*Sir?*" the chief exclaimed.

"The little jigaboos shouldn't go where they're not wanted. Maybe this experience'll teach them. Did you lock the other jigs up?"

The chief shook his head. "They got away. I wasn't the first on the scene, as I said, sir."

"Why not? Why weren't you the first on the scene, is what I want to know. Why weren't you *anywhere* to be found earlier this evening!"

"I had to do a bit of carpentry work," the chief said sheepishly. Bella hid her smile.

Abe was rigid with indignation. *"Carpentry* work? I don't remember your exact salary, Boyd, but as I recall, it's a substantial one. Is it paid to you by the borough of Lakestown to do carpentry work?"

"No, sir." Taking refuge in supercorrectness, the chief pulled a notebook out of his pocket. "Eleven thirty P.M.," he read aloud. "Proceeded to subject's house on Merchant Avenue. Noted fire in adjacent field. Four fire companies at the scene. Found subject and minor child at home, in spite of fire. Attempted to proceed with Board of Health eviction, but met with resistance on the part of subject. Drew weapon in self-defense, accidentally shot out rear window. Attempted to contact headquarters, but subject had no telephone. Remained on premises until one A.M., repairing window, as requested by subject." He snapped the notebook shut and returned it to his pocket.

Bella could not repress her laughter, picturing this tall, dignified man dirtying his dapper uniform, glazing Vinnie's window.

Abe glared at her, and she stopped laughing.

"Is the subject dead?" he asked Boyd.

"No, sir."

"Why not?" Abe demanded. "I thought you shot in self-defense."

"Only at a window, sir."

"You should have shot *her!*" Abe screamed. "I told you that woman was dangerous. The woman, not her windows."

"Yes, sir," the chief said meekly. "It was a mistake, sir."

"The . . . er . . . subject had spare glass on her premises, I suppose."

"No, sir. I had to go home to get it. I got your message from Dispatch at home and tried to call you, but there was no answer."

"I'm not answering any phones tonight," Abe announced. "A phone call might be a trap."

"Sir?" the chief asked in astonishment.

"When you came up just now, did you notice anything unusual? Anyone hanging around my house?" The haunted, fearful look had returned to his eyes.

"No, sir," Boyd said.

KRISTIN LATTANY

Abe seemed to relax for a moment. But only for a moment. "You haven't touched your drink," he said, and raised his own. "To the ruling class."

"To the—*what*, sir?"

"To *us*, dammit! Because that's what we are. Boyd, before this night is over you are going to take care of business, and you are going to understand exactly why you are doing it. Let me tell you how you have to treat niggers. You have to keep your foot in their asses constantly. Or you'll find yourself dealing with a mindless, murderous mob, like the one out there."

Bella and Boyd both turned involuntarily to glance at the shaded windows, silent except for the night songs of insects, then back at the speaker.

"Don't you know why God created people like us, Boyd?" Abe shouted. "To rule over the unruly. Because they're incapable of ruling themselves!"

Bella, unable to take any more, covered her ears and ran to her room.

"That's right, get out!" her husband called after her. "Go to bed. The chief and I have important business to discuss."

Bella lay down on her bed fully dressed and stayed there, shaking, for what seemed like hours. Gradually the shaking stopped, but sleep was out of the question, so she did not bother to undress. The voices in the kitchen rose and fell indistinctly, but eventually there was silence. Then, an apologetic knock at her bedroom door.

She sat up. "Come in, Boyd."

"Sorry to disturb you, ma'am," he said, "but he needs looking after."

"Do you think you can get Doctor Thompson over here?"

The chief shook his head. "I already suggested it, ma'am. He refused. Said the doctor is one of his worst enemies."

Bella shuddered, then became still, feeling strength for whatever was necessary gathering inside her. "I see. Thank you, Boyd. Good night."

He tipped his hat somberly. "Good night, Mrs. Lakes. Good luck."

15

"Now whose idea was it," Lukey Hawkins asked, "to go back and throw garbage in the pool?"

He spoke softly, but with an edge of menace. His six-and-a-half-foot height lent his words considerable authority. So did the cracking of his knuckles, which made sounds that suggested fists cracking skulls.

"I'm waiting."

The cozy loft room in which the Young Warriors met seemed to have been transported from another world. No one would have known it was in a church in America, except for the organist practicing downstairs, whose muted hymns were masked by the throbbing of drums from a tape recorder. There were soft lights, African wall hangings, comfortable low cushions and rugs. But no one in the room was comfortable that morning. The members of the club sprawled in the shadows at distances from one another, as if unwilling to make contact.

"Was it you, Nazzam?"

Tommy Adams, the most dispirited of the group, shook his head. "You, Sulik?"

Alfonso Telford, a long, loose-jointed boy, stood up. "Not me," he said. "I wasn't even in it, chief. I was home all night. First time I heard about this mess was today, when I got here."

"Doesn't matter, Sulik. We're all in it now, whether we want to be or not. Two brothers in the hospital. Two trials waiting for them when they get out." The knuckles cracked again, sharp as gunshots. "Trials in *their* courthouse. Cells in *their* jail. And then this morning some fool decides to throw garbage in *their* pool."

Pint-sized Rudy Merchant spoke for all of them when he said in his high, squeaky voice, "I'm scared. Boyd wasn't there last night, but all he had to do was hear about it. He knows we're all in this club. I figure any minute he'll show up to arrest us. I don't know about the rest of you fools, but I'm leaving."

"Where you going, Hamid?" Lukey asked the youngest Warrior, who was more like a mascot than a member.

"Baltimore," the freckled, rusty-haired Runt replied. "I got relatives there. I ought to be on that bus right now. I just came by this morning to see if anybody had a better plan."

"Lie," Foxy Carter offered.

"Huh?" Rudy asked.

"Say we wasn't in it. We don't know anything about it."

"What about our brothers in the hospital?" Lukey reminded him.

Foxy shrugged. "They got caught. That's the breaks."

"Yeah," Telford agreed. "Let them go for theirselves."

"You all make me *puke!*" Tommy Adams cried. "Some Warriors. Some unity. You got about as much unity as a bunch of tomcats. Less."

"Thank you, Nazzam," Lukey said. "You said it better than I could. Unity is our main principle. Let's have no more talk about leaving town or making up alibis. Our problem, as I see it, is first to find out how we got into this situation; second, to decide how to conduct ourselves after this, and third, to figure out how to help our brothers deal with this trouble after they get out of the hospital."

Tommy said in a barely audible voice, "Lou's *really* my brother."

"We're all your brothers, Nazzam," Lukey said, putting a giant hand on the shaking shoulders. "Whatever happens, remember that."

"I just got to thinking—my brother might die, and for what? We don't deserve to call ourselves Warriors. We were actin' like a bunch of punk kids last night. Playin' games."

"Will any of you, do you think," Lukey asked, "be tempted to act that way again?"

"No!" a chorus responded.

"Then maybe, at least, we've all learned something."

Foxy Carter came forward and faced up to Lukey. "I did it, man. I threw the garbage in the pool this morning. Nobody was with me. I did it by myself."

"Why?"

Confronted with this calm, thoughtful question, Foxy stumbled and stammered. "I—I dunno. I guess . . . uh . . . I guess it seemed like a good idea."

Lukey merely responded with another soft, "Why?"

"Well . . . uh . . . because when I woke up, I was still mad."

"At whom?"

"The whiteys."

"The ones at the swim club?"

"Well—no—not them. The ones who moved our house."

"We're all mad at *them*, Hakim," Lukey told him. "But we have to control and direct our emotions so we can deal with them. Hopefully, even, stop them from moving more houses. What happened last night was a bad case of misdirection. It got us nowhere, and I can't tell you how much it's cost us. The community is afraid to trust us now. We're going to have to show plenty of control and good sense after this, or we'll be left completely out of the main action."

"Aaaah!" Foxy exploded in disgust. "What main action? Them moldy old heads ain't gonna do nothin'."

"You worry me, Hakim," Lukey said in that same mild voice. "But first I want to know exactly what happened last night, and why."

"Crump started it," Tommy Adams said.

"Who on earth," Lukey wanted to know, "is Crump?"

"You mean you don't know spooky old Crump, lives with his old man in a shack down by the creek? I thought everybody knew him," Tommy said.

"I haven't had the pleasure," Lukey replied.

"It ain't no pleasure, man, believe me," Tommy told him. "He like somethin' you wouldn't even want to see crawl out of your garbage can. Folks say he and his old man are the Devil."

Lukey was beginning to remember something. "His father, he took out some time a few years ago, right?"

"Right," Alfonso said. "For shootin' the little Brown girl. Blossom Brown."

"How," Lukey wanted to know, "did Crump get into the picture?"

"Nobody knows," Tommy replied. "He comes and goes like he's made of smoke or something. One minute we were all standin' around talkin' on the baseball lot and the next, Crump is there sayin', 'Let's go swimming.'"

"And because he said it, of course you had to do it," Lukey said sardonically.

Foxy spoke up. "It was my fault, Rashid. If I hadn't been so mad about them movin' our house, I wouldn't have gone for that okey-doke of Crump's. But I did, and I talked the rest of them into it. Except Tonio.

Nobody can talk Tonio into nothin'. He's strong, man, strong! I can't stand him bein' hurt when I was the one who started it. I take the blame, Rashid. Punish me any way you want."

"Do you have anything else to say?" Lukey asked him.

"No. Except that—it ain't over with. I told Crump he could be a member. I even gave him a name—Karim—and told him he could come to our meetings."

"When was this?"

"Last night. And again this morning, before light. It was so hot down there in Froggy Bottom I couldn't sleep, and our house is near his shack now, so I stopped by to see him. He was fishin'. He gave me the idea to put garbage in the pool, since we didn't get a chance to pollute it last night. He's full of nasty ideas, Crump is. But he didn't come with me. He had a carp on his line, he said, or maybe a catfish. So I picked up all the garbage bags I could carry from behind the Blue Moon and dumped 'em in the swim pool myself. I was pitchin' grapefruit rinds and rib bones over that fence till the sun came up."

Some of the fellows laughed at this, till Lukey silenced them with a look. "This Crump certainly has a lot of influence on you, doesn't he?" he observed.

"Yeah, he did," Foxy admitted. "But no more. I got my head together now."

"Well, then, this is your punishment," Lukey decreed. "Crump is your problem. Deal with him."

Foxy looked up in astonishment. "How?"

"I can't tell you how. You must become strong, like brother Tonio. If he tries to influence you, resist him. If he comes to our meeting, find out what he's after, then get rid of him. You invited him, Hakim, so getting rid of him is up to you. Of course, if you need help, we'll all back you up."

"Rashid, that's too heavy," Tommy said.

"Why?"

"Can't nobody deal with Crump. Best thing to do is leave him alone. 'Cause we only human, and he's the Devil. Don't nobody beat the Devil."

"Ain't no such thing as the Devil, Adams," Telford argued. "Crump ain't nothin' but flesh and blood, same's you and me."

"Yeah? Then how come he sneaks in and out of places without anybody seein' how he does it? You see how he got away last night? He turned into a *shadow!*"

"Yeah, well, he's shady enough," Telford cracked, eliciting a few laughs from the others, "but he's still just a human person."

"Last night he turned into a shadow. But he can turn into anything he wants—a snake, a frog, a puff of smoke."

"Haw!" Telford laughed. "Better watch out your superstitions don't run away with your brains, Adams. You can't have both in the same head."

"If you don't believe in the Devil," Tommy retorted, "then you can't believe in God, Telford."

"This is getting serious," Lukey decided. "We need some expert advice. Hakim, go downstairs and ask the Rev to come up here a minute."

The Reverend William Bream was in his little office at the rear of the church trying to work on the next day's sermon but finding it difficult to concentrate. The boys upstairs had him too worried. He knew he ought to do something about their escapade of the night before, but was not sure what that something should be. It was a relief when the Carter boy knocked on his door and asked him to come upstairs.

The Reverend Bream was one of those short, bald, fleshy men who appeared ten feet tall in the pulpit, where he acquired a symbolic power that could convince anyone of anything, but who without his vestments might be mistaken for somebody's humble yard man. On unofficial occasions and informal days like Saturdays he wore tan Hush Puppies, baggy corduroy pants, and a plaid sports shirt. Principles, not appearances, were all that mattered to him.

The brown dome of his head emerged through the trap door of the boys' loft, and his faded plaid shoulders followed. He did not look like a figure of authority who could guide them, except, perhaps, an authority on weeds and hoes. His mild moon face with its prominent eyes wore a perpetually startled expression, as if the world were a continual source of amazement. As, to the Reverend Bream, it often was.

But the moment he spoke, his mediocrity and shabbiness fell away. His rhythmic, sonorous voice had a riveting authority. "Now you boys know I've never interfered in your activities. But last night's carrying on was something I can't defend. Something that isn't up to me

KRISTIN LATTANY

to defend. You boys are going to have to answer for this to the *Lord!*"

The Reverend's voice dropped to a compelling whisper. "I've been studyin' on this all last night," he said, "and prayin' on it all morning. Studyin' to figure out how it could happen. Prayin' to git the right words to speak to you about it. Now you boys know I've always given you plenty freedom. You-all said you wanted this club for constructive purposes, and I gave you this room because I trusted you. But now you've taken your freedom too far. Last night's recreation was definitely out of bounds. And that fits right in with my sermon for tomorrow, on freedom and limitation. Y'know, you can't have one without the other."

He had been rocking on his heels, building up a rhythmic momentum as his voice gained power. He was preaching.

"As Peter said, 'For so is the will of God, that with well doing ye may put to silence the ignorance of foolish men. As free, and not using your liberty for a cloak of maliciousness, but as the servants of God.' Hah! No man is supposed to be so free that he forgets he is a servant of God! Hah! I think last night was not well doing, not at all. And I think this morning you showed maliciousness."

The boys were swaying in rhythm with the Reverend's preaching. Lukey interrupted him before they all became hypnotized. "Reverend, we agree with you. We're all ashamed of last night. I think we've gotten ourselves together now. But we have another problem. There's a guy who wants to join our group. One of us invited him to our meetings. But we wonder about him."

"What sort of character does he have?" the Reverend asked.

"Bad," Lukey replied.

"Well, then, there's your answer," the minister said.

"It's not that simple, sir."

"Did this young man have anything to do with last night's foolishness?"

"Everything to do with it, sir. He started it."

"Luke Hawkins, you surprise me," Reverend Bream said. "I thought you were in charge of this group. How could you let someone else lead them?"

For the first time, their chief seemed ashamed. "Actually, I'm not around enough to lead them. Not anymore, not since I started college.

I've been thinking I should step down and let Tonio take over, if he—"

"Yes, yes, I understand. If he recovers."

"Besides, last night I was helping the fire department, so I wasn't around."

"And this person took over in your absence. Too bad, Hawkins, but I don't see what your problem is. Refuse to let him join. Bar the way with flaming swords."

"It's more complicated than that, sir," Lukey said. "Fact is, it's sort of a theological question. Some of the fellas here think he's not just a man. They think he's the Devil. So we want to know, how can you tell a person from a devil? And if he is a devil, how can we get rid of him?"

The Reverend Bream chewed on one of his ragged nails for a minute, then said, "You invited him, you say? Here?"

"Yes, but he didn't come."

"Then invite him again."

"Sir?" Lukey questioned in surprise. "I thought you said to keep him out."

"This is the house of *Gawd!*" the Reverend roared startling them all. "If this creature is a devil, he won't enter it. If he is merely a man, he will, and you can deal with him as you would any other mortal being."

"I knew you'd know what to do, Rev," Lukey said admiringly. "Hakim, get going. This is your job."

As Foxy rose to his feet, the preacher complained, "I do not understand why you have abandoned your Christian names. That may be why you were open to temptation last night. As for me, I will call you what I christened you. Mark Forrest Carter, come here. I have something for you to take with you."

"Rashid, let me go," Tommy Adams said unexpectedly. "I believe and he doesn't!"

"In what?" Reverend Bream asked softly. "In God, or the Devil?"

"In both," Tommy answered. "And I believe this guy is a devil, 'cause my mama said so."

The minister reached inside his shirt to raise a heavy silver chain from his neck and place it around Tommy's. From it depended his large silver ecclesiastical cross. "Then wear this, Thomas. You'll be all right. Return it to me when you come back."

"Thank you," Tommy said, tucking it inside his shirt. "Will you pray for my brother?"

"I have. All night." The redness of the minister's eyes attested to his lack of sleep. He bowed his head. "Let us pray now. Almighty God, we beseech Thee to preserve the life of Carl Lucinda Adams, in all his robust youth and health. And to restore Antonio Farmer to the full strength of his young manhood. But if it be Thy will to take them, we pray for the strength to accept it, and to let it make our faith even stronger. Amen."

"Thank you," Tommy said again, and started down the ladder. Reverend Bream turned to follow him.

"One more thing, Rev," Rudy cried out. "Is it true you can't be arrested in church?"

"The church is still a sanctuary, yes," the minister answered. "Only God's law applies here. However, when Chief Boyd called and woke me up with the news at three this morning, he mentioned that he might want to drop in on your meeting, and I agreed."

Rudy almost knocked Reverend Bream down in his rush for the ladder.

The Reverend caught him by the shoulders. "What's your hurry, Rudolph? You haven't done anything to be ashamed of, have you?"

Rudy shook his copper-wool head.

"Then stick around a while. Trust me."

Rudy nodded sullenly and the benevolent brown sphere of the Reverend's head disappeared below the floor of the loft.

Moments later, Chief Benson Boyd started coming up the ladder, coming up, coming up, as if there were no end to him. But finally his entire blue-clad length was in the loft. "Listen," he said tersely. "That's all I want you to do, keep quiet and listen. I expected everyone to be here. Where's Tom Adams?"

"He went on an errand."

"Maybe it's just as well. Makes what I have to say easier. His brother died at ten forty-five this morning. He never regained consciousness."

The impact of this announcement was so powerful that the chief did not have to repeat his demand for respectful silence. Looking around at the stricken young faces, he deliberately made his speech as impersonal as if he were a witness in court. "The family's already been notified," he said. "All except Tom. Maybe you'll have to be the ones to tell him. Now, I have only one thing to say to you. And that is, I don't want to hear anything at all about last night. As far as I know, those two were the only ones in the pool. I don't want any rumors going around to contradict me. Do you understand?"

"Yes, sir," Lukey said.

"Lou jumped in, hollered for help, and Antonio tried to save him. Is that clear?"

"Yes, sir," Lukey repeated.

"Tonio will be all right, by the way. And that will be his defense. He was not trespassing; only trying to save a life. No one else was involved. No one. Do you understand me?"

The chief swept the room with his pale eyes. "I don't want anyone to get the urge to confess just to make himself feel better. Bad feelings are something we all have to learn to live with sooner or later. It might as well be sooner with you kids. So not a word about what really went on last night.

"And one more thing. I don't want any repetitions. Reverend Bream has promised me that he will keep a very close watch on you all from now on. And, believe me, so will I. I'll do even more, if necessary."

"It won't be necessary, Chief," Lukey promised. "Would you do us a favor?"

"Maybe." said the chief in a tone that implied he was not inclined to grant them any favors.

"Tell Tonio he's the new president. By unanimous vote."

"Tell him yourselves," Chief Boyd said. "He's allowed to have visitors." His mission completed, he went down the ladder and closed the trap door behind him. He had been gone a full fifteen minutes before the Warriors realized that his stern manner had masked kindness.

He had let them completely off the hook. They were free. But as their numbed brains returned to life and they began to think about Lou Adams, they realized that they would have preferred almost any kind of punishment.

16

The list of conspirators was growing, beginning, in fact, to resemble an army. Fess, the main recruiter, chuckled and did a little skipping dance step in celebration of his success, then counted off the recruits on his fingertips. There was himself, of course. Bella Lakes. Vinnie Coddums. Mame Porritt. Ikie Lakes, though he was not convinced of that one's reliability. Doc Thompson, naturally, and at least three of the six other members of the Borough Council, whom the doctor had instructed him to approach first. Four out of seven added up to a clear majority. He felt like cheering.

Not that it had been easy. Fess had foreseen this. It had been difficult for Doc Thompson to persuade him to undertake the recruiting project. Doc had finally succeeded by pointing out that only Fess knew how to concoct the sort of sophisticated questionnaire that would put the respondents off-guard and elicit their true feelings, and that he alone had the perfect excuse—his dissertation—for interviewing them. Many times today, Fess had regretted accepting the assignment. It was hot, dusty, irritating work, and he was far from finished.

His first interview had been with Forrest "Dunce Cap" Carter, Sr., now serving his second term on the council. Cap could not be found at home, of course. Where his home had been was now a large, gaping hole. Home is where the hole is? Fess wondered absurdly, hoping he was not about to decerebrate into silliness, an occasional, involuntary failing that could not be stopped until his derailed brain ran its course of free associations, puns, and other nonsense. But it was true that where the Carter home had been a hole now was. Overnight the brave patriotic decorations had been buried and crushed by bulldozers, with only a red shell here, a blue can there, to attest that loyal Americans and true had once lived here. Fess doubted very much that the Carters would use a patriotic motif to decorate the new site of their home. If they did, he would have to cross them off his list as hopeless.

Not that Cap Carter, working at his service station, had been easy to convince. Approached with the questionnaire, which purported to have both official and academic reasons for ascertaining how respondents felt about the new highway and its possible effect on the town's economy, Cap had been more than optimistic.

"Wonderful prospects," Cap had said, pausing in his job of kicking the tire off a jacked-up Buick. "It's progress, and progress can't help but improve things. You get a lot of people passing through on a road like that, some of them are bound to stop. And when they stop, they'll spend. For meals, souvenirs, things like that."

"And gas?"

"Well, of course," Dunce Cap said complacently, kicking the tire to the ground with a satisfying *thunk*. "What else? Americans are people on the move, and the country travels on gas. Confidentially, I've already got a man drawing up plans for a bigger station. I'm thinking of putting in nine more tanks and six bays."

"I read somewhere recently," Fess said, "about a car that can fly. But it's still only on the drawing boards."

The grizzled mustache that bisected Dunce Cap's face quivered. "What? A car that can fly? Make sense, man."

"You push a button," Fess said serenely, "and these rotors on the roof start turning. Wonderful. Just like a helicopter. In fact, I think that's what they call it, the Auto-Copter."

Dunce Cap straightened up, lean, mean, and wiry, wearing an angry expression on the fox face his son had inherited, its sharp features crowded into the center of a long dark triangle. "What the hell are you saying, Roaney?"

"I'm saying," Fess said, "that a car like that Auto-Copter thing is the only kind that'll come off the highway to buy gas in Lakestown. A car that can fly. Because I-27 is going to be way down there." Fess pointed in the presumed direction of hell, which he expected the highway to resemble—a hot, stinking source of smoke and fumes. "Depressed at least two hundred feet below Lakestown. Edgehill Road will pass over it, but nothing else will be left for fifty feet on either side."

Cap removed his trademark, the greasy cap that always clung precariously to his steepled skull, threw it to the ground, kicked it, stomped on it, and swore eloquently to do the same thing to the mother-raping sons of beasts who had lied to him.

Fess added casually, "Oh, and the nearest access ramps will be ten miles from here, somewhere over in Dorset Township. You can check it if you want, but I think you'll find the best service station locations have already been taken."

"Of course. By white men." Dunce Cap swore some more, then paused for thought and glared at Fess narrowly. "But why the hell should I believe you, Roaney?"

Fess shrugged. "You don't have to. Just come to the council meeting tonight. Copies of the highway plans will be passed out."

"I'll be there," the frustrated businessman said. "The trouble is, I believe you already. Because that's the way it always goes. The way the white man always does things. And what can a black man do but take it?"

"Keep practicing on that cap," Fess suggested. "We'll think of something."

Cap Carter clearly was a convert. But Fess had been forced to put question marks beside the names of the next two councilmen he visited.

The Reverend Bream became obstinately and obtusely theological when an appeal was made to his sense of town pride, quoting scripture liberally and refusing to deal with worldly issues.

"The Christian doctrine is clear," he informed Fess. "Render unto Caesar what is Caesar's."

"Yes," Fess protested, "but Lakestown's land doesn't belong to Caesar. It belongs to us."

The minister slammed his large Bible shut and glared at Fess as angrily as he could with those large, mild, watery eyes. "All worldly projects and the profits from them belong to Caesar," he declared. "We are instructed to render them unto him. We are to take care only for the preservation of our immortal souls, which belong to God."

Fess felt himself becoming angry. "Well, then, you should want your flock to stand up and fight this outrage. If they lie down and take it, they'll have no souls worth rendering unto anybody."

"What do you know about it?" Reverend Bream asked scornfully. "A soul is never worthless in the eyes of God."

"Maybe not, but . . ."

The Reverend held up a hand for silence, then used it to rub his reddened eyes. It was evident that he needed rest. "I have a funeral sermon to write this afternoon as well as my regular sermon. I have just come from calling on the bereaved family. I tried, but I could not make their son's death make sense to them. I failed because it does not make sense to *me*. This kind of terrible waste is what comes of meddling in Caesar's business. I am convinced there will be more tragedies if the meddling continues. Now, if you will excuse me, I must get back to my sermon."

Fess felt he could have convinced the Reverend if given more time, but after such an abrupt dismissal he had no choice but to leave.

Josh Hawkins was the other council member beside whose name Fess was forced to place a large question mark. Today the laconic store-keeper was more confusingly noncommittal than ever. Asked whether he felt the highway would help the town, he said, "Might be a good thing, and then it might not. Some say it'll bring money in, and some say it won't."

On the one hand, Fess thought, there's the other hand. "You planning to expand your business when the road comes through?" he asked Josh.

"Been thinking about it. Might put in a little sideline or two, a couple of restaurant tables, maybe some souvenir knickknacks. But I ain't in no hurry. I always say, no sense in bein' greedy."

"What would you say," Fess inquired, "if I told you there was no way the highway could bring more business to you or anyone else in town?"

"Heeee," Josh cackled. "I'd say it didn't bother me a-tall. Mae and me, we're doin' all right here as it is. We make a dollar here, a dollar there, enough to keep goin'."

I'll bet you do, Fess thought. Just Mae, and me, and ITT makes three.

"Long as I've got enough to get by, I don't go chasing all over for a dollar. And I don't let little bitty things upset me, no sir. T'ain't worth it."

"What about big things? Do you ever let big things make you mad?"

Josh stood up and cracked his knuckles: a fearsome sound resembling gunfire. "Well, now, Professor, you wouldn't want to see that happen."

"Maybe I would," Fess said bravely, though his eyes barely came up to the giant's navel.

"Last time that happened, I woke up on the chain gang down in Georgia. Heeee," Josh said. "Spent most a year there. Would've been more, 'cause I had a life sentence, but I got away. Found me a way to snap them little bitty leg irons, and lit out for the North fast as I could go." He lifted one of his trouser legs to show the ugly scars.

Fess was awed. "What did they sentence you to the chain gang for?"

"Oh," Josh said with a laugh, "they claimed I'd killed three men in a fight over some gamblin' money."

"Did you?"

"I don't remember," Josh said and laughed again. "I don't know what they put in that stump-hole likker they make down there, but it makes you forget everything. Even makes you forget your mama's name. Heee. So I don't remember whether I killed them or not. I think maybe I tapped 'em a little. But how could a little bitty tap on the head kill somebody?"

Fess thought he knew how. "You came here to be free, isn't that right, Josh?"

"Right. Got shet of them chains, and didn't slow down or stop movin' till I crossed the Mason and Dixon."

"Well, that's why everybody else came here, for freedom. Now suppose I was to tell you the white man was getting ready to put those chains on you again?"

"That wouldn't be nice," Josh said gravely. "No, that wouldn't be nice at all."

"Well, not chains exactly. But he might be taking away your freedom, just the same. Tricking it away, this time. Suppose you believed that. What would happen?"

"Wouldn't be nice," Josh repeated. His eyes had a narrowed, far-off look, like a sailor's on lookout, squinting at the horizon. "If I believed a thing like that, I'd get mad. Then I'd have to tap somebody. Maybe a whole lot of somebodies." He flexed his foot-long hands and studied them reflectively, as if they had a life of their own.

Fess shuddered. "Are you mad now?"

Josh grinned "Shoot, no. What I got to be mad about? I'm studyin' nobody's business but mine."

"So," Fess concluded, "you haven't made up your mind yet."

"About that road? Shoot, no. It ain't botherin' me none yet, so why should I worry about it? Guess I'll just wait and see how it turns out.

And now, if you'll excuse me, I got to wait on Miz Lula Farmer. Mornin', Miz Lula. How you feelin'?"

The gentle-voiced giant eased from behind the counter to help Nunc Farmer's wife choose some pinto beans, and Fess, puzzled and defeated, made his exit.

Clutching his clipboard a little more tightly, he headed toward Grimes Road, the elevated part of town, elevated both socially and geographically, since the precincts of Grimes Road consisted of a small hill topped by several large houses that used Edgehill instead of Lakestown as their mailing address.

The only authentic colonial house in Lakestown belonged to Morris Merchant, the senior member of the Council. It was square as a box, sheathed in weathered drab gray shingles and trimmed with correctly murky gray blue shutters.

Grinning over his shoulder like a jack-o-lantern, Merchant's aunt Essie Mae looked, with her moronic agelessness, far younger than her nephew. She had not a wrinkle on her face nor a tooth in her head nor a stitch of clothing on her gaunt frame. Nor had she a fan or a feather even, to cover her ancient nudity. *Ou est la plume de ma tante?* Fess wondered idiotically. At a time when he needed all his diplomacy, Fess knew his mind had slipped its rails and was coining nonsense faster than a meat grinder spat out hamburger. He was powerless to stop it until it exhausted itself.

The oldest member of Lakestown's Borough Council had the instinctive aplomb of the upper classes. "My aunt," he said with simple dignity, "is suffering from a fever."

"Oh, I understand. I couldn't be more understanding," Fess babbled, wishing he could shut up. "She should starve it, shouldn't she? Or should she feed it? I never can remember."

"What she needs, I think," Mr. Merchant said, "is a cool bath. Tepid, rather. And a pitcher of lemonade." He patted Essie's shoulder. "Go upstairs now, Esther. I think Rudolph has run your bath for you."

As she obediently turned her withered buttocks, old Mr. Merchant bent with surprising agility, picked up a small, rich Oriental rug, and wrapped it around her shoulders. "Wear this, dear. So you won't catch a chill."

"Lovely," Fess said, unable to stop being trivial. "The rug, I mean. Is it Persian?"

"Chinese," Mr. Merchant said. "It's been in my family for three generations. Are you interested in carpets? I have a few good specimens I might show you. But you didn't come here to discuss carpets, did you?"

"No, sir," Fess said.

"Well, then, what can I do for you, Mr., er?"

"A great favor, sir. It won't cost you a cent. Only about fifteen minutes of your time."

That was a mistake, Fess realized as soon as he said it. Disavowal of the profit motive was the most time-worn ploy of door-to-door salesmen, and it had only convinced Mr. Merchant that he belonged to that pestiferous tribe.

The old man ticked off the things he did not need on his fingers. "We are, as you can see, fairly comfortable here. Our house is in excellent repair. Our kitchen is well stocked with pots, pans, and cleaning implements. My aunt has all the costume jewelry she requires, my grandson has an excellent set of encyclopedias, and I already subscribe to more magazines than I can read. I have been of the Anglican faith all my life, and am too old to be converted to another. I am also—" this with a slight smile of long but authentic teeth, "—too old to be beautified by Avon Products. Have I covered everything?"

Fess found his natural tongue at last. "Please, Mr. Merchant. I am honestly not selling anything. My name is Ronald Roaney. I am a candidate for a Ph.D. at Syracuse University, and I was hoping to interview you as part of my doctoral research."

The old man gave him a handshake and a full, genuine smile. "Why didn't you say so in the first place, Mr. Roaney? Delighted to meet you. And, if I can help you in your scholarly research, even more delighted. I was just about to have my lunch. A poor meal—my doctor has denied me almost everything that tastes good—but won't you join me?"

Disclaiming hunger, Fess followed him to a darkly gleaming oval table, where Lakestown's senior councilman sat down solemnly to a cup of tea, a hard-boiled egg, two tomato slices, and one lettuce leaf on a large, delicate china plate. A maid—a maid!—brought an extra cup for Fess and filled it. For a moment he regretted not having pursued his academic ambitions to the point of affording such an elegant life-style. But only for a moment; he knew he really preferred the redolent warmth of the B.M.

"Diets," Mr. Merchant said with disgust, shook his head, and began his austere feast.

"I sympathize, sir. Or rather I empathize. I am on a diet, too. Several, in fact. Bland for my ulcer, low-cholesterol for my blood pressure, low-sugar for my diabetes, and another that escapes me for the moment."

Morris Merchant *tsk*'d. "A young fella like you? What a shame." He wiped his mouth with his linen napkin. "Oh. Please pardon my forgetfulness. Would you prefer something stronger than tea? I can offer you some sherry."

Fess, delighted both at being called a young fella and at being in a house that served sherry, really wanted to see the maid come in again, bearing, probably, a lead-crystal decanter and two thimble-sized, gold-rimmed glasses, but he declined. "Not this early in the day, thanks. I think I'd better get on with my survey, if you don't mind."

"Go ahead, sir," Mr. Merchant said, lighting up a fat cigar while the maid cleared.

"Well, sir, since you're one of the most distinguished citizens of this community, I'm seeking your opinions."

"Don't give me that BS," Mr. Merchant said, surprisingly. "I guess I should have mentioned that I'm also too old to be susceptible to flattery. Just what constitutes my distinction, young man? Other than wisely investing my mother's money, which she inherited along with her good taste from the family she kept house for, how have I distinguished myself?" He spilled ashes on his lap and brushed them away angrily.

"Other people might disagree with you, Mr. Merchant."

"I don't give a fart for other people's opinions," the old man said. "At my age I don't have to."

"Well," Fess said in an attempt at mollification, "you have served the longest term on Borough Council of anyone in Lakestown's history."

"That's true. Getting pretty sick of it, too. Those meetings go on too long. Too much talking and beating around the bush. They keep me out past my bedtime. One more year to serve, then I'm getting off. Quitting that part-time dispatching job, too. So you know something of Lakestown's history, do you? What is your subject? Something to do with black history?"

"Something like that," Fess said evasively.

"I don't hold with this idea of teaching black history, myself," the old man said. "I think history should simply be *human* history. Teach the true history of this country and give the black man his rightful place in it. *That's* what needs to be done."

"I agree with you. But it'll never happen."

"You have a point there," Mr. Merchant agreed. "Too many influential whites would be embarrassed. Trace any important white family in this country back far enough, you'd find slaveholders, if not slave traders. Not to mention an admixture of Negro blood. Ha!"

Fess went directly to Question Nine on his sheet. "Would you say," he asked, "that you are in favor of historic preservation? Or do you prefer the modern trend toward change and progress?"

"Words, words," the old man said, waving them angrily away along with a cloud of smoke. "Mere generalities. How can you expect an intelligent person to answer a question like that? Preservation of historic *what*, versus progress in what form?"

Fess was liking old Mr. Merchant more and more. He decided to skip to the very end of his questionnaire. "Would you agree that Lakestown is a historic community worth preserving?"

"Yes, of course. But not because of its history. Because it's a damned fine place to live. Take a boy like my grandson, Rudolph. He's fourteen and, I don't mind telling you, full of the devil. If we lived anywhere else, he'd have been in fourteen different kinds of trouble by now. Here, the minute he gets out of bounds, someone notices and the phone rings. So he stays within bounds, more or less. A small town like this, all black, is like one large family. That's a great help to an elderly man raising an orphaned boy. But what are we preserving Lakestown *from*, Mr. Roaney? That's the question."

"Progress," Fess said, "in the form of an interstate highway. Which, I might add, will come right past your front door."

"You should have omitted that last statement, young man. It would prevent me from giving an unbiased opinion. Except that I know it is not accurate. So here it is."

The old man touched his fingertips together. "My opinion. There are too many goddamned cars and highways in this country already. I sold my last automobile in 1963. Now I walk everywhere. Better for my constitution and for the other drivers, since my vision has deteriorated considerably. Hindsight is easier than foresight, of course. If we could have foreseen, back in 1925, that highways would chew up as much of this country as they have, we would have outlawed them. Or at least restricted them severely. As for running one through this little town—it's *execrable.*"

Fess thrilled at the rich pronunciation of that old-fashioned word.

"But talk of historic preservation," Mr. Merchant went on, "is a luxury for upper-class whites in towns like Edgehill. They have eight square miles of historic real estate. We have four. Those with more have always had the power to take from those with less. 'From he that hath not,'" he quoted, "'even that which he hath shall be taken away.'"

"Not my favorite selection from Scripture," Fess said wryly.

"But true, just the same. You want to know how I feel about the road coming through here? Well, the answer is—it makes me *furious!* If I were a younger man, I'd commit sabotage. I'd put sugar in their infernal engines. I'd do worse things. But I'm not a young man."

"Thank you, Mr. Merchant," Fess said, putting his pen away. "Thank you very much."

"That's all?"

"Yes. Except for one thing. That, er, prejudicial statement I made was accurate. Come to the council meeting tonight and find out for yourself."

Mr. Merchant closed his eyes and sighed. "I'm afraid," he said, "that you have angered me enough to raise my blood pressure, young man. Yes, I definitely hear a ringing in my ears. I will have to take a pill and lie down for the rest of the afternoon. Because I do intend to be at that meeting. And I hope that when I get there I'll find out you've been lying to me."

17

Fess practically bounced next door to the rambling old Grimes place, thinking he might get around to writing that dissertation after all. He had just discovered a new truism. Everyone knew the old one, scratch a white liberal and you'll find a die-hard bigot. However, scratch a black conservative and you'll find an angry radical was news.

Scratching Greta Grimes was not going to be so easy or safe, though. She had her own claws, usually sheathed in white gloves. Today, however, she was in full-dress rehearsal for her favorite role, the southern belle. She wore a girlish white eyelet dress, a lacy wide-brimmed hat that filtered the sun onto her seamed face with misty kindness, and, flowing to her shoulders, the kind of long auburn curls that could only be called tresses. The effect clearly intended to he picturesque; succeeded at a distance. Only a close inspection revealed that the tresses were synthetic and that a dirty bra strap poked from beneath the lacy bodice. There was, Fess discovered, a reason why the town cynics usually dropped the final *s* from her name.

That Greta was cutting roses from the bushes near the house was one picturesque touch too many. She looked up from her task and tossed her curls in simulated confusion.

"Oh, my goodness, Mr. Roaney, you surprised me. That's not *fair!* I wasn't expecting visitors this early."

With an inward groan Fess realized he was expected to play the gentleman caller, a role the Grimes girls had a way of forcing on all eligible men who came into their vicinity. He struggled for a gallant remark. "I was just wishing I had a camera with me. You make a beautiful picture."

"Why, thank you, kind sir," Greta said with a curtseylike bob. "Flattery will get you everything. Just let me finish this bouquet, and I'll make you some iced tea."

Having received the obligatory tribute to her vanity, Greta went on to her second favorite pastime, gossip. "Have you heard about the poor Adams boy? What a shame. And so *unnecessary.* I don't see why these young people have to behave so recklessly. After all, it's not as if the place were prejudiced. Anyone can swim there. I have many lovely white friends who are members, and I've been a guest there, oh, dozens of times."

Snip, snip, snip went the shears, lopping off the youngest roses.

"Lovely place you have here." Fess said, squinting across their large lawn. "A perfect setting for you and your sister. It must make you very sad to know you will lose it."

Greta dropped her girlish performance along with her garden shears. "What on earth are you talking about? We have always kept up our taxes."

"Oh, not the house, of course. And I imagine the highway authority will pay you a good sum for the land. But money isn't every-thing. It can't replace all this—" he waved his hand toward the lawn "—tradition."

"I think," Greta said abruptly, "that we had better have something stronger than iced tea. Come on the porch, Mr Roaney, while I get my sister."

Greta yanked off her hat, skewing her wig slightly, and marched up the steps with the brisk tread of a WAC sergeant. "Jane!" he heard her calling inside. "Jane! Where the hell did you put the gin?"

Greta soon reappeared with a tray and a hard expression that did not match her romantic costume. Jane, following her with an ice bucket, looked almost pleasant in contrast, in a plain seersucker housecoat and no makeup.

"Why, Mr. Roaney," Jane said, beginning the charade all over again, "what a pleasant surprise."

Greta finished what was probably a straight slug of gin before pouring herself a ladylike mixed drink. "You won't think so," she said, "after he repeats what he has just said to me. Go ahead, Professor. You were saying," Greta prodded him, "something about money coming to us from the highway authority."

"Well, of course, I wouldn't have mentioned it if I hadn't thought you ladies already knew."

"You mean a road is coming through here?" Jane said with a gasp. "How close?"

"I always believe in thinking positively and counting our blessings," Fess said piously. "Let's thank the good Lord you'll be able to keep this beautiful porch. Of course, I doubt if it'll be as pleasant sitting out here next summer, with all that traffic roaring by."

"Where did you get your information, Mr. Roaney?" Greta asked.

"I'm not at liberty to divulge that. But it'll be confirmed for you tonight at the council meeting. You'll be there, of course."

This was hardly a safe assumption. What with her crowded social calendar, Greta's absenteeism from the council was notorious.

"Oh," Jane fluttered, "we're invited to the Hendersons for dinner tonight, Greta."

"Screw the Hendersons and their dinner. She's a rotten cook anyway. Excuse me, Mr. Roaney, but if I have to eat another of her stuffed chicken breasts I'll choke to death. I think she stuffs them with poison gas. Yes, I'll be there. *Both* of us will be there. And when I find out who's responsible for this, I'll invite you to the viewing. Unless, of course, you've made it all up for some ridiculous reason. In that case, we'll have to order a casket for you." She measured him with a practiced eye. "As a matter of fact, I think we have one in stock that will do."

It was clearly time to leave. He finished his weak gin and tonic and rose. "Thank you for the hospitality, ladies. It was charming. But I must be off now."

Mainly to soothe his shattered nerves, Fess headed next for Lonnie Jenkins's snug little Cape Cod bungalow. Lonnie was not a councilman, though his house was in the path of destruction, and Fess ambitiously planned to alert every threatened homeowner after he had seen all the council members. But his main purpose in going to Lonnie's was to relax in the easygoing atmosphere. He could always count on a warm welcome there.

Today, though, the Jenkins's house was as grimly quiet as if they had had a death in the family. Jerutha met him at the kitchen door with whispered instructions.

"I sure am glad to see you, Professor. Please come in and talk to Alonzo. He's in the front room, just settin' by himself. He used to have all his friends in to talk and joke around on his days off, but now all he does is stay by himself. The TV's on, but he don't even watch it. He don't go out to see nobody, and don't nobody come to see him. Yesterday I gave a cookout to try and bring some people by, but nobody came."

Fess regretted his decision the day before to resist the tantalizing aroma of Jerutha's barbecue. It only proved once again that when a man felt he was being most righteous he was most likely to be doing wrong. "Why didn't they come?"

"Because he's helping to dig that road, that's why!" Jerutha cried then shushed herself with a finger to her lips. "People see him in there shoveling dirt and it's like he's throwing it in their faces. I tell him, 'It's not that bad, Lonzo, most people understand, they know it's just your job.' But he always knows when I'm lying, and when I tell him stories like that he won't even talk to *me*. Please go in and see him, Professor. You know my Lonzo is a sociable man. It ain't natural for him to be stayin' by himself all the time."

The little house, usually so vibrant with the thumps and screeches of playing children, had an uneasy silence like a funeral chapel. Fess found himself proceeding on tiptoe to the small, dark parlor where the television flickered like a blue votive candle, with a single penitent slumped in front of it.

"Hey, Lonnie, it's Fess," he called. "Who's winnin'?"

The voice that answered him had a hollow, tired resonance. "Cleveland, I think. No, Minneapolis. Hell, I don't even know who's playin'. I ain't been payin' attention. Draw up a chair, Professor. Have a sitdown."

"Lonnie," Fess said, "a man's got to earn a living."

"Why?" the man in the shadows said, and waved away the answer. "Oh, I know, I know. I got five kids. I got to keep grits on the table. But I swear, if I didn't have a family, I'd hop a freight and leave town. Been thinkin' about taking out some more insurance and makin' sure they collect it."

"Don't think that way, Lonnie."

"What other way is there to think? Yesterday we dug up some of the best farmland around here, the old Henry Lakes place; you know, old George's brother. Nobody works it anymore, but it's still good land. Was hopin' to buy a piece of it myself and work it when I retired. Then here comes this freaky little Jew to talk to the boss. He's in the cement business. Seems like he wants to cover the whole earth with cement. I swear he's the Devil. He hates trees and anything else that grows, and he preaches about cement like it's his Jesus. Cement it all over, he says. All of it. Middle of next week, we start pouring."

Fess cast about for some kind of strategy and reached out and gave Lonnie what he hoped was a Masonic handshake, adding a second grip, reversed, for black power.

Lonnie backed off uneasily. "What kind of handshake is that, Professor? You ain't funny, is you?"

"Lord, no," Fess said. "I love women. Even though they don't usually love me back."

"I didn't think you was funny. I never heard nothing like that about you, but for a minute there I didn't know what to think. First I thought you was a lodge brother, but I ain't ever seen you at meetings, and then you put in that extra little flip, and it confused me."

"It's a new brotherhood, Lonnie."

"Is that so? How come I ain't heard about it?"

"We're just getting it together. Me and a few other folks in town. I wanted you to know about it, because I don't want you to give up hope. And whatever you do, don't give up your job. Not just because your family needs you. *We* need you. We need a man on the inside."

"You mean a bunch of peoples is getting together to . . . Oh, Professor, please say it's true."

"I'm not saying," Fess said enigmatically, "but I'm not playing either."

Roused from his apathy, Lonnie began to talk feverishly. "I know the work schedule. I know how to drive all their equipments. They won't let me, on account of the union rules, but I know how. I know when all the shipments come in and where. I know where all the blasting equipment is, too, the dynamite and the rest of it. And I know how to get hold of keys to all the locks. Shoot, ain't nothin' old Alonzo can't do if he gets the chance. And if I did get the chance, all this shame and humiliation would be worth it."

"You'll get your chance. Believe me."

"Whoeee!" Lonnie cried in joy, leaping from his chair like Lazarus raised. "Man, am I glad you stopped by to see me. Jerutha! Jerutha! Fix the professor a little something!"

The couple's gratitude was so effusive that Fess had to consume three beers and four helpings of barbecue, plus mountains of potato salad and greens, before he could leave. When he left, he could barely walk. But it had been delicious. More important, the children had sensed the lifting of their father's depression and come out of their hiding, and the little house was normally noisy again.

Retracing his steps back up Edgehill Road, Fess paused indecisively at Carl "Bunky" Adams's corner lot. Adams was a councilman and his underground house lay in the monster's path, but Fess hesitated to burden him with more bad news today. He decided simply to pay a condolence call. If, that was, he could figure out a way to get inside.

Since he had last inspected it, the entire lot seemed to have been covered over with vegetation. He circled it several times, from the kale and collards to the snapdragons and daisies and back again, but saw nothing that resembled an entrance.

Until, at his feet, a patch of marigolds moved. As he watched, fascinated, a thirty-inch square of orange pom-poms began to rise. The youngest Adams child, six-year-old Louise, came up beneath it and steadied the slanted marigold patch with a stick. Her ten-year-old sister Marian followed with a basket of laundry.

"Why don't you come in, Mr. Roaney?" Marian invited. "Everybody's downstairs. I'll show you."

She led him beneath the blossoming trapdoor, down some ladderlike stairs, into a large, cool, cavelike room. As his eyes grew accustomed to the dimness he saw that it contained a great deal of junk furniture and a great many Adamses. But it was blessedly cool, and so large it did not seem crowded.

"Just came to offer my sympathy," Fess said to the progenitor of all these subterraneans, a short, bald, habitually gloomy man. To Bunky Adams's pretty, normally cheerful wife he added, "Don't get up, Doretha. I'm only staying a minute."

Bunky Adams shook Fess's hand and nodded his thanks, there being nothing more he could say except, "It's a hard thing to get used to. Hardest on my wife, of course."

"Nonsense, Carl," Doretha said valiantly, as if she needed even now to keep up her spirits to balance her husband's chronic gloom. "I'm fine. Have a seat, Professor. Will you have some of our homemade dandelion wine?"

"Of course," Fess said, understanding how important it was to offer and accept hospitality at times of bereavement: it was a ritual like Holy Communion, a reconciliation to life. To her husband he said, "I think an underground house like this is a wonderful idea. So cool and restful. If it were mine, I'd let it stay this way."

"Hah!" Bunky's laugh was bitter. "I keep it this way only out of necessity, believe me. I sodded over the roof to save on fuel this winter. I always thought . . ."

He was interrupted by a loud clattering down the ladder stairs, the rude arrival of his eldest, seventeen-year-old Tommy.

Ignoring him, his father repeated, "I always thought my two oldest boys would help me raise the first story. But now . . ." His voice broke.

"I'll help you, Dad," Tommy promised. He seemed oddly brash and exuberant for this particular day. "I'll say one good thing about our house. They can't pick it up and move it to make room for the highway. Maybe they'll have to build us a new one."

"You shut up," his father said roughly. "The less you say around here, the better. You should've been looking after your brother last night. Where've you been all day, anyway?"

"The boy's got a point, though," Fess said. "Actually, I had another reason for coming to see you, Bunk. I didn't want to disturb you with it today, but there's a good chance you'll be affected by the highway. In spite of your bereavement, I'm hoping to see you at the council meeting tonight."

"Council tonight? I hadn't given it a thought," Bunky said. "At a time like this, what should I care what they do over there?"

"Because the highway will be coming right through here."

"Let it come. I don't care," Bunky said. His depression had apparently sunk to a new low.

"Carl, no!" his wife cried. "We've struggled too long and too hard to get this place. And you know they won't give us anything for it, half-finished like it is."

"She's right, Carl," Fess said. "You should be there. Your family needs you there. The rest of us need you, too. Will you come?"

There was a pause. "Yes," Bunky finally agreed. "Why not? I'm all right." He was not usually an excitable man, but today the muscles of his jaws showed strong emotions working under the surface as he looked at his oldest son. "I'd be fine if I could just get that . . . that thing over there out of my sight."

"He's your son, Carl," Doretha reminded him.

"Don't you think I know that?" he answered her roughly. "That's what's driving me crazy. If he were a stranger, I could stand this. I could beat him up or kill him and feel better about the whole thing. But he's me all over again. Look at him standing there. He looks just like me. I can't stand the sight of him."

To save both of them more anguish, Tommy retreated into the shadows.

"Excuse me," Fess said, "but I think you're being too hard on the boy."

Bunky Adams stood up, only an inch taller than Fess but seeming to tower in his rage. "And *I* think you're way out of line, Roaney. I think you'd better mind your own business. I'm in a mood to punch somebody out this morning, and if you don't get out of my way, you'll be it."

Fess began to scramble for the ladder to freedom.

"I'll come to your damn-fool meeting," Bunky called after him. "Just don't come to my house anymore. And don't try to tell me how to raise my family."

18

MEETING OF

LAKESTOWN BOROUGH COUNCIL

Saturday, July 10, 1965

PRESIDING:	Abraham Lakes, Mayor
RECORDING:	Mae Hawkins, Borough Secretary
PRESENT:	Carl Adams, Rev. William Bream, Forrest Carter, Miss Greta Grimes, Joshua Hawkins, Morris Merchant, Walter Thompson, M.D., Members of Council Floyd Crudup, Esq., Borough Solicitor Lester Porritt, Borough Treasurer
ABSENT:	None

That last item was noteworthy in itself. Rarely in the history of Lakestown had all the members of the council been present at any one meeting, nor within Fess's memory had Borough Hall's small council chamber ever been so packed. Every seat was filled, standees packed the walls and aisles, and in the hall a decorous but determined crowd tried to get in.

Fess glowed. His feet hurt from a day of tramping Lakestown's mostly unpaved roads, but the ache was almost pleasant. It had been worth it. After all those years of steadfastly refusing to get involved in local politics, especially the Board of Education, on which everyone felt he should serve, he had found his proper civic role: rabble-rouser. He was ideally suited for the job. The combined assets of a government pension and a short life expectancy gave him enough independence not to care whom he offended.

As the turnout proved, he had done his job well. It had not been necessary to visit all the homeowners whose property lay in the highway's path, or Fess would be walking on his kneecaps by now. He had visited only half a dozen families, and the town's reliable network of gossip, more efficient than Western Union, more mysterious than the talking drums of Africa, had done the rest. They were all here: the ones who had already lost their homes, the ones who were about to, and the others who were not sure. Over two hundred people, probably half the town's adults—for a town of two thousand residents that was not bad.

Mayor Lakes rose, looking a bit paler than usual but clear eyed and crisp in a beautiful beige linen suit, and pounded his gavel. After calling the meeting to order, he suggested that those who did not have specific business with the council should leave in order to alleviate the crowding.

He was immediately forced to recognize Councilman Thompson, M.D., who had an alternative suggestion.

"With all due respect, Mr. Mayor, let me venture to suggest that these people would not be here if they did not have some good reason. After all, everyone knows our people usually have better things to do on Saturday nights."

This remark drew appreciative laughter, which caused the mayor to frown.

"And since, under the latest statutes, all council meetings are open to all interested citizens of the borough, they have every right to be here, Mr. Mayor. Therefore, I respectfully suggest that we move this meeting to the school auditorium, where everyone can be accommodated."

"That is a most unusual suggestion. I can recall no precedent for it," Abe said, as if he were in a courtroom. "Besides, the school is locked."

A gaunt, striking apparition rose up on the front row. It was Baron Sam Potter, the Grimes girls' embalmer and man-of-all-work, as well as the school's night watchman and janitor. Known throughout the county for his sinister reputation as a witch doctor, the Baron had a skull-shaped face and hypnotic eyes whose gaze caused even the bravest youngsters to cross to the other side of the street when they saw him coming. He was well over six feet tall and straight as an iron pole, even though he had already lived past his allotted three score and ten, and he always wore a black suit—in order, some said, to be ready at a moment's notice for his funerary duties. He also wore a black cape in cold weather and, after dark, a top hat.

"I'll open her up," Potter said in a gravelly voice, jangling his huge ring of keys, and moved off with a long-legged lope that carried him rapidly out of the chamber. "By the time you-all get there, the doors will be open and the lights will be on."

KRISTIN LATTANY

The mayor opened his mouth, only to close it again. The exodus had already begun, streaming toward the school, leaving him in the awkward position of a leader scrambling to catch up with his followers.

However, once restored to his place at the head of a council table that had mysteriously appeared on the school auditorium stage, Abe took command. There was old business to be gotten through, and he dispatched it quickly. The council moved unanimously to ask the state to install a traffic light across from a school on Edgehill Road, to resurface the section of Laurel Road that was pocked with potholes, and to levy a five-hundred-dollar fine on Rowdy Row tavern owners who did not observe 2:00 A.M. closing hours. The audience was getting noticeably restless at this point.

"What you gone do about my house, Mayor?" called a woman far back in the auditorium. "The state only offered me five thousand dollars. Where can I get another house today for that kind of money? Where am I gonna live?"

"Move in with him and Bella," another irate citizen suggested.

Bella. Where was Bella? Fess wondered. Although the mayor's wife did not usually appear at these meetings, Fess had somehow expected her tonight. But she was conspicuously absent.

"Order!" the mayor shouted. He looked around for a gavel, saw none, and banged his fist on the table instead. It must have been painful, because he sucked on his knuckles before continuing. "We will deal with all of your questions in the proper order. First, let me say that compensation for houses that are not being moved has been arranged by the state on the basis of fair market value. There's a hardship provision, however, Mrs. Jenkins, which might apply in your case. The state will provide supplemental funds if you can prove you need them.

"These are difficult times for all of us," the mayor went on. "The temporary inconvenience of the highway construction is hard on everyone, I admit. But I beg you to remember that it is *only* temporary. When it is finished, Lakestown will enter a new era of progress. I envision dozens of new businesses. Expansion of existing businesses. Better jobs for all our employed citizens and new jobs for all our unemployed!"

Dunce Cap Carter forgetting Roberts' *Rules of Order,* leaped to his feet and shouted. "How the hell can I expand my business when the traffic will be depressed two hundred feet below my station?"

The mayor paled visibly. "Councilman Carter," he rebuked, "I should not have to remind you that you are out of order. But let me say that I think you have been seriously misinformed."

"Well, somebody set me straight, then," Dunce Cap said truculently. A small, angry man, he stood there defiantly refusing to sit down, looking for all the world like a fice hoping for a fight with a doberman.

"With your permission, Mr. Mayor."

"Yes, Dr. Thompson?" There was a hint of weariness in the mayor's voice.

"I have prepared a little exhibit that might clear up a lot of these confusions. Are you ready, Professor Roaney?"

Fess moved to the slide projector that had been set up in the center aisle by the Baron. "Ready, Doctor."

"Then let us have the screen, please, Mr. Potter."

Baron Potter danced up the stairs to the stage and glided across it, flourishing his top hat as if doing a vaudeville turn, and pulled down a large screen at the rear of the stage.

"And now, Mr. Potter, the lights, please."

As the lights went out, the last thing to vanish was the Baron's grin, spectacularly white in his taut black face. Fess projected the first slide, a simplified version of the first set of plans Vinnie had purloined from her employers.

"Now this," Doc said, using a pointer he had probably purloined from one of the classrooms, "is the original plan for the Dorset County section of I-27. Note the date on it—October of last year. I ask you to note, also, that it bypasses Lakestown completely, and goes right through the heart of Edgehill instead. I think you will agree that this plan was sensible. If we must have more highways, which I seriously doubt, this is the way they should be built. This section would have been a straight north-south line. The shortest distance between two points."

"Potter," the mayor warned, "if you don't turn those lights on this minute, you can forget about working for this school board."

"I wouldn't advise you to threaten me, Mr. Mayor," the Baron rasped from his post at the light switches. "I might decide to take offense. Besides, I always got work." But he switched the lights on anyway.

The mayor addressed Doctor Thompson sarcastically. "Since you speak with such authority, Doctor, let me ask you—are you a highway engineer?"

"As a matter of fact, I am. Or could be," Doc replied calmly. "I took a double major in college, engineering and pre-med, in case I couldn't get into medical school."

"I'd have to see proof of those credentials before I accepted them, Doctor," the mayor snapped back. "In any case, that slide was not an official state plan. It was the rendering of some crude artist."

"Your brother, Mr. Mayor, is hardly a crude artist," the doctor said in a whisper not intended to carry over the PA system. "He has won the Salon de Paris and two Guggenheims. But you are essentially right, of course. He simplified the plans to make them clear to everyone." Doc raised his voice to address the audience. "That was a simplified drawing to help me get certain points across. Copies of the *official* plans will be passed out at the doors as you leave."

The mayor stepped forward and clung to the rostrum at the edge of the stage as if he needed its support. His voice shook slightly, but it gathered strength as he continued to speak. "That original plan you just saw," he said, "was changed because Edgehill has many historic sites that must be saved. *Certified* historic sites. Certified by the *United States Government* as national historic shrines!" He banged his fist on the rostrum for emphasis, sucked his knuckles again, and went on, "I will mention only a few. The King's Grant Inn, where a suite was kept for George the Third. The town hall, where both Royalists and Federalists met. Dozens of irreplaceable houses, built in the time of King George and carefully kept up ever since."

"We ain't subjects of no damn king!" cried one of the Young Warriors, who were stationed at the rear exits with stacks of copied plans. Fess turned his head and saw that it was Tommy Adams. "This sposed to be a democracy, where everybody who rules has to get elected and can get *de*-lected. Including you!"

Councilman Merchant raised his hand and was recognized. "The young man has raised an interesting point. The state and federal governments are using the privilege of eminent domain to acquire our land. There is no such doctrine to be found in the United States

Constitution. Eminent domain was established solely as the privilege of the English king."

"I thought they had a revolution in this country," Foxy Carter cried. "What right's some old dead king got to make us move?"

"That's not the point," the mayor shouted, growing livid. "The point is, the United States government has declared all of Edgehill a national historic shrine. Therefore, the highway had to come here."

Lukey Hawkins raised a polite hand.

"My name is Luke Hawkins, Mr. Mayor. And I have a question. Doesn't Lakestown have a history too? Wasn't it the first northeastern stop on the Underground Railroad?"

"Yes, yes, of course. So what?" the mayor said irritably.

"Well," Lukey said, "the Underground Railroad dates back to before the American Revolution. Way back to the seventeenth century, not just the eighteenth. Seems to me like the white folks' revolution didn't amount to that much anyway, if they still admire that king enough to preserve his houses and enforce his laws. But *our* revolution is still going on!"

Lukey's speech opened the floodgates. "Right on!" was shouted by several young voices at the back of the hall. "Hear hear!" acclaimed older voices scattered throughout the room. And on the front row, Lakestown's most senior citizen, Mrs. Baretta Farmer, leaped to her feet and cried, "You tell 'em, young man!"

The mayor chose to ignore it all and recognize another council member. "Yes, Miss Grimes?"

Elegant in a patriotic tricolor print and matching turban, Greta stood up. "He's right," she said. "Our house was built in 1850, but the cellar is a hundred years older than that. And some of the first runaway slaves to come to Lakestown are buried there. Their names were Jubal Lakes and his wife, Tullah, and their son, Abraham. Your ancestors, Mr. Mayor."

"I know who my ancestors were," the mayor rebuffed her, "and I didn't come here to hear about them."

"He don't play that," Mame Porritt commented, eliciting some laughter.

"Silence!" Abe demanded. "Yes, Reverend Bream?"

"Mount Moriah," the Reverend said, "is the oldest church in Lakestown and the oldest Methodist church in the state, the spiritual home of our freedom-loving ancestors. With due respect for your feelings, Mr. Mayor, its first pastor, in 1762, before the present structure was built, was the same Jubal Lakes. And its last pastor before me was your father, George Lorenzo Lakes, who loved freedom so much he incorporated this borough. I believe the church will be spared by the highway, but I am told that the cemetery will not. Half the families here have graves in that burying ground. I say, let's defend it! Let's preserve our heritage at all costs!"

Fess was startled by the Reverend Bream's turnabout and wondered what had caused it. Perhaps he, Fess, had gotten to some of his congregation, and they in turn had gotten to their pastor.

Not to be outdone, the Reverend LeRoy Bird rose and was recognized. "We do not need," he orated in a sonorous voice that rolled like thunder, "the official approval of the u.s. government to make us value our history. We do not need real estate appraisers to tell us the worth of our land. We know what Lakestown is worth. It is beyond price, because it was paid for in suffering, toil, and blood! And we do not have to take second place to Edgehill in the value of our homes, our history, our land, or anything else. If my understanding is correct, their revolution was a mockery. Their history is a fraud. They are still kneeling before royalty over there in Edgehill. The people in this town bend their knees only to *Gawd!*"

His speech turned the audience into a congregation. There were a half dozen amens, three cries of "Yes, Jesus!," and one fainting in the congested center of the crowd.

While Doc Thompson went to revive the victim, the mayor protested, "This is turning into a circus. We will have an orderly meeting, or we will have no meeting at all. I now move to adjourn . . ."

"Not till I get *my* say in you don't," shouted Vinnie Coddums, bounding up in the twelfth row, where she had been restored by the doctor's ministrations. "Abe Lakes, when I get finished tellin' these people what a hypocrite you are, you'll wish you'd never laid eyes on this town *or* on me."

Abe swayed and clutched the rostrum for support. The blood had drained from his face and his eyelids were fluttering as if his turn to faint had come.

Doc Thompson, returning to the stage, took him by the elbow. "Mr. Mayor, you look unwell. I suggest you sit down for a moment while I show my next slide. It gives a clear picture of all the progress you were telling us about."

The school public-address system may have been faulty—it often was—but Fess thought he heard the mayor say, "Anything you want. Anything. Just get her out of here."

Baron Potter extinguished the lights, Fess clicked the next slide into place, and the audience was treated to as pretty a piece of deception as they had ever seen.

The artist's sly rendering was almost wicked in its glorification of the highway plan. Stores, restaurants, gas stations, factories, and lush plantings blossomed on either side of the future highway. Where the devastation now lay, Ikie had pictured prosperity and charm, depicted in such exquisite, pastel-tinted detail it was like an aerial view of fairyland.

Dr. Thompson addressed the mayor. "Now this second plan, Mayor Lakes, which I note is dated June of this year—is this an accurate picture of the progress we can look forward to?"

Abe rose, casting a long shadow on the screen, which was extended by the pointer Doc handed him. "Yes," he said. "Most of this is not promised, of course, and nothing is guaranteed. But the state has promised to put in all the landscaping you see here, and I know that two fast-food chains are interested in setting up franchises here and here. Also, two national retail operations want to open up braches here, with the intention of developing a shopping mall around their locations. And I have had several inquiries recently from manufacturers wanting to move into an industrial park on land the borough owns here. Now, if all these things come about, and I see no reason why they shouldn't, they will mean lower taxes and higher income for the citizens of this borough. More money in the borough treasury. More jobs for our residents. And there will be room for even more ribbon development on both sides of the highway, as you can see here, here, and here. Banks, I might add, are willing to lend money to responsible investors. The business prospects for these locations look very lucrative, with an estimated traffic of thirty thousand cars every day and more on weekends. In the long run, I am convinced, Interstate twenty-seven will be a great asset to the economic future of Lakestown."

Abe had swung a large portion of the audience over to his side, judging by the long and enthusiastic applause. In the midst of it, a small, cool hand gripped Fess's and thrust some crumpled papers into it. "From Miss Bella. Only . . ."

With astonishment Fess recognized the pert profile silhouetted in the backlight of the projector. Cindy. *Talking*. "Only what?" he whispered.

"Only if you need 'em," she said clearly.

"And if I don't?"

"Give 'em back." Then, quickly and lightly as a moth, she slipped out of the aisle and back into the blackness.

The applause was over. "What," Dr. Thompson was asking, "are the boundaries of the highway, Mr. Mayor?"

"Approximately the ones you see here. Occupying a width of sixty feet, beginning at Nestor Avenue and proceeding westward to Piney Road, and beginning at the northern bank of Crump's Creek and proceeding in a northeasterly direction to the Dorsettown-Lakestown border on the south side of Edgehill Road," the mayor recited.

"Then why have they begun to dig on Merchant Avenue?" Reverend Bird wanted to know. "It's at least fifty feet away from this plan."

"I don't know," the mayor said. "I was not aware of any excavating on Merchant Avenue. But I assume the highway crew needs the dirt for its landfill operations."

"You a dirty lie, Abe Lakes," a woman howled.

"So far they've only disturbed borough property on Merchant Avenue, not private property—am I correct, Reverend Bird?"

"You a double-damned dirty-dog lie!" cried Vinnie. "You just said you didn't even know about them digging on Merchant Avenue."

"Please calm down, Mrs. Coddums, before you faint again," the doctor said. "Next slide, please."

Fess quickly clicked the third and final slide into place. On it the extent of the prospective damage was dreadfully clear. The town would be split in two and devastated by the highway, with nothing left but a few clumps of houses around its edges. The gasp that rose from over two hundred throats was like a strong wind sweeping away the cobwebs of politicians' promises.

"This is the latest plan," Dr. Thompson said. "Note the date: this month, this year."

"I would like to know," the mayor said icily, "how this plan was obtained, Doctor."

"I am not at liberty to say. But it is authentic."

Dunce Cap Carter's steepled shadow appeared on the screen. "Mr. Mayor, this new plan is as much a shock to you as it is to me, I guess. But if it's correct, it changes everything. I got eyes like everybody else in this room, and I can see clearly what it says right here: 'Depressed two hundred feet below grade level.' If the highway's going to be depressed, what happens to all that progress you just said we could expect?"

"I can tell you what happens to it. I could have told you all along," Carl Adams said. "It rolls right on up the road to white country, like it always does. Leaving us depressed. In a depression."

"I don't see any benefits coming to Lakestown from this plan," Dunce Cap continued. "I don't see anything in it for us but losses. Looking at this diagram here, I don't even see any access ramps within the borough. All I see are 'Overpass' and 'Underpass.' How are we going to gain anything from that?"

"We ain't," Adams interjected mournfully. "The benefits are gonna pass us over, like they always do. And we gonna be put *under*. In the hole, like we always been."

"Gentlemen of the council," the mayor said, "please don't jump to conclusions. At this point we don't even know whether this plan is fact or fiction."

"Well, this *lady* of the council wants some facts fast," announced Greta Grimes, jumping up and snatching the pointer from the mayor's hand, "because that piece of that road is on my property, mine and my sister's."

"May I ask the council again to refrain from jumping to conclusions and have patience? This matter must be checked out with the authorities. I suggest we table it until I have a chance to go to the appropriate officials and find out whether this plan has any basis in fact, which I doubt. And now, may we have the lights, please?"

Baron Potter complied, flooding the hall with light that turned the slide into a pale ghost of itself, almost completely exorcised by the mayor's calm reasoning. You had to hand it to Abe, Fess thought grudgingly. He was smooth to begin with and grew smoother under pressure. Fess was half convinced the mayor was innocent of this latest development.

But not everyone else was convinced. "Sellout! Sellout!" one of the Young Warriors shouted. "Don't let him sell us out, y'all!"

"That's right!" old Baretta Farmer echoed, shooting up from her seat with incredible energy. "He might go to the Man and get money to hand the council under the table."

Josh Hawkins rose, dwarfing everyone else on the stage, and said in his soft accent, "I know you got to check this thing out before we can discuss it proper, Mr. Mayor, but I been wondering. Suppose the doctor is right? Suppose that plan we just saw is the one the state is using. What can we do about it?"

"I'd like to refer that question to solicitor Crudup," the mayor said.

The simian borough solicitor, known as Crud to the victims of some of his shadier deals, stood up. "I haven't had a chance to study the matter, of course. It's as new to me as it is to the rest of you. But an educated guess would be—nothing."

"Nothin' at all?" Josh said, with the exaggerated astonishment Fess always considered play-acting.

"Nothing at all," the lawyer repeated. "The right of eminent domain still prevails. We are only a small borough. There is nothing we can do to stop a combined state and federal project."

"You mean," Josh said, "there's nothing we can do to stop it *legally*." The cracking of his knuckles was picked up by the microphone and amplified throughout the auditorium until it sounded like a barrage of artillery. "That's right," lawyer Crudup said, nodding a patchy skull from which the hairs had irregularly eroded.

"Thank you," Josh said with ironic courtesy. "Thank you very much."

Abe said into the microphone, "The matter under discussion is tabled for further study until the next meeting. As there is no other new business, I move to adjourn. Do I hear a second?"

"Second," Doc Thompson said cheerfully.

"Then this meeting is adjourned." The mayor and lawyer Crudup strode hastily from the stage, followed by Chief Boyd and an almost equally gigantic patrolman, Lukey Hawkins's brother Matthew. No doubt they would have needed protection if they had stayed a minute longer, judging by the comments coming from the floor.

Fess pocketed the slides and hurried back to the main rear exit. He needed to talk to Lukey Hawkins immediately.

Fess found him asking Tommy Adams, "What happened with you and Crump this morning?"

"He ran," Tommy said. "Maybe 'cause he saw the Rev's cross, maybe not. What he said was he was late for school."

"What school?" Lukey demanded. "Crump dropped out three years ago."

"Embalming school," was Tommy's amused answer. "The Baron's getting old, so the Grimes ladies decided they needed somebody young to help him out around the funeral home. But Crump got to get his license, so they're sending him to school for it."

"Perfect job for creepy Crump, I'd say," Lukey observed. "And it'll keep him busy. Good. Now get back to the other door and hand out those papers, Tom. Yes, Professor?"

"Secret meeting at the poolroom tonight, after this one breaks up. You know who to tell. No youngsters . . . except," Fess added as an afterthought, "you."

The broad smile this produced on Lukey's dark face was more radiant than the sunrise over the neon-lit Blue Moon, which Fess had always considered the most scenic view in Lakestown.

"Somebody's been lyin' to us!"

"I bet not find out who, if they know what's good for 'em!"

With each shouted comment, the rumblings of the crowd grew louder. As if he were deaf, Doc Thompson moved serenely and ponderously around the stage, speaking privately to each of the other members of the council. Fess both rejoiced and trembled at what he had done. Almost single-handedly he had turned Lakestown's complacent citizens into an angry mob. How to lead that mob and channel its anger in a useful direction was the problem now, one he hoped somebody else could handle.

19

Bella floated about her house as if trapped in a dream, a nightmare. She still wore the clinging ivory satin gown she'd put on last night, the first night she'd spent in her husband's bed in four years. Over it she wore a matching satin housecoat trimmed with the same ecru lace. The set had cost fifty dollars and had never been worn before.

Bella's feet, usually bare at home, were encased in high-heeled satin mules with pom-poms. As if hoping to shock herself awake by bringing the soles of her feet into contact with hard, solid reality, she kicked the slippers away. But the house was thickly carpeted wall to wall, and walking barefoot gave her an even more dreamlike sensation.

Her house, like her image, seemed falsely perfect, Saran-wrapped. There were no scattered papers, no dirty ashtrays, no dust or lint anywhere. Of course not, since she had spent the entire morning cleaning. But the order and perfection she had created seemed unreal to Bella. The house made her uneasy, as if she were a stranger who did not belong there. This room was blue, with a Wedgwood-patterned wallpaper and matching Wedgwood plates arranged on a ledge above French doors. The highly polished table, usually dusty and littered with projects, was set for eight with blue linen place mats, crystal goblets, gleaming sterling, and the silver-rimmed china she had not used since her wedding. It was a magazine-page room, admirable and threatening.

There were no dirty dishes in the kitchen either, because she had eaten nothing all morning.

Why not? It was noon. By now, usually, she would have had a hearty breakfast and the first of several light lunches.

At least the kitchen had a cold tile floor, which roused her enough to remember. Abe had said she needed to lose weight. He had said a lot of things last night. But the speech she remembered distinctly at the moment was, "You're going to need a lot of new clothes. And the kind of clothes I want you to wear don't come in stout sizes."

Bella walked around the kitchen, deriving some comfort from the unpleasantness of the cold floor under her feet, though the tidiness and cleanliness of this room was just as disorienting as the perfection of the rest of the house. Her kitchen smelled of wax and pine oil instead of cooking; her appliances gleamed like packed snowbanks in the sun. Rather than sully them she opened a cabinet, took out a six-ounce can of tuna, opened it, and ate its entire contents with her fingers, standing up at the sink. Then she rinsed her hands, poured herself a tall gin and tonic, and lit a cigarette, less because she wanted one at the moment than because she wanted to chase the ghost of disinfectant from the room.

On what TV program was it that which black comedian had said in what way white folks were different from blacks?

"Their houses don't smell."

"And they don't smell, either," Bella added from her own observations. Oh, the rule did not include poor or working-class white people—they often stank, all right—but the whites who lived in houses like hers, the well-off ones in the suburbs, were usually as clean and odorless as wax fruit. You felt dirt would not cling to them if you threw it at them; it would simply slide off without leaving a trace.

She bent and sniffed her own armpit for reassurance. She had worn this gown for twelve hours, had slept, cleaned, scrubbed, and, yes, fucked in it—yet it was spotless and she had produced no odor.

She was, suddenly, thoroughly frightened. What had happened to her? She didn't know. What was she feeling? Nothing. Anything, even drunkenness, would be better than this robotlike trance in which she seemed to be sealed like a photograph in someone's wallet. She reinforced her drink. What had happened last night? At least she could reconstruct that.

She had helped her shaken husband to his bed and there acceded to his plea that she stay with him, not abandon him to spend this particular terrible night alone. She could see his tremors, could feel them, too, because his scrawny arms had seized her and held her close. Even at the moment of his greatest weakness, Abe was strong. Bella, feeling nothing but pity, failed to observe this at the time. She had undressed and slipped into bed beside him, had held him, rocked him like the baby she would never have, soothed him with meaningless phrases, soft bits of nonsense to convince him that everything would be all right, when both of them knew nothing would ever be right again.

KRISTIN LATTANY

What happened next almost anyone could have predicted except Bella, and even she about any man except Abe. It began timidly, very timidly, with little, scared, shy touches and immediate withdrawals of the possibly offending hands. Polite requests worded almost like formal invitations: "Would you mind very much, Bella?" "Do you think I could?" "Would you—?"

Of course she could. After watching in horror while he went through a crisis that sent him over the edge, if this was all he needed to bring him back, why of course she would. Sholy, Lakes. Ain't no big thing. After all, as Mame Porritt often said, it was the one thing you never ran out of, the one thing you could always give away and keep too—so why be stingy with it? Bella was prepared to do almost anything to bring her husband out of his state of shock, and what he asked turned out to be the easiest thing in the world.

Well. The shock was soon to be hers. Abe the pitiful became powerful. The need that had been dammed up in him for too many uptight years broke through with the force of a torrent and the polite requests soon gave way to demands. "Move your hips. No, not that way, this way. Goddamn you, move!" As if he were giving an army its marching orders.

The first time he took her he hurt her. The second time was worse: she enjoyed it. Her unwilling body felt a pleasure that threatened to turn her entire life upside down. Confused and sated, she barely heard him complaining, "You're wearing a *thing*. I can feel it. I want you to take it off."

And then, shockingly, he added, "I don't care who else you wear it for. Just don't use it with me. I don't want to feel anything artificial when I'm inside a woman."

It startled her out of bed and into the bathroom. When she came back, he said, "Turn on the lights. I want to see you."

He studied her for a minute that seemed like an hour, then sighed and said, "Turn off the lights."

Bella felt as if she had been slapped. Perhaps because she had always taken her good looks for granted she was vulnerable, and this seemed like the worst insult she'd ever received. She fled to her own bedroom, where she covered herself against his critical scrutiny in the fifty-dollar nightgown and peignoir. She was moving toward the further safety of her own bed when she heard him calling. "Bella, come back. I want you. You promised to spend the night with me, remember?"

"Don't you think it's time we got some sleep, Lakes?"

He was lying on his back, his hawk profile highlighted by the bedside lamp, smoking. "No. I think it's time we had a talk."

She came in, but stayed warily on the other side of the room.

"You know, Bella, your figure would have been considered ideal in the nineteenth century. But this is the twentieth, and you're obese."

Somehow that particular word was the cruelest he could have chosen, far more cutting than *overweight* or even *fat*.

"How many pounds have you picked up since we got married?"

She took refuge in drawling. "Ah don' know. Twenty or thutty, Ah guess."

"Forty or fifty is more like it. I want you to take them off. And for God's sake, cut out the fake Southern accent. I have plans for you. They don't include country talk and crude manners."

"What sort of plans?" she asked.

"Bella," he observed, "we've been married twenty-five years, and you don't know a thing about me."

"That's true," she had to admit.

"But what bothers me more is, you don't know a thing about reality. Sometimes I think you're completely out of contact."

Thinking back to his performance in the kitchen only a few hours ago, Bella didn't know whether to laugh or cry. She chose the former as a way of dispelling the strange authority he had suddenly acquired over her.

"Don't laugh at me," he ordered. "I know I was crazy a little while ago. Of course I snapped. Anyone would snap after the strain I've been under. And why have I been under so much strain lately? If you'd ever tried to be a wife and a partner to me, you would know."

"How was I supposed to know what was on your mind, Lakes? You never bothered to tell me anything."

"Maybe I have kept too many of my concerns from you," he conceded. "But you seemed determined to thwart and frustrate me at every turn. So I left you alone."

"How—?" was all he allowed her to utter of her indignant response.

"You know damned well how you've frustrated me. And don't pretend you don't. The higher I've tried to rise in the world, the lower down you've tried to get: the sloppy way you dress, the ignorant way you talk, the low companions you choose, the immoral establishments you spend your time in."

She opened her mouth, only to close it again.

"You were going to ask how I know? I'm not stupid, Bella. And I have my informants."

"I never said you were stupid, Lakes."

"And neither are you. So stop acting stupidly."

"I was going to ask you for your definition of 'immoral.'"

"At least you're talking like an intelligent woman for a change." He smiled his grim smile of satisfaction. "You first. What's yours?"

Bella, feeling power over him and, therefore, safety, moved closer to the bed. She lit a cigarette and took a long pull on it before she spoke. "I'd say," she said after a long pause, "it's fathering a child and then refusing to own her."

He gripped her arm. "And *I'd* say that's none of your business. At least I've been discreet about it."

"Like hell. The whole town knows. I was the last to find out." She blew smoke in his face, but it did not dim the belligerent glare in his eyes.

"That makes us even, then," he said. "You've treated me like a fool, and I've done the same with you, and neither of us was fooled for very long. So we can quit playing that particular game." He pinched the flesh of her upper arm.

"You're hurting me, Lakes."

"I don't mean to," he said, without lessening his pressure. "I'm measuring something. Look. A person of normal weight has about three-quarters of an inch of pinchable flesh right here. Each additional quarter-inch equals fifteen pounds of excess weight. You have to lose forty-five pounds, Bella, and you have to start tomorrow."

She hated him for coldly analyzing her flesh right after wanting and having it. "It's my body. Maybe I like it the way it is. Let go my arm, Lakes."

"Of course," he said, releasing her. The blue mark on her arm made him smile gain. "It bruises nicely, doesn't it? No matter how hard you try, you can't get black . . . Of course it's your body, Bella. I don't care what you do with it, as long as you get it in shape and groom it properly. I mean, I don't care as long as you use discretion."

"Immorality is what shows, then, according to you. Is that right, Lakes?"

"Exactly. According to me and all the rest of the civilized world. If you met your lovers at good New York hotels it wouldn't matter to me. If you flew over and met them in London or Paris, I might even like it. But meeting them at vulgar cafés around the corner hurts my future."

"Maybe I *like* vulgar cafés," she replied defiantly.

"From now on," he stated, "you are not going to like *anything* vulgar, Bella. Not if you intend to go on being my wife."

"Are you asking me or telling me?"

"Telling you, of course. It's rough out there in the world of politics. It's a jungle. If you stay with me, you're going to have to help me compete, and that means you're going to have to acquire some style and some class."

"Why should I do all that? Why should I start making myself over at this late date?"

His smile was that of a card player to whose hand she had inadvertently lost a trump. "You just said it yourself. Because it's late. Much later than you think. Face it, Bella, you're middle-aged. I don't know what your motives are—and frankly, I don't care—but you're much too old to rebel. It's time for you to stop fighting me, or the system, or whatever you're fighting, and start cooperating. At your age, I don't think you really want to start facing the world alone. Think about it."

"I will," Bella said coolly.

"I want you to do more than that."

"What, for instance?"

He reached under the bed, came up with a mouse-sized lump of dust, and dropped the evidence in her lap. "For instance, I want you to clean up this filthy house. I want you to clean it thoroughly today. Can you do that?"

"Of course, Lakes," Bella said.

"I hope so. Although I haven't seen any evidence in twenty-five years to make me believe you. Well, do your best," he sighed. "After that,

I want you to fix a late supper for eight people, and I don't mean chitterlings and potato salad. I mean some good hors d'oeuvres, smoked oysters and paté and foreign cheeses, and some rare roast beef, and a big green salad, and French bread, and good wine. You wouldn't know a good wine if you drowned in it, so . . ."

"Would you like a light wine, she interrupted sweetly, "say a Mouton Rothschild or a Margaux? Or would you prefer something stronger, a Chambertin or a Chateauneuf-du-Pape?" She smiled, knowing Abe would never guess that she had acquired this part of her education from his truck-driving, pool-shooting brother.

Abe smiled too. "By God, I believe there's hope for you, Bella. You really surprise me. Get beer, too. Nothing domestic. Danish or German, light and dark. And liquor, of course. The best brands."

"What else?" she asked, knowing the money he thrust into her hands was for shopping, yet unable to keep from feeling he was paying her for sex, like any whore.

He frowned. "This is going to be the hardest part. I want you to get your appearance in order, Bella. Eventually you're going to lose all that fat, of course, but right now you'll have to cover it up the best way you can. One of those long, flowing hostess things should do it. The simpler the better. Get it here." He dug into his wallet again, plucked out a card, and flipped it at her. It bore, she saw, the address of an overpriced women's clothing shop in Edgehill.

"Oh, and get something to wear under it. You know what I mean, something that keeps you from jiggling so much when you walk."

"When you walk across a room, shaking all that fine stuff you got, I just melt," someone had said to her. Her head began to whirl with confusion and to throb with the beginning of an all-day ache.

"Take a bath before you get dressed. Scrub your nails. Wash your hair. Better yet, have it washed and set while you're over in Edgehill. And while you're cleaning up your appearance, don't forget to clean up your mind. Try, for once in your life, to talk and act like a lady. If you can't do that, just keep your mouth shut and say nothing. I want you to be ready for my guests at ten. Do you think you can do all that?"

"Of course I can," Bella said calmly. "I just want to know what I'm doing it *for.*"

"Survival, that's what!" he shouted. "Your survival and mine. I don't know who you think is in charge of this country, but it isn't your precious Negroes. The people in Lakestown don't have any power, Bella. White men are the ones who make the decisions. I want the decisions to be in our favor. I want to be in a position to make decisions myself fairly soon, and I don't care what I have to do to get there. For all I care, they can take Lakestown and . . ."

"Hush," Bella said, and covered his lips with her hand. "Don't tell me any more, Lakes. Please."

"You're right," he said. "You have enough to remember as it is. You don't have to think about my part. Just do yours. Promise!"

"I promise."

"That's a good girl," he said sleepily. "Come here."

Bella was so slow to respond that Abe never carried out his intentions, though apparently he was dreaming that he had. "Aaah," he said. "That was good. I didn't feel anything but you that time." Before her astonished eyes he rolled over into a deep, sound, snoring sleep.

Bella went to her own room but found that she was unable to sleep more than half an hour. After that she got up, douched, and methodically set about her cleaning, still wearing the lavish gown and housecoat that resembled a bridal costume.

Her dusting, straightening, scrubbing, and vacuuming went on all morning, interrupted only by Cindy's usual Saturday visit. Bella refused the puzzled child's help. She sent her off instead with the scraps of paper for Fess and a note care of Fess for Ikie, and went back to mopping and polishing like an efficient, high-speed machine.

Now, at noon, Abe still slept. Flinging on the first thing she could find in her closet, Bella drove over to Edgehill, did her shopping and had her hair done by an effete Frenchman whose incomprehensible babble contributed further to her dreamlike state. It was as if her mind had been turned off and some master control center was directing her movements, making her do all these unnatural, detestable things.

When Abe arrived at ten that night with a loud herd of tightly suited white men, the repast was ready and so was Bella, scrubbed, perfumed, girdled, coifed, and gowned in a graceful float of powder blue chiffon, chosen less because she liked it than because it matched her dining room.

"My wife, gentlemen," he said, and bent toward her in an alarm-ingly unfamiliar gesture of affection.

Bella recognized the cue and held up her cheek for the first husbandly kiss he had ever given her.

"Wonderful," he whispered, sniffing. "You even smell like a white woman."

20

Ikie's Pool Room, along with Bobo Wright's Barber Shop and the Crump's Creek Rod and Gun Club, was one of the few stag retreats in the community. Women and girls were intimidated by the place. They seemed to feel that insults and damaged reputations, if not actual rape, would be their fate if they entered it or even paused in front of it. And, Fess thought, they were probably right.

As it turned out, the gathering that convened there after the adjournment of the Borough Council did not tarnish the poolroom's record. As a member of the council who had voiced opposition to the highway, Greta Grimes was automatically invited, but an unfortunate remark kept her out.

As Greta was leaving the school, Fess overheard Mae Hawkins say to her, "Wasn't it a shame about the Adams boy? Are you going to the funeral?"

Greta, who had paused to repair her lipstick, replied in a tone as hard and metallic as the clicking shut of her purse. "No. Why should I? We didn't get the body." She moved on down the school steps, her heels tapping like an adding machine; dragging her reluctant sister. Jane.

But Fess was not the only one who had overheard the exchange. Bunky Adams had too, and he stood there like the proverbial baboon, thick, hairy arms folded, barring the poolroom door.

"Try to get by me," he said, "and there'll be another body to be buried next week."

Greta tried to disarm him with her sugary southern belle act. "Why, Mr. Adams," she said sweetly, "surely you wouldn't use physical violence against a lady."

"No, ma'am, I wouldn't," he agreed. "But everything that wears a dress ain't a lady. The way you carry yourself, I do believe you got the same things under that skirt as me."

A knot of male loungers was present as usual in front of the poolroom. They drew closer as Bunky continued.

"You got two choices if you want to come in here. You can fight me like the man I think you are. Or you can pull up that dress and prove me wrong."

Greta looked as if she were about to take him up on the first challenge. Eyes narrowed, pocketbook poised for swinging, she took a step toward him.

She had one supporter who shouted, "Go ahead, Miss Grimes. Hit him up side the head. Give him a *good* lick."

But the rest snickered and gave her lewd encouragement to follow the second suggestion.

"Go 'head, show it, baby. It ain't nothin' to be ashamed of."

"Yeah. Let us see it. Bet it's fine."

"Greta," her embarrassed sister said, "please. I don't belong here. I'm going home."

"So am I, Jane," Greta said. "All right!" she called to Bunky. "You win. But you lose, too. You had my support, but you just lost it. I'm going over to the other side. And I think you'll find I can be a dangerous enemy."

As if to lend substance to her threat, the gaunt Baron, looking twelve feet tall in his top hat, materialized out of the blackness to escort the girls home. The street-corner loungers stopped laughing the moment he made his appearance. Within half a minute the sidewalk was cleared.

It was not, Fess thought, an auspicious beginning, but at least it eliminated the sidewalk gang and ensured the secrecy of the meeting. Ikie put the last pool players out, dismissed his house man, and turned the sign on the door to CLOSED to discourage additional customers. He admitted the invited few only after peering at them through a slot in the door.

Like a school of fish, they gathered in the aqueous green light that illuminated the big green tables. Bunky Adams and Fess and the Reverend Bream, who took a deep breath and held it before crossing the poolroom's threshold, as if he expected to breathe the sulfuric fumes of hell inside. Cap Carter and Morris Merchant; Josh Hawkins and his son Luke. When Doc Thompson arrived with Lonnie Jenkins and Nunc Farmer, the room was beginning to get crowded.

Ikie, running balls to relax the tension that showed in his set expression and slanted eyes, called to him, "Hey, Doc, this is just our first planning meeting. We don't need the whole town."

The humblest man in Lakestown turned to leave, saying "You gemmans know where to find me if you want me."

"Come back, please, Mr. Jenkins," Morris Merchant said. "There's no room for class distinctions in here."

"There's no room for all you niggers in here," Ikie said, completing a vicious bank shot. "That was why I raised a question about the last bunch that came in. Now can we cut out the crap about etiquette and get down to business?"

"Don't you have an apartment upstairs?" Fess inquired boldly.

"Those are my private quarters, Roaney," Ikie answered with an angry scowl.

"So much the better," Doc rumbled with that jovial heartiness that could usually cover all differences, like thick, gooey frosting applied to a cracked cake. "Privacy is exactly what we need. Freedom from observation, so we can conspire in comfort."

Throwing him an evil look, Ikie tossed away his cue stick and went to a side door near the front of the poolroom. From a massive ring of keys he selected one that opened the door's cylinder lock and another that unfastened a huge, rusty padlock that hung from a thick hasp. Then he bounded into a hall and up some dark stairs, where more keys were required to open a second door.

"You guys wait a minute. Gimme time to clean up in here," he called.

But his fellow conspirators were right behind him, and Ikie was interrupted in his frantic effort to drape a tarpaulin over the large granite statue that dominated the center of the room.

"Oh, what the hell," he said with a shrug. "Come in."

So there was a female presence at the meeting after all, and an overwhelming one at that. Bella in stone, twice life size, was even more compelling than Bella in the flesh. Ikie had done her as Eve accepting an apple from a serpent coiled cozily around her left breast. Her expression was not coy but open and serene, as if she knew exactly what she was doing, and she wore no fig leaf or other trace of shame. She had not been prettied up, either; her flanks and rump were massive and her loins and abdomen, rippled and dimpled with fat, seemed capable of populating the earth. This was no sickly Virgin Madonna but a real woman. Yet,

　　　　　　　　　　　　　　KRISTIN LATTANY

after their first stares, the men averted their eyes, refrained from lewd comments, and seemingly gave the statue as much respect as a church icon.

Its presence, however, was impossible to ignore. "Amazing," the irrepressible doctor said. "that you could create the effect of softness, working in such a hard material."

Ikie grunted. "Some other time, Doc. We're not here to discuss stone. The subject was land."

Fess, meanwhile, having suddenly remembered something, was rummaging through his pockets. The crumpled scraps of paper in a strange, loosely scrawled handwriting did not make sense to him. Neither did the note, which he read before realizing it was not meant for him, though his conscience would probably not have restrained his curiosity anyway:

> Dear Ikie,
> I don't know how I feel about you right now, or about anything. I'm staying away until I'm sure.
> Good luck.
>
> Bella

"I was trying to cover it up," Ike was complaining to Doc. "They didn't give me enough time."

"Would you put a bra on the Venus de Milo? A Mother Hubbard on a Gauguin woman?" Doc asked him.

"No," Ikie said tonelessly.

"No more would I," Doc replied.

Ikie shrugged, as if the baring of his intimate secrets meant no more to him than a change in the weather, and began tossing cushions around the floor of his studio. "This place isn't set up for hospitality, you guys. But these'll keep your behinds off the floor and the dust off your clothes. There's a fifth over there in the kitchen cupboard, and I think there's some beer and some ice in there." He pointed to a square-foot cube of a refrigerator that was tucked under an apartment sink.

The ceiling light gave a brief flash and a sputter, then left them in darkness except for the moonlight that streamed in through the high windows and half-glazed ceiling of the studio. "There's some candles and matches in the sink drawer, Josh," Ikie called.

The resourceful storekeeper found a stub of a candle and lit it, lit two larger ones from that, and brought them in saucers to the center of the area where the others squatted. Then he went back to his bartending duties, which were quickly completed. He returned with a glass dangling from each of his long, hooked fingers, a fifth of whiskey under one arm, and a six-pack under the other.

Fess, who had been edging toward Ikie in the shadows, finally reached him and handed him the scraps of paper, with Bella's note on top.

"Where did you get these?" Ikie demanded, snatching up a candle and reading quickly. "Did you read them?"

"They were passed to me at the meeting. By your niece."

"Well, at least she can't read. But you can."

"Does it matter?" Fess asked, growing weary of the unabated hostility between them, especially since Bella's message had made him feel slightly sorry for Ikie. So okay, you're an Indian, he was thinking, but do you have to act like a wooden one? "I'm on your side, man. When will you get that through your head?"

"It would help if we knew who wrote them," Ikie said, stuffing Bella's note into his pocket.

"The only message was," Fess said, "to return them to Bella if we don't need them."

Ikie showed no reaction at the mention of his lover's name. "Cindy said that?" was all he asked.

"Yes. I wouldn't be too sure she can't read. She can certainly talk now."

Ikie grunted noncommittally at this news and stood up to address the group. "I figure I'll just toss out a few suggestions and see how you react. You all heard Crud tonight. He may be wrong, but I doubt it. No legal maneuver can stop that project. However, as I understand it, if we can manage to stall it long enough, we may be able to bring it to a screeching halt."

"That's correct." the doctor said. "Basically, it's a federal project, with some money from the state treasury. If it falls too far behind schedule, Washington may withdraw the funds."

"Now," Ikie continued, "I assume all of you are against the final highway plan we were shown tonight. Assuming that it *is* the final plan. Otherwise you wouldn't be here. Am I wrong about anyone? If so, let me know right now."

There was no response.

"All right. I have some notes here that seem to indicate they intend to do to Lakestown exactly what Doc said they were going to do."

"Highway robbery. In the most literal sense," Doc commented.

"These notes also indicate that certain parties in Lakestown are in league with the robbers, incredible as that may seem. Is anyone here familiar with the mayor's handwriting?"

"He's your brother," Fess remarked, then regretted it.

"I'd rather not be the one to make the identification. For obvious reasons, Roaney."

Old Morris Merchant raised his hand and was passed the slips of paper while he was studying them by the light of the other candle, Ikie went on, "I believe Crud was right. It would be pointless for us to go to court."

"Then it's war," Bunky Adams said.

"We can't afford all-out war. It's a David-and-Goliath situation. Our objective is to stall the highway construction as long as possible. So what I propose is a compromise." He flashed a rare grin that in the flickering light looked satanic. "You might call it malicious mischief."

"Malicious mischief!" Cap Carter snorted. "What the hell is that? Sounds like kid stuff."

The impact of the statue was heightened by candlelight. Above their heads, those mighty haunches loomed like mountains. Fess was not surprised when Ikie began to voice Bella's ideas.

"That's the beauty of it," Ikie explained. "Kids can help. Listen. We're in the middle of a heat wave, with no relief in sight. Monday is supposed to be a real scorcher. Suppose we get three or four of the cutest kids in town. Wait till the hottest part of the day, then send 'em out on that construction site with thermos jugs of cold lemonade."

High above Ikie, the statue's mouth seemed to curve in a gentle, tolerant smile.

"Heh, heh," Lonnie Jenkins chuckled, as if his mind worked the same way as Ikie's and Bella's, and he knew exactly what was coming next. "What's in the jugs besides lemonade?"

"Something," Ikie said, "that will knock the crew out for the rest of the day."

"Ethyl alcohol's the best." Doc suggested. "I can get you all you want from my lab."

"Is it stronger than Mame Porritt's home brew?" Fess wondered.

"That I can't guarantee," Doc admitted. "If there's anything stronger than that Mason-jar liquor she gets from Georgia, they must use it for rocket fuel. But lab alcohol is better, because it's absolutely tasteless."

"My Lindy and my Bessie would sho love to help," Alonzo volunteered.

"Fine," Ikie said. "Nobody would be suspicious of those little dolls of yours. And the next day the kids come back with more lemonade, plus some sandwiches. 'Cause we're a friendly community, see? We're nice, friendly, *helpful* nigras."

"Sho," Josh said with a low, evil chuckle. "We gone help 'em to death."

"Death, you say?" the Reverend Bream exclaimed in alarm.

"Just an expression, Reverend," Josh explained.

"And we're curious, too, like all ignorant darkies," Ikie went on, inspired. "Friendly and curious as hell. Poking our noses into everything. Asking hundreds of questions. Showing a lot of interest in the work, enough to slow it down. And constantly getting in the way."

"Mis-tah," Josh whined, standing up, his figure even more elongated by candlelight. "Hey, mis-tah, what do you call this heah thing? A earth movah, you say? Hey, I never heard tell of one of them before. How do it work? Oh, it looks so easy. You think maybe you could let me try it a little while? . . . Got it in gear now, speedin' up, headin' straight for that cinder-block wall behind the Grimes place. Jump off at the last minute. *Blam!* Ooh, mis-tah, Ah sho didn' mean ta do that. No *suh*. Ah'm *so* sorry! Heeee!" He and his shadow, which added up to sixteen feet of man, shook with delighted laughter.

"Josh, that's great. You ought to go on the stage," Fess said, with sincere admiration.

"Been on the stage all my life. Like any other black man who lives past thirty. Heee."

"Not the earth mover, Josh," Cap Carter interjected suddenly.

"Huh?"

"I said, don't wreck the earth mover. At least not right away. I think I have an idea. Lonnie, how many tons of dirt does that crew take out every day?"

"Depends," Alonzo Jenkins answered. "Four, six, sometimes as much as ten."

"Do they haul it all away the same day?"

"Sometimes, but mostly they don't. Mostly it just sets there, in case we—in case they need it later on."

"Suppose," said Cap, "we had a night crew working, putting the dirt back in."

"Hee hee," Josh cried delightedly. "Ah hee hee hee. Pass me some more of that nasty liquor."

"I like it, Carter," Ikie approved. "While the night crew is working at full speed, half the day crew is out sick. So they start falling behind and can't catch up."

"Sick from what?" the Reverend Bream demanded.

"The sandwiches, man, the sandwiches," Ikie said irritably. "Chicken salad. Ham salad. Tuna salad. Whatever has mayonnaise in it and can be left out long enough to turn."

"I won't betray you," Reverend Bream answered. "But I personally refuse to do anything that will make people ill. And I don't feel comfortable with the idea of destroying government property, either."

"Good God, man, they're destroying *our* property!" the doctor exclaimed, leaping up with unusual alacrity and spilling a trail of cigarette sparks down his front. Brushing them off and stamping on them, he went on, "If our land isn't worth fighting for, what is? I personally promise you that nothing fatal will be fed to the work crew. As for the machines, they're only machines. Paid for by your taxes and mine. In a sense they belong to us."

"And as soon as we destroy one, they'll replace it with another," Bunky Adams interjected gloomily.

"Ah, but each one of those monsters costs money. A lot of

money," Doc Thompson told him. "This project has cost limits as well as time limits. If it goes too far over budget *or* schedule, the government will send some inspectors around."

"What makes you so sure?" Adams wanted to know.

Fess said, "We can see that the right agencies are informed. Along with the newspapers."

"Isn't there a danger that the press might get too interested in us too, Roaney?" Ikie asked softly.

"Awww," Lonnie drawled, "who gone suspect us? We just a bunch of nice old ignorant Nee-grows. Playin' harmonicas and eatin' fried chicken and singin' hymns."

"*There's* something you can do to help, Reverend," Cap Carter suggested. "Lead the hymn singing. Save the infidels' souls. You could walk around buttonholing the work crew, asking them, 'Brothers, are you saved?' You and your deacons could pass out tracts, give them the full evangelical treatment, even hold a revival meeting. That ought to hold up work for a week or two. If you won't do it, I can guarantee you Reverend Bird will."

"I'll do it," Reverend Bream said, surprisingly. "But I'm still concerned about those tainted sandwiches. Doctor, couldn't you give us some sort of harmless drug to use instead?"

The doctor considered this, then shook his head. "Nope. Ethics are a funny thing, Bream. It might surprise you after some of the things I've said tonight, but I do have them. I'll check the sandwich filling to see if the level of contamination is safe. I'll treat any victim who suffers unusually bad effects. But I won't contribute a single item from my drug cabinet for human sabotage. Maybe I should drop out of this project."

"Nonsense, Doc," Ikie told him. "You're the moving force behind this entire operation. Yes, Lukey?"

"Sir, I know the Young Warriors would like to help."

"That crazy bunch of hotheads? No way. After what they pulled off at the swim club? Impossible. They'd get us all killed."

"Sir," Lukey insisted, "I know they want to be in on this action, and I think they'll do exactly what you say. They need a chance to prove they can be trusted. They're more likely to get out of bounds if you leave them out of it."

KRISTIN LATTANY

"Is that a threat, fella?"

"No, sir. it's just what I know."

Ikie considered this. "You may be right. But don't tell them anything yet, you hear? Wait till we get this thing organized. We've got to lay it out from A to Z, plan it carefully, and make sure we do everything in the right order. The way I see it, we ought to start with the small things, the little harassments, and work up to the big ones. Save our biggest guns for last. Like good generals."

"Yeah, take it nice and slow," Josh Hawkins said. "That way we'll avoid mistakes."

"But not too slow," Ikie said, "because we have to figure that at some point they're going to catch on. Are you making any headway with those notes, Mr. Merchant?"

"My eyes are not as good as they used to be, but with Mr. Adams's help, yes, I have made a positive identification. This is definitely Mayor Abraham Lakes's handwriting. Distorted by stress or drink or both, but indisputably his. We have put the pages in order, and they clearly indicate that the highway will be as enormous as we feared it would. I'm afraid they also prove the mayor had full knowledge of it tonight when he was pretending otherwise."

"I'm sorry to hear that," Fess said.

"So am I," said Ikie, as a look of truce passed between them. "Pass me that bottle."

"It's bone dry," Josh said regretfully, holding it up to the candle. "Not even a little bitty corner left."

"Then," Ikie said, "I propose that we move this meeting to the Blue Moon. We can iron out a lot more of the details there. We have to brief Mame Porritt, anyway. She and her girls can be a big help to us."

"And besides," Fess could not resist adding, "you won't have far to stagger to bed."

"Neither will you, Roaney," Ikie shot back, with less animosity than usual. "But at least you're used to sleeping alone."

21

"We are going to church today. Together!" Abe commanded, the first thing Sunday morning. Church to him meant services at the Protestant Episcopal Chapel of Saint Ignatius (High Church), where he worshiped a complex deity called the Holy Trinity. Bella was sure he believed Baptists, Methodists, and members of all other lower denominations would be yard men and cooks in heaven as on earth, though she was not sure he believed in anything else.

Often Bella had asked him to join her in making the circuit of Mount Moriah African Methodist Episcopal and Peace Baptist and even the holy-rolling Assembly of God, where he might at least get to know and understand more of his constituents. But he had always refused.

So this morning there would be all those head bobbings and genuflections, all that ritual self-crossing, all that spastic kneeling, sitting, standing, *repeat*, like jacks-in-the-box. Services at Saint Ignatius were more like military drills than spiritual communion, Bella thought. Well, at least she would get some much-needed exercise.

And there would also be, she thought with a yawn, the nasal chanting of Father Andrew Merchant, elder brother of Councilman Morris Merchant. Bella rather liked both of the quaint old geezers, but Father Andrew's chanting was so incomprehensibly twangy it might as well be in Latin, and he himself was so ancient he really should be embalmed in a glass casket, like any other holy relic. The chapel was a one-story stucco building without a single gorgeous stained-glass window, only a narrow series of leaded crenels with diamond-shaped panes in muted colors. Architecturally it was the lowest church in town, but it was High.

Bella felt she needed to get high in order to endure it. Perhaps a few drinks would allow her to observe the service passively and with good deportment, as a pleasing blur of colors, scents, and sounds. She beseeched her own god, who was also three persons but more intimate ones—the god who dwelt within Bella, and a mother and father who resembled her parents—to prevent her from giggling at the implications of all those males in swishing lace skirts.

Abe had frequently urged Bella to become confirmed, to which her silent reply was, I already exist, God knows it, and I don't need man-made rituals to confirm it. Besides, at her age the procedures would be humiliating. She had never been baptized in the Episcopal or any other church. Her parents had never even seen fit to have her christened. At maturity, she refused to go through the embarrassment of one ceremony intended for babes in arms, another usually administered to toddlers, and, finally, a series of confirmation classes composed of children younger than Cindy. She poured herself a double shot of vodka in a glass of orange juice.

She needed it to kill the pain. It was better than yesterday's numbness, but the transition was too sudden for her to make without chemical support. On awakening, she had already felt herself coming out of Saturday's stupor. She recalled every detail with stinging clarity. She had cleaned house like a machine, dressed like a mannequin, and behaved like a well-programed robot for that herd of hunky buffaloes Abe'd brought stampeding into her house last night. Mostly large, rude men with huge appetites, they'd helped themselves to her exquisite buffet like pigs jostling at a trough. They were even greedier with the liquor. Soon she realized she was merely an overdressed accessory to the evening and began to recede into the decor.

She listened and learned to attach names to faces. And learned other things. The tall, beefy one with the deep voice was Harry Grafton, state senator from the Fifth District. The pair of short, stocky ones who might be twins, except that one was fair and one dark, were, respectively, county freeholders Sam Moscowitz and Joe Luciano. The little dark one with a pinched face that looked like it had been pulled through a knothole was Joe's older brother, Dominick Luciano, who had (guess how?) been awarded this particular road-building contract by the county. With the gnome were two of his aides, an accountant named Nick Nussbaum, with square black-rimmed glasses, a square face, and square-cut black bangs that gave him a gloomy hound-dog look; and his cement subcontractor, Bill Moscowitz, a youthful, slender, hyperactive version of his broad brother, Sam. Bill's glasses were gold rimmed, modish, and he bounced around a lot.

The one who stood apart from the others, the tall, mustached one who was graying with distinction at the temples and could have modeled for a men's fashion magazine, was Oscar Clarkson DeWitt III, the state highway commissioner. He was the most genteel and the most ill at ease, for reasons that presently became clear.

"Harry," he asked the senator in one of those well-bred, faggoty voices, "are you sure this meeting is wise?"

"Sure, Oscar," the senator boomed back like a foghorn. "Abe here is our man. Isn't that right, Abe?"

"Of course. Have another drink, Harry," Bella's husband said.

"Don't call me Oscar. Call me Clark," the commissioner told the senator.

"Hell," the senator said, ignoring him and staring into his newly brimming glass, "Abe's the whitest nigger I know."

Abe turned his face away. Bella badly wanted to see her husband's expression and whether his complexion was turning paler, darker, or red.

"I get a call from him tonight," Grafton continued, "and I expect him to raise holy hell because he's seen the new plan, and instead he says, 'Come on over to my house tonight and let's talk about it.' That means he's willing to make a deal."

"Too many deals have already been made," the highway commissioner replied shrilly, "and too many of the people who made them are in this room. I thought we agreed that long before things reached this point, you and I were going to get strictly out of it."

"That's the trouble with all you tight-assed WASPs," Grafton replied. "Always want to turn the dirty work over to the dirty ethnics so you can keep your hands clean. If you'd keep your hands in things instead of being scared of a little dirt, your deals would go a lot smoother and you wouldn't get cheated so often."

"I believe you're a WASP yourself, Grafton," the commissioner retorted.

"So does everybody else." Harry Grafton chuckled. "The truth is, I'm three-quarters Irish. That's why I've got three times as much balls as you, DeWitt. Can hold three times as much liquor, too. Gimme another drink, Abe. Just walk the vermouth past the glass."

Abe silently poured Grafton his third martini while DeWitt continued to sip fastidiously from his first goblet of wine.

"Well, if they ever sprang a grand jury investigation on us, all they'd need would be a list of the people in this room."

"Oscar, you know what's wrong with you?" the senator said. "You're too uptight. You can't even go to sleep without checking for federal investigators under the bed. And you haven't done anything in bed *but* sleep for years. What you need is a real drink."

"This *is* a real drink. But you wouldn't know about that," the commissioner said pettishly.

Bella had bought the light wine, the Chateau Gloria Margaux. It was appreciated by at least one of Abe's guests, but not by all.

Dominick Luciano made a disgusting gesture, a combination of picking his nose with his thumb and spitting. "I tasted it. Like cheap toilet water. Phewww. Gimme some good Chianti or nothing."

"You'll always be an ignorant paisan, Dom," his younger brother Joe said. "This is special stuff, much better than your crummy old dago red. But you're too old and crummy yourself to change."

"Well, I don't care what you call me," Dom retorted. "I don't mind being a crummy old dago or a dirty ethnic—or even a dirty nigger—as long as I keep on making lotsa dat dirty money."

"You're making too much of it, Dom," the accountant, Nussbaum, put in glumly. "That dirt you're digging up is literally worth its weight in gold. We gotta find us some more tax shelters fast."

"I'm a partner in two restaurants and a night club. Go burn 'em down or something. Just don't bother me about taxes while I'm eating."

"The big money is in the cement, Dom," the younger Moscowitz said excitedly. "Every time you pave over three square feet of land, you make two bucks profit to my one. And then, when you break up the cement and pave it all over again, our profit doubles. It's beautiful. I tell you, I'm going to cement over this entire township. Throw up some houses on the slabs, move all the slobs out of their city rowhouses, call it Mosky's Bosky Dell or something, and make millions."

The handsome highway commissioner looked at young Bill Moscowitz as if he would like to see him encased in cement. "Half of Dorset Township is farmland, you young idiot. Productive farmland. After you cover it over with cement and sell it to the city slobs, as you call them, what are they going to eat?"

Bill shrugged. "That's their problem. All I know is, it'll sell. Because city people don't really like grass and trees. They think they do;

that's why they want to move to the suburbs, but what they really like is what they're used to. Cement."

"Shut up, Willie," the older Moscowitz said. "How do you know there isn't a tape recorder in this room?"

"I was thinking the same thing," Commissioner DeWitt said, finally accepting a brandy.

Abe, handing it to him, smiled. Bella knew that self-satisfied little smile of his, like a cat's with a belly full of pet goldfish. And suddenly she also knew where the gadget was. He had pointedly told her to leave the dining room wall sconces alone when she was cleaning.

"What I want to know," Grafton growled, "is how he got hold of the plan."

"That," Abe assured him with the same slight smile, "is something you'll never know."

"You drink too much, Grafton," DeWitt said. "Too many things slip out of your mouth. And out of your hands."

"Stop being so nervous, you prick. Relax. And mind your fucking business."

"This is my business," Commissioner DeWitt said, allowing Abe to pour him another snifter of Remy Martin. "I wish all these people weren't here, Lakes, but let's get to the point anyway and get it over with. You got hold of the new highway plan somehow. Now the whole town is on your back about it, or soon will be. Yet you don't seem in the least disturbed. Why? What do you want?"

Abe touched his snifter to the commissioner's, sipped from it, then stared at him levelly over its rim. "Your job," he said.

"You're pulling my leg," the patrician white man said.

"Not at all," Abe replied. "I'm perfectly serious."

"Now look here, fella," DeWitt said patronizingly. "I'm all for integration, but this is pushing things too far. There *are* limits, you know. There's never been a black highway commissioner in this state."

"Don't call me that," Abe said, betraying sudden anger.

"Well, what the hell am I supposed to call you?"

"Mister Lakes. Until you start calling me Mister Commissioner." Although Bella hated everything else she'd witnessed tonight, she could not help admiring the way he talked up to this arrogant aristocrat.

"This is ridiculous," the reddening commissioner said. "It's outrageous. I'm not staying here a moment longer."

"I think you ought to hear me out, Mr. DeWitt. Excuse me, I distinctly remember hearing you say you prefer to be called 'Clark.' Well, then, Clark, we all know you're going to make a very nice bundle out of this project—enough to buy yourself a successful campaign for the u.s. Senate or a cozy diplomatic post or a whole island all to yourself to retire on. And I think you'll want to leave your present job in Trenton once the heat starts coming your way."

"He's right, Oscar," Grafton said. "You really ought to resign. You don't have the balls for this kind of action, the way you're always worrying about grand juries and guilt by association."

"And tape recorders," young Bill Moscowitz added, with a loud, braying, imbecilic laugh.

Above Bella's head one of the sconce lights flickered. Simultaneously she heard a soft click as the tiny reel reversed itself, followed by a muted whir as it resumed spinning. No one else in the room noticed.

"Yes, and tape recorders too," Grafton continued. "You worry about everything, when nothing at all has gone wrong. If anything does go wrong you'll probably fall apart. Why not take your share and get out now, while you're clean? Step down. Or up. Or out. It's up to you, Oscar. You can go anywhere you want and forget you ever knew anything about this road."

"As long as you make room for me," Abe reminded DeWitt.

"A colored commissioner?" DeWitt wondered. "The governor will never go for it."

"The governor will go for anything Washington goes for, Commissioner," Abe told him coolly. "And you're the one with all the connections in Washington. You got this project approved by your friends in the Department of Commerce. You're the guy who brought in the funds, and that means you can name any successor you choose. I don't mind being called 'colored,' by the way."

Bella thought she heard the kitchen door open softly. It startled her heart into skipping a beat. But she remained still, and no one else reacted.

"I call you an impudent, upstart, pushy nigger, Lakes."

No one but Bella, who was already alerted, seemed to hear the soft steps in the kitchen. Big as he was, Chief Benson Boyd could move as silently as a panther when he wanted to. Suddenly he appeared, towering over the swinging Dutch doors. He raised a tiny camera and took three pictures in rapid succession, then ducked back out of sight.

"Who," Dom Luciano demanded, "was that great big monster with the little spy camera?"

Abe shrugged. "You might as well come on in, Boyd. Gentlemen, meet my best friend and chief of police, Benson Boyd."

Boyd, in sneakers and clownish sports clothes, managed to be almost as impressive as in uniform. He nodded politely, said, "Good evening, gentlemen," and extended a boulder-sized hand. No one took it.

"I want that camera!" DeWitt shrieked in a high, hysterical voice, and moved toward the towering chief.

Boyd reached inside his improbable purple-and-pink silk sports shirt and drew out not his camera but his .38. "Sorry, sir," he said politely. "You can't have the camera. It's police property."

"How do I know you're a policeman? You're not in uniform," the highway commissioner demanded.

"I've been off duty since ten o'clock," Chief Boyd said, flashing his badge.

"I think you'll find," Abe said, "that Chief Boyd will be invaluable in keeping order in Lakestown until the project is finished."

"How many of your people know about the new plan?" DeWitt wanted to know in a calmer voice. Boyd put his sidearm away but went on watching him carefully.

Abe shrugged. "Whether it's two, two hundred, or two thousand, what difference does it make? They all have eyes. They'll find out what's happening pretty soon anyway. The point is, you don't want any interference. Disturbances or demonstrations might get attention in the press and other places. I promise you there won't be any—if you keep your part of the bargain."

"How can you back up that promise?" DeWitt demanded.

Abe flickered an eyebrow at Chief Boyd, who drew his handgun again and gave it an elaborately casual inspection before putting it away.

"Hell, he's got us by the balls, Oscar. We underestimated him. This is one smart nigger. Better draft that letter of resignation," the senator advised, "and start making plans to move on to better things."

KRISTIN LATTANY

The commissioner's voice again lost its well-bred modulation. "Wait a minute. What has he got, exactly? A couple of pictures? One witness?" His eyes rested on Bella and seemed for the first time to see her. "All right, two witnesses. His best friend and his wife. So what?"

"Those, yes," Abe said smoothly, "and some other things. Such as a town full of people who'd like nothing better than to cause trouble for every single one of you."

Bella could not help admitting that her husband had played a masterful game, even making his local opposition work for him. But somehow she felt he had overestimated the strength of his hand.

"Told you, Oscar." Grafton chuckled, clearly enjoying twitting the commissioner by using his least favorite name. As a matter of fact, Bella thought, he was enjoying the entire evening too much for her peace of mind. He might, of course, be drunk. "This is the smartest fucking nigger I ever met. Let's agree to give him what he wants. We know we'll get ours. Then let's all have a drink to that."

"Just one more thing, gentlemen," Abe put in urbanely. "It would be useful in maintaining order if I could make the prospects sweeter for some of my most influential citizens—like Boyd, here."

"Sure, sure," Dom Luciano agreed, as if it were all up to him. "Makes me feel better, to tell the truth. I was beginning to wonder what fucking kind of town this was, on account of the cops never came around. It made me nervous. I always feel nervous until I've done business with the cops."

"You're not in the gambling racket anymore, Dom," his brother Joe reminded him. "You're a legitimate businessman now."

"Gambling, graft, what's the difference?" Dom retorted. "It all comes down to the same thing—money. You always got to spread some around."

"Money will satisfy some of the people I have in mind," Abe said. "But there are others to whom I should be able to offer positions in state or county government. I can put a few on my own staff, of course, but it wouldn't look well if they were all in my department."

"So it's your department already, is it?" DeWitt snarled.

Grafton cut him off. "We'll work out all those little details later, Mayor," he said briskly, suddenly sober and businesslike while DeWitt, who had seemed so abstemious, was gulping down his fourth brandy and melting into an alcoholic puddle. "It's getting late. Where's your lovely missus? Oh, there she is, over there. Mrs. Lakes, thank you for a delicious treat. The most delicious part of the evening was meeting you, of course. I'm afraid we've bored you to death with our business discussions."

"Not at all," she said, with a slight smile that caused a frown to appear on Abe's forehead.

"I hope," Grafton added to Bella, "that you and your husband can be our guests for dinner sometime next weekend. I've always given Abe hell for not bringing you over, but now that I've finally met you, I can see why he's kept you all to himself. I don't blame him. I'll tell my wife to give you a call."

It was all over very suddenly, like the dropping of a curtain on a play. Bella rose to see her guests out and stood beside Abe in the open doorway to watch them get into their cars. She almost spoiled the per- fection of her role at the very last moment, when she observed that the men's positions in the hierarchy of corruption could be discerned precisely by the cars they drove She stifled a giggle as DeWitt climbed unsteadily into a gray Bentley, whereas Nussbaum and the younger Moscowitz got behind the wheels of identical scarlet Cadillacs, the kind known all over the East Coast as the Petty Mobster Model. The rest had larger late-model Cadillacs of more somber hues, except Grafton, who drove a middle-aged dark blue Lincoln the same year, size, and color as her husband's. Abe had obviously been choosing his models and making his plans for a long, long time.

He surprised her by ending the evening as he had begun it, with a dry kiss on the cheek. "You were wonderful, Bella," he told her. "Everything was perfect. And we won, girl. We won! Did you hear him? He invited us to dinner!" The excitement he had suppressed all evening was overflowing like a little boy's.

Bella answered softly, "Don't order your Bentley yet, dear."

22

At Saint Ignatius's, Bella went through the correct motions with only an occasional nudge from her husband and endured the interminable service in a pleasant alcoholic daze, right up to the recessional of altar boys, vestrymen, priest, choir, and congregation, in that order. Anglican services, she thought, waiting for their turn to file out; Anglophilia: sounds like a fatal disease. Well, niggers who have it *are* sick. I have Anglophobia, I think. Must mean I'm healthy.

Old Father Andrew had taken up his post at the chapel door to mumble incoherent greetings to each parishioner. Bella, sober now, wondered if he drank before services, too. But his comment to her was quite clear. "So glad to have you with us again, Mrs. Lakes. I see you've taken advantage of the recent relaxation of Pauline doctrine."

"Pauline who?" she answered ignorantly, causing Abe to look severely pained.

"I meant Saint Paul's dictum that women attending worship should cover their heads in shame."

"In shame of what?" Bella asked him, tossing her unruly mane. "Why should I be ashamed of being a woman, if God created me that way?" That Paul, she thought, was no saint. He was a dirty-minded old man. And so, probably, are you.

Old Father Andrew chuckled appreciatively. "Your point is well taken, my dear, though I do not think Paul meant it exactly the way it sounds. I would enjoy having a discussion with you about it sometime. But all I meant to say was, 'Welcome back, with a hat or without one.' Because the archdiocese has ruled that you are now free to choose. Mayor, thank you for attending, and for bringing your wife."

Jane and Greta Grimes were just ahead of them, dressed almost identically in large-brimmed straw hats, print silk dresses, and white gloves, though Greta, as usual, looked smart, whereas Jane merely looked dowdy and bewildered, like a little girl dressed up in her big sister's clothes.

Greta turned and said, "I remember you never *would* wear a hat,

Bella, even when you were a little girl. Father Andrew always used to have to put a choir hat on you."

"Maybe that's why I've always hated hats," Bella responded coolly.

But Greta had turned away from her and was shamelessly flirting with Abe, batting absurdly long false eyelashes. "My, Mr. Mayor, don't *you* look handsome today."

Anyone can look handsome if he has nothing else to do but order his breakfast and put on a shirt someone else ironed and a suit someone else picked up for him at the cleaners, Bella thought hotly. You should have seen Humpty Dumpty the other night before I put him back together again.

Greta, cozily linking arms with Abe, said, "I want to talk to you, Mayor. I did some thinking last night after the council meeting and I want you to know you have my wholehearted support. If there's anything Jane or I can do, anything at all . . ."

The four of them had walked a dozen paces from the church. "There is," he said firmly. "I notice you and your sister are always, er, presentable."

"We try, sir," Greta said coyly. "We try."

"Well. my wife isn't. Not as presentable as she needs to be. She needs instructions in grooming. Beauty routines, hair arranging, clothes shopping, all that sort of thing. I was wondering if you could find the time."

The bastard. She knew she was a thrown-together mess again this morning, but it was his fault. She'd just begun to dress after fixing his breakfast when he told her to hurry up, he was ready and it was getting late. So she'd grabbed the first clothes she could find, with the results that her skirt was rump-sprung, her stockings laddered, and her jacket stained. And of course there were no white gloves on her sink-reddened hands. If Bella had ever owned any white gloves, she'd long ago forgotten where she'd put them.

"Why, of course!" Greta exclaimed with a glee that would grant Bella, she was sure, a verdict of justifiable homicide. She turned to her with a vampirish smile and said, "Bella, it *is* a shame the way you neglect yourself. If I had half the material you have to work with, I'd be the toast of three continents." She laughed girlishly, then cast a critical eye at her intended victim. "All that lovely hair, just *hanging*. What you need is a good blunt cut. Or—have you ever worn an upsweep?" Before Bella could guess what she was about to do, Greta reached out an ungloved hand, took a handful of Bella's hair, and tugged firmly, as if making sure it was attached to its owner's skull, before lifting it.

That did it. Bella's self-control snapped like a taut rubber hand. Knocking the other woman's hand away, she screamed, "Let go my hair, you body-snatching bitch! You won't get to lay your buzzard claws on me till I'm dead, and not even then, if I can help it. Get this corpse polisher away from me, Abe, before somebody has to sweep *her* up off the sidewalk! The idea. Asking her to clean me up! I *am* clean. *She* smells like Charnel House Number Five. I won't let her grave-digging hands touch me, and I won't be your whore either, do you understand? I'll be your wife, but I won't be your whore. If you want one, you'll have to come looking for me in vulgar cafés. I'm taking the car. You can walk home."

Behind her she heard Greta commiserating with Abe and offering him a lift, but she did not care. Maybe Anglophilia and necrophilia went hand in hand, like Abe and Greta, like pimples and chicken pox. All she knew was she did not care to come in contact with either disease again.

23

One more time, Lord,
One more time.
You know I'm glad
To be in the number
One more time.

Mount Moriah A.M.E.'s choir of thirty voices sounded like three hundred as they swayed and sang to the accompaniment of their jiggling, sweating organist and director, Randy Barnes.

"One more time!" echoed the Reverend Mrs. Baretta Farmer, the oldest woman Methodist preacher in the county, maybe in the world. "Yes, Lord, you know I praise you every morning just for letting me open my eyes. And for letting me get up and walk to church, so I can be with this congregation again. You know it's sweet to be in the number one more time, and I thank you Jesus!"

"Thank you, Jesus!" repeated Vinnie Coddums with brisk little claps of her hands. She felt less uncomfortable than she had thought she would in this strange church. Cindy had insisted on coming here today, to Lou's church, instead of to Vinnie's beloved Peace Baptist. Just this once, because the child was heartbroken about her sweetheart's death, she had given in. But she had an uneasy sense that Cindy's will was growing stronger daily and that there would be more giving in in the future.

To make matters worse, Lou's older brother, Tommy, seemed to have taken on the responsibility of consoling Cindy. Yesterday she and Tommy had wandered off together in search of unspecified things to do. Vinnie had been grateful at the time that someone was offering to distract the child from her grief. After a night of listening to Cindy's sobbing and a morning of watching her mope around with a blank expression as if she'd been struck dumb again, she was relieved to have someone take her out of the house. Only later—much later, for Tommy had brought Cindy home around midnight—did it occur to her that the

KRISTIN LATTANY

older Adams boy might have other ideas about her daughter besides consolation. But Cindy had found her tongue again, and the words it spoke in response to Vinnie's clumsy questions were definite, sharp. "Good night, Mother. I want to go to Lou's church tomorrow."

Reverend Baretta was growing hoarse, but her voice still carried throughout the church. "But there is one who is not able to be in the number this time. Oh yes! It's always sad when someone passes over. We always wish we could be with them one more time. But when a person is as old as I am, there's no reason to fuss and grieve. When these old bones are laid to rest, I don't want nobody to cry. Just say, 'Old Baretta's walked more than her share of miles, and now she's walking her last mile to glory.' Hallelujah!"

There were scattered responses of enthusiasm from the congregation.

"But when a *young* person passes over, it's hard. Oh yes, it's hard to accept and understand. But remember, people, it's not meant for us to understand God's ways. We're only supposed to praise Him!"

"Oh yes! Praise him!" came several echoes from the front bench, while just behind it Vinnie, Cindy, Tommy, and the rest of the Adams family sat in stolid silence.

"Now y' know I'm not going to preach little Lou Adams's funeral here and now. The time for that is Tuesday night at seven P.M., and Reverend Bream will be preaching the service. But I do want to say a few words about young Lou. He was one of the nicest young men I ever knew. Always willing to do favors and run errands for old ladies like me, always helping out around the church here, always respectful and obedient to his mommy and daddy, who raised him in a good Christian home."

To her left Vinnie observed Lou's parents holding hands and then, closer to her, Tommy and Cindy doing the same. She got up clumsily from her aisle seat, pointed Cindy toward it, and changed places with her daughter, placing herself firmly between the young pair, like a wall of enforced virtue. Except that the wall did not feel as strong and solid as it once had.

"The best thing," Reverend Baretta was saying, "you can do for young Lou Adams is raise your children to be like him. Help all our young people, Lord! Help them to grow up straight and strong! Talk to them, Lord! Talk to their parents; tell them to bring them to church and pray with them!"

"Yes!"

"And now a selection by the choir, with a guest soloist, another lovely young person, Miss Lucinda Coddums."

Vinnie did not realize her daughter's name had been called until Cindy rose, walked confidently to the choir box, shook her head when offered the microphone, and filled the church with her unaided voice.

> Come, Lord Jesus,
> Walk by my side.
> Come, Lord Jesus,
> And be my guide.
> Days are dark,
> Nights are long.
> Good friends are few,
> And they all are gone.
> Come, Lord Jesus,
> And walk with me.

When the choir's last echo had died away, Reverend Baretta Farmer sat down, mopping sweat from her brow, and Reverend William Bream took her place.

"Lord help us," he said, expressing everyone's appreciation for Cindy's moving solo. "Thank you, Jesus. I had a sermon prepared for this morning, but I think Reverend Farmer has said it all for me. And that young lady just sang it better than either of us could preach it. But I will touch on the subject a little anyway. My text is from the first book of Peter, the second chapter, the fifteenth and sixteenth verses. 'For so is the will of God, that with well-doing ye may put to silence the ignorance of foolish men. As free, and not using your liberty for a cloak of maliciousness, but as the servants of God.'

"Now Peter is talkin' here about freedom. Not the freedom to run around steppin' on everybody else's rights, or to go talkin' behind people's backs, but the freedom to live as servants of God! And the time and place to learn the limits of our freedom is when we are children, in our parents' homes. In line with what Peter said, we can't expect our children to know the limits of their freedom unless we set limits on our *own* behavior. We should be both models and lawgivers to our children—and we should send them to church to learn God's laws, so they will just naturally want to use their freedom in the right ways.

"And talking about God's laws brings something else to my mind. After some of the things that have been happening lately, I find myself growing less and less concerned with *man*-made laws." There was a slight stir in the congregation as he thundered, *"God's* laws are supreme, and when men's laws contradict them men's laws must be broken!"

Reverend Bream waited for the excitement to die down before he continued, in a sober voice, "I'm talkin' 'bout racism, people. I'm talkin' about the injustices of mighty Whitey. I'm tired of waitin' on the Lord to bring down the mighty from their seats of power and exalt the rest of us. I want to be one of the servants the Lord helps because they help themselves! And I am so determined that justice must be brought to bear on this matter of the high and mighty trampling on the rights of the lowly, and some people building highways all over other people's *right*-of-ways, that I'm about ready to call for an all-out revolution!"

Alfonso Telford, the least likely of the Young Warriors to show emotion, leaped up and cried, "All *right!"*

"People, you know what I'm talking about. Our town is being destroyed right under our eyes. I'm convinced it's the Devil's work, and that to sit back and let it happen would be cooperating with the Devil. I say, they have broken God's commandment by coveting their neighbors' land. Our land. I say they got a lot of trespasses to be forgiven, 'cause they're trespassin' on just about everybody in this town. And I say God's law commands me to fight this injustice! I will not commit aggression, but I *will* fight to defend what is yours and mine. I will not commit violence, because God's law limits me by telling me, 'Thou shall not kill.' But I will oppose this evil in every other way that is consonant with God's law speakin' to me through my conscience. I call on you to join me and all the others who are in the fight with me."

What followed was the loudest pandemonium permissible in a Methodist church, most of it enthusiastically assenting. When it finally died down, Reverend Bream said, "There will be a meeting in the basement immediately after services for those who want to participate. And now we will have another selection by our choir and our guest soloist, Miss Lucinda Coddums."

Vinnie watched with mixed emotions as Cindy rose, confident and glowing in the bright coral dress Bella had bought her, and walked forward while the pianist, more skilled than Vinnie but with no more spirit, struck up the majestic, rolling chords of "We Shall Not Be Moved."

Vinnie was proud of her daughter, yes, but disturbed to discover there were so many things she did not know about her. The more Cindy learned to talk, it seemed, the more secretive she became. She had not told her mother, for instance, that she would be singing at Mount Moriah this morning. No doubt she and Tommy Adams had planned it. And probably Cindy had spent a good part of yesterday right here, rehearsing. Fine. But Vinnie stole a sideways glance at Tommy, whose features were no longer childish, whose smooth, tan cheeks seemed to grow darker every minute with their imminent beard, and wondered what else those two were planning. Vinnie did not know, but she had a feeling a lot more surprises were in store.

24

A massive hangover with a life of its own kept Fess pinned to his bed most of Sunday. Each time its victim tried to get up, it sat on his chest and bared its fangs like a vicious police dog. Fess tried to appease the beast with one of its hairs, only to find the insides of his head slipping loose from their moorings and sliding back and forth like a cargo of Jell-O in a storm. His head was full of words floating in a medium of unbearable clarity—words left over from the night before, far too many of them, the most preposterous and embarrassing ones, being his.

"God's rump print!" he had declaimed in response to some pious counsel of restraint offered by the Reverend Bream. "The indisputable indentation of the Deity's derriere. That's what that excavation is, my friends. And if we do not erase it, there is no reason to believe the Deity is going to do anything but defecate in the same spot. On us, that is. And anyone who thinks otherwise is a fatuous fool. What else is there to do with a desecration of creation but defecate on it?"

The Reverend Bream was showing signs of discomfort: a nervous fingering of his collar, frequent glances over his shoulder, and constant swallowings of air.

Fess, however did not shut up. Oh, no, not he. In his best professorial jargon he ranted on, "Look around you, gentlemen. Behold the parameters of progress, once mere traceries on some dolt's drawing board, grown fat in their passage through the bowels of bureaucracy and now solidifying into permanence with the inevitability of cement.

"I have studied all the available data, gentlemen, and found that the useful contributions of cement to human life are limited to two or three basic functions. One, the economical construction of buildings. Two, the mass manufacture of sewer pipes. And a possible third—if you will pardon me, Doctor—the creation of objects of somewhat dubious artistic value.

"There is a fourth use of cement, the one that concerns us here. I refer to the paving of paths for gasoline-powered vehicles that the depletion-level tables of the earth's fossil fuels have already shown to be obsolete. There are those who insist on ignoring the statistics because ours is a progressive society, and it is the nature of progress to proceed with ever-accelerating speed. There have always been such fools, and there always will be.

"However, gentlemen, since we presumably are not fools but intelligent beings in pursuit of knowledge, let us not ignore the statistics. Opposed to the two or three functions of cement that are useful to society I have found one thousand, eight hundred, and thirty-three that are inimical to human life. They consist of the various forms of edible matter that cannot be nurtured on cement. One cannot, for example, plant yams or other tubers in it, or peanuts, or melons, or collards, or mustards, or lettuce, or other greens.

"Yet we are told that we must henceforth do without the vegetables that sustain us for the sake of an artificial need, the incessant movement to which this go-go society has become addicted. But why? Are you going anywhere? Am I? Are we not content to stay in this pleasant place where we are? Of course we are, unless the cement mixer starves us to death with its life-destroying excretions! And that is why I say we must change the parameters of progress. We must develop a new paradigm!"

He was shoved down into his seat by Ikie's broad hand. "I don't know what a parameter is, but I do want to talk about the perimeter and how we can infiltrate it," Ikie said. "I guess, now that Ronald Running Mouth is quiet, we can have our meeting."

But the way Fess remembered it, it was less a meeting than a brawl.

Mame left the bottle on the table and retreated to a quiet corner to go over the books with her ex-husband, Lester. The Porritts were one of the many couples Fess knew who seemed to get along much better after than before their divorce. They lived apart, but Lester Porritt retained a half share in the Blue Moon, and his careful handling of money probably kept it going.

Another odd couple that were unfortunately still wed were Big Bertha Barnes, the three-hundred-pound blues singer at Loveland, and her husband, Randy, who was the organist and choir director at Mount Moriah A.M.E. and two other churches. While his wife lapped pink gins with the tip of her tongue, like a cat daintily sipping milk, Randy gulped ginger ale and exhorted her to give up show business and return to the righteous fold. "Come back to the church, Bert," he urged, "and I'll come back to you. The Lord gave you that voice to sing His gospel and nothing else."

"Will you listen to this faggot?" she demanded of no one in particular. But as she turned on the bar stool she surrounded rather than sat upon, her very hugeness forced everyone to pay attention. "What makes him think I want him back? I put him out in the first place. Know why? He never looked at me. He spent all his time in the bedroom looking at his own behind in the mirror. Now, I ask you, what's so goddamned cute about his rear end?"

"Bertha, dear, please stop blaspheming. And please keep our business out of the street."

"I'm a mind to put *you* out in the street, you pious-ass pansy."

"Whore of Babylon!" he shouted.

A solid fist at the end of Big Bertha's dimpled arm connected with her husband's paunch and he toppled backward to the floor. His foot came up, only to collide with Booty's satin-upholstered rear end. She whirled, pulled him to a sitting position with one hand, gave him a rapid one-two punch with the other. Booty was preparing to finish Randy off. Big Bertha moved her aside with the ease of an elephant brushing off a fly, picked up her husband tenderly, and carried him out the door.

"Ain't love grand," Mame observed from among her ledgers.

Seizing his opportunity, Fess rose to his feet and resumed his lecture. "Let us enumerate the possibilities," he began, "which might enter into our paradigm. We can create a new modality of existence, or we can revert to an old one. The latter course seems to me the most productive. Bring back the horse, if necessary. Bring back the plow and the mule! Bring back the rubbing board and the scald pot, and get rid of the washing machines! Bring back the . . ."

Ikie cut him off with a blood-curdling war whoop. That was the last thing Fess remembered. Probably he had passed out and been put to bed by someone, because he did not recall getting there himself.

Now, slowly, painfully, he got up again. His left foot seemed to have died while he was asleep, and he could move only by dragging it. It would be a miracle, he thought as he hobbled into the Blue Moon's dining room, if anything at all had been organized here last night.

Today the place bore a startling resemblance to a hospital, which was probably, Fess thought, where he belonged. Mame, her girls, and Big Bertha were lined up in a row in dazzling white uniforms, and Randy Barnes at the piano was leading them in singing "Nearer, My God, to Thee."

All this was so bewildering that Fess began to wonder if the rest of him had died along with his foot. But he returned to life when Bella Lakes tumbled in and collapsed into a nearby chair like a marionette who had lost her supporting strings. She was no longer the Bella he had known. All her handsomeness, he decided, had been held together by her proud carriage. But now, as she slumped and drooped spinelessly, he saw not only the disarray of her hair and the rumpled state of her clothing but the wrinkles around her eyes and the pouches beneath them, and the sagging cheek muscles that had made deep grooves from her nose to the corners of her mouth, pulling them downward. Age had suddenly caught up with Bella. And so, judging by the frightened look in her eyes, had something worse.

Because she was no longer a goddess, merely another mutilated mortal, Fess had no qualms about addressing her.

"You look," he said, edging his chair closer to hers, "as if you could use a friend."

"So do you," she said bluntly, taking him in with a direct gaze that did not drive the specter of fear from her eyes.

"Well, then, we have something in common."

"I doubt it."

"Let's have a drink together anyway," Fess said boldly, and called, "Mame!"

"I'm busy right now," the proprietress called back. "Bella, why don't you join our choir? We're gonna sing that highway straight on to Glory."

"I can't carry a tune," Bella said flatly.

"Then how come you were in here the other night belting out a solo?"

"That," Bella said, "was the other night."

"Can't you see the lady needs to be left alone? And, maybe, a drink?" Fess said.

"My license says I can't serve liquor on Sundays without food. And I got no cook. But," Mame relented as she took in Bella's condition, "I won't notice if you go behind the bar and serve yourselves. Now, Lily, see if you can stay with the tune this time. You been throwin' all the rest of us off."

"Maybe I'm not the friend you want," Fess said, after they had touched glasses and sat for five minutes of awkward silence.

"It's not you, Fess. It's not anybody. It's me," Bella said, each word sounding as if it cost her great effort. "I think—I've got to—to learn to be friends with myself again, before I can learn to be be friends with anybody else."

"That seems sound," he murmured.

"I need to get away. But the only place I could think of to come was here. Do you think Mame would rent me a cabin for a few days?"

Fess considered this idea. "Probably. She seems to be training the girls for a different line of work next week."

The notes of "It Will Be Glory" bounced to their ears. It sounded pretty good to Fess, except for Lily's off-key soprano.

Randy, quivering with outraged artistic sensibility, leaped up from the piano stool and told her, "You better not sing. You better just stand there and shake a tambourine."

"Don't have a tambourine," Lily told him.

"Shake a couple of pot lids, then. Rattle a fork and a spoon. Or a set of false teeth. Anything. Just don't sing. You look all right, but you got about as much soul as a cold boiled potato."

"Don't be so hard on the child, Randolph," Big Bertha cooed. "She's trying."

"Don't tell me how to direct a choir, Bertha," he retorted. "*I'm* trying to turn this bunch of tone-deaf hookers into gospel singers, and trying to get used to you again, too. Neither one is easy, believe me."

A brash new voice intruded itself. "Bella, I see you're here. Does that mean you've made up your mind?"

"No, Ikie," Bella said. "I'm not even sure I have a mind anymore."

"You were pretty damn emphatic about having one the last time I saw you."

"That was years ago," Bella said, filling her glass to the brim with a shaking hand.

"Hey, take it easy. *I'm* supposed to be the drunk. Remember?"

"I don't know what I am anymore," Bella said, and downed half a tumblerful of vodka.

"That won't help you figure it out. I know, believe me. Listen, baby . . ." Ikie slid an arm around her shoulders. At his touch, Bella began to shudder violently.

"Hey, baby, what happened? What I got? Leprosy, all of a sudden?"

"It's not you, Ikie. Please believe me. I just need some time to . . . to pull myself together."

Ikie withdrew his arm. "Sure, sure. Take all the time you need." His tone was icy, covering, Fess was certain, hurt pride.

"Oh, I'm so tired of explaining." Bella's voice peaked to a high, hysterical note. "I'm so tired of everything. How can I make you understand? Remember, I said to you one time, hands that touch dead bodies will never touch mine?"

"Yeah, yeah. It was a joke or somethin'."

"It was no joke. I meant it. But it happened today. I've always had this thing about undertakers. Ever since I was sixteen, and had to go to the funeral parlor by myself to . . . to look at what was left of my family . . . and sign permission for what they did to them. Stuffed them, sewed them up, painted them. It was obscene! And it took every cent I had. Now I don't want anybody to touch me again, ever, unless—until—" Unable to complete her sentence, she shuddered and covered her face with her hands as a long, gaunt shadow fell across their table. Booty, the first to see its owner, screamed.

In his ebony masklike face, the Baron Potter's eyes were as bright and hypnotic as beacons. "Miz Grimes sent me to fetch you, Miz Lakes," he said. "Your husband wants you home."

Bella's face was ghastly. "I'm not ready to go home."

"You heard the lady, Potter," Ikie said. "She doesn't want to come with you, and nobody's dead around here that I know of, so go away." He did not succeed in budging the Baron or in dimming his disquieting grin.

KRISTIN LATTANY

Mame was more direct. "Death, you get off these premises right now. Nobody around here's got time for dying today. We got too much work to do. So you just move on to somebody else's house. You hear?"

"You mistake me for someone else. I am just an assistant," the Baron said softly. Just the same, he backed away as Mame approached him vigorously with a broom with which she clearly intended to beat or sweep him away.

After he had left, Mame went on sweeping a path that followed his to the door and over the sill. When she was finished, she closed the door, propped the broom against it, and complained, "Now ain't this a mess? With all the other work we got to do, now I got to do a lot of spirit work, too. Got to burn a mess of candles and scrub down this whole place with drive-off water. Got to put things at all the doorsills to keep that buzzard away. Thank Jesus I had me a little Four Thieves Vinegar to pour on that broom, but I ain't got the rest of the stuff I need. Drat the luck! Lily, I'll make up a list. You run over to Josh Hawkins's store and get it for me."

She licked a pencil stub and wrote as she thought out loud. "A dozen sulfur candles. A dozen green driving-off candles. Four quarts of Four Thieves Vinegar and two cans of Guinea pepper. That oughta do it."

Josh Hawkins now seemed more enigmatic to Fess than ever. Obviously, he had stock on his shelves that Fess had never heard of, with uses he could not imagine. If he could ever figure Josh out, he thought, he would finally understand his people, or at least that portion of them who resided in Lakestown. Then, because Bella appeared near collapse, he called, "Excuse me, Mrs. Porritt, but do you have a spare cabin out back that Mrs. Lakes could use?"

Mame came over to their table, took a close look at Bella's devastated face, and said, "Lord this is more serious than I thought. Gimme that list back, Lily." She wrote down more items. "Some white mustard seed, and a half gallon of blue scrub water. Some White Rose incense, and some of that five-fingered grass for herb tea." To Bella she said, "You can have Cabin Four, but you got to let me prepare it for you first."

Bella rose shakily to her feet. "I don't care what it looks like, as long as it's got a place to lie down. I'm sure it'll be fine the way it is now."

"Looks ain't what this is all about," Mame told her. "Death is been here huntin' for you, woman. And you look like you been touched by him."

Mame bustled back and forth between the dining room and the kitchen, lighting sulfur candles, sprinkling sulfur powder at all the doors, placing cut onions and garlic cloves in odd corners. Then she came over to their table and set a cup of tea in front of Bella. "Drink this. It's not as good as what I sent for, but it'll help."

"Ugh. It smells funny, and it looks strange," Bella said. But she drank the orange liquid anyway and admitted that it tasted good.

"Did you eat today?" Mame asked her.

"No, I'm on a diet."

"What?" Ikie roared. "Woman, if you lose a single voluptuous ounce, I'll find a way to punish you, and so will God."

Mame agreed with him. "This ain't no time for dietin', Bella. You under attack. You need all the strength you can get to fight it off. Booty, heat up those pig tails and limes I got on the stove and bring Miz Bella some. Bring an extra bowl, too. . . . After you eat, you can have some more liquor if you want, Bella, but pour the first sip out of each glass in the bowl I'm gonna put on the floor. And it'd be best if you switched to rum."

"Why rum?"

" 'Cause that's his favorite taste. Put the first spoonful of your food in his bowl, too. See, if you feed him, he won't be so hungry and he won't be in such a hurry to come back lookin' for you."

"When can we start rehearsing again?" Randy Barnes wanted to know.

Mame straightened up. "Right now. Least till Lily gets back. Then we got more important work to do."

"Devil work," Randy muttered. "Left-handed religion. But what else can a person expect in a place like this?"

Ignoring him, Mame requested, "Please pick some other hymns besides them old sad ones about leavin' this world, Randy."

By the time she had finished her food and tea, Bella was smiling. After her first rum, she began humming along with the music. Ikie was encouraged enough by this to put a hand on her shoulder. She flinched, and he withdrew it.

"I'm sorry, Ikie, but I still can't stand for anybody to touch me."

"It's okay. Have another rum." He poured one for her carefully, remembering to put the first few drops into the Baron's bowl. He poured one for himself, too, taking the same precaution, then touched his glass to hers. "Here's to you, baby. You'll come through. I can wait till you do."

"Thanks, Ikie," Bella said, smiling, though tears appeared in her eyes.

Bella's second rum brightened her eyes. Her third put her on her feet and inspired her to add her voice to the choir, singing with great feeling that she was glad to be in the number one more time.

Fess stomped his numb foot on the floor, keeping time to the music and also trying, vainly, to restore circulation. He had been watching Ikie for reactions to Mame's procedures and had been disappointed when he saw none.

"I take it," he said, "that you share Mame's beliefs."

"Let's say I respect them, Roaney. It's not a matter of belief, anyway. It's a matter of knowledge. I *know* there are unseen forces of evil in this world. I have my ways of dealing with them, Mame has hers, and I hope you have yours. It probably all amounts to the same thing. Lighting candles to chase away the darkness. Let's have a drink together. I've decided to be your friend. You pour. Don't forget to give Death his due."

Fess solemnly poured the skimmings of each drink into the bowl, then touched his glass to Ike's. "To what," he asked, "do I owe this surprising decision?"

"It takes me a long time to make up my mind about people, Roaney," Ikie answered. "But once I do, I'm your friend for life."

"I'll drink to that. I'm grateful. Although," he added after swallowing, "in my case, you probably aren't making a long-term commitment."

Ikie had either too much delicacy or too much stoicism to give this information any response but an expressionless stare. Instead he provided an explanation for his offer of friendship. "Bella's in trouble. I care about that woman, and I could see you were trying help her.

"Besides," he added quickly, as if to keep the discussion from becoming emotional, "we can't afford petty differences right now. There's a lot to be done, and it calls for a united effort. We drew up a tough schedule last night after you fell asleep, and I think it looks pretty workable. Tonight the work crew starts refilling operations. Tomorrow morning the children show up, along with all the adults we can get. Tomorrow afternoon we start confusing them with religion. Tomorrow night our crew works all night, hopefully undoing whatever the day crew's managed to accomplish. Tuesday morning we really start to blitz them with religion. And then, when the preaching begins to wear thin, we lead them into temptation. Of course we can't have a rigid schedule, we have to see how it goes, keep it flexible, but it looks pretty good to me."

"Sounds good to me, too. What do you want me to do?"

"Nothing but observe, tomorrow. After that, I want you to supervise the daytime activities. The able-bodied men will have to rest as much as possible in the daytime so they can work all night."

Fess was stung by Ikie's last remark in a way that no amount of friendship and trust could assuage. But he knew it was realistic.

"Well," he said, pouring drinks for himself, his new friend, and their enemy, "this disabled body is at your service."

25

Fess did not really believe that the previous night's session had produced any serious planning until much later, after Bella had been bathed nine times in Waste-Away tea and made to drink almost another tubful of the same liquid. She seemed better for the treatment, though Fess did not like the hysterical note in her laugh when she was loaned one of Lily's nightgowns, a clinging ruby red number with a center-front slit almost to the crotch. She accepted it without complaining, though, and went meekly to her chaste bed in the thoroughly fumigated Cabin Four, after lending him her car keys without question.

Fess had borrowed them because he was still too hampered by his frozen foot to walk all the way to the construction site. So he drove there instead, to find that his fellow conspirators had indeed infiltrated its perimeter and even began to shrink it, with the help of Lonnie Jenkins's inside knowledge and Dunce Cap Carter's mechanical genius. Lonnie had opened the trailer that held all the keys. While Ikie Lakes and Lukey Hawkins stood guard, Lonnie operated the power shovel and repeatedly loaded two dump trucks with dirt. Bunky Adams, Cap Carter, Josh Hawkins, and Nunc Farmer took turns driving the trucks, and Cap relieved Lonnie for a while at the controls of the power shovel, at which operation he proved adept.

Long before dawn, they had replaced all the dirt that had been dug up the week before. Fess longed to help, but he knew he would be useless in this particular effort. He tried to take a turn standing guard but, finding his lameness a hindrance even there, reluctantly gave up, drove back to the stall he called home, and went to bed, after carefully parking Bella's car in front of Cabin Four.

He did not fully appreciate the extent of Ikie's strategy until the next morning, when he arrived just in time to observe Lonnie Jenkins's reaction when the foreman asked what had happened to their hole. The rest of the illicit night crew was presumably snoring the morning away, but Lonnie, who of course had to report to work on time, was just wide awake enough to pretend sleepiness. Fess wished he had a camera to record his expression, a masterpiece of dissimulation, as was his response: "Hole, suh? Is dey a hole missing? Mus' be around here someplace. Le's us take a look."

A crowd of spectators gathered and continued to gather until it became a mob. Conspicuous among them was Essie Mae Merchant in the most arresting combination of Black Power colors ever worn: a long red satin gown, a black sash, a green feather boa, and bare feet. All the others—a third of Lakestown's population, he judged, including most of the night crew, who probably preferred missing sleep to missing this— imitated her wide vacant grin and seemed to share her simple-minded amiability. Chewing gum or tobacco according to preference, laughing and chatting casually as visitors at an amusement park, they wandered across the moon-crater site of the highway construction, aggressively friendly and inquisitive.

One young white workman seated at the controls of an impressive diesel-powered machine painstakingly explained its functioning at least ten times to as many male questioners. Pride made him an easy victim—he was proud of his skill at operating the marigold-yellow dynamo, proud of the pay it earned him (which was, he said, triple the wages of unskilled laborers), and as proud of the machine itself as if he owned it.

"What'd he say that thing's called, Nunc?" asked Cap Carter, who had operated it so expertly the night before.

"A power shovel, Cap," Nunc Farmer replied.

"A power shovel! Imagine that. Never heard of one of them before. How's he say it work?" asked Cap.

"You tell him, mister. You can 'splain it better than me," Nunc requested.

Patiently, proudly, the young man went over the control panel of the monster once more, pointing out the levers and switches that arched and swiveled its neck, the ones that opened its jaws and shut them, and the fourteen gears that moved it back and forth and in circles.

At that point Fess joined the others and asked to have the machine explained to *him*. He listened gravely to a repetition of the lecture, then asked in awe, "You say it goes in *circles?* That must be something. I sure would like to see that!"

KRISTIN LATTANY

Visibly puffed up with pride, the hairy young man gave him a demonstration, driving his golden beast in endless circles while the black men applauded and cheered. They would have cheered him all day long if the foreman had not come trotting over.

"Corrigan! What the hell are you doing?" the foreman demanded.

The young man shut off the engine. "What you say, McCoy?"

"I said, what the hell are you doing? Riding a merry-go-round?"

"Aw, I was just showing them how this thing works, McCoy."

"Well, this isn't a circus. Nobody's paying you to put on a show. I'm docking you for the last two hours, and I'm docking you fifteen minutes' pay for every minute you waste from now on."

The workman grumbled something about complaining to the union, but McCoy did not hear him. He had already rushed off to another sector of the battlefield to deal with another problem. In the very center of the man-made crater squatted a dozen small children, industriously pouring water into the dust bowl and making mud pies. At first they had a sort of midget bucket brigade going from the Adams's house on Edgehill Road to their play area, passing the buckets of water from hand to hand, until that clever runt, Rudy Merchant, opened a fire hydrant for them. Then the water flowed freely down the sides of the crater into their play kitchen, giving the children a chance to splash and slosh and get gloriously messy while making their pies.

When a workman ordered the kids to move, their lack of reaction was so singular they seemed stone-deaf. But when he picked up one to *make* her move, she let out a yowl that rent the air and became contagious. All the other toddlers joined in with ear-piercing screams that brought forth a contingent of indignant mothers from the crowd.

"What he do to you, Alex? What that man do?"

"What that man do to you, Louisie?" Doretha Adams asked her daughter. "Did he hit you?"

"Yes!" cried Bunky's youngest, and pointed a chubby accusing finger not at the workman but at the innocent foreman, McCoy, who until a minute ago had been a hundred yards away, trying to break up a marbles tournament that was in the way of another piece of equipment, failing because the winners—the middle Adams child, twelve-year-old

Quincy, and Rudy Merchant—both refused to budge until they had found their favorite shooters.

"Jeeee-sus!" cried McCoy jumping up and down in frustration. "Where are the police? Isn't there anyone who can control these people?"

As if by magic, his request was fulfilled. Patrolman Matt Hawkins, Lukey's twenty-year-old brother, called Tiny because he was a mere seventy-four inches tall, appeared. Innocent of the weekend's intrigue, he strode into the ruckus and asked, "What's going on here?"

"He hit my baby!"

"And mine!"

"And mine!"

"And he hit me," Doretha Adams calmly lied.

"Now wait a minute," the foreman said, reddening. "I didn't hit anybody. These children were in the way of my work crew, and I was trying to get them to move."

Looking from Doretha's bland face to the foreman's scarlet one and back again, Matt made some notes. "Are you prepared to come down to Borough Hall and testify to that, Miz Adams?" he asked her respectfully.

"Sholy, Tiny," she said.

"She's lying!" McCoy screamed. "We were working here. These people were in the way, and they had to be removed."

"Was it necessary to use force against women and little children, sir?" Patrolman Hawkins asked.

"You've got this all wrong, officer. Nobody used any force against anybody."

"I've known Miz Adams all my life," Josh's older son said, "and I know she wouldn't tell a lie. Would you, Miz Adams?"

"Certainly not, Tiny."

"You see?" Tiny said to the foreman.

"This is ridiculous! I demand my rights!" the foreman cried.

"Certainly," Matt said, and recited in the same soft-spoken, courteous tone his father and brother always used. "You have the right to remain silent, and anything you say may be held against you. You have the right to avoid self-incrimination. You have the right to legal counsel . . ." as he led the foreman to his patrol car. As they got into it, Matt called over his shoulder, "I don't think we'll need you to testify, Miz Doretha, but if we do, I'll come get you."

"This is insane!" the foreman screamed. "I can't believe it, after all I've done for you people! Lonnie! Lonnie Jenkins! Help me!"

Fess suddenly recognized McCoy as the patient boss man who had performed all that volunteer labor in Lakestown several summers ago and felt momentarily sorry for him. But Lonnie, he noticed, had kept his back carefully turned to avoid seeing McCoy in his moment of trouble, and he was now slipping into the explosives shack so as not to hear him, either.

The Lakestown patrol car sped away, taking the foreman to the two-cell jail, and young Bill Moscowitz, the cement subcontractor, was obliged to take over his job. Fess saw Doc Thompson ambling toward him and decided to follow at a discreet distance. Sure enough, just as he had expected, Doc was engaging the new foreman in a rambling, distracting conversation.

It was amazing to learn how many things there were to be said about a dull topic by those who shared a love for it. Cement, for instance, was a subject that bored nearly everyone, but it seemed to hold endless fascination for Doc Thompson and Bill Moscowitz. They discussed its cost, its textures, its ingredients, and the various recipes for combining them. The ways of speeding up or retarding its hardening. When it should be patched, and when it was best to break it up and start over. The problems of transporting cement; pouring it, molding it. The many ways of reinforcing it so that it would bear exceptional stresses or hold unusual shapes. Doc, of course, led the conversation, at the same time leading Moscowitz farther and farther away from the site and positioning himself so that the younger man's back was always turned to it. Behind it, more monkeyshines were going on and more monkey wrenches were being tossed into the works. Out of the corner of one eye, Fess saw Josh Hawkins climb into the driver's seat of a crawler tractor after a long conversation with its operator and braced himself for the crash that would soon follow. But he was too fascinated by Doc's strategy to move out of earshot.

Very casually, Doc tossed something new into the conversation, "I realize you are familiar with all the uses of cement in building construction.

And, of course, you understand all the ramifications of cement as a profitable commodity. But have you ever seen anyone exploit it as an art form?"

Art probably meant so little to Moscowitz that he did not even hear the word. It must have been that other word, *exploit*, that caused his eyes to goggle with greed.

"I'm only an amateur compared to you, of course," Doc went on, "but I think I've pruduced some interesting effects with cement. Just muddling around for my own pleasure and relaxation, you understand; nothing serious. Everything I've done is purely decorative, but some of the techniques I've developed, just puttering around, might have commercial applications. My place is only a few steps away from here. I'd be happy to show you around, if you can spare a few minutes."

Fess observed the moment when Doc's fish was firmly hooked by the term *commercial applications*. They ambled off together toward Doc's place, where, Fess was sure, Moscowitz would be lost for hours in Doc's crockery-studded maze of cement wishing wells, vases, pagodas, towers, baskets, fish ponds, follies, and waterfalls. Where, if he or anyone else let a careless foot slip, he might find himself permanently embedded in the latest solidifying dream. He badly wanted to follow them but was afraid his presence might break Doc's spell, and also thought he had better stay where he was and pay attention to what was happening.

The crash he had been anticipating came at that moment and was followed by another. Josh Hawkins had managed to run the tractor into an embankment and turn it over. For a moment it hung in the air, upended, like a ship about to sink, giving Josh time to jump clear. Then it flopped over on its back and lay there, helpless and pathetic as an overturned turtle, while Josh stood nearby, declaring loudly that he couldn't understand how a thing like that could have happened. Neither, apparently, could anyone else in the crowd of workmen and citizens that quickly surrounded him. But Fess, who knew Josh had driven enough tractors enough miles to plow under all the southern states, would not have been surprised to see him make one fly.

The lunch hour was approaching, as was a contingent of cherubs in their Sunday best, with all traces of the morning's mud-pie making scrubbed away. No one would have recognized Lonnie and Jerutha Jenkins's Bessie and Lindy or the youngest Adams girls, Louise and

Marian, or any of the others as the same youngsters who had been knee-deep in mud three hours ago. They wore starched pinafores in a rainbow of pastels and matching knee socks and hair ribbons on tightly greased braids. Stepping daintily in patent leather Mary Janes, they approached in pairs, each lugging a heavy thermos jug between them.

Behind them, like guardian angels, came the Blue Moon's ladies of the evening, dressed for day in the white uniforms worn by waitresses and Baptist deaconesses. They carried large picnic hampers and, instead of their normal sensual languor, walked with a brisk, righteous strut in rhythm with their singing:

> Children, go where I send thee.
> How shall I send thee?
> I'm gonna send you two by two . . .

This was, of course, in line with a long and honorable tradition. In the days of slavery there had been a code hymn to convey almost every type of information. Fess hoped he could remember to suggest to Ikie that they revive this valuable method of communication, because Ikie was not around. He should have been, but Fess figured he was hovering anxiously around Cabin Four instead. Luckily, so far everything was proceeding splendidly without him. The workmen, who had done no work at all that morning, must have been overly hungry from sheer frustration. They fell so ravenously on the provender that Mame had to send the girls back for more sandwiches and lemonade.

By the time the contractor arrived, though, the cherubim and seraphim had vanished. Half his crew had passed out in peaceful drunkenness and the other half were doubled over in acute distress, groaning and throwing up. Luciano brought his Cadillac to a screeching halt, got out, swore, and stared in disbelief at the black citizens who swarmed over his project and the shambles they had made of it. He turned to the driver of the car that had parked behind his, a plain black Ford decorated only with the yellow-and-blue state seal, and began gesticulating wildly. Fess moved close enough to the hill on which they stood to overhear that the little contractor was hopping mad about being unable to get his foreman out of jail, because the county circuit judge could not be located to hold a hearing, and that the other man, the state engineer in charge of the project, was less concerned with the foreman's fate than with the setbacks the work had suffered.

"It's my fault, Luciano," the latter said. "I shouldn't have been running all over the county with you trying to bail out that foul McCoy. I should have been right here, supervising the work. And from now on I will be. All day, every day."

The contractor apparently wanted to discourage this resolve. "You don't have to sweat it, Berger. I'll get on top of it and get it moving. Don't I always finish my jobs on time? This is just a temporary foul-up. I've seen worse. Things go wrong. Things can happen."

"That may be, Luciano, but dammit, holes don't just disappear. Maybe some of these people know something."

"Them? They look like they wouldn't know a hole if they fell in one."

"Well, let's ask them anyway."

The contractor expressed his skepticism with an astounding burst of profanity in at least three languages, but he scrambled down the embankment behind the engineer anyway.

He was soon proved right. Trying to get information from the likes of Josh, Jerutha, Nunc, and Lula, let alone Biker Boyd and Essie Mae Merchant, was like trying to tread water in a sea of molasses. And getting angry with them was like hitting the tar baby.

The more the white men swore, the more they were put off by smiles and friendly greetings.

"Hello there, Mister Bossman, sir. How you feelin'?"

"Good day to both of you. Hope life is treatin' you all right."

"Nice day, ain't it? A little hot, maybe, but it won't bother you if you take it easy."

"Yep. Good day to be layin' in the shade. Gone find me a big old tree. Heee."

"I hear a lot of children were out there playing today. How come?" Berger wanted to know. "Wasn't school open?!"

"School, sir? I dunno," said Essie Mae Merchant.

"It was one of our holidays, sir," said Lula Farmer. "Black Independence Day."

"Black Independence Day? I never heard of that one," the engineer said, while Fess smiled and restrained himself from proclaiming, "We just invented it!"

"All I know is," Berger said, "a hundred-foot excavation was filled in over the weekend." He turned to question the nearest person, who was, as it happened, Jerutha Jenkins. "You live near here?"

"Yessir. Just up that way."

"Did you hear any loud noises over the weekend, like this equipment makes when it's moving? Noises at night, maybe?"

"No, sir, didn't hear nothin'. Slep' sound as a baby, all three nights."

"You can believe her, Berger," Luciano said. "Her husband is one of my best boys. I've been to their place with McCoy a couple of times. Boy, can she cook!" He kissed his fingers into the air.

"Glad you liked my cooking, sir. Glad to have you over anytime," Jerutha said. "Why don't you come by tonight? I got something real nice in the oven."

A time bomb, probably, Fess thought.

"I don't understand it. This equipment makes a lot of noise. And somebody had to use it, to move all that dirt in two days."

"I tell you, this woman's all right, Berger. I know her."

"Maybe so. But I just thought of something. To these people, *near* might mean anything from ten feet to ten miles. Maybe she doesn't really live near enough to have heard anything." Raising his voice, gesturing with his arms, and speaking very slowly, as if addressing the natives of a newly discovered isle, the engineer asked, "Does anybody live close to where we're working here? *Real* close? Close *by?*" He brought his hands together in a kind of sign language, in case these natives didn't understand any English at all.

"I do," old Baretta Farmer volunteered. "Right up there on that hill. It wasn't a hill before, but now since you dug the land away, well . . ."

"Yes, yes, I understand. Did you hear any strange noises over the weekend, any heavy equipment moving? Anything like that?"

"No, sir, I ain't heard nothin' but the crickets crickin' in the weeds out back, since I got too old to chop 'em down. Every year before this one, I chopped 'em and dug 'em out and planted my garden. A real nice garden, too, fifteen rows, yielded so much crops I had plenty to give away. Corn, tomatoes, peppers, collards, snap beans . . . But this year, somehow, I didn't have the strength or the spirit to chop and dig and . . ."

"You said the right word though, Miz Farmer," Vinnie Coddums interrupted.

"What word was that?"

"*Sperit.* Sperits is what done it. Sperits picked up that dirt and moved it back where it was before."

"Why would they do that?" Josh Hawkins asked in pop-eyed innocence.

"'Cause, long 'bout the end of last week, them shovels started diggin' up old graves in the corner of Mount Moriah churchyard. It wasn't people done it, mister. People ain't been out after dark all weekend, 'cause they knew the graves was disturbed and the sperits was restless."

Vinnie could not have timed her remark more perfectly. Without anyone's noticing, the sky had turned dark. A roll of thunder and a flash of lightning bracketed one white man's deprecatory shrug—meaning, "What's the use of questioning these superstitious darkies?"—and the other's.

"Down on your knees!" she shouted. "Down on your knees and pray for forgiveness! The Lord is givin' us a sign! He gonna punish all sinners and trespassers!"

The rain was coming down in sheets, the construction workers were indisposed, and all the potential sources of information were deeply absorbed in prayer. After a brief consultation, in which Luciano tried to convince the state engineer that his constant presence on the job would not be necessary, the two men in charge agreed to do the only sensible thing: call off work for the rest of the day. Reiterating his resolve to be present thereafter, though, Berger climbed into his little state car and Luciano into his Cadillac, where he appeared to engage in a shocking pantomime, cursing and gesturing obscenely at the white plastic Virgin who swung from the mirror. Only after they and every member of the wretched crew had driven off did Vinnie and her faithful flock get up from their knees.

"I'll have rheumatism for a week," Baretta Farmer observed.

"So will I," said Vinnie, "but it was worth it. Come on home with me, Baretta. I got some extra-good liniment."

Ikie, after reprimanding Josh for disabling the tractor prematurely ("I just couldn't resist it, boss. That thing drove so *eeeasy!"),* told the night crew to go on home from the Blue Moon and stay home. The rain, he said listlessly, would do more damage than they could.

"Hey, this looks like an all-night rain, though," Lonnie Jenkins said. "We could dig a few trenches in the walls of that there crater. Then the runoff would settle in the bottom and make a nice big mess of a puddle."

Fess thought it a pretty good suggestion, but Ikie vetoed it, saying that too much suspicion had already been aroused that day. Let the bosses come back in the morning and find everything exactly the way they'd left it. Give them a chance to get complacent, and give the hard-working men of Lakestown a chance to get some rest.

"Shoot," asked Lonnie, the only one who'd put in twenty-four straight hours, "who's tired?"

"Go home and get some sleep anyway," Ikie ordered with a distant irritability that suggested he had far more important things on his mind than debating with them.

Ikie was their general, and so far no one was mutinous enough to disobey him. They grumbled, but finally, reluctantly, left. Only Fess, who was home already, stayed.

"Well, how'd it go today?" Ikie asked him in an abstracted way, as if he barely cared.

"Great. Score one for our side, zero for theirs. They had a day of total confusion, with nothing accomplished. The bosses couldn't figure it out, the foreman got arrested, and the entire crew got sick. I don't think they'll go for the sandwiches and lemonade again, though."

Ikie focused on the subject at hand for a minute. "We won't use sandwiches next time. It'll be barbecue. Show me a white man whose stomach can stand up to Mame's sauce, and I'll show you a man with some dark-skinned ancestors he doesn't know about."

The cook whose recipe he was discussing came in, looking distraught and rubbing her hands against her gory apron.

"What's the matter?" Ikie asked her.

"That old sanctified Randy Barnes quit on us. Said he couldn't stand the sinful atmosphere around here. I told him we couldn't stand him, either."

"That's okay," Ikie told her. "You already sing good enough to fool white folks."

"I think we ought to drop the singing," Mame said. "Those men are dumb, maybe, but they ain't *that* dumb. They ain't gonna fall for the same scam twice in a row."

"What else do you have in mind?"

"Why can't we just be our natural selves? Let my girls wear their regular get-ups so nobody won't recognize 'em, and let 'em go ahead and do what they're best at. Which ain't singing. After those men spend a little time in the cabins, they'll be in a mood to eat and drink whatever we give 'em."

Fess was convinced Mame was right, but Ikie was not. "All right, you can skip the picnic baskets next time. But I need you all out there singing and saving sinners."

"Ain't Reverend Bream got his own choir? My girls got to get their rest in the daytime, if they gonna have a heavy night in the cabins."

"All right, all right. Have it your way," Ikie said brusquely, as if tired of the subject.

The second mention of the cabins gave Fess an excuse to broach the question all three of them had been skirting. "How's Bella?"

Mame's expression was troubled. "Not so good. She just lays around sighin' and cryin' and lookin' like her own grandma. I got to find out who's throwin' it at her."

"Pardon?" Fess asked.

"Mame believes," Ikie explained, "that someone has put a curse on Bella. To cure her, she must find out who that person is and make them remove it."

"How would you go about doing that?"

"I got ways, Professor," Mame said inscrutably. "I'm workin' on 'em right now. Betcha, whoever the snake is, they'll show up before the sun goes down another time." She took off her apron and laid it on a chair. "I left the sauce on simmer, so it'll be all right for a while. I better go and see to Bella now."

"Would it be all right if I came with you?" Ikie asked.

Mame shook her head. "Better leave her alone."

Ikie's glowering expression was a clue to Fess that it was best to treat him the same way. He hoped fervently that Bella would soon be cured of her mysterious ailment, because as long as she was ill, Ikie would clearly be giving their subversive enterprise less than his full attention. And that meant that entirely too much of the responsibility would fall on him.

26

Ikie had been right about the rain's causing more damage than his crew could. Fess made this observation with a tinge of resentment, acknowledging to himself an uncharitable wish for Ikie to be wrong just once. But apparently this was not going to be the day for it.

Softened by its double removal, the earth they had replaced had been mixed with enough rain overnight to become a morass in which the scattered pieces of road-building equipment were stuck, helpless as frozen dinosaurs in the ice age. On Fess's left a big, blunt-nosed *Triceratops* of a bulldozer wheezed impotently, unable to budge. On his right, the power shovel that looked like *Tyranosaurus rex* seemed capable of only one movement, opening and closing its jaws like a dying creature gasping for air. Straight ahead he saw that the big red Caterpillar tractor Josh had overturned yesterday had been righted somehow but was still useless: the more its operator spun its treads, the deeper it sank into the mud.

As he watched, reinforcements arrived in the form of a half dozen new tractors. Calf-deep in mud, swearing and yelling, the men maneuvered them into position to push and pull the mired machines free. It was slow work. After an hour, two tractors managed to move the bulldozer out of its sinkhole and forward a grand total of two feet. And the rest of the new equipment seemed to be sinking into the giant mudhole as deeply as the other machines.

Trust Ikie, the sort of conscious Indian who could read animal footprints and hear messages in the wind, to know that nature could undo more man-made work than any human effort.

Plenty of human effort was also being expended by the rebels of Lakestown, however. Reverend Bream, his choir, and the pillars of his congregation were already deployed at the north end of the crater, with the choir lined up in a semicircle behind the Reverend and the deacons and deaconesses stationed like guards at ten-foot intervals.

Never one to be outdone, Reverend LeRoy Bird had already set up a gigantic tent at the opposite pole of the perimeter. On arriving, Fess had been puzzled to see a half dozen empty chartered buses lined up along Edgehill Road. Now before his dazzled eyes four more buses arrived, and scores of out-of-town worshipers poured out of them and streamed toward the tent.

Crow certainly did not do things halfway. "Week-long Summer Revival!" screamed the red-and-gold satin banner that decorated his tent. "Nonstop Healing and Baptism! Evangelist LeRoy Bird, Three Healers, Four Preachers, SIX CHOIRS!" If there were any human power equal to the forces of nature, Fess reflected as the faithful continued to flow down the sides of the crater like a dark river, it had to be the collective ardor of a flock of heaven-bent Baptists. He doubted whether even the Pentagon could produce anything like it.

But it was Vinnie, whose ideas of proper deportment had kept her away from the planning sessions at the poolroom and the Blue Moon, who came up with the day's most masterful strategy. She had set the stage yesterday for today's most showy performances, and now her unerring instinct aimed her in a beeline toward the man with the most authority, Maxwell Berger, the highway engineer assigned by the state to supervise the project. She asked him, "Do you know what time it is?"

He checked his watch. "Ten thirty."

"Wrong!" Vinnie answered triumphantly. It's one minute to midnight, unless you're saved! The clock of eternity is tickin' away those last few seconds right now. It's much later than you think, man, unless your soul is ready for the day of judgment. But there's still time for you, if you come with me right now and accept Jesus as your savior!"

A slight smile of amusement relieved the chronic tightness of Berger's expression. "Is a man saved if he's a Lutheran?"

Vinnie pondered this. "Is that one of them sprinklin' churches, or do they baptize you all over?"

"They just sprinkle," he replied.

"No good!" Vinnie exclaimed. "You got to be washed all over. You got to get every inch of you clean for salvation. You got to get your head down under that muddy water and *drown* before you can be born again!" She grabbed the man's arm and tugged it, pointing toward Bird's tent. "Your soul is in danger, man! You better come with me right now!"

"Waalll," Beger drawled, "I might's well walk over there with you. Got to see what's goin' on in that tent anyway. Lead on, lady."

And, amazingly, he allowed himself to be led off by Vinnie, even tolerating her continued grip on his arm as they sloshed through the mud. Fess, following them by a circuitous route, noticed that the Reverend Bream's flock was making a quieter but no less effective approach to the construction crew.

"We're all praying for you," one earnest young deacon said to the driver of a stalled tractor. We're praying for your sins to be redeemed in the sight of God."

"I ain't sinned," declared the bewildered young hard hat who was told this news. But under the deacon's relentlessly sympathetic gaze, he became defensive. "Maybe I have a few beers after work on payday, but what's wrong with that? I know the wife and the kids need every cent I make, but I deserve to relax a little after working hard all week, don't I? So maybe the barmaid flirts with me. Is it my fault I'm attractive to women? Is it my fault barmaids don't have any morals? If she invites me to her place after she gets off work, am I a sinner for going? I figure God made men that way for a purpose. I believe he wouldn't have put that urge in us if we weren't supposed to slip it in every time a woman gave us a chance. I know I always feel bad afterward, but I don't call it a sin. Am I wrong, Father?"

"I'm not a father. You don't have to confess your sins to me. Just call me 'brother.' I'm just another ordinary sinner like you," the young deacon said. "Let me take you to meet our pastor. I promise you he'll make you feel better."

"What's he charge?" the young white man asked suspiciously.

"Nothing. Unless you feel like making a donation."

"Hell, you can't beat a deal like that. Let's go," said the tractor driver, leaping out of his vehicle. "This damn rig isn't going anywhere today anyway."

All over the work site, Fess observed as he approached Bird's tent, Methodist church workers were using the same quiet tactics and achieving the same results, separating men from their jobs and bringing them to the satin-draped shipping crate that was Reverend Bream's makeshift altar. None of which Berger, who had already been led into Crow's tent, was able to observe. Fess wondered if the Baptists had him bound and gagged in there.

When he went inside, the effect was dazzling. Bird's revival tent was a portable palace, a cloth cathedral. Scarlet and gold strips of satin had been stretched from the center pole to the sides to create a ceiling like a Valentine's Day candy box, and half the folding chairs in the world had been sprayed with gold to accommodate the large assemblage. No expense had been spared in erecting a gorgeous portable altar complete with a glowing white neon cross and a shimmering blue baptismal tank. The choir was arrayed in scarlet robes, and the Reverend himself wore layers of scarlet, gold, black, and ivory lace. Moving closer to him, Fess sniffed the odor of ambergris, cologne or whale-oil pomade, about his person.

Berger, he said, was not tied up, but the Reverend Bird seemed involved in a slight dispute with him.

"I realize you have a job to do," he told the state engineer, "but this meeting was arranged weeks in advance. Plans were made, buses were chartered, tickets were sold. Hundreds of people have traveled great distances. I can't disappoint them."

"I don't care how many people came," Berger told him. "You'll have to put them somewhere else."

"Where?" Bird asked, his jeweled fingers catching fire in the sunlight. "My church only accommodates two hundred people."

"That's your problem, Reverend. You can't hold your services here. This land belongs to the state."

"Show me the papers to prove that, young man!" Bird rumbled, gearing up to roar.

"I don't happen to have them on me," Berger admitted.

"Then," he asked, "would you mind coming up front to help me explain this problem to my people?"

Berger nodded his assent. "This land belongs to Gawd!" Bird thundered, with impressive amplification from the tiny microphone pinned to his chasuble. "Neither you, nor the state, nor the President of the United States and his army has the right to prevent us from worshiping here. *We* are the army of the righteous!"

The choir began to belt out "Onward, Christian Soldiers" as Reverend Bird strode toward his neon-lit altar, with the engineer scrambling to keep up with him. Once there, he raised his arms for silence, displaying yards of scarlet satin.

"This man," Bird orated, "says we have no right to worship God here, on God's land, under God's sky. What do we say to that, people? What do we say, Sister Cindy?"

Reverend Bird snapped his fingers, and Cindy's voice came over the microphone, singing Woody Guthrie's "This Land Is Your Land, This Land Is My Land," to a rousing gospel beat. After her voice died away to an echo, Reverend Bird again gestured dramatically for silence. "What is your name, brother?" he asked the engineer with infinite kindness.

"Maxwell Berger, Reverend, Highway Engineer One, New Jersey State Highway Department, Supervisor, Dorset County Section of Interstate 27."

"Now never mind all that, brother. We don't need titles in here. The Lord doesn't recognize titles. The Lord knows all His children and treats them all the same. Now, what was the little problem you were just telling me about?"

Patiently, the engineer repeated his statement that the state had acquired the land on which the tent stood and that the assembly would have to move.

"Would you repeat that, please?" Reverend Bird requested. "I'm not sure everyone heard you, and I want all my people to understand. Did you hear him back there, Sister Coddums?"

"Not a word, Reverend!" Vinnie called back.

"Please say it louder. Right into this little microphone."

The engineer complied.

"Are you aware," Reverend Bird intoned, "that this doctrine conflicts with the First Amendment of the United States Constitution, which says, and I quote 'Congress shall make no law respecting an establishment of religion, or prohibiting the free exercise thereof; or abridging the freedom of speech . . . or the right of the people peaceably to assemble . . .'?"

"I don't know anything about that." Berger said, beginning to look uncomfortable.

"Well, then, let me ask you this. Are you aware that this conversation is being broadcast coast to coast on network radio? One hundred and twenty-seven stations, brothers and sisters, carrying the good news of the gospel all over America!"

Berger looked at the microphone in his hand, saw that it bore three letters of the alphabet, and dropped it as if it had caught fire. "Omigod," he said. "This is outa my department. I gotta call my Public Information office, get a PR man down here." As he ran back up the aisle, the choir hastened his exit with

> You better run,
> You better run,
> You better run to the city of refuge,
> You better run!

What showmanship, Fess thought. And what a clever maneuver. Only now did Fess notice the radio engineer, almost invisible with his earphones on, crouching behind his bulky equipment.

He wanted to congratulate the Reverend Bird but thought it wiser to follow the highway engineer outdoors, where Berger rushed up to the contractor, Luciano, and tried to get his attention.

But Luciano, like his cement contractor Moscowitz the day before, was deeply involved in a talk with that most engaging of conversationalists, Doc Thompson. The only difference today was that Doc, to Luciano's utter enchantment, was being loquacious in Italian.

"Mi chiamo Dottore Thompson," the doctor introduced himself.

"Uno dottoro?" Luciano asked in amazement. "Medico?"

"Si."

"Nero?"

"Es evidente," the doctor said with a shrug.

"Parla Italiano?"

"Si, parlo un po. Capisco un po."

"Uno medico nero, parlando italiano. Miracolo!" the contractor shouted. Berger was tugging at his sleeve, trying to interest him in his public relations problem, but he was rebuffed with a loud, "Andate via! Go away! Quit buggin' me! Fermatei! I just found me a miracle. The only Italian nigger doctor in the world! Say somethin', Doc. Parla!"

"Come sta, signore?" Doc inquired politely.

"Aah, don't ask him. The dummy non capisca. Ask me!"

"Come sta?" Doc repeated.

"Malata, malata," the Italian said. "Mi stomaco," he said, pointing to it. "Io mi dolgo. Indigestione."

After a long, grave pause, Doc spoke. "Raccommando . . . non pasta."

"Non pasta?" Luciano echoed in disbelief.

"Si. Non pasta, non vino, non salsa di pomadoro, non olio di'olivo. *Specialmente* non olio."

No grease for white folks, Fess translated roughly, while Luciano screamed, "Moriró di fame!"

Doc, who had just sentenced him to starvation, shrugged. "Tengo una buona medicina a mi ofiza. É la mia. Una buona preparazione . . ."

"Per favore, mi porta là."

"Con felicita!" Doc said gleefully. "Vi essaminaro là. Essaminaro tutto. Andiamo!"

"Hey, Berger, this is some find, huh? This guy's gonna fix up my stomach. Maybe he can cure the rest of the crew, get 'em all back on the job tomorrow," Luciano called over his shoulder toward the place where Berger had been. But the engineer had vanished in search of his PR man. "Wonder where he went? Oh, well. Half my crew called in sick this morning, and the other half can't move anyway, in this fuckin' mud. The hell with it. Andiamo!"

Linked by linguistics, an even stronger bond than cement, he and Doc left the site arm in arm like old friends. Thus another supervisor was lured into the labyrinth from which Moscowitz apparently had not yet emerged. Fess hoped Doc had not encased him permanently in a pyramid or a wishing well. But with the bosses gone, he realized happily, the field was clear for the forces of good and evil to engage in mock battle.

Fess could predict at a glance which side would gain the most converts. There was plenty of glamor under Reverend Bird's tent and about his person, but none of it equaled the allure of Booty's posterior in very short yellow shorts. There was something about the extra little hip flip she put into each syncopated step, something about the visible v of her black bikini panties underneath the shorts, that galvanized all eyes. What Booty displayed below the waist was matched only by what Lily flaunted above. Propped up by God alone knew what mechanics or magic, her regal breasts floated as serenely as helium-filled balloons, perfectly parallel with the earth, in a red halter narrow enough to use as a shoestring. Everywhere he looked, workers could be seen shutting off machines and muttering exclamations as Booty jiggled in one direction and Lily glided in another.

He stopped their choreographer to congratulate her and ask, "How's Bella?"

"Like a new woman," Mame said. "Up early this morning, singin' and bouncin' around like a teen-ager. She wanted to come with us, but I told her it wouldn't be proper. She and her old stiff-necked husband might decide to get back together again. So she's back at the kitchen, stirrin' the pots and turnin' the ribs." Pulling him closer, she whispered, "I drew the snake what spelled her. She showed up at daybreak."

"*She?*"

"Yes, it was that Grimes woman, the old one, Greta. I had to do some extra-hard work to draw her and make her tell me what she was up to. The dirty snake was hopin' to widder the mayor and marry him. She had that evil old Baron Sam helpin' her. Him and that sneaky Crump boy that follows him around like the shadow of a shadow. But Grimy Greta won't give Bella no more trouble for a while. I threw somethin' at her to keep her plenty busy."

"Busy doing what?" Fess wondered.

"Scratchin', that's what!" Mame chuckled. "I gave her an itch that'll last seven days and seven nights, and I can keep it goin' longer if I want. Before she left my place, she was already diggin' and scratchin' and jumpin' like a snake trying to shed its skin. She gonna have so many welts and scratches and scabs before the week is out, she'll be uglier than a alligator. Not that she ain't ugly enough now, but I say if a woman's got a husband and that woman's a friend of mine, I ain't gonna make it easy for no other woman to grab him."

Fess could think of nothing to say except, "Mame, you're a magician."

"Well, of course I am!" Mame gave him a playful punch on the arm. "Ain't I always told you that? Here comes some reinforcements for you, now they ain't got a sick woman to worry about. Me, I got to go load up the girls and the johns in my car. 'Spec I'll be making a few more trips today. Catch you later."

Sure enough, as Mame hurried off, Ikie appeared at the rim of the crater and surveyed the scene with tightly squinted eyes, as if his mind were finally capable of concentration.

"Beautiful," he said to Fess after he had taken it all in. "This is the most beautiful motherfucking mess I ever saw in my whole life. Look at that big mother of a backhoe, sinking in the mud. Look at those three Cats, trying to pull it out and sinking right along with it. At this rate, they'll all be buried by evening. Hah! Look at that horny idiot following Booty, with his tongue hanging out like a hound dog's. And look at those other hypnotized fools, down on their knees. They'll never straighten this out, Roaney. Never. It's better than I ever dreamed. Congratulations."

"Thanks. But I didn't do it," Fess said. "It seemed to happen all by itself, like a miracle."

"No miracle," Ikie said. "Just a couple of basic sociological facts you of all people should understand. One, every black person in this country is by nature an outlaw. Most of us don't dare risk overt action, because we're outnumbered, but the more we have to conform outwardly, the more we want to rebel. So, dig it: there's nothing we love better than finding sly ways of getting over on the Man. And nothing we're better at doing.

"Two, conspiracy is hard for white folks, 'cause basically they don't trust each other. They have to keep the numbers small to make it work for them, and even in small groups every dude has to have something to hold over every other dude's head. And even then, half the time they blow it, 'cause they got no loyalty.

"But black folks are different. We can organize a whole town in a conspiracy, or even a whole continent, because no matter how much a few individuals dislike each other, we all dislike white folks more. And ain't none of us fools enough to trust 'em."

"Especially if we remember the South," Fess added. "Slavery and all that came after it. *Real* oppression."

Ikie's jubilation was short-lived. His face took on a brooding expression. "That's the trouble. Some of us have short memories. Some fools born in the North got nothing to remember from the git-go, so they're dumb enough to trust Whitey."

"For a while, maybe," Fess said. "But they learn, they learn. You know what we're watching, Lakes? A reenactment of history. Think of the organization it took to escape from slavery. Think of all the strategies and tricks it took to move all those people. A network stretching for hundreds of miles and ending right here. And now we're starting it up all over again."

"Don't get carried away, Roaney," Ikie said. "That was then. This is now."

"Yes, but maybe we could use some of the old strategies. The code hymns, for instance. There was a gospel song to convey every signal imaginable. One for leaving, one for hiding, one for safety, one for danger . . ."

Ikie cut him off. "Aah, who remembers all that old stuff?"

"*I* do. I looked it all up years ago. I've got it all in a box under my bunk."

"Leave it there. You can't have a chain this big without a few weak links. That's what worries me."

"Greta Grimes, for instance," Fess said, though he knew Ikie was thinking about his brother, and perhaps Bella, too.

"And God knows who else. We have to locate them, isolate them. But how?"

They were distracted momentarily by the Reverend Bream's choir singing, with a sudden increase in volume,

Will the circle be unbroken,
By and by, Lord, by and by?

Looking intently in that direction, wondering whether it was a trick of the wind or whether the sudden loudness had any meaning, they did not see Jane Grimes coming until she was right upon them. She looked scared. Breathlessly, she said to Ikie, "My sister would kill me if she knew. But I just had to tell someone."

"Tell someone what, Miss Grimes?"

"About the awful things she's doing to stop you."

"Stop me from what, ma'am?"

"Oh, I don't expect you to trust me. I've been a foolish, frivolous woman all my life." She drew her short body erect with touching dignity. "But I've also been a Christian woman. And Greta wants revenge on you people so bad, she's made a pact with the Devil."

Fess said, "What?" so loudly Jane knew he thought she had lost her mind.

"Please don't think I'm crazy, Mr. Roaney. That's what Greta wants everybody to think. But she's getting that old Baron Potter to hex you, you and all the others trying to stop the highway from coming through. Him and that horrible young man she hired—the sorcerer's apprentice, I call him. They do awful things down in the basement late at night. Things with the bodies. And other things down in Froggy Bottom. You may think I'm talking nonsense, but I know it's real. Every time they're working down there, I feel this horrible negative force, like a weight on my chest, holding me down so I can't get out of bed. That's why I had to run off early this morning. I just hope you believe me."

"I believe you, Miss Grimes," Ikie said. "I just don't see how it affects me."

"Thank you," Jane said hoarsely. "Maybe somebody can do something. I've got to get back now, before she misses me." The choir was strangely silent as Jane scrambled off, a brave, pathetic figure in her backless, flapping house shoes.

"You know, that's a nice woman," Fess commented. "Too bad she has to live under her sister's shadow."

"A rich woman too, Roaney. Why don't you propose to her?"

"That's not a bad idea. But it wouldn't be fair to ask someone to share my future, when I know I don't have one. Of course," he added after a pause, "I've believed that for fifteen years."

"So why not believe the opposite for the next fifteen?"

Fess, for whom walking these days was like dragging a block of ice around, did not respond. Instead he said, "So there's a real battle under way between the forces of good and evil, not just our mock engagement between the saved and the sinners. I wonder which side will win?"

"In my experience," Ikie said sourly, watching a fresh troop of men follow the girls to Mame's waiting Cadillac, "evil always does. There goes what's left of the work crew to prove it. Of course we have to try and fight it, anyway. Let's go talk to the esteemed madam. Mame!" he called, trotting toward the car. "Wait a minute."

Lowering her power window, she said irritably, "What is it, Ikie? I'm busy. This is the fifth trip I've made today. I got a dozen drunk johns back at the house to keep an eye on, and here come three more. That makes fifteen."

Ikie bent and whispered in her ear. When he straightened up, Mame's lips were grimly compressed, as if she had removed her false teeth. "I shoulda known she was after somethin' besides Bella. There's been funny things goin' on the last couple of nights: things walkin' down by the creek, lights shinin' where they ain't supposed to be. I may have to call in some help, some people I know in the country. I hope they can get here in time." Her voice rose an octave as the girls arrived with their walking trophies. "All aboard for the Joyland Express!" she sang out sweetly, then rolled up the window as they piled in and, mashing the accelerator, sped them away.

Next, a loud roll of drums shattered the silence, so loud it stopped everything, including, for a moment, Fess's heart. It presaged the singing of an ominous hymn by the choir beneath Bird's tent, joined, in a matter of seconds, by Bream's:

> There's a Man,
> Goin' rou-ou-oun'
> Takin' names;
> There's a Man goin' roun'
> Takin' names . . .

"I wonder what direction trouble is coming from this time?"

"All of them," Ikie said grimly. "I knew this was too good to be true. You can leave your research in the box, Roaney. They remember."

> Don't you let him catch you with your
> Work undone,
> When he takes your name.

On the artificial hill above their heads, a cobalt blue Lincoln sped into view, coming from the direction of Edgehill. An identical car approached from the opposite direction with equal speed, driven so recklessly it almost tipped over the edge of the crater. The twin cars squealed to a stop inches away from a head-on collision. A large, red-faced white man got out of the first one. Lakestown's mayor got out of the second.

"That's State Senator Grafton," Ikie whispered. "Get as close to them as you can without being seen. Try to hear everything. I don't want Abe to see me out here." Softly whistling a familiar tune, he headed rapidly for the cover of Bird's tent.

The two men had squared off to face each other like opponents in a classic western, as if measuring the distance between them before drawing their guns. Fess ducked behind Grafton's Lincoln to get as close as possible to the confrontation.

Before it could erupt, though a third car bore down on them, one of those small, inconspicuous models that always signify real authority. A tall man in one of those nondescript gray suits that conveyed the same message got out and introduced himself, displaying his opened wallet. "James Redfern, U.S. District Engineer, Region Three, Bureau of Public Roads, Federal Highway Administration."

"Harry Grafton, New Jersey State Senator, Fifth District."

"Abraham Lakes, Mayor of Lakestown, New Jersey."

After they had exchanged the briefest of handshakes, Redfern said, "I got a memo this morning to drop everything and come down here and check on this project. Not just one of our routine spotchecks, a memo marked *Urgent*. Now that I've finally found this little place, I can see why— looks like nothing's getting done. What exactly's been going on here?"

"I was about to ask the mayor the same question," Grafton said coldly.

"Where's the contractor who was awarded the job? Where's the state engineer assigned to the project?"

Both of the other men shrugged.

"Isn't *anybody* in charge?" the federal inspector asked incredulously. "I don't even see any workmen down there. Where is everybody? And who are all those other people?"

From the tent into which Ikie had disappeared, the choir picked up the tune he'd been whistling and sent it surging across the field:

> People, get ready,
> There's a train a-comin'
> People, get ready,
> Time to get on board.

Its effect was instantaneous. Making haste while seeming to move slowly, the conspirators began to disappear. Soon nothing was left but Bird's tent, and it, Fess guessed as he heard the buses begin to rumble, was probably empty.

"Well, they'd better show up soon, if they want to go on working here," the federal inspector said calmly. "Looks like a case of outside interference to me. I want fences thrown up around this job immediately. I want armed security guards with dogs around the clock. And all of it has to come out of the existing appropriation. Not one penny more is coming to this project from Washington. And if the security requirements I just outlined aren't met, or if this project comes in one day over schedule, or one dime over budget, the present funding will be cut off. Do I make myself clear?"

"Perfectly," Grafton said, with such grim control Fess wondered how he kept his head from exploding.

"Good," Redfern said. "Of course, I have to tell them myself. I'll just go back to my car and wait for—what are their names?" He dug a piece of paper trom his wallet. "Oh, yes. Berger from State Highways, and Luciano of Luck-Tex Construction." He took a long time to get his pipe lighted before he strolled back to his car. He didn't have to hurry or get excited. He was the Man, taking names.

"You let us down, Abe," Grafton said softly, with ominous Peter Lorre overtones. "I hope you know what that means. If you don't keep your promises, we don't have to keep ours."

When Redfern's car door closed, Grafton released his fury, screaming, "You promised to keep these people in order, Abe! I believed you. I thought we could stop worrying about Lakestown. I thought your big cop had everything under control. Jesus, I had faith in that monster. He looked big enough to control King Kong and a hundred other gorillas. Where is he, anyway, Abe? Where the hell is he?"

"I sent him," Abe said sheepishly, "to raid the whorehouse."

27

Foxy Carter had grown quite a few inches since the last time he'd hidden under the front porch to eavesdrop on the grown-ups. Back then, right after his bedtime, which always seemed to be the same as his age—eight or nine or ten—the hardest part had been climbing soundlessly out of his bedroom window and crawling and wriggling undetected into his favorite spot. Now the main problem was finding space for his additional length—that and the damned mosquitoes that plagued the Carters' new homesite in Froggy Bottom. He managed to solve the first problem by folding himself up like an accordion, and resolved to ignore the second. But he was also worried about whether the temporary blocks that supported the porch would hold up all the weight that was on it. His father didn't weigh much, and neither did that professor guy, but old Doctor Thompson and Ikie Lakes and Lukey's father were all heavyweights, even though one was all fat, one all muscle, and one all sinew and bone.

They might come crashing down on him any minute—he'd never heard the porch rocker creak as loudly as it did under Doc—but Foxy was compelled to remain where he was, directly beneath the creaking, legs drawn up and cramped, the damp earth soaking his skin. He had to endure this discomfort long enough to learn what, if anything, the older men had accomplished with all that play acting and grinning in the white men's faces, where all that shucking and jiving had gotten them.

His father's voice confirmed Foxy's suspicions that it had gotten them exactly nowhere. "Well." he said, "we're back to square one."

"Worse than that," said Fire Chief Farmer in his deep, rumbling bass. "We ain't even in the game no more. They've gotten too suspicious. You better believe they won't be fooled by no more games."

Jesus, thought Foxy. Counting Tonio's old man, there had to be at least three tons of flesh up there.

"Timing. Bad timing," Ikie Lakes growled. He sounded good and angry. Foxy wouldn't like to get on the wrong side of him. Even when he smiled, the mayor's brother looked mean. "We underestimated them. We spent too much time on the gentle stuff, playing around. We should've gotten rough a lot sooner, before they caught on."

"Ah," the professor said dreamily, "but it was beautiful while it lasted."

"It was too beautiful to last. I should've known that. I let it go on too long, and we lost our chance to get in there and do some real damage. That's what I get for listening to dreamers and women and preachers."

"Now don't blame the peoples what helped us, Ike," Lukey's father drawled. "They had good ideas, and most of them worked out good."

"Yes," the professor put in, "and nobody got caught, either. Except Mame's girls, and Les Porritt had them bailed out inside of an hour. They even had their hearing first, before the judge got around to that foreman, McCoy, and fined him."

"Heh heh," Lonnie Jenkins chuckled ungratefully. "Bossman sure do seem to keep on catchin' hell, don't he?"

"A small victory, but a nice one," the professor said, then added, "of course, Bella's still in the lockup."

"What?" Ikie Lakes roared like a lion, startling Foxy so badly that he jerked upward and banged his head on the porch floor. Fortunately, no one heard the crack it made.

"Well, naturally she got caught in the raid, along with the others," the professor explained. "She was still wearing that red nightgown Lily had loaned her, and it made her look like one of Mame's working girls. The chief was very apologetic about taking her in, but I think he had his instructions. Abe's been trying to get her out of the Blue Moon all week, you know. But when he came to the jail for her, she refused bail. Insisted on serving her thirty days."

"Good Lord," Ikie said. "The woman's crazy."

"I don't think so," Fess said. "I think she knows exactly what she's doing. Trying to get her husband to see the light, maybe. Embarrassing him, at least. Anyway, she's in good spirits. Mame and I took her some lunch today and a bottle of wine, and she was laughing and joking like she was on a thirty-day vacation. She sent you a message, by the way, Ikie. She said the weak link in the politicians' chain is right at the top, a guy named DeWitt, the state highway commissioner. Said he's scared of everything—investigators, reporters, even his own shadow. She thought it might be a good idea if we could get to him."

"If there's one thing I don't need at this point," Ikie grumbled, "it's more advice from my crazy sister-in-law."

"Now Ike," Josh said, "I told you before, stop blaming the other peoples."

"I'm not," the mayor's brother said fiercely. "You all put me in charge, so I'm blaming myself for not seizing our opportunity while we had it. We should have sabotaged everything in sight right away."

"It might not be too late for that," Doctor Thompson said in his wheezing voice. "Carter, you were just up there. Is the site completely fenced in?"

"Not quite," Foxy's father said. "They work fast, but not that fast. At least half the south end is still open."

"How many guards on duty?"

"Only one, and he knocks off at midnight. I heard that ratty little contractor say he can't afford three shifts of guards, no matter what the government inspector says. He's lost too much time and money on this job already. He's hoping if he skips the graveyard shift they won't know the difference."

"What time is it?" Lonnie Jenkins wanted to know.

"Ten minutes to midnight," Foxy's father said.

"Well, then, what are we waiting for? Let's go," Ikie urged.

"Patience, patience," the doctor said. "And for heaven's sake, man, stop despairing. If Luciano has lost time and money, our previous efforts were not wasted. But I've been sitting here thinking while you were all talking, and I've concluded that this situation calls for delicacy. Suspicions have been aroused. Federal authorities have been called in. We can't afford to be obvious. We have to use subtle methods, or we'll be sitting around discussing our strategy in a government prison instead of on your pleasant porch, Carter. Any bourbon left?"

"There's plenty," Foxy's father said curtly. "Help yourself."

There was a click, a splash, and a gurgle as the doctor satisfied his thirst. "Ah. Excellent. Now then. Is there anyone here besides me who is familiar with hydraulic systems?"

"Of course," Foxy's father responded. "What the hell do you think I do for a living?"

"Fine, fine. But let me elucidate for the benefit of the others. All those man-made monsters you see out there, all those bulldozers and backhoes and tractors, have circulatory systems, just as you and I do. Only in their case the life-giving fluid is not blood but oil. What I'm driving at is a way of paralyzing those mechanical beasts by clogging their circulatory systems. Earth-moving equipment runs on heavy oil—seventy weight or even higher. Therefore, we must introduce an oil of a lighter weight and a thinner viscosity into its arteries."

"Like number-ten cutting oil?" Foxy's dad asked.

"Perfect," Doc said. "A piece of that equipment will run only as long as all the oil in its lines is of the same specific weight and viscosity. If someone were to introduce a lighter-weight oil into its lifelines, he would clog them and literally gum up the works. This would have to be done, of course, while the machine was in a state of homeostasis . . ."

"'Homeo what?" Lonnie Tenkins asked.

"Rest," Fess translated.

". . . because it is only possible to interfere with the hoses that are not under pressure. The unpressurized hoses are usually the top ones, which lead from the reserve oil tank to the monster's heart, the pump that supplies power to the controls. The results of this interference will not be immediately apparent. First the machines will have to be put in operation. Heat will have to build up in them before the molecular structure of the oil breaks down and becomes goo. But once this happens, a vicious cycle will begin. Excess water vapor will build up, causing air bubbles and oxidation. Cavitation will devastate the gears, pistons, and other moving parts."

"You lost me with that last long word, Doc," Lonnie Jenkins complained.

"Cavitation? The creation of cavities, Lonnie, like the ones that used to be in the teeth you used to have. Pits will destroy those moving parts the way they did your uppers and lowers. Repairs will be difficult and time-consuming, if not impossible. Replacement will probably be the only answer, just as it was in your case. A very small admixture of the wrong weight oil would do the trick. But it would have to be introduced undetectably. No one should even be able to figure out how such, er, accidents happened."

"How do you propose to manage that, Doctor?" Ikie Lakes wanted to know.

"With some equipment I happen to keep on hand in large quantities. Ideally suited to making small punctures that will reseal themselves quickly and leave no traces, because that is exactly what they were designed to do. I am referring, of course, to hypodermic syringes."

At least half of the men reacted to this plan with excited shouts and foot stompings that drowned out the others' words. But Foxy had heard all he needed to hear. With swift, silent cunning that matched his small, sharp features and made his nickname doubly appropriate, he wriggled out of his hiding place and rolled down the damp slope of their new yard to the very edge of the creek that bordered it.

> Thirty days in jail with my
> Back turned to the wall,
> Thirty days in jail with my
> Back turned to the wall.

Bella sang cheerfully.

> Look here, Mister Jailkeeper, put
> Another gal in my stall.

"Please, Mrs. Lakes," Chief Boyd pleaded. "You're disturbing the other prisoners."

"What other prisoners?" Bella wanted to know. "I thought they were all out on bail but me."

"Benny Mingle's in the next cell now."

"Sleeping off a drunk?"

The chief nodded.

Bella's raucous laugh bounced off the concrete walls of her cell in a cascade of echoes. "I have a better chance of waking the dead than I have of waking Benny." She glanced at the lunch box and wine bottle Fess and Mame had brought her, both empty. "Can you get me another bottle?"

"Not now. Mrs. Lakes. Your husband's outside, waiting to see you."

"I told you twice before, I don't want to see him. I don't want him to bail me out. I want to serve my thirty days. And when I leave the House of Many Slammers, I want to go work for the House of the Rising Moon."

"You don't mean that, Mrs. Lakes," Chief Boyd said.

"How do you know what I mean? I do mean it, I do. I never had so much fun in my whole life." She laughed again, joyously recalling the parade of dazzled johns, the pile of muddy boots they'd left at the door, the honky-tonk music that had lifted her spirits, and the even greater joy of serving the already besotted white men food and drink that turned them into total zombies. She hadn't turned any tricks—Mame's orders were strict—but the sore bruises on her frequently pinched behind were evidence of her diligent service. "Bring me a pig's foot and a bottle of beer," she half shouted, half sang at Boyd.

The big chief was doing his best to deal with her calmly, but his broad, handsome brow, wrinkled like a bulldog's, showed that it was not easy. "You're making things awfully hard for me, Mrs. Lakes. I didn't want to arrest you in the first place. But there you were, dancing and carrying on, with that nightgown pulled up so high you didn't give me any choice."

Bella looked down and studied herself. "It was the only way I could move in this skin-tight thing." She stood up and demonstrated. "Oops. Guess I forgot about the slit in front. Whatsa matter, Chief, did you see the hairs on my whiskbroom?"

"Please, Mrs. Lakes," the reddening chief said with averted eyes. "I'll get you a bottle on one condition. No, two."

"What are they?"

"You see your husband. And you, uh, cover yourself more modestly."

"Oh, all right," Bella said crossly, yanking the garment down to her calves. "Send the old fusspot in. But send the bottle in with him. I prefer imported vodka, a hundred proof. And some juice to mix with it, if that's not too much trouble."

Chief Boyd did not return. When the door of Bella's cell swung open, it admitted only Abe, laden down with a bottle, a briefcase, a bouquet of roses, and a gigantic cardboard box.

"I've come to take you home, Bella," he croaked.

"Straight from Greta Grimes's bed, I'll bet," she said. "I hope you've washed the grave stink offa you."

"I haven't been in any bed but ours," he said humbly. "And it's been damned lonesome without you. I've already paid your bail, dear. Please come home." Awkwardly, with an audible creaking of his joints, he dropped to his knees as if proposing.

"For God's sake. Lakes, get up from there. You sound arthritic, and you look ridiculous. Sorry I can't offer you a chair, but . . ." she giggled, "this place doesn't offer much in the way of hospitality. Sit on my bed, why don't you? At least we can have a drink and talk about it."

He rose, still creaking, and lowered himself and his packages onto her bunk.

"Aren't you going to scold me for my behavior?" she asked him. "I thought you had me locked up for lewdness."

"Not lewdness, Bella. Jealousy. It hurts to admit it, but that's what it was."

"Hmmmmmm," she said. "Jealousy, or pride?"

"Well, maybe a little bit of both," he conceded. "Dammit, Bella, I didn't want you locked up at all, but it was the only way I could get you back. I never thought I cared for you as much as I do, but when you left, it almost killed me. All I could think of was, 'I want my wife back.' And it's still all I want, Bella."

"I doubt that," she said. "Of course, I don't expect you to believe me, either, but none of the men at the Blue Moon touched me, except for pinching my rear end. It still hurts. That's why I'm standing while you're sitting."

"I believe you," he said after a long pause, finally looking her in the face. "But I didn't know that, and I was jealous. I wanted you back in the worst way, Bella. Physically and every other way. You'll never know how much it cost me to go after you. Maybe everything."

"And maybe nothing," she said dryly. "Can we have that drink now?"

"Certainly," he said, pulling, with his typical efficiency, two shot glasses from his briefcase. "To us," he said, after pouring and clicking glasses.

Bella drained hers without responding to the toast. "Abe, before I come home with you. I've got some conditions."

He did not respond except for a slight raising of his graying, expressive eyebrows.

"I won't play any more roles for you or with you. If that interferes with your ambitions, it's just too damned bad. I'm Bella Lakes, your black wife, not some silly white society whore. Plain old funky natural me is who you'll be getting, not a mock-up of some painted white doll. How white I happen to look has nothing to do with it. I'm a black woman inside, a real *down* black woman, and you're just going to have to live with that. And if there's a little bit of the Devil in me, you'll just have to live with that, too. If I have to do any whoring after this, I'll do it for myself, not for you or for some other man. Especially not for some phony-ass *white* man, no matter how much you think he can help your career."

"My career," he said, "may already be wrecked because of you. I sent Boyd and the whole force to the Blue Moon to get you, when they should have been keeping order at the construction site."

"I'd be sorry," she said "if I thought you'd ever had a chance to get that state job in the first place. But if you want my opinion, the career you're hoping for is a fantasy. You said once I don't deal in reality, Lakes. Well, I think you're the wildest dreamer I ever met. I could smell the phoniness on those white men the minute they walked in our house. But you still think they'll keep their promises, don't you?"

"There's still a chance," he said stubbornly. "If I keep mine."

"You're incredible, Lakes. Pour me another shot. Those men don't need you. They don't have to give you anything. Oh, they can offer you promises, but they don't intend to follow through on them. The only career ahead of you is the one you already have right here in Lakestown. And that's something I *can* help you save. I know the people here, and they trust me. I may be able to get them to trust you again, in spite of all the shit that's gone down. But you still haven't given up on that other thing, have you?"

"No," he admitted. "But I want you home, too."

"On my terms or yours? Pour me another shot, please."

"Your terms, Bella. I need you just as you are."

Bella finished her vodka and said, "Okay. Let's go."

"Please open the box first."

She noted the elaborately scrolled gold label of an extravagant Edgehill shop, then lifted the lid and the layers of tissue paper and stared in wonder. Beneath them was the most seductive thing she'd ever seen, except her husband's brother: a full-length coat of jet black mink. She knew she was being seduced by it but could not resist lifting it out and rubbing her cheek against its softness.

"Please put it on," her husband said.

"In July? I'll swelter."

"Please."

"Oh, I get it. You want me to cover up my shame."

"No, I just want to see how it looks on you."

She didn't need a mirror to know it looked magnificent.

"Will you wear it home, please? Just as a favor to me?"

"You old prude, you just don't want me seen on the street in this sexy nightgown. To tell the truth, I don't blame you. Did Boyd give you my handbag?"

He nodded.

"I think there's a lipstick and a compact in there."

She took them, colored her face, then mischievously offered him the lipstick. "Don't you want to paint an *A* on my forehead?"

"What for?"

"For a college man you sure are ignorant, Abe. For *Adultery*, of course."

"No," he said, moving close to her, giving her a moist kiss on the cheek, a definite improvement on the dry one he'd given her the night they entertained, "but I'd like to put it there for 'Abe's.'"

She sniffed him thoroughly. "Well, at least you don't smell like embalming fluid. Just the usual soap and Old Spice. But that doesn't mean you can brand me with your initial. I'm not your property. I don't belong to anyone but me."

And, swinging on her husband's arm, she walked jauntily down the jailhouse steps, singing, to the tune of "Tonight I Belong to You":

> You may
> Think that I belong to you
> But no matter what you say

And no matter what you do,
I'm free,
I be- lo- ong
To me.

"So that's the plan," Foxy finished expounding, having enjoyed his friends' rapt attention for half an hour. "I heard the old heads work it out tonight. They gonna go on talking about it all night, I expect. But while they're still talking about it, we're gonna be *doin'* it."

"It's their plan. Maybe we should let them carry it out," Tonio Farmer advised.

"*Damn,* Tonio! Ever since you got out that hospital, you sound like the doctors stuck some gray hairs in your 'fro. Is you still a Young Warrior, or is you an old man now?"

"No call to be disrespectful to the new chief, Carter," Lukey Hawkins reproved him.

"Sorry, Hawk. Didn't mean to be disrespectful, Chief. But this sittin' around doin' nothin' all summer's been drivin' me crazy. All this time we been hangin' back, lettin' the old heads take charge, waitin' patiently for a piece of the action. And what they been doin' in the meantime? Shuckin' and jivin' and clownin' like a bunch of old Toms in a minstrel show. And what did it get 'em? Nothin' but a ten-foot fence and a bunch of armed guards. I say it's time us young bloods took over."

"They were gonna let us in on the action, Carter," Lukey told him. "They promised me they would."

"When?" Foxy demanded. "When it was all over? Hell, man, we got to do it now or never. The last guard just went off duty. Tomorrow night they'll have the fence finished. Are we gonna be like the old heads and stand around all night and talk and talk, and never get around to doing anything?"

"Who was there when you were listening?" Tonio asked.

"Everybody. Your pop, and Hawk's, and mine, and Mr. Lonnie Jenkins, and the mayor's brother, and that professor guy, and Dr. Thompson."

"My pop too?" Tommy Adams asked.

"Naw, Adams. I heard somebody say he was out lookin' for you for staying out all night three nights in a row. And when he catches you, won't be enough left of you to put in a pee pot."

All the young men laughed except Tonio, who was, as usual, serious. "These old heads you're talking about are our *fathers,*" he reproved Foxy. "Even if we've dropped our African names, I'm going to insist that we stick to our African principles. And one of them is having respect for our elders."

"I respect 'em, all right," Foxy grumbled. "They're just too slow for me."

"You know, the last time we listened to you, we got in serious trouble, Carter," Tonio continued. "Maybe we should have learned a lesson from that. Maybe it would be better if we all went home."

"I don't want to go home," Foxy said.

"Why not?"

"Well . . . I saw something down by the creek near our house."

"What?" Tonio asked.

"I don't want to talk about it."

"Talk," Lukey commanded.

"Well, the trouble is, I'm not sure exactly what I saw. I was layin' in the weeds, and looked up and there was Crump and that old Baron killing a chicken. Twisting its head off and drinking its blood, and sayin' some funny words I never heard before. The first time I looked, it was just the two of them, I know that. But the second time, it seemed like at least ten people was down there, jumpin' around, singin' and dancin'. That was when I told my feet, 'Feet, get me out of here.'"

"I bet they stole Croquignol!" Lukey exclaimed.

"Croaky *who?*" Rudy Merchant wanted to know.

"Our frizzly-tailed rooster, Croquignol," Lukey explained. "He was our protection against bad luck. He's been missing all week."

"Well," Foxy said, "I don't expect you'll recognize him when you see him again. He's probably in somebody's stew pot by now."

"Wasn't enough of him to make a meal," Lukey said sadly.

"Well, are you *all* a bunch of chickens, or are we still the Warriors?" Foxy demanded. "That's what *I* want to know."

"We'll take a vote," Tonio decided. "All in favor of Foxy's plan say 'Aye.' All against, say 'No.'"

There was a chorus of *ayes*.

"The *ayes* have it," Tonio said, not too happily. "All right, Carter. You get the oil from your dad's service station. I'll get the hypodermic needles."

"Let me get 'em, Chief," Rudy Merchant volunteered. "You're too big to crawl in Doc's little bathroom window, and that's where he keeps 'em. I know 'cause I was in there last week to have him look at my tonsils. And he don't never lock that window. Only the door. Carter, you sure Doc is still down at your house?"

"Sure. They had three bottles of whiskey on the porch. When I left, he was just getting started on the first one."

"All right," Tonio decided. "Telford, you go with Merchant and stand lookout while he's in the doc's office. Adams, you go with Carter and help him get the oil from his father's station. Don't waste any time. Meet us at the south fence inside half an hour."

Left alone, the two oldest Warriors walked slowly and talked quietly, expressing apprehensions they had not shared with the younger boys.

"I hope this turns out better than the last caper the club pulled off, man," Tonio said.

"You ain't lyin'. I hope so too."

"I'm not thinkin' about myself. I'm here, walking, talking, breathing. But somebody else got put underground behind that caper. I hope we're not making more bones for graves."

"I wish you hadn't said that, Farmer," Lukey said. "I feel like somebody just walked over mine."

"You?" Tonio mocked, trying to tease him out of his mood. "Are you superstitious and scared of the dark? Hell, Hawkins, you *is* the dark! I don't understand how a man can be scared of himself. You so big and black the sun calls you to help him put the stars out."

"You pretty shady yourself, Farmer. You're so shady the grass won't grow where you go. And if you stand in one place too long, toadstools spring up around your feet. *Blam! Blam! Blam!* A whole forest of toadstools."

They both laughed at this equal exchange, but their basic mood was still somber. They walked in silence for a minute. Then Lukey said, "I ain't afraid, man. It's not that. It's just . . . I had that rooster such a long time. He was my pet from the time I was five years old. And my dad said he was our good-luck bird, so I always felt safe long as he was around."

Everything seemed to go very well indeed; almost, Tonio felt, too well. When he and Lukey reached the fence, Rudy Merchant and Alfonso Telford were already there with a half dozen hypodermic needles they were sure Doc would never miss. Tommy Adams and Foxy Carter arrived shortly with a case of oil and a pair of flashlights.

Foxy, who worked afternoons and weekends at his father's service station, apparently knew as much about hydraulics as Dunce Cap and the doctor did. He demonstrated on a tractor, showing the other boys where the transmission lines were and how to foul them by injecting the light oil. They worked in pairs, quickly and efficiently, sabotaging the big machines first and the small ones last, and were finished in less than two hours.

"Let's leave now," Tonio urged. "We'll bury the needles. You put the other stuff back where you got it, Carter."

But Foxy was not satisfied. The sabotage was not spectacular enough to suit him. The machines did not look harmed or even tampered with. No one could tell the Warriors had been there.

"That's the whole point," Tonio told him. "You said so yourself. The road crew's not supposed to suspect anything."

"But how," Foxy argued, "are we gonna know it works, unless we try it out?"

"We'll know tomorrow," Tonio said. "Come on, you guys, let's haul ass out of here."

But Foxy defied him and climbed aboard the power shovel. "I know what I'm doing," he asserted. "I can drive anything. I always wanted to drive one of these big mothers anyway. This is my chance."

"Carter, come down from there!" Tonio ordered.

But Foxy, high in the cab of the machine, even higher on the power of sitting at its controls, was past hearing him. He started the engine cautiously, put it in low gear, and began to inch forward, squinting ahead into the darkness. The drive gears on this monster worked fine. They had not tampered with its transmission lines, only with the ones that operated the boom. Foxy wanted to go faster but could not see where he was going. He fumbled around on the control panel and found a lever he thought would turn the lights on.

The boom rose majestically to its full height. Foxy fumbled frantically for another lever, found one, and pulled it as hard as he could. The boom trembled and fell to earth with the impact of a giant sequoia tree.

Before any of them had recovered from the shock of the crash, they heard an even more terrifying scream.

The men, alerted by Tonio's frantic phone call, got to the scene in record time. While everyone else grubbed in the earth, digging a hole beneath Lukey, his father and Freeman Farmer heaved and grunted until they managed to lift the crane that pinned his leg. Doc instructed Tonio to pull the unconscious Lukey out of the hole by his shoulders as fast as possible.

"Shine the flashlights here," Doc ordered. Tommy Adams and Foxy Carter complied, but when Foxy saw what the light revealed he began to retch. Tonio angrily snatched the light from his hand, releasing Foxy to go off and puke in the darkness.

"Sorry, Josh," Doc said as he tightened a tourniquet above Lukey's ankle. "That foot's just hanging by a thread. There's no way to save it. He's lost a lot of blood. Let's get him to my place and transfuse him. You know his blood type?"

"O positive," Josh said tonelessly. "Same as me."

"Good," Doc grunted, getting to his feet. "That will help. I have some whole blood and some transfusing equipment at my office. It's primitive, maybe, but we can't waste time getting him to the hospital. Let's go."

Josh Hawkins's silence as he carried his son to Doc's car was more chilling than Luke's screams.

Except for an occasional call to one or the other of them to help, there was no relief from the tension in the crowded waiting room. The boys and men sat and smoked tensely, not speaking to one another, for what seemed like hours, while Doc worked on Luke inside.

In the little room Doc had turned into a temporary surgery, he turned to the father who lay on the next table, giving his second pint of blood in an hour, clamped off the tube in Josh's arm and said, "He's had five pints now. That ought to do it. I think he's coming out of shock. His pulse is almost back to normal. I'll just give him some glucose to be safe, then I'll call the ambulance. Jesus! What strength. Just like his old man. Don't sit up too fast, Josh. You might get dizzy."

The senior Hawkins ignored this warning. He swung his long legs to the floor and said, "Just get me some whiskey."

"Cap!" Doc called. "Bring the Scotch from my desk drawer."

Josh took a heavy swig, wiped his mouth, and asked with a tremor in his voice, "Why couldn't it of been me, Doc? Why couldn't it of been me?"

"Ask me some easier questions, Josh," Doc said. "Like, what are we going to tell the hospital? I have to call the ambulance now. How am I going to explain this accident?"

Josh thought for a moment. "Hit and run car?"

Doc nodded. "That'll do."

Cap Carter offered Josh some more whiskey. Josh took another drink, passed the bottle to Doc, then said, "What I want to know is, who was driving that thing that hurt my son?"

"My boy," Cap said sadly. "My damn-fool boy. He admitted it to me."

Josh leaped to his feet, ripping Band-Aids and tubes from his recently drained arm, and rushed into the waiting room. Before anyone could stop him, he had Foxy down on the floor, first pummeling him, then shaking and choking him with those gigantic fingers. All the while he kept pleading strangely, in a soft, crooning voice, "Get me off him, please, somebody. Please get me off him before I kill him."

It took the combined strength of Alfonso Telford, Tonio Farmer, and his father, Nunc, to accomplish what Josh asked. When they finally succeeded, Foxy was a crumpled, whimpering wreck in the corner.

"Now what do I tell the ambulance crew?" Doc mused, checking him over. *"Two* hit and runs?"

"I don't care what you tell 'em," the giant grocer said, trembling, his hands quivering as if they wanted to choke someone else. "Just tell 'em he's lucky to be alive."

"He is, at that," Doc said. "Two broken ribs and a dozen contusions." He put his hand on Josh's back and guided him gently into the surgery.

"I got to go home now, tell Mae," Josh said brokenly.

"Well, when you do, tell her *right,*" Doc said. "Tell her he'll recover and walk again. Tell her we'll get him one of the new prostheses, a flexible one that'll have him walking as good as ever. He won't take any Olympic medals, maybe, but he won't have to spend his life in a wheelchair."

"How do you know that?" Josh demanded.

"Shhhh," Doc said. "He's coming around."

Sure enough, Lukey's eyelids were fluttering, and he was trying to speak. Briefly, his eyes opened and focused on his father. "A stockbroker don't have to run, Pop," he whispered.

"*That's* how I know," Doc said triumphantly.

"A stockbroker," Lukey said dreamily, "pays people to do his running for him."

"Shut up. Save your strength," his father said roughly. "I want you to be lookin' and soundin' that good when I bring your mother to see you at the hospital."

28

"Well, Abe," Senator Grafton boomed over the phone. "I wish I could say you've done a good job for us. But the work's been stalled for over a month now, and Dom's had to replace nearly all his equipment. I don't have to tell you what that means, do I?"

"Yes, you do," Abe said evenly, fanning flies away from the kitchen, which Bella had left in the habitual state of slovenliness to which she had returned after he brought her home. Just before the phone rang he had been contemplating, with a faint degree of pleasure, rolling up his shirt sleeves and plunging his arms up to the elbows in sink suds. The chore would be so simple and satisfying, compared to the complications in his life.

"It means we're all going to take one hell of a beating on this project. It means you can probably forget about that state appointment, Abe."

Abe brought the flat of his hand down on an unusually fat August fly, succeeded in stunning it, then crushed the life out of it with his long index finger before replying, "I don't see why you're taking it out on me, Harry." He enjoyed emphasizing the first name. "It's not my fault you picked a contractor who cuts corners and uses second-rate equipment."

"You have a point, Abe," the senator admitted grudgingly. "Dom suspects sabotage, but he can't prove it. Mechanics who work on earth-moving equipment are scarcer than emeralds. It took Dom two weeks to get hold of one, and when he did the man couldn't find any indication that those machines had been tampered with."

"Well, then," Abe said, "probably none of them *had* been tampered with. Probably it was junk equipment in the first place."

"Possibly," Grafton conceded. "But if the machines weren't sabotaged, why did they all blow at once?"

Abe had been out there that morning, along with most of Lakestown's other citizens, and had seen the machines stall, collapse, and, in three instances, explode and catch fire. It had been a far better

Fourth of July show than Lakestown had ever been able to afford, though only Biker Boyd, waving flags and setting off sparklers, seemed to think that was the occasion.

"I have no idea," Abe said. "Apparently the experts have no idea either. So how can you expect *me* to explain it?"

"Abe, I don't know what those darkies have been up to over there if you don't, but I suspect something. Dom does too; but he can't afford to push an investigation, because he was supposed to have twenty-four-hour security, but he didn't have anyone on duty at the time. He can't afford to let the government know that. Do you read me?"

"I'm listening." Abe wished he could tell Grafton how much he hated listening to his phony, syrupy radio-announcer voice.

"Jesus, everything seems to be going against us all of a sudden. The governor has decided to come out against the highway, and he's been leaning on DeWitt. Our boy Oscar is wavering. That faggot is afraid to drive on anything wider than two lanes anyway, and he won't go within ten miles of a traffic circle. But I've got half my life tied up in this project, so I've decided to give you one more chance, boy."

Boy. Abe felt the muscles of his stomach contract, felt its juices churn and converge painfully at the tender spot where two doctors had told him he was developing an ulcer.

"You know all the delays this project has suffered. After all that's happened, we're going to have to work double time, maybe triple time, to get back on schedule. Right now there's only one obstacle standing in the way of our progress."

Abe belched. He had gone to Thompson about his incipient ulcer and thrown up his hands in disgust when that black quack gave him a single-word prescription: "Grease." Then he had gone to an Edgehill doctor, who prescribed Maalox. It hadn't helped much. Doc's irrational advice—"Take it easy, and go greasy"—still echoed maddeningly in his ears.

"I think I'll ask Bella to cook some pigs' feet tonight," he said, momentarily forgetting he was speaking into the phone.

"Abe, aren't you listening to me? All the homeowners on this month's schedule have cooperated except one. Woman named Vinnie Coddums. Refuses to move out of her house. We've offered her double the state allocation, but she won't budge. From what I hear, she's armed in there, and she has all the doors and windows barred. I want her moved out, Abe. Today."

"With pleasure," Abe said, belching up some more bitter bile and wondering whether fried chicken would be easier on his tender gut than trotters.

"She's squatting right in the center of Merchant Avenue, guarding her shack twenty-four hours a day. Funny thing about it, I used to trust that woman more than I trust my wife. She was our maid for over twenty years. I would have fired her when this came up, but she quit first. Made me feel like a damned fool. I want her moved out of there if you have to blast her out with dynamite. Do you hear me, boy?"

"Consider it done," Abe said, and belched again. Yes, he would ask for fried chicken, and some greens from Bella's garden boiled with fatback. Steaks and salads were definitely not helping him.

"After all that's happened, I don't consider anything done until I see it with my own eyes. Her shack isn't worth five hundred, but you can offer her up to five thousand. Write her a check on the spot. I'll make it good. I'll be waiting to hear from you, boy. It better be soon." *Click.*

While he was doing the dishes, a towel neatly tucked into his waistband, his dangling cigarette dropping ashes into the water, Abe succeeded in turning his rage away from Grafton and toward Vinnie. When he thought of all the trouble that cat-eyed witch had caused him over the years, the most violent means he might use to evict her seemed justified. She had seduced him when she was a lowly kitchen mechanic and knew he was a married man with three degrees and a promising future. But that didn't stop her from shaking her hips and her hair at him, that long silky tail of hair that irresistibly reminded him of his mother's, until he surrendered. Then had come the embarrassment of the afflicted child, complicated by his wife's inexplicable attachment to it. Bella would never know, but it was his own genes he mistrusted, not hers, especially after Cindy's retardation became evident. He had never believed that coal-black man with his fits of fiery evangelism was his real father. How could he, even now, looking at his own wrists, blanched white by dishwater?

Isaac had enough color to be Freedom George Lakes's son, but Abe did not. And since no white man would want a squaw, his mother must have been playing around in Claypool to produce him. And Claypool being what it was, a tiny hotbed of close mulatto incest, he and Bella were probably cousins, another reason for refusing children.

But he and Vinnie had crossed paths and produced a defective child anyway.

Abe put the first pile of dishes away and started on the second while he continued to enumerate Vinnie's crimes. This sleepy little town would never have become aroused about the highway if she hadn't stolen the plans somehow and circulated them. They would have accepted it the way they accepted the weather and the ways of white folks, as indistinguishable acts of God.

But she had stolen the plans from her employer, who was also his political patron, and now the patronage would end unless he could move her out of the highway's path.

It would give him great pleasure, Abe thought as he dried and polished the last glass, to follow the senator's suggestion and blast her loose with dynamite. It was only what she deserved. Vinnie was the source of all his troubles, *all* of them. And all his successes were outweighed by the defeats she had brought on him.

As he removed the towel and put on his jacket, he felt his shoulders sag with the knowledge that Vinnie had always beaten him. He was conscious, too, that his putative father's preachings about damnation had made such a deep imprint on his mind that he had never stopped expecting retribution for his sins. His guilt over his trespasses with Vinnie and his neglect of their child had become a massive weight over the years, one he could not shrug off. He would try his best to get Vinnie out of there, but he had a deep sense of hopelessness and futility about it all.

The bride wore white, a hasty, haphazard construction of dotted Swiss curtains and elastic in which she looked ravishing. She carried a bouquet of wild white field daisies.

The groom wore tattered white sneakers, patched jeans, and a strained, brave expression. He carried the rings.

The mother of the bride wore a pink chenille bathrobe and carried a shotgun.

The stepmother of the bride wore a blue chiffon float from an exclusive Edgehill shop and carried a bottle of imported champagne. When the banging at the door commenced, she opened it and called out sweetly, "Come in! You're just in time to give the bride away!"

And the father of the bride, who had come to attack, found that he had walked into an ambush.

"You stand over there, to the left of Cindy," Vinnie ordered, indicating his position with the barrel of her rifle, "and don't speak till your turn comes. I'll tell you when."

Abe did as he was told, sneaking a sheepish look at the father of the groom, who sat in a corner, scowling. Carl Adams looked as if he had been angry for twenty years and intended to stay that way for another twenty. Abe felt his own face take on a matching expression.

"Proceed, Reverend," the person in charge directed, placing her shotgun at parade rest.

"Dearly beloved," the Reverend LeRoy Bird intoned sonorously, "we are gathered here to . . ."

But Abe, whose eyes had just grown used to the dimness of the cluttered little room, was startled to see another scowling figure in the farthest corner. "Dom!" he cried. "What are *you* doing here?"

"Same thing you are, I guess," the little man said sourly. "I came here first thing this morning to offer this woman a bonus for moving, and she and the Reverend there held me prisoner."

Vinnie swung indignantly and pointed her gun at him. "We did no such thing," she said. "All we did was quote Scripture to you and try to point out the error of your ways."

"I always heard money talks," Dom said. "So I brought three Presidents here with me to talk to her. Jefferson, Jackson, and Madison. But she wouldn't listen to none of 'em."

"You wouldn't listen to Ezekiel, Daniel, or Isaiah. Three prophets," Vinnie stated.

"We were only concerned, the Reverend said suavely, "about the state of your immortal soul."

"I go to Mass," Dom said with a quaver of defiance.

"How often?" the Reverend Bird asked.

"Often enough. Two, three times a year. I give lotsa money to the church. I'm the biggest contributor in the parish."

"Money," the Reverend said severely, "has nothing to do with it. If you were truly devout, you would not be trying to put this poor woman and her daughter out of their home."

"He's stubborn, that's his trouble. He's a hard one to teach. That's why we had to keep him here so long," Vinnie said. "He still thinks the Gospel is written on a dollar bill. But we're gonna teach him yet. You ever seen pictures of Matthew or Mark or Luke or John printed on a piece of paper money?"

"No, ma'am," Luciano said with surprising respectfulness.

"You ever see the Virgin Mary on a coin?"

"No, ma'am," he said again.

"Then stop thinking money can buy your salvation," she told him.

"Look, lady, I respect your beliefs. But they don't happen to be mine, and they don't give you the right to kidnap me."

"No one has kidnapped anyone," Reverend Bird said. "You're free to go at any time."

Dom stood up, looking like a fire hydrant in his red knit suit and white silk shirt, only to sit down again quickly when Vinnie swung her gun in his direction.

"You see?" he said to Abe with a hopeless shrug. "It's a clear case of kidnapping. Somebody call the FBI."

"I will," Abe said, starting for the door.

But the hostage himself called him back, "Hold it! Leave the FBI outa this. They already got a file on me thicker than the phone book. I don't want no more trouble."

Abe recalled the reason he had come. "Well, I'm not in anybody's files, and I have a job to do. Vinnie, you're holding up the highway construction. I'm prepared to offer you ten times the market value of your property to move. If you'll just sign this paper I have here, I'll write you a check for five thousand dollars."

"Tsk, tsk." Reverend Bird chided. "All this talk of money."

"When," Abe demanded, "were you ever offended by money? You live like a king. You ride around in a Cadillac. You have enough antiques in that parsonage to break all the sales records at Parke-Bernet."

"I ask for nothing," Reverend Bird said silkily. "Everything I possess comes from the generosity of my flock and, through them, from God."

"Maybe I'd better get acquainted with this God of yours."

"Praise be!" Vinnie exclaimed. "I never thought I'd hear it from Abe Lakes, but it's never too late for a soul to seek Jesus!"

The Reverend Bird cleared his throat. "If the mayor wishes to seek salvation, he can consult with me later in my study. Right now I have a ceremony to perform."

"Yes," Abe said, "and it looks like I walked in just in time to stop it. You preach about sin, but if I ever saw one being committed, this is it. Why are you marrying these children? Lucinda's only fourteen—"

"Fifteen," her mother corrected.

"Still. She's just a child. And that boy there is only—what, Adams? Fifteen?"

"Seventeen," his father said grimly. "Old enough to stay out all night, every night, all summer."

"I couldn't stand it at home anymore, Pa," Tommy defended himself. "I don't mean any disrespect, but you kept blamin' me for Lou gettin' drowned and sayin' you hated the sight of me. I couldn't stay there anymore."

"Then why the hell didn't you join the army? Huh?" his red-faced father roared.

Tommy shrugged. "I wanted to finish high school."

"Imbecile!" his father shouted. "They shouldn't even have let you out of *grade* school. Irresponsible idiot! All you've done is get yourself and this poor girl in trouble."

"I'm going to do the right thing, Pa," Tommy said sturdily.

"Damn right you are," Vinnie said, and patted the barrel of her gun. "Excuse my language, Reverend. Let's get on with the wedding."

"Now just a minute," Abe said. "Nobody's asked me what I think about this. I say they're too young. I say they're still children."

"Abe," Vinnie said, "this great big *child*, as you call him, 's been sneakin' in Cindy's window every night after dark. Spendin' the night with her, and sneakin' out again in the morning before I went to work. They was so quiet and sneaky about it I never would've caught 'em if I hadn't quit work. Then I noticed Cindy had gone six weeks without showin' blood in her drawers, and I took her to Doc and found out she was pregnant. Excuse me for talkin' so plain, Reverend, but the mayor's such an educated fool you practically have to draw him pictures. Poor thing, she still don't even know what's happened to her."

"I do, too," Cindy said clearly. "I'm going to have Tommy's baby."

Abe, suddenly dizzy, reeled backward and sank into Vinnie's ancient sofa. It had protruding springs that stuck him in several tender places. He sprang up again, spluttering. "How did she learn to talk? And how did she learn to, to—? Vinnie, you should have supervised her more strictly. And you, young man, how do you intend to support my daughter?"

A babble of voices ensued from which Bella's, the loudest, emerged stridently. "She learned to talk from listening to me, of course. Nothing's wrong with her mind, nothing ever was. It was just that nobody else ever took the time to talk to her till I did."

"Yeah? What did you talk to her about?" Vinnie asked belligerently. "Things she had no business knowin', I bet."

"I told her some of the facts of life, yes. I thought it was time she knew them. I'm afraid I didn't get around to telling her all of them, though."

"Then it's all your fault!" Vinnie raged. "If you hadn't told her about them things, she wouldn't have done 'em."

"That's ridiculous," Bella said calmly, though her face flushed. "Of course she would have done them. She only did what everybody else does. The difference is, she *knew* what she was doing."

The babble became deafening, with Bella and Vinnie raging at each other, and Carl Adams shouting new accusations at his son, until the Reverend Bird interrupted by raising his splendidly robed arms for silence. "Peace, Mrs. Lakes. Peace Mrs. Coddums, Mr. Adams. Peace, everyone. Let us all stop casting blame, and bow our heads in prayer."

They obeyed.

"Our Heavenly Father, Your ways are not for us to understand, only to accept and praise. We ask You to look down and bless this young couple and the new life they are going to bring into the world. We ask Your assurance that only good will come of this union. We ask Your blessings on every member of this company, and especially on those who must help these young people make it to maturity. Let Thy holy peace descend on this company. May the Holy Ghost descend and take up residence in this dwelling, to keep it in safety and blessed happiness. And may Thy holy spirit reside harmoniously within these walls and within every member of this company, now and forevermore. Amen."

"Amen," they all echoed. Luciano crossed himself.

"I had another question," Abe said when it seemed tactful to break the silence. "I asked you, young man, how you plan to support my daughter." His emotions were so turbulent that he failed to notice until the words were out of his mouth that he had admitted the inadmissible twice in two minutes. When he realized what he had said, he felt better than he had in years, as if at least half the load he carried around had slipped from his shoulders.

"I'm going to be a lawyer, sir," Tommy said.

"I mean in the *meantime*," Abe growled.

Bella interrupted sweetly, "Didn't you say something about a check, dear? Five thousand dollars is a nice round figure. It ought to get them off to a good start."

"That check," he told Bella, "was to pay Vinnie for leaving her house."

"But of course she can't give up the house now, darling. Her family's growing. She needs it. She may even need to add a room."

"That's true," he grumbled, feeling himself propelled by forces beyond his understanding or control.

"Well, then," Bella said brightly. "You *do* see my point, dear. Even half that amount would help Tommy and Cindy a lot, though five thousand sounds much nicer. And of course you'll send Tommy to college."

"I'll do what?" Abe roared.

"I know you," she said. "I know you don't want a disadvantaged grandchild. So of course you're going to help Cindy's husband finish his education."

"I am? I am?"

"I did hear you rightly, didn't I, darling? I *did* hear you say Cindy is your daughter? Your *only* daughter?"

"Yes," Abe growled, "I guess I am." He looked from young Adams's face to his father's, both the same shade of saffron, and thought, at least it won't be dark skinned.

For the first time in months, the shadow of a smile flickered around Carl Adams's mouth. Abe felt the corners of his own lips turn upward to the same minuscule degree.

"Of course," Abe said almost dreamily, "an abortion would be cheaper."

The face Bella turned on him was contorted with awful, unnamable emotions. "I didn't hear you say that, Abe. But if you say it again, I *will* hear you, and I'll probably go berserk and kill you. All these years you wouldn't let me have children, and I kept wondering, what's it all for? What good are all his achievements and ambitions, if he won't leave any posterity? No, Abe! *No!* You're not going to deny us grandchildren, too!"

"I didn't say anything, Bella," he retracted hastily.

"Good."

The Reverend Bird cleared his throat. "I hope everything has been settled now. We were about to have a solemn ceremony."

"Yes, let's get on with it," Vinnie urged, "so I can stop hatin' that little sneak and start tryin' to love him."

Bella clapped her hands in delight, like a child. "Oh, but now that everybody's here, we can do it right! Vinnie, put that silly gun away and go put a nice dress on. Abe, go out in the kitchen with Cindy. Wait, and don't come back in till you hear the music."

She seated herself at Vinnie's piano and experimented with a number of chords until she found ones that circumvented the broken keys. Then she called out, "Everybody ready?" Without waiting for an answer, she began to hammer out "Here Comes the Bride."

Vinnie emerged from her bedroom, wearing her best blue Sunday dress and carrying her prayer book instead of her shotgun.

And Abe, walking with a stately, steady tread but feeling as if he were tottering, came out of the kitchen with his daughter on his arm. Her arm on his felt as light as a butterfly. She seemed too small and fragile to be a woman, but nature had proclaimed that she was, and God was about to add His official endorsement to that awful decree. Abe wondered where the years of her childhood had gone and why he had allowed them to fly by without even watching. He did not hear the words of the ceremony that handed her over to someone else. He was too busy regretting the stiff-necked pride and propriety that had made him miss all those lovely years. Adams had to nudge him in the side to tell him it was time to give the bride away, moments after he had claimed her, and then retire, forever it seemed, to the darkest corner.

He watched the beardless groom kiss the baby-faced bride through a moist film.

"There's a collation in the kitchen, everybody," Vinnie announced. "Bella brought the wedding cake and wine, and I made pigs' feet and potato salad, and Doretha's bringing fried chicken and greens."

"Pigs' feet? Fried chicken?" Abe echoed, brightening. "Oh, wonderful. Just what I wanted."

Bella gave him a sharp, disbelieving look. "I couldn't eat now, Vinnie," she said. "I'm crying. Oh, look. I believe Abe's crying, too. Are you crying, dear? Wonderful! You must be human, after all." The bright, brittle tone Bella's voice had taken on lately grated on Abe's nerves, but he kept hoping, as he wiped his eyes on his cuff, that it was only a temporary symptom of strain.

A strange sound like "Bawwww" issued suddenly from Luciano's throat.

"Shut up, you insect," Abe said roughly. "What have *you* got to cry about? Why are you still here, anyway? Why didn't you run when you had the chance?"

"Because," Dom answered, "I'm a sucker for weddings. I love 'em. I'm not cryin' over the wedding, though. I'm cryin' over my road. If they won't move, how'm I gonna finish it? Bawww."

"Build a bypass," the Reverend Bird suggested.

"Yes, do," Bella agreed. "See if you can make it bypass Lakestown altogether."

"I'm beginnin' to think," the little contractor said. "that might be a smart idea."

29

But the road did not bypass Lakestown. It merely bypassed Merchant Avenue, extending only one narrow tentacle southward almost to the edge of Crump's Creek. Then, in temporary deference to Vinnie's obstinacy, the workmen withdrew and began to expand in the opposite direction, their insatiable machines chewing up turf and houses and gardens as if they were hamburger, all the way to the Lakestown-Dorsettown border, enlarging and deepening the desolate dust bowl until it seemed vast as the Mojave Desert, bottomless as the Grand Canyon.

It was late, late August now. Summer was growing frowsy and ragged around the edges, and, Fess observed morosely, the town's mood was already as gloomy and autumnal as late November. Signs of neglect were everywhere: the broken stained glass in the Grimes girls' front door; the torn blinds in Les Porritt's office windows; the shingles, blown off by a rainstorm, still missing from Josh Hawkins's roof. Conspicuous among the many unweeded gardens was Carl and Doretha Adams's crowded lot of gone-to-seed greens and parched, yellowing flowers, unattended since the funeral cortege had carried their second son past it to the Mount Moriah Cemetery. Civic works had come to a standstill, too; potholed streets and cracked sidewalks had gone unrepaired all summer. The general attitude seemed to be: why bother to fix up the town, since it's about to be destroyed?

Fess could not take his long walks anymore and had to settle for short ones, but there was nothing beyond the environs of the Blue Moon that he cared to see these days, anyway.

He knew what lay behind him: a barren, sunken arena, bigger and more barbaric than the Circus Maximus. But if he turned his back on it and the Blue Moon, he could still gaze at a small spot of wilderness where life not only survived but thrived. The banks of Crump's Creek were thick with vegetation, from weeping willows and wild blackberries to jack-in-the-pulpit and poison ivy. Dragonflies hovered over the moving water, a family of ducks owned by Bobo Wright swam in peaceful circles on its surface, and fat carp and catfish scavenged the mucky bottom. Crump's Creek was not as attractive as the lake it had once fed, but it was still a peaceful, pleasant scene, though its days were probably numbered, just as, Fess knew in his bones, his own were. He had deprived himself of his best friend's company for more than a month to keep from learning just how little time he had left. But if the one remaining natural spot in Lakestown was about to be cemented over and replaced by belching engines whizzing north and south, he did not really care to be around to see it happen.

An improbable cylinder of black silk appeared over the edge of the creek bank, followed by the grim visage of Baron Sam Potter, who tipped his tall hat to Fess. "Good morning," he croaked.

Fess stared him straight in the sunken eye sockets of his skull without returning the smile. "I am not," he said clearly, "afraid of you."

It was amazing how quickly the old ghoul disappeared.

Fess grinned behind his back and hobbled over to his favorite rock, a large, flat hulk of gray limestone. He seated himself in the sun and spoke to his friend Bulgy the box turtle, the only creature in town that moved more slowly than he did.

"Old buddy," he said to the familiar patterned back, "I hope you don't lose your home, too." Maybe they would bridge the creek over, rather than ram the road right through it. But that was not Whitey's way; he was Magog, the great destroyer. With distaste Fess began using his cane to hook the many beer cans that lay at his feet and arrange them in a neat, collectible pile. These were droppings left by the intruders, he knew; Lakestown folks generally had too much respect for nature, or at least too much dependence on it, to abuse it.

Labor Day was almost upon them, he reflected, but there was little for Lakestown's laborers to celebrate this year. Lonnie Jenkins, for instance, had gone back to walking to and from the job with his hat pulled down almost to his nose as a disguise and to staying in his house all weekend with no visitors and drawn shades. Lakestown's tempers were as frayed as its gardens, it seemed. These days, people greeted each other with surly grunts instead of gossip and smiles.

Fess wondered if there was something wrong with his own attitude. Maybe he was just an old crank, stubbornly opposed to progress. It would certainly be better for his state of mind if he could accept the inevitable gracefully. What, after all, was so special about

Lakestown? What made it worth saving? What did it consist of, except a few clumps of houses and churches and a couple of municipal buildings? The people seemed unique and valuable to him, but what, after all, had they built? The town had plenty of Adamses, but no scholars or statesmen. Quite a few Merchants, but only two stores. Plenty of Farmers, but no farms. Hundreds of Lakeses, but no . . .

Bulgy and the ducks and the scavenging fish were not the only permanent inhabitants of Crump's Creek. A colony of frogs had lived there so long and multiplied so extensively that the area was called Froggy Bottom after them. One of the frogs, leaping into the water, had made a loud splash that set off a corresponding chord in Fess's mind. Long after the creek had returned to its normal silence his head resounded with hopeful echoes.

Fess stood up and stumped off with unusual briskness toward the place he'd been avoiding for nearly six weeks.

Office hours were not over, but Doc was already in his garden sculpture gallery, applying a trowel to a new hump-backed creation that resembled a thirsty camel kneeling to drink from the fish pond at its feet.

In his eagerness to talk to his friend, Fess bumped into one of the many concrete obelisks that littered the place and fell sprawling, luckily on what was left of Doc's grass.

"How long have you been limping like that?" Doc asked him.

"Anybody would be bound to limp, trying to get around this obstacle course of yours," Fess retorted, getting up and seating himself on a concrete garden bench. "What's that you're working on now? A dying camel?"

"A waterfall, of course," Doc said, applying more touches with the trowel.

"Oh, of course," Fess said mockingly. "How could I have been so blind? Did you close your office early to work on this masterpiece?"

"Had a slow morning," Doc replied calmly. "It's the dog days in more ways than one. I had three dog-bite cases, and that was all. Boyd and Matt Hawkins are out now trying to catch the first two dogs. The last case was Greta Grimes. I cauterized her lip where her toy French poodle bit her, and she objected to my dirty office and unsanitary appearance. I told her anybody who would kiss a dog had no right to criticize anybody else's hygiene, and she left in a bit of a huff."

"I just wonder what condition the dog's in," Fess said.

"Well," Doc said, "it wasn't rabid *before* it bit Greta. By now—who knows? Meanwhile, while I'm waiting for a report on the two loose dogs I can work on this. It'll trickle into the fish pond and recycle itself with the same water, aerating it for the fish at the same time."

"How's it going to do that?" Fess asked.

"I'm hoping," Doc said, "that it won't require a pump of any kind. I'm hoping to do it all with gravity. See, there'll be another pond up here, in this basin at the top of the waterfall, and this water pouring down will push that water back up, with the help of the slopes I've dug out underneath. I saw you from a distance. You were limping badly before you got here. Let me just put these ornaments in before the cement hardens, and I'll have a look at you. Which do you like best for decorations, the scallop shells or the cones?"

"Why do you have to stick any decorations in it at all?"

"Oh, that's the whole point of doing these things. The impulse to stick things into wet cement is absolutely irresistible and, I think, primeval. That's why we have kids' initials in sidewalks, movie stars' footprints in front of Hollywood theaters. And, probably, 'Kilroy Was Here' in Latin on the old Roman viaducts. I think I'll alternate scallops and cones all the way down both sides. Do you like the effect?"

"It's okay," Fess said, "if you like dying porcupines."

"Critics, critics," Doc complained. "The bane of the artist. Those who can't create, criticize. When did your foot first get cold?"

"Who said it was cold?"

"Don't be cute. *When?*"

"Last month sometime," Fess admitted.

"Any feeling left in it at all?"

"Not really," Fess admitted.

"Has the skin changed color? Texture?"

"No."

"Come on inside." Doc put his trowel down abruptly and led the way through the maze of cement sculptures to the back door of his office, where he put Fess through a thorough examination, including numerous pokings, jabs, and pin pricks. Then he picked up the phone.

"What are you doing?" Fess asked in alarm.

KRISTIN LATTANY

"I'm trying," Doc said, "to find out how fast I can get you an appointment with a specialist I know. And whether they've got a bed for you over at Edgehill Hospital. They've got a pretty good vascular team over there. With luck, you can have a bypass done this weekend."

"Hold it!" Fess cried, clamping his hand on top of Doc's and forcing the receiver down. "Not so fast, Doc. What are you getting me into? What's a bypass, anyway? And why do I need one?"

"It's a fairly common procedure nowadays. They stick a new artery in there to replace the one that's blocked. And you need it, fool, because there's practically no circulation in that foot."

"Will it work? Will I survive it?"

"Don't ask me impossible questions, Roaney," Doc said brusquely. His glum expression told Fess all he needed to know.

"Then don't ask me to make impossible decisions. You talk a lot about not interfering with nature, but when it gets right down to actual cases you're just like all the other doctors. Always anxious to try out their latest gadgets and discoveries, even when they know they won't work. Well, don't subject me to extra suffering. Don't waste what's left of my time."

"Dammit, Roaney, there's always a chance," Doc said, slapping his thigh in frustration. "And if you don't have an arterial bypass done, that foot will have to come off. Have you seen Lukey Hawkins lately? He's walking better than you are. But he's also about thirty years younger than you are. If you lost a foot, I doubt you'd ever get out of a wheelchair."

"I didn't come to see you about my foot, anyway," Fess said. "I came to see you about something more important."

"I don't know what that could be," Doc said. "But since you've neglected yourself this long, I guess another twenty minutes won't matter. What is it?"

"Tell me again," Fess requested, "about your new waterfall, how it's going to work."

"I'll never understand you, Roaney. But you have three main factors to deal with in controlling the flow of water. Slope, perimeter, and velocity. Now, if the slope is steep enough and the perimeter is small enough, the water will flow fast enough to keep itself moving—even uphill and over obstacles."

"I'm not sure I understand you, either," Fess said.

"It's simple. Where do you usually find rapids? In narrow gorges with steep descents."

"Okay. Gotcha. Now listen to me a minute."

The upshot of their discussion was that Doc made a number of phone calls to his cronies instead of to his colleagues, because Fess absolutely refused to go into the hospital and miss any of the excitement.

"It's your decision, Roaney," Doc said, after trying three more times to persuade him. "Funny how few people realize medical decisions are up to them. Most patients do whatever their doctors tell them; that's why they talk about 'doctor's orders.' But I can't bully you, can I?"

Fess shook his head. "Not this weekend. Next week, maybe, but not now."

"You realize what you're risking? Gangrene can set in overnight. Next week might be too late to save your foot."

"It's my foot, and it's my right to risk it," Fess said firmly.

"Well," Doc said with a sigh, handing Fess a bottle of pills, "take one of these after each meal."

"What is it?"

"Coumarin. It thins the blood. The dosage is very critical, so I'll have to check you over every day till we get it exactly right. See how much extra work you've made for me?"

"Sorry," Fess said insincerely, since he had no intention of entering any hospital. "Do you think my crazy idea might work?"

"It's just crazy enough, and simple enough, that it might. All we can do is try. Come on, let's go."

The men who were gathered around the Blue Moon's largest table were not favorably disposed to Doc's latest proposition.

"I don't want to hear nothin' more about that highway," Josh Hawkins declared. "It's caused us too much trouble already."

"I feel," Carl Adams said, "exactly the same way."

"That's understandable, Adams," Doc said. "How's Luke coming along, Josh?"

"He's fightin' hard and comin' back fast," his father said. "He works out with his therapist every day, and yesterday he threw away that walker and started usin' a cane. He won't hear about takin' a term off from school, and he's talkin' about gettin' on the swimmin' team next year. Can you feature that? *Swimmin'!* I know that thing they strapped on him hurts. But he ain't complaining."

"Then why are you?"

Josh's mouth fell open and closed again slowly. He looked suddenly hard and angry, a big improvement on his former depression and listlessness.

"Thanks for not socking me, Josh," Doc said. "I deserved it."

"No, it's me who deserved the sock. Thanks for what you said. You were right. But it sure would help if I could sock somebody."

"How about socking it to that highway one more time? One last try for Luke. And for my foolish friend here, who ought to be in the hospital this minute."

"I dunno," Josh said, rubbing his chin, which bristled with three days' worth of gray stubble. "What you got in mind?"

"Let's go out back. I can show you better there."

Together the men walked out to the bank of the creek. Fess perched on his rock and the others gathered around him.

"Throw this stick in the creek, will you, Roaney?"

Fess did as Doc asked. The doctor watched the stick intently, clocking its movement with his stopwatch until it swirled out of sight.

"Pretty good velocity," he announced. "It traveled ten yards in twenty seconds. I thought the creek was sluggish, but it's not. And downstream is the right direction, too."

"So all we have to do," Ikie asked, "is open up that channel all the way to the creek, right?"

"I wish it were that simple, Isaac. But we've got more than one factor to deal with. Slope, for one thing. That channel has to slope downward from the creek to the center of the cavity. Then there's the perimeter we want filled. It's huge, so we need to narrow the channel to speed up the flow as much as possible. And, of course, the stream has to be dammed up just below the channel to divert it in the direction we want it to go. *Then* we have to start praying for three things."

"What are they?" Fess asked.

"Rain, time, and freedom from interference. We'll need plenty of all three."

"Boss men ain't watchin' so careful no more," Lonnie Jenkins reported. "We stopped messin' with 'em so long ago, they just about forgot to take care of security. The guards go home when we do now. Ain't a guard to be found up there after five o'clock most nights. And I don't think any of 'em are workin' this weekend." Lonnie pulled a gigantic steel turnip from his pocket. "Lunch break's over. Got to get back on the job now."

"Do you think," Ikie asked him, "you could manage to leave a few things unlocked when you leave tonight, Lonnie?"

"Oh, sho," Lonnie said. "I'm gettin' mighty forgetful in my old age. Everybody says so, specially Jerutha. I can forget to lock the gate and the shack where they keep the keys. Shucks, I can even take the keys and forget to put 'em back."

"Beautiful, Lonnie. But I don't want you to get in trouble, lose your job or anything like that," Ikie cautioned.

"*Me* get in trouble? Shoot. Boss man ain't never gonna blame me." Lonnie winked. "He thinks I'm his personal nigger. Anything else you want?"

"See if you can leave us a loaded dump truck," Doc requested.

"Why, sho," Lonnie agreed. "I'll leave two of 'em."

"Great," Doc said. "We could do the work with hand tools, but power equipment is a lot quicker." He got a pair of scabby old fishing waders out of his trunk, put them on, and waded into the water with his fishing pole.

"Whatcha doin' now, Doc?" Josh called. "Fixin' to catch some catfish?"

"Nope," Doc answered, making marks on the pole as he walked. "I'm measuring something. I think we're in luck. The creek slopes downward right to here, just below their channel. Then it levels off. Right here is where we build our dam. All we need, besides some of their equipment, is the fire truck."

"What's the fire truck for?" Freeman Farmer wanted to know.

"You'll see when the time comes," Doc said, lumbering up the bank slowly like a pleased hippopotamus.

"What's it *for?*" the fire chief insisted on knowing.

"We need it," Doc explained, "for our dam. I think a simple earth-fill dam will do the trick. But we need streams of water under high pressure to compact the earth and make it hold together."

"I'm only supposed to use the fire truck for fires," Nunc Farmer said stubbornly.

"Good Lord, Farmer," Doc said irritably. "Are you going to get officious on us at this late date?"

"I have my responsibility," Nunc said with folded arms. "I take it very seriously."

"Well . . . what the hell are you doing, Roaney?" Doc asked in sudden wonderment.

Fess, crawling around on his hands and knees, which was speedier for him these days than upright locomotion, was rapidly amassing a large pile of paper, cardboard, and leaves. "What Mame's always wanted me to do," he replied. "Picking up the trash out here. It's very combustible trash, you notice. When I'm finished, it'll probably catch fire. Spontaneously, of course. You've all heard of spontaneous combustion?" he inquired, holding up a matchbook.

"Never mind, never mind," Nunc said hastily. "I'll bring the truck whenever you say."

"Five thirty should be about right," Doc said. "Lonnie can't get here much before then. Earth fill is the most primitive kind of dam, but I think it'll work with those high-pressure hoses. The soil around here is mainly fine sandy loam, the easiest kind to compact; that's why it makes such great cement. Damn! I wish we could get started right away. I wish there were time to build a *real* dam, a real cement beauty." Doc stomped in circles, shaking water on everyone, like an angry Saint Bernard.

"What are you waiting for?" asked Ikie, leaping into the ditch the road crew had dug. "Get me a shovel, somebody."

Obligingly, Baron Sam, chillingly dapper in his rusty black suit and tall silk hat, appeared from around the corner of Cabin One and threw Ikie his gravedigger's spade.

Ikie tossed it back. "Keep it, you old snake. This isn't a cemetery."

"Besides," Fess said bravely, "you'll need it soon. For me."

The Baron bowed gravely to Fess and walked off with his spade on his shoulder.

"God, he gives me the creeps," Ikie said. "I thought Mame had exorcised him by now. Her country cousins have been here all week. Do you think he heard us?"

"It doesn't matter," Fess said. "You can't exorcise him, but you can appease him temporarily. I just did that."

"How?" Ikie asked.

"By promising him a fresh body. Mine."

None of the men had the poor taste to contradict him with false assurances. Instead they simply went to work. Josh set off at a trot for Bobo Wright's shack, three hundred yards downstream, and returned with two shovels. Bobo, sleepy-eyed as a lizard but strong, followed him with a third shovel on his shoulder. Doc went back to his office to minister to the victims of dog bite, and Carl Adams disappeared into the comforting gloom of his cellar, but Josh, Bobo, and Ikie, cheered on by Fess, worked all afternoon.

By four thirty, when they knocked off for supper, only four feet of dirt remained between the highway excavation and Crump's Creek.

At five o'clock the deep, refined rumble of Nunc Farmer's voice was heard throughout the town, raised in a fine rendition of "Shall We Gather at the River?"

At five fifteen a less euphonious rumble announced the arrival of Lonnie Jenkins in a loaded dump truck. "Where do I dump it, Doc?" he called.

"Right here, in the creek, Doc said, pointing. "We'll need the fire truck soon."

"Fire truck coming right up," Fess promised from atop his rubbish heap.

"Roaney! Put those matches away! You don't have to do that," Doc said just in time. "We'll need quite a few loads of dirt, Lonnie. We have to build up our dam *and* the channel, to make it narrower and give it the slope we need. What do you think? Can we get at that equipment now?"

"Sho," Lonnie replied. "Everybody knocked off early. Holiday weekend. They left one guard behind, but I gave him a fifth of Wild Turkey. Told him the boss man had forgot it."

"Wild Turkey!" Doc exclaimed. "My God, what a waste of good bourbon. I haven't tasted any since Christmas 1955."

"What I gave him," Lonnie said, grinning evilly with the only two upper teeth left in his head, "was a Wild Turkey *bottle*. I never said what was *in* it. But what it was was a mixture of Old Overcoat, smoke, and Mad Dog wine. . . . Speaking of dogs, he got two of 'em up there. He probably thinks they pink bunny rabbits by now, but what they is is mean old German shepherd attack dogs."

"What do you think, Doc?" Ikie asked. "Can we get past the dogs, or deal with them somehow?"

Doc rubbed his warty chin in thought, then said, "Matt had to stun one of the dogs he caught for me today. He used one of those dart guns that shoots tranquilizers. Does he still have it, do you know, Josh?"

"Yep. He brought it home tonight when he came off duty."

"Think we can borrow it?"

"You know it."

"Good. Let's get going, then. We'll just stop by your place and mine on the way."

"I think I got the keys to everything," Lonnie said, pulling a hefty key ring from his pocket. "And everything is brand new, A-1 condition, too. They had to get all new equipments after . . . after . . ." he said, and faltered.

"After our damn-fool kids destroyed the old equipment," Cap Carter finished for him. "I would be proud of my boy, if he hadn't gone too far."

Ikie decided to cut this conversation short. "What I want to know is, who can drive that equipment."

"You know I can," Lonnie stated.

"Just lead me to it," said Cap Carter.

"I get first choice," Josh Hawkins declared, "and I want to drive that big dipper thing."

"You got it," Ikie said. "Let's move out."

"Hit it a lick for Luke!" Fess cried after them as they rode off in the back of the dump truck with Lonnie driving.

It was not long before an impressive parade came rumbling back, with the fire truck in the lead. Behind it were Josh driving the long-necked power shovel, Cap Carter driving a backhoe, and Lonnie, Ikie, and Doc each behind the wheel of a loaded dump truck.

"Hey, that was great, the way you fixed them dogs, Doc," Lonnie said admiringly as they climbed out of their respective cabs. "They keeled right over soon's you shot those darts in 'em. And that guard was so drunk he never even felt the shot you gave *him*."

"Shut up, Jenkins," Doc growled. "I never thought you were the blabbermouth type. Don't tell anybody else, please. Animal sabotage is one thing, but I never intended to commit human sabotage."

"Awww, he'll just sleep like a baby all night and wake up feelin' real good. Ain't that what you said?"

"It's what I *expect*," Doc said shortly, "but I'm not infallible, Lonnie. Chloral hydrate's pretty harmless stuff, but I don't know how it will react with that dreadful mixture *you* gave him. Well, Farmer, how about it? I've compromised my most sacred principles. How do you feel about yours? Are you staying with us?"

"I'm here, ain't I?" Nunc said in his deep voice. "I ain't got nowhere else to go right now. Let's just hope nobody turns in an alarm. I got my radio on in case they do."

"Fine," Doc said. "Shine your lights over here on the creek."

It was not dark yet, but fog was already rising from the creek and its banks. "Move out of the way, Bulgy," Fess whispered as the second load of dirt was dumped into the water. He was strangely comforted when he found that the turtle had crawled up on the rock beside him.

"We have to give the dam a pyramid shape," Doc explained. "While Nunc aims the hoses, we ought to get in there and pack it down with shovels. Anybody want waders? I have an extra pair in my trunk."

"Shoot, no! I'm waterproof," Josh said, and strode into the creek. Ikie followed his example.

"Aim the stream of water right there, Nunc," Doc directed. "Glad you decided to join us, Adams. Give me a hand with this hose, will you? Thanks. Got to do everything we can to pack it tight." The men on the bank manipulated the hose while those in the creek swung at the dam with the backs of their shovels. Then, to add the final touch, Ikie and Josh trampled the dam with their huge bare feet.

"That's the way dams used to be built in the old days," Doc commented. "I mean in ancient Rome and medieval Spain. How did you guys know about it?"

"'Cause that's the way we used to do it in the old days down in Lowndes County, Georgia," Josh called back.

"I bet that place was plenty medieval, too," Ikie added. "Right, Josh?"

"You said it. Them crackers was plenty mad *and* plenty evil when I left. This here job looks near 'bout finished, Doc. Come take a look."

Doc made his inspection and pronounced Josh right. "Yep, it's tight as a drum. Hardly any seepage at all. Look."

Sure enough, below the dam, the bottom of the creek was visible, with fish flopping and gasping in the shallows.

"Sure wish we had time for a fish fry," Josh said wistfully.

"Tell Mame. She'll take care of it," Doc said. "The problem is, how do we keep the creek from overflowing before the channel's ready? We need a lock, a gate to hold it back." He socked himself in the forehead. "Damn it, I should have thought of it before. Now what do we do?"

"Take the door off my cabin," Fess suggested.

"What?"

"Take it. I don't need it. Take my mattress too. It's three inches thick. Go on, take it. I won't miss it."

"Mame'll have a baby, but take mine, too," Ikie offered. "In fact, take all the doors and mattresses you need. We'll square it with her later, somehow."

Four doors were stealthily removed from cabins One through Four. Hinged together, they became the bread in a mattress sandwich that was placed against the narrow barrier of earth between the stream and the future highway.

Fess crawled on top of the sandwich and sat there swinging his short legs.

"What the hell are you doing, Roaney?" Doc cried in alarm.

"Holding my finger in the dike," was Fess's silly answer. "Besides, I get a better view from here."

"What's next, Doc?" Lonnie Jenkins asked.

"Now we have to prepare the channel," was the answer. "Make it narrower and smoother, and give it a steeper slope. I think a couple more truckloads of dirt should do it."

"Let me at it," Josh said.

"Why don't you take a rest, Hawkins?" Ikie said. "Let me work for a while."

"My son don't rest. Why should I?"

"Because," Ikie said, "he's eighteen, and I'm thirty-eight, and you're—what? Fifty-eight?"

"Can't say," Josh replied. "They never kept regular birth records down in Lowndes County. For all I know, I'm younger'n you. I look and act it, don't I? Heeeeee."

"Yes," Ikie was forced to admit. "But I still think you've done your share."

Josh shrugged, and Ikie climbed into the cab of the power shovel.

"Hit it a lick for Luke and Lou!" Fess cheered.

Ikie, in spite of his truck-driving experience, was not as skilled with the earth-moving equipment as Cap, Josh, or Lonnie, and the fogs that shrouded Froggy Bottom after dark made his work even more difficult. Still, he made fairly good headway, biting the channel deeper to create the slope Doc wanted and depositing the earth on its banks.

Doc's back was turned as he made his calculations aloud. "Let's see if I remember my fluid mechanics. Liquid velocity equals the roughness coefficient times the square root of the slope times the perimeter. We can't do anything about the perimeter; it's already determined. All we can do is make the slope as steep as possible, smooth out the roughness on the bottom, and hope we don't have too big a hydraulic jump."

"What kind of jump was that you mentioned, Doc?" Lonnie asked.

"The hydraulic jump," Doc explained, "is the slowdown in the flow of water when you've got a huge perimeter to fill. All we can do to reduce it is make the channel slope toward the center as much as we can."

"And try to jump back in time," Josh quipped.

"That's right," Doc said. His back was still turned when Ikie, like Foxy before him, found himself stymied by darkness and unable to locate the correct lever on the monster he was driving. He swung the shovel blindly and bit out several chunks of the narrow barrier that remained between the channel and the dammed-up creek. There was an ominous rumble, the growling of underground water that had been waiting for eons to be released, a sound like the collective complaint of centuries of repressed black rage; then a pause and an almost human cough. Then refusing to submit to further delays, the water bubbled and spouted over their improvised rock, gushing with such force it took the gate with it.

KRISTIN LATTANY

"Jump-back time!" Lonnie Jenkins cried.

Everyone obeyed him with alacrity.

"So much for my precise engineering," Doc said ruefully. "All we can do now is let 'er rip. Let's put those machines back where we got them and go home, everybody."

"Hey, where's the little professor?" Lonnie Jenkins asked.

"Oh my God. He was sitting on the lock when it went," Carl Adams said.

They had done their work well, almost too well. The water was flowing rapidly down the channel as they walked along its banks, searching with flashlights and the fire truck's floodlights. Three hundred yards from the creek, they caught up with it and found Fess, floating face downward. When they hauled him out and turned him over he was smiling blissfully. But he was not breathing.

"Oh, no," Carl Adams moaned. "Why does something bad have to happen every time?"

"And why," Lonnie wondered, "does it always have to happen to the nicest people?"

"Why are you all looking at me?" Doc asked. "I'm just a man like the rest of you. I can't answer questions like that."

"My son Lou," Carl reflected, "never had a chance at a happy life. But neither did the professor, from what I could tell. He was about the loneliest man I ever knew. Never even had a wife or a child. I doubt he ever had any happiness at all."

"That's where you're wrong, Adams," Doc said. "I think Roaney had enough fun this summer to make up for everything he'd missed."

"That's the most presumptuous crap I ever heard," Ikie told him. "Can't resist playing God after all, can you, Doc? Who else could be so sure about a statement like that?"

"I'm not absolutely sure, Isaac. I just have a strong feeling about it. I think I knew Roaney better than anybody else did."

"What kind of fun," Ikie asked angrily, "is worth paying for with your life?"

"The best kind, maybe," Doc answered. A sad and thoughtful silence descended on the men for several minutes.

Finally Josh asked, "What do we do now, Doc?"

"I don't know," Doc said sadly. "He was my best friend. He had no next of kin."

"Who's that?" Ikie cried out suddenly. He shone his flashlight on the trees, lighting up the gaunt, grinning figure of the Baron. "Scat!" he cried, and threw a rock at it as he would at a cat. It worked. The specter vanished into the shadows.

"That settles it," Doc said grimly. "I think I can speak for Roaney. I know he wouldn't want to land in that buzzard's claws. We'll dig a hole for him over there, under those trees, and simply say we couldn't recover his body."

"It was my fault," Ikie said. "Me and my big ego, thinking I knew how to operate that thing."

"Don't flatter yourself, Lakes," Doc told him. "I think Fess planned this accident. He had a serious condition that called for immediate surgery, but . . . let's just say the operation might have been a success, but with all the other things that afflicted him, the patient would probably have died. He very sensibly refused to have the operation."

"He was smilin' when we turned him over, remember?" Josh reminded them.

"Then," Doc said, "let's try to smile with him. He got to choose the way he went. That's more than the rest of us will get to do."

They returned the equipment to the construction site, then came back and dug the small grave with hand tools. Each man wanted to take a turn preparing his friend's last place, and did. Reverend Bream was summoned to say a few words over the unmarked mound. Then the weary men tramped into the Blue Moon's common room. As they seated themselves around the large round table with one empty chair, they heard the first splatters of rain on the roof. It soon became a hard, steady drumming, at once somber and cheering.

30

The rain poured down all Friday night, all day Saturday, and most of Saturday night. Sunday morning dawned fair and clear, allowing Lakestown's faithful to dress up and go to church without raincoats or umbrellas. Doc Thompson went instead to the edge of the construction site and saw that only the tip of the tallest boom now showed. He was no churchgoer, but he knelt in the grass and said a prayer of his own.

"More rain, Lord," he whispered. "Hit it a lick for Roaney, please."

The word quickly spread around the congregations of Lakestown. In their sermons that morning, Reverend Bream and Reverend Bird both made considerable references to Noah, the Ark, and the forty days and forty nights of rain that were required to cleanse the earth of its wickedness, inspiring their congregations to concentrate on the same prayer as Doc's.

Their prayers apparently had collective power and were answered. Shortly after church was over, the skies opened up once more and delivered another all-night rain.

Labor Day dawned bright as a newly minted coin, with the gleaming freshness of recent rain. All over Dorset County, abandoned picnics were hastily reorganized and baskets packed and loaded with thermos jugs into station wagons. A sunny day was forecast, but the station wagons did not get very far. They were forced to turn around and go home again when the bright sky turned black and more torrents descended.

On Tuesday morning the radio reported that they had been the victims of an unpredictable storm called Hurricane Bella, which had defied the forecasters and refused to be dissipated at sea, unlike her docile predecessor, Alice.

Serves 'em right for naming it after me, thought one amused listener. She reached out to turn off the clock radio and looked with cool speculation at her husband, who had awakened with a broad, self-satisfied smile.

"Why are you looking at me like that?" Abe asked.

Before she could answer him, the telephone rang. It was Harry Grafton, resonating so deeply he sounded like a pipe organ, informing

Abe that he could forget about his political ambitions and that he wished *all* of Lakestown were under water. Bella, her ear close to the receiver, marveled at the equanimity with which her husband received this news.

"All right, Harry," Abe said calmly. "Have a nice day."

"Don't call me by my first name, Lakes," the senator told him. "In fact, don't call me, period."

"I won't," Abe responded. "But don't forget, I still have those tapes and photographs. If you ever try to run for governor, I'll run you out of the state."

"Who do you think will believe you," Grafton said, pausing dramatically before adding, "nigger?"

Bella saw her husband turn white as the pillow case his head rested on. "He called me a nigger, Bella," he said in a voice as shocked and small as a five-year-old's.

The moment had come, forty-odd years too late. Bella decided to withhold what comfort she might give. "Let him feel the pain," Ikie had advised. "Let him crack up and break and feel the pain."

"*Me,* Bella," Abe said, and began reciting his credentials. "Me, Abraham Lincoln Lakes, B.A. Howard, 1937; M.A. Rutgers, 1939; Ll.B. Yale, 1941; Major, u.s. Army; Phi Beta Kappa; Alpha Phi Alpha; thirty-third degree Mason; *and* Boulé. *Me!*"

Moisture appeared in his eyes. Although he neglected to add it, she felt sure he was thinking, *"Me,* with my features keen as razor blades, my lips thin as paper, my skin the color of heavy cream."

So she said, "Remember those parties in Claypool when we were young, Abe? I always thought they were awful. The stuffiness, and the pretentiousness, and all those beige blondes and green-eyed nappyheads pretending they belonged to a special, superior race. I always felt I had walked into one of those sideshow tents at the circus—you know, the ones with the trick mirrors. Everybody at those parties seemed to want to be freaks. My parents were that way too, but I always remembered something my grandmother used to say, 'Don't forget, when you get bigger, you'll only be a bigger nigger.'"

"Why," Abe asked in shock, "would you recite a nasty, vulgar little verse like that to me at a time like this?"

"Because," she said calmly, "someone else should have done it a long time ago. You shouldn't have been allowed to grow up without knowing you'd always be a nigger—to Harry Grafton or to any other white man."

"But that's not true, Bella. They don't all think the same." He pulled a letter from under his pillow. "Look. This is why Harry couldn't really upset me. I don't need him anymore."

It was a letter from the prestigious Edgehill law firm of DeWitt, Eaton, Haskell and Hill, offering Abe a partnership. Now she understood why he had been smiling so smugly that morning.

"Very nice," she said, handing the letter back to him. "I wonder what you have that Oscar wants?"

"Brains, of course," Abe shot back. "Training. Talent. And the right kind of deportment, the kind that will be acceptable to his clients. Are you trying to disparage my qualifications, Bella?"

"Of course not, dear," Bella answered. "You have all those qualifications and more. You're brainier and better trained than *any*body. But take a look at that stationery. It's so heavy I could use it for table napkins, and it's not printed, either—it's engraved."

"So?"

"Well, a partnership in a firm like that usually costs money, doesn't it? I mean big money, more than we have, or else a list of rich clients. Forgive me if I'm ignorant, but am I wrong?"

"You're not ignorant," her husband said after a long pause. "You're right. And I don't have that kind of money or those kinds of clients."

"But you do have the pictures Boyd took here that night, and the tapes of the meeting. I think Oscar is scared, dear. This is a trade-off. He doesn't want a scandal, doesn't want to be forced to resign his job."

"Are you saying my ability counts for nothing?" he demanded, with a hard glare.

"Of course not, dear. I'm just saying you'd better learn you're a nigger. Or at least start thinking like one."

"Nigger. Coon. Smoke. Darky. Spade. *Never!*" he shouted, his face red with fury. "I'm none of those things, and I never will be. And I'm not white, either. You're wrong if you think I want to be. I'm a mixture, and that's better than either one. And I'm going to take this job, no matter how much you try to talk me out of it. Dammit, Bella, you're not going to drag me down anymore!"

"But I want you to take the job, dear," Bella said sweetly after this tirade had ended.

"You do?" he asked in amazement.

"Yes, of course I do. It's a marvelous opportunity. I just want you to be smart about it, and never, never trust white people again. You know, I've always thought our people were called coons because coons are by far the smartest animals in the forest. I'm not saying you have to be a coon, dear. Just try to be as smart as one."

"What are you saying?" he asked her.

"I'm saying," she said patiently, "not to let old Oscar have all the tapes and pictures at once. Only give him a few at a time: say, one or two a year. Or, if he insists on having them all at the start, which he probably will, make duplicates and keep them in a safe place. And get a twenty-year contract from him in return."

She leaned over and kissed his lined forehead. "I do have faith in your ability, dear. Knowing how good you are, I'm sure you'll be indispensable to Oscar long before that contract runs out. He'll come to rely on you, and so will his other partners and his clients. In time, they'll probably even forget about your race—most of the time. But always keep those tapes and photos, just in case. Keep them for insurance. And never get complacent; never relax and think you've been accepted into his exclusive little WASP club. Because I heard him call you a nigger myself, right here in this house."

"You know, I'd forgotten that," Abe said. "I guess I forget things I don't want to remember."

"That's human," she said, "but it's dangerous. Always remember: 'Even if you do get bigger, you'll only be a bigger nigger.' It's bitter, maybe, but it's the truth."

He meditated on what she'd said for a few minutes, then said suddenly, "All right. If I have to be one, I'm going to be the biggest nigger in this county."

"Why settle for the county? Why not the state? Why not the country?"

"Why not?" he echoed, laughing. "Where are you going?"

"Well, you know," she said seriously, "if you'd decided to keep on trusting white folks, I think I'd be leaving you. But since you didn't, I'm just going to make our breakfast."

When she returned with their coffee, he said, "I wonder what Harry meant about wishing all of Lakestown were under water?"

"I have no idea," she said, snuggling contentedly against the pillows with her coffee. "I expect we'll find out one of these days."

Like most people in the area, they'd stayed indoors behind closed curtains all weekend. The rain had done its work in relative secret. But they found out about it much sooner than Bella expected.

There was a frantic knocking at the back door and a familiar voice calling, "Mr. Mayor! Miss Bella!"

The mayor answered it in his Liberty of London paisley robe and his soft leather slippers, his pale, hairless legs looking like leeks between them. "Come in, child," he said, admitting Cindy.

"You've got to come see what's happened!" Cindy insisted. "You've got to come right away!"

"What is it that we have to see?" he asked.

"I can't tell you. You wouldn't believe me. It's just too much! It's a miracle! Just walk across Edgehill Road and see."

Bella, suddenly mindful of her husband's position, said, "Finish your breakfast, Abe. Let me go first. I'll come back and brief you."

She wrapped her nudity in a tie dress, started out of the house barefoot, then came back and slipped into sandals.

She and Cindy had to push their way through an enormous crowd of people, about forty feet thick, it seemed, to find out why it had gathered.

At last they stood at the edge of what had been the construction crater and saw a deeper shade of the blue sky reflected in a shimmering sapphire mirror at least a mile wide. All of Lakestown seemed to be standing there, hypnotized by its crystalline beauty. Many of the young people wore bathing suits and a few men had brought fishing rods, but no one was wet, and no lines had been cast. It was as if one and all were afraid the lake were a mirage that would disappear if they touched it.

"Oh, Miss Bella," Cindy breathed, "isn't it beautiful?"

"The most beautiful sight I ever saw," Bella answered.

"Do you think it's real?"

"I think so. I hope so." She gave Cindy's hand a squeeze.

"Do you think we'll go skating on it in the wintertime, the way you used to?"

"Absolutely," Bella said firmly. "You and Tommy and your little one will skate on it, and swim in it, and fish in it, and take boats out on it, and have picnics beside it . . . and . . . and so will I, and so will your father, if I can ever teach him how to have fun." Out of the corner of her eye, she saw a knot of official-looking white men gathering and gesticulating angrily. "I have to go now. Be right back. I hope Abe can stand two shocks in one day."

"Get dressed, dear," she told him breathlessly, having run all the way back to the house. "You have a speech to make. Your Palm Beach suit is clean, I think."

"What? What?" Abe exclaimed.

"You can use the same old speech you used the last time. The one about development and prosperity and all that. You just have to change one word. Every place you said 'highway' the last time, this time say 'lake.'"

He choked on his English muffin and had a long fit of coughing while Bella convinced him she was not joking. Finally he stopped coughing, stood up shakily, and got dressed.

They went out together into the glorious sunshine and made their way through the crowd, which still stood as if mesmerized, afraid to test the miracle.

Ikie nodded curtly to his brother, grabbed Bella's arm and pulled her aside. "I've got the van all packed up to leave town. You coming with me?"

She had never seen him in an angrier mood. "What's the hurry, Ikie? Where are you going?"

"New York, for starters. If I don't like it there, Canada. I can't stay around here anymore. They know about us, and they know I'm an artist. Besides, my bungling killed a man last night."

As usual, Ikie's most violent anger was directed against himself. "Who?" she asked, placing a gentle hand on his arm.

"The professor."

"Oh, no," Bella said, and sniffled and wiped her eyes. "He never did anything to hurt anybody. Why did it have to happen to *him*, Ikie?"

"It doesn't matter. It happened, that's all. Because of my clumsiness and my stupid ego." He grabbed her arm again, painfully. "Make up your mind, Bella Are you coming with me, or not?"

"No," she said. "Your brother needs me. Besides, haven't you heard? We're going to have a grandchild."

Ikie shrugged as if to say, "So what?"

"I don't want to miss the event, Ikie. And I'm getting more grandmotherly every day. Look at me: overweight, gray hairs coming in by the dozens, and my eye doctor just prescribed bifocals. You need a woman at least as young as you are."

Ikie gave her a hard, uncompromising stare. "I don't want any woman but you."

She gave him a warm, strong kiss they both knew meant good-bye. "Well," she said, "maybe I'll meet you sometime at a good New York hotel. Or even a grubby one."

His expression did not change. "No, you won't. But if that's your decision, okay. I hope you'll ask Doc over. He needs friends now."

He looked at her for another long moment, then turned and surveyed the immobilized crowd. "Well, somebody has to break the spell. It might as well be the black sheep."

Oblivious of all the shocked stares, Ikie began to strip. He took off everything but his Jockey shorts, then mumbled to himself, "Why do things halfway, Lakes? Might as well leave town in *total* disgrace," before stepping out of the shorts too.

Ikie walked to the water's edge, turned, cast another glance at the crowd and his small but growing immediate family—Bella, Abe, Tommy, and Cindy. Then he lifted his arms and bounced on his heels.

"I christen thee," he howled, "Lake Lucinda!"

He bounced up in a high, graceful arc, brown penis flapping against mahogany thighs, then descended in a matching curve into the water. When he came up and shook himself, droplets glistened like diamonds in his hair and across his broad shoulders.

Bella thought to herself, God, he *is* a beautiful man. Maybe I will go to New York and meet him someday. Then, remembering another rapidly approaching birthday, she sighed, stepped back, and took her husband's arm.

Luke Hawkins, leaning on his cane at the water's edge, said to his best friend, "Lemme lean on your shoulder a second, Hoss."

"What you think you doing, fool?" Tonio asked as Lukey stepped out of his own pants (keeping his shorts on, though) and unstrapped the contrivance he wore.

"What you think? Gimme a push."

"Are you sure?" Tonio asked doubtfully.

"I said, *push* me," Luke cried with all the ferocity of his determination.

Tonio did as he was bidden, and Luke plummeted into the water. His mother and several other women shrieked, and his father cursed, but when Lukey surfaced and began to churn the water with a rapid, powerful freestyle, leaving a wake behind him like a motorboat's, a cheer rose from a thousand throats.

The spell was broken, all right. A hundred splashes followed Lukey's. Convinced at last that the mirage was real, most of the people under twenty and quite a few over decided to cool off. The patrons of the Dorsettown Swim Club, whose oasis now looked like a birdbath in comparison, pressed against their fence in wonder and envy, probably feeling for the first time fenced out instead of in.

Abe seemed to be frozen in a trance. "What happened, Bella?" he asked her. "Who did it? Where did it come from?"

"It doesn't matter, dear," she said, squeezing his arm hard to rouse him. "Just call it an act of God, a miracle. And make your speech about progress."

"Who will listen to me?" Abe asked sadly, watching all the joyous splashers.

"Everybody. Here comes Tommy now with the amplifier his rock group uses. Just talk into the mike and tell everybody this is the best thing that ever happened to Lakestown. That water *does* look inviting, doesn't it? Do you think it would be all right if I went home and put on my bathing suit?"

"I hardly think," Abe said, "that would be proper, Bella."

Out of the corner of her eye Bella saw the angry white men approaching. Harry Grafton was in the lead, followed by the state and federal engineers, Berger and Redfern, with Luciano and his aides bringring up the rear.

"On second thought," she said, "I think I'll stay with you till this is over."

Harry Grafton was the first to reach the spot where they were standing. "Well, boy," he said, "I guess you know you blew it."

Abe did not honor that remark with a reply. He simply stared at the face that was no paler than his own without blinking.

"Let me tell you something I couldn't say on the phone this morning," Grafton said, unaware of the microphone Bella was holding. "You never had a snowball's chance in hell of getting that state appointment, anyway. You and your little pigsty of a town simply aren't that important. We were going to wipe it off the map and leave you with nothing."

Abe remained silent, giving Grafton plenty of rope—no, wire, amplified wire—with which to hang himself.

"This state," Grafton pronounced, "will never appoint a nigger commissioner."

Abe still refused to react.

"Nigger!" Grafton shouted, seemingly trying to force a response from him. The epithet boomed out of Tommy's three speakers and stilled most of the activity in the lake.

"Ethnic!" Abe shouted back, his eyes bulging. "Vulgar, pushy, greedy, immoral ethnic! Why don't you get back on the garbage scow that brought you here and leave America for us Americans!"

Redfern and the others were drawing closer. "Hey, buddy, quit that ethnic talk, will you?" Grafton asked. "Most people don't know about my background."

"Ethnic!" Abe shouted even louder, the word reverberating through the speakers and echoing back to him across the lake. "This isn't your country, so you don't care what happens to it. You'll destroy every inch of it if we don't stop you."

Grafton grabbed the microphone. "There will be no highway running through here, folks. You have my solemn assurance of that. Vote for Harry Grafton, State Senator, Fifth District!"

Lukey, dangling from the bank, said, "Tell that man we wouldn't vote for him for Snake of the Fifth District. And tell him to get his junk out of the water, too. I only got one foot left, and I just banged it on a crane or something. We don't like littering in Lakestown."

"That is one of our young heroes, Luke Hawkins," Abe said. "You heard him, Grafton. Get your litter out of Lakestown. And you, Luke, please do me a favor. Get some of your friends up here to act as life-guards. We don't want any more accidents."

"Yes, sir, Mr. Mayor," Lukey said. "Watch me do the butterfly!" And, lunging up and down like a dolphin, he charged off to the other side of the lake, where the other Young Warriors were gleefully dunking Ted Crump without mercy.

"All right, Lakes, I'm leaving," Grafton growled, relinquishing the microphone. "I don't know how this latest sabotage was accomplished. Redfern's men can't get anything out of your people, they all seem to be hopelessly retarded, but this section of the highway is definitely abandoned, finished. I promise you one thing, though. Next week I'm cutting Lakestown's state budget to the bone. And the first thing to go will be your police chief's car. He's useless! Let him ride a bike!"

"Good-bye, Harry," Abe said, "and good riddance. We don't need you." Abe meant it. He did not need the acceptance of men like Grafton any longer, and he no longer even craved their respect. It was meaning-less, since they really respected nothing, not the land, not the law, not even their own backgrounds. He felt suddenly elated as the other half of his lifetime burden, the shame and self-hatred over being classified as black, slipped from his shoulders as rapidly as his guilt about Cindy. As he looked at the shimmering marvel his people had made, all that misery now seemed as absurd as a peacock's being ashamed of its tail, imagining it to be drab and ugly instead of a rainbow-colored glory. He felt light and buoyant enough to leap in and float, but of course after all those wasted years that was impossible. Instead he put one arm around his daughter and another around his wife, who was holding up the mike again, and began.

"We," he called out, "are the real Americans!" His voice rolled out over the lake and came back to him further amplified: "—mericans!—mericans!"

"This is our country! Some of our ancestors were here before for-eigners ever set foot on it. . . ."

"Wahoo!" shouted his shameless brother, just getting into his clothing. "Hear, hear!"

". . . and the rest worked hard enough and long enough without pay to buy it a thousand times over! This is *our* land, and here we will

KRISTIN LATTANY

build the finest minority resort in America! We will build a beach and a marina. We will build hotels, motels, and restaurants! We will build facilities for banquets, parties, and picnics! We will really put Lakestown on the map!"

"And in the history books!" interjected Reverend Bream, who had managed to grab the microphone. "If we prosper, fine, but we should never forget the sacrifices that have brought us this far. The Lakestown Rebellion belongs in the history books along with all our other great rebellions—Gabriel Prosser's, Denmark Vesey's, and Nat Turner's!"

After the applause had died down, Abe continued, "Yes, we will build a museum to our history, too, because Lakestown has come through many harsh struggles before and since slavery. But now I predict an era of unprecedented progress and prosperity! I foresee that lakefront property in Lakestown will soar to tremendous value! And to prove my faith and commitment to this prospect, I will build the first lakefront home!"

Bella whispered something in his ear.

Abe looked at her questioningly.

She nodded her head vigorously.

Abe gave in. "All right," he said. "Since the weekend was ruined by the weather, and since everyone seems to have stayed home from work today anyway, I declare this an official holiday. I proclaim this the first Black Independence Day in Lakestown!"

Cheers greeted this announcement. Bella whispered to Abe again.

"The Borough Council, of course," Abe continued, "will vote on the time and manner of next year's celebration. But to start this one off right, I will personally supply free beer and soft drinks to every citizen."

"Well, all *right!*" cried some of his thirstiest constituents.

Lukey, treading water with one arm hooked through a Styrofoam life preserver, was the first to accept a free beer from the mayor.

"Come out of that water, fool," Josh said to his son. "Now you fixin' to get high, and you ain't even healed right yet."

"I'm fine, Pop," was the answer. "Watch me do the sidestroke with one arm and one leg." He glided off smoothly as a canoe, resting his beer on the life preserver.

"Stop worrying about that boy, Josh," Doc counseled. "Don't forget, he's had pool therapy every day. By now he's literally unsinkable."

Bella took the doctor's arm and drew him aside. "I'm sorry about the professor," she said.

"I'm troubled about him," was the doctor's answer. "I'm not a religious man, and neither was he, but still I think maybe he should have had a funeral. There's something atavistic about black funerals that makes everybody feel better. All that preaching and singing and crying, and then those majestic processions of Cadillacs to the cemetery, like barges along the Nile. And then the feast, to reconcile the living to life again. Maybe I'll have a memorial feast for him every year."

"Fess would like that," she said. "But not the first part. Greta doesn't know how to do a real black funeral anyway."

"Do you think so?" he asked hopefully. "I think I'll have the party at the Blue Moon. I've been sketching a design for a grave marker. Cement and glass. See?" He pulled a crumpled prescription blank from his pocket. "It looks like a cross, but it isn't, really. It's a jeweled sword. Because our friend the professor was a fighter."

"We'll miss him. You will, especially."

"I'm afraid," Doc said, "I'm not the only one who's just lost a close friend."

His eyes rolled meaningfully toward Edgehill Road, where Ikie's van, sagging under its load of sculpture and possessions, was ready to roll. The engine coughed twice, then turned over with a great rumbling fart. Soon the van was gone.

"I'm going swimming," Bella announced. "If I'm wet all over, no one will notice if I cry."

But they noticed other things when the mayor's wife unwrapped the dress beneath which she was naked. Briefly, she struck the pose in which Ikie had sculpted her, then raised her arms over her head and eased gracefully into the water.

"Bring her back, Boyd," Abe ordered his giant henchman. "Bring her back and wrap a towel around her."

"Not me, Mayor," the chief said. "I can't handle that wife of yours. Nobody can."

"Embarrassed, Mayor?" Doc Thompson asked softly.

"Not really," Abe said with a faraway look, watching his wife as she flipped onto her back and floated voluptuously. "Just sad, Thompson. You see, I never learned to swim."

"I hate to play analyst," Doc said, "but I can't help thinking swimming stands for a lot of other things. Dancing, singing, playing, carousing, making love—all those activities our people do so naturally when they're enjoying themselves."

"Yes," Abe said, "and it's too late for me to learn."

"Not necessarily," Doc said, his eyes irresistibly drawn to the sight of Bella doing the backstroke, her spectacular breasts rising alternately with each lifting of her arms. "Not when you're blessed with one of the world's best teachers."

"Do you think so? Do you really think so?" Abe asked eagerly.

"I do," Doc said.

Bella paddled to the shore and emerged dripping, taking the large towel Chief Boyd handed her. "Thanks, Chief. Sorry if I embarrassed you, dear. But that was something I just had to do."

The mayor blushed furiously. But he did not stop smiling.

COFFEE HOUSE PRESS
Black Arts Movement Series

THE POSTWAR 1920S was the decade of the "New Negro" and the Jazz Age "Harlem Renaissance," or first Black Renaissance of literary, visual, and performing arts. In the 1960s and 70s Vietnam War era, a self-proclaimed "New Breed" generation of black artists and intellectuals orchestrated what they called the Black Arts Movement.

This energetic and highly self-conscious movement accompanied an explosion of urban black popular culture. The Coffee House Press Black Arts Movement Series is devoted to reprinting unavailable works of this period. We have tried to choose work that is masterful, that deserves another chance and other audiences, and that will help us keep the windows to the future open.

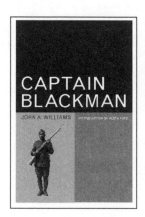

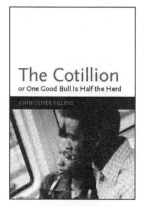

Captain Blackman, JOHN A. WILLIAMS

FOREWORD BY ALEXS D. PATE

ISBN: 1-56689-096-9 | TRADE PAPER | $15.95

Named "among the most important works of fiction of the decade" by *The New York Times Book Review* when first published in 1972, this novel revisits the contributions and experiences of African American soldiers in each of America's wars.

ALSO AVAILABLE: *Clifford's Blues*

ISBN: 1-56689-080-2 | TRADE PAPER | $14.95

dem, WILLIAM MELVIN KELLEY

FOREWORD BY JOHN S. WRIGHT

ISBN : 1-56689-102-7 | TRADE PAPER | $14.95

Originally published in 1967, this surrealistic satire lays bare the convoluted and symbiotic relationship between whites and blacks. "One of the outstanding comic novels of the [sixties]." —*The Boston Globe*

Bird at My Window, ROSA GUY

FOREWORD BY SANDRA ADELL

ISBN : 1-56689-111-6 | TRADE PAPER | $14.95

"This book was welcomed when it was first published in 1966. Its brave examination of a loving, yet painful, relationship between a Black mother and her son is even more important today."—Maya Angelou

ALSO AVAILABLE: *My Love, My Love* OR *The Peasant Girl*

ISBN: 1-56689-131-0 | TRADE PAPER | $11.95

The Cotillion or One Good Bull Is Half the Herd, JOHN OLIVER KILLENS

FOREWORD BY ALEXS D. PATE

ISBN: 1-56689-119-1 | TRADE PAPER | $14.95

"The current crop of young readers will be amazed to discover Lumumba's rapping prowess that precedes hip-hop culture by some ten years. In this way, and in so many others, Killens forged an alternative style, a new way of distilling black culture, and making it resonate with fresh vigor and integrity."

—*Black Issues Book Review*

Reading group guides available at coffeehousepress.org